CABAL OF LIES

CABAL OF LIES

OPUS X™ BOOK FIVE

MICHAEL ANDERLE

LMBPN

DISRUPTIVE IMAGINATION

Cabal of Lies (this book) is a work of fiction. All of the characters, organizations, and events portrayed in this novel are either products of the author's imagination or are used fictitiously. Sometimes both.

LMBPN Publishing
PMB 196, 2540 South Maryland Pkwy
Las Vegas, NV 89109

First US edition, April 2020
eBook ISBN: 978-1-64202-405-0
Print ISBN: 978-1-64202-406-7

THE CABAL OF LIES TEAM

Thanks to the JIT Readers

Dorothy Lloyd
Jeff Eaton
Peter Manis
Dave Hicks
John Ashmore
Lori Hendricks
James Caplan
Micky Cocker
Larry Omans
Deb Mader
Paul Westman
Kelly O'Donnell

If I've missed anyone, please let me know!

Editor
Lynne Stiegler

To Family, Friends and
Those Who Love
to Read.
May We All Enjoy Grace
to Live the Life We Are
Called.

CHAPTER ONE

July 19, 2229, Neo Southern California Metroplex, Johansen's Personal Flitter and Transport Emporium

Change could often be painful, but that didn't make it any less necessary.

Jia had learned that lesson well from Erik during their time together. If she'd never met him, she might still be the same deluded, naïve person being led around by corrupt, lazy people who dishonored their oaths and their badges.

However, understanding the necessity of change wasn't the same thing as easily *accepting* it, which was why she'd waited months before purchasing a long-overdue new flitter.

Jia rubbed her chin as she strolled between the long lines of flitters arrayed in the lot. The variety was staggering. Different sizes. Two-seaters. Four-seaters. Even larger. Every color of the rainbow was present, along with every color of hair she might see at a club on the weekend.

A few colors should never have seen the light of day, and certainly not on the shell of any of these flitters. There was no accounting for taste, but Jia had a hard time believing those colors were selling well.

Four different major flitter manufacturers were represented on the lot, including the oxymoronically named Off-World Systems, the German makers of Erik's flitter. There were no cheap brands present, but Jia wasn't there for an economy vehicle.

A bright yellow Taxútnta MX 60 was parked a few meters to her right. The vehicle was more slender than her partner's. She puzzled over that for a moment before recalling that a year's worth of heavy modifications had all but turned Erik's ride into a military vehicle.

If he could get away with sticking in a hidden turret or missile rack, he would.

He was already hauling around prototype military weapons in hidden compartments, and that was only quasi-legal. There wasn't an MX 60 in the entire UTC like his. Probably no one else had even thought to modify one as much as Erik had. Why bother when you could just get a tank?

Babe magnet? Unlikely. She was pretty sure she knew the truth of that statement.

A bright-eyed salesman in a crisp suit trailed Jia. His smile hadn't dared to leave his face during their short time together. "So, Jia, you mentioned you wanted a new vehicle, and you made your generous price range clear, but you could give me a little better idea about what kind of vehicle you're interested in? I could help narrow it down. We have a wide variety of vehicles to meet a wide variety of needs. We'll do everything we can to make sure you leave today happy with your choice."

Jia wanted to poke him over his presumption, but there was no reason to be rude. He was just doing his job. She couldn't blame him because of her own lingering discomfort.

She stopped and frowned at the yellow MX 60. "I need something new. My life's changed a lot this last year, and my old flitter doesn't reflect those changes." She eyed him for a moment. "It's too…boring and blue." She shrugged. "I need something a little flashier. Sportier? It needs to fit my new lifestyle, too. I need good performance."

Jia wasn't sure if *she* was flashier and sportier, but at the minimum, she wasn't the same person she had been previously. Replacing her flitter was a way of acknowledging that truth and of gaining a small advantage over Erik, but she didn't want the salesman to know that yet.

He already had too many preconceived notions. She would pull the trigger on the full truth when the time was right.

A knowing smile took over the salesman's face, and he nodded. "I understand. A beautiful woman like you deserves a flitter that can enhance her beauty. One that tells the world, 'I'm Jia, and I'm here. Pay attention to me, world!'"

She agreed, her voice not reflecting what she was thinking. "Uh-huh. Sure. Something like that."

Jia strolled toward a huge green flitter across from the MX 60. The green monstrosity was so large it bordered on being a cargo hauler. It made a statement all right, but not one she wanted to make. She scoffed and continued past the overcompensation-mobile.

"I understand that in today's complicated dating environment," the salesman began, "it's hard to know what kind of signal you're sending. But you're right—your flitter should reflect you. May I be brutally honest, Jia?" He threaded his fingers in front of him.

She shrugged. "Go ahead. I doubt you'll say anything that shocking."

"The flitter you arrived in is the kind of thing your mother would drive." He shook his head, a look of pity on his face.

Jia grimaced. His words struck deeper than she'd anticipated. She wanted to complain, but he was right. While her mother didn't drive the same make and model, she *had* recommended it and approved of the purchase. Was she that easy to see through?

"That bad, huh?" Jia sighed.

"Don't worry," he assured her. "You're here now. You're doing what you need to make the outward expression of your recent inner changes correct."

She needed to regain control of the situation. That was what she *needed* to do.

While she might not be her mother, she wasn't looking for some cutesy ride to zoom around in on dates. Her needs were particular, and it was time the salesman understood that. Form was one thing, but function was far more important.

Jia pointed to a two-seater crimson flitter to her side. "Could that survive a collision with a tower? Not like the side of a tower, but say you had to crash through a window in an emergency situation?"

The salesman let out a quiet chuckle. "Excuse me? Did you just ask if it could smash through a *window*?"

"I get that it can smash through. I'm just trying to get a feel for how much damage the flitter would take and if the auto-repair systems could get it up and running in a few minutes. That kind of thing."

Jia narrowed her eyes at the flitter, trying to imagine crashing into a tower filled with terrorists, gangsters, or *yaoguai*. Her life had gone from boring to colorful. An image of a Tin Man with a blade arm ripping through the top popped into her head.

"If it runs into a tower?" the salesman repeated. He coughed into his hand while his eyes searched around the lot. What he was looking for, Jia had no clue. "Am I hearing you correctly, ma'am?"

Jia slammed her fist into her palm to demonstrate the collision. "Yes. Like that." She held her palms up and slowly moved them away from each other. "I'm presuming a decent-sized window, maybe a long, wide hallway that could accommodate the flitter inside, but if you had to crash through," she looked at him, "how much damage do you think it'd be able to take? I'm just trying to figure out if I'd be able to take off again, or if it's more of a last-ditch desperation move."

"That's a very unusual question. Have you had to crash into a tower before?" Confusion and doubt dripped from the salesman's voice. "I can't recall any other customer ever asking me something like this."

"I wasn't the one who crashed the flitter, but I was in the flitter at the time. Stuff happens." Jia considered her question. "I'm not asking for the technical information, but you know, extrapolations from crash tests."

This was what she got for not doing her research ahead

of time. She should have shown up at the emporium with a specific vehicle already in mind, but she'd thought picking one out without excessive preparation would be more spontaneous and in the spirit of why she was purchasing a new vehicle.

"I see." The look on the salesman's face suggested he didn't believe her, but his smile returned. "I will note that every vehicle here has top-notch safety features, whether you're colliding with a building or getting into a crash with another flitter, and the autodrive in all of our vehicles is the best on the market. If you're having trouble with accidents, don't worry. This flitter can assure you'll never hit anything ever again." He shook his head. "I almost never fly on manual. Why take the risk? If you ask me, it's insane that it's even legal for people to fly their own flitters."

"I don't fly most of the time," Jia replied. "But every once in a while, I don't have a choice. Sometimes you don't want to trust your life to an AI."

The salesman chuckled. "I'd rather trust my life to an AI than a human."

Jia couldn't ask him how well the flitter would operate when controlled by a military-grade experimental AI, but she doubted she needed to.

Emma had demonstrated little trouble adapting to everything from Erik's flitter to a lunar transport. She wouldn't have trouble running Jia's new flitter. For that matter, properly interfaced, Emma could probably handle multiple flitters at once, but Jia wasn't sure she wanted to rely too much on the AI in a situation where transmissions could be jammed. There were other, more immediate vehicular concerns anyway.

She tapped her lips. "You didn't explain if it could take the crash, but more importantly, how resistant is it to small arms fire?" Jia asked. "I'm not saying it has to be perfect. I just want to make sure it can take at least a few shots. I don't want the thrusters or grav emitters cutting easily. It's a long fall around here."

"Excuse me?" The salesman blinked. "First, crashing into buildings and, now, if I understand you, guns?"

Jia walked over to the flitter and squatted. "I will say there's a nice, narrow profile on the grav emitters. That makes for a harder target. You should read up on why the military doesn't use many flitters versus dedicated ground or air vehicles. I was dubious for a long time, but now I've lived it." She clucked her tongue. "And yes, guns. I'm talking basic pistols, rifles, and slug-throwers, not stun weapons. Any decent flitter can defend against those already. I just don't want to plummet to my death because some idiot street tough gets a lucky shot. There's only so much grav fields can do when you fall straight to the ground. I've seen it."

The salesman didn't respond. She could almost hear the gears turning in his head.

"So, you want to know how resistant the flitter is to getting shot?" the salesman inquired. "In addition to if you can crash it through large windows?"

She wondered if flitter salespeople had panic buttons, and if they did, was he pressing his like a maniac at the moment?

"To be clear, I'm not planning to crash it through any windows." Jia offered a quick bob of her head before hopping back up. "As for the guns, yes, exactly. I'm not expecting it to take rockets or military-grade EMP, but I'm wondering about random gunfire. Think lucky punks rather than heavily armed Tin Men." She furrowed her brow and tapped her lips once more. "Or *yaoguai*? But they wouldn't be using guns. These things have to be pretty resistant to acid attacks, though, you'd think."

"I...honestly don't know the answer to that." The salesman glanced at the door leading into the building, licking his lips nervously. "Every vehicle we offer has top-of-the-line self-repair for standard damage. Is being able to take, uh, small-arms fire something you'll anticipate needing on a semi-regular basis? I'm sure the general anti-corrosive capabilities of the vehicle would help you with any acid-spitting monsters you might run into." He blinked several times, realizing what was coming out of his mouth.

"It'd just be nice if we didn't have to lean so much on *his* vehicle." Jia folded her arms and shook her head. "And also if I don't have to take it to the shop every week just because some ass-tastic anti-government civilian decides to take a shot at me." She snapped her fingers. "It's fine if it can be modified. I know a guy. Technically, somebody I know knows a guy, but I'd prefer if I could have the dealer do it, so I would at least like some bulletproofing. Trust me, I'll need it."

"I'm unsure if we offer that kind of modification." The salesman tapped on his PNIU a few times before murmuring, "Show options: bulletproofing." After a few seconds of looking at something only he could see, he nodded. "Huh. It turns out we do. It's part of a VIP protection package. It's not something that comes up all that often. It's not as if we sell to people who live in the Shadow Zone." He let out a quiet scoff. "You *don't* live in the Shadow Zone, do you?" He shook his head. "Of course, you don't. There's no way you would be here purchasing a flitter if you did."

"No, I live Uptown." Jia waved a hand. "And to be clear, price isn't a consideration when it comes to the modifications I want." She looked up, and another flitter caught her attention. She jogged toward a bright red four-seater in the distance, a Tachyon Transport Aurora. Insofar as a machine could be sexy, the flitter was. Great curves, nice symmetry. It'd be a great change from her Mom-mobile, and she'd be able to prove a few things to a certain judgmental partner.

"Is there anything else you might want?" the salesman asked, his voice trembling with faint trepidation as he caught up with the young woman.

"Custom antiprojectile sensors? Maybe some sort of decoy launcher to distract guided missiles?" Jia snickered. "Even Erik doesn't have that. Maybe that's not a thing, but you do see it in military transports." She rubbed her chin. "It wouldn't be impossible to install."

"We don't have anything like that, but I can talk to someone if you're really interested."

"Don't worry about it." Jia waved a hand.

"And Erik?" the salesman asked, desperation in his tone. "Is he your boyfriend?"

"Kind of." Jia didn't want to admit in public that she was fake-dating her partner. She never knew who or what might get back to her mother, and she wasn't sure if the salesman recognized her. He hadn't reacted when she'd introduced herself.

"Ah, a competitive relationship." The salesman nodded

sagely, some of his confidence returning. Maybe he believed this was all just a big game she was playing. "I think I'm getting a better feel for you, Jia. The Aurora is a great choice for you. It's a perfect vehicle for a modern woman like you who needs to prove to her man that she doesn't need him."

I might not need him, but I might want him, regardless.

Jia suspected the price tag made it a perfect fit for the salesman, but she wasn't going to let a few credits sway her. Her pride was on the line.

"It's not quite like that," Jia explained.

The salesman cleared his throat. "Might I ask what kind of work you do that you need your flitter to be bulletproof and avoid missiles? Or is this just something you want to show off at parties?"

"No, this is about saving my life. I'm a police officer." Jia looked up at him and smiled. She resisted asking if he watched a lot of news. She didn't want to come off arrogant. "I'm Detective Jia Lin of the Neo SoCal PD. I've dealt with a lot of dangerous cases in the last year, and it's made me more cognizant of my on-the-job and personal-time equipment needs."

The salesman took a sharp breath, understanding dawning in his eyes. The corners of his mouth curled up in the smile of a man who smelled even more money and opportunity. "I see. Everything makes much more sense now." He stepped closer to the Aurora and patted the side. "In that case, I still recommend this vehicle. Excellent acceleration. Great handling. We can get it bulletproofed for you, Detective, with no degradation in handling. I know when you're doing one of those high-speed chases, you need good performance. You wouldn't want to let a terrorist get away, now, would you? This might not top out at the same speed as, say, an MX 60, but it's got better handling under most circumstances."

Jia grinned and her voice dropped, practically purring. "Does it now?"

He really could see through her.

"Let me guess, your boyfriend has an MX 60?"

"It's not so much my boyfriend as my partner," Jia replied. "It's heavily modified, but yes."

"Of course." The salesman offered a quick nod. "I understand how competitive police officers can be."

I bet if I told him I was a gardener, he would have mentioned how competitive gardeners could be.

She slowly circled the flitter, taking it in from different angles. She and Erik would probably mostly stick to the MX 60, but it would be nice to have the option, and she never knew where she might be when a call came up. The police might be strangling crime and terrorism to nothing in the city, but that didn't mean it was entirely gone. Snakes always slithered in alleys, ready to strike. Terrorists didn't care about how peaceful a city was. In some cases, they preferred it wasn't.

"We can get this any color you want," the salesman offered as she continued looking but was quiet.

"Red's good. I don't care about it being camouflage-capable like my partner's. Sometimes being flashy is its own kind of camouflage." Jia nodded slowly. "I'll definitely take it, along with that VIP protection package." She ran her hand over the side of the flitter. "If you can get it to me within the week, it'd be helpful, and I'll win a bet with my partner, too."

The salesman's brow lifted. "A bet?"

"Yes, a bet," she confirmed.

The salesman tapped his PNIU with renewed passion. "I'm sure we can get it expedited, Detective Lin." He tapped a few more times, paused, then tapped again. A moment later, he looked up. "How does tomorrow sound?"

"That sounds *perfect*."

The salesman inclined his head and extended his hand. "Just feel free to let all your friends know about us. We live to place the perfect vehicle with each customer."

CHAPTER TWO

Erik let out a hearty laugh as he stepped onto the parking platform, pushing a hoverdolly carrying numerous long, sealed crates.

A bright red flitter waited in the spot nearest the door, Jia sat behind the control yoke with a huge grin on her face. He shook his head and made his way over to the flitter. She'd actually gone and done it. He'd been sure she wouldn't.

"I knew you would lose the bet," Emma commented.

"Why were you so sure?" Erik scoffed. "She's been talking about getting a new flitter forever. I figured a deadline would prove she was bluffing. And then she shows up in this thing?" He gestured toward the vehicle. "I'm surprised she didn't have a heart attack when she chose the color."

"Perhaps Detective Lin's tastes are wider than you believe."

"Looks like it." Erik arrived at the flitter, wheeling his dolly opposite the driver's side. He stepped away from the dolly and slipped into her passenger's seat. Honesty compelled him to admit the seats were damned comfortable, although that wasn't a huge problem. He didn't intend to spend any more time in Jia's new vehicle than he had her old one. He hmmmd and huh'd before sliding back outside and over to the dolly

"Huh?" Jia frowned. "You hate it that much?"

Erik pointed to his dolly. "I wasn't pushing this for my health. Open the trunk. I'll have to put some of this in the back seat. Good thing you bought a four-seater."

Jia gestured toward one of the crates. "Are those what I think they are?"

"Guns, guns, and more guns." Erik patted a square crate. "And grenades. Tightly-packed death."

"Are you a rolling gun show today?"

"I told you to clear your schedule for something fun." Erik smiled. "And these crates are filled with fun."

Jia offered him a grin so wide it belonged on a shark *yaoguai*. "Before that, we have a little business to discuss." She leaned forward in her seat to tap the screen on her console. The trunk popped open.

Erik grabbed a wide and long case that likely held his laser rifle. "I hate losing, but yeah, bring it on." She could hear him just fine as he walked around to the back.

Jia waited for him to deposit the case in the trunk. "I believe the terms of our bet were quite clear. If I didn't buy a new, sexier," Jia made air quotes around the word, "flitter by the end of July, I would pay for your breakfast, including at least two beignets, for a month. If I won, you would pay for *mine*."

Erik picked up another crate. "I was just trying to motivate you, and I was successful. In a way, we both won the bet." He opened the back door on his side to access the back seat.

"You've motivated me to let you repay me after I buy more expensive breakfasts for the next month." Jia laughed. "And don't feed me a line. You totally thought you were going to win."

"No soldier wins every battle." Erik continued ferrying his supplies into the flitter, filling the trunk and the back seat with deadly cargo. "Let me run this dolly back to the utility room, and I'll explain where we're going."

He departed with a quick nod to finish his errand. A couple of minutes later, he jogged back to the parking platform, settled into the passenger seat, and swiped over his seatbelt.

Jia tugged on the control yoke, and the Aurora began to rise. "I'm surprised you were so willing to let me pick you up." She nodded toward the back. "Especially with the arsenal. This thing might be able to take a few bullets, but it's not nearly as souped-up as your baby."

Emma appeared in the back seat, arms crossed and partially obscured by boxes. "Alas."

"The MX 60 is in the shop," Erik explained. "I needed more hidden cargo space, and some of the electronics reinforced. It was one thing when we were just running into basic criminals, but now we also have terrorists and high-end cyborgs sent by conspiracies. I want to make it harder for them to kill us."

"Funny. I was thinking the same thing when I bought the Aurora." Jia pulled her flitter away from the parking platform. "Why do I have a feeling I'm going to end up spending half my savings improving my new flitter?"

Erik shrugged. "You don't *have* to. We can just use the MX 60."

"Sometimes I like to be in control," Jia complained.

Erik laughed. "You don't even use manual control most of the time."

Jia's hands tightened on the control yoke. "Well, it's not like I *never* do. I am now. But let's forget about all that. Care to explain why we loaded the arsenal into my new flitter on our day off? Unless there's some secret syndicate raid I hadn't heard about, I thought we were supposed to go to the tactical center?"

"The tactical center is useful, but it has its limits." Erik pulled back his duster and patted his pistol. "All the fancy nanotech, holograms, and misdirection allow us to be anywhere, but it's all fake in the end."

"I'd hope so." Jia chuckled. "We put our lives on the line often enough during our job. I don't want to risk them for a training exercise."

Erik shook his head. "Even the guns are fake, though—the weight, the feel, the recoil. It's close, but not the same as the real thing. In the beginning, I only cared about getting you to shoot without reservation and making sure you had better tactical resources. The center is good for that, but we need to take it to the next level."

"Meaning what?"

Her PNIU chimed.

Erik looked into the back seat and nodded at Emma. "Sent her the address already?"

Emma nodded back. "I figured we could discuss everything on the way."

Jia's eyes darted between them. "The Shadow Zone? Please tell me we aren't doing some rogue raid."

"Nothing like that." Erik looked out the side window, a wistful expression on his face. "Live fire is important. I know you already get that, so it's time to mix live fire with the training scenarios. The best simulation in the world can't trick the human brain, and sometimes it's good to train when you're not getting shot at."

Jia accelerated, and her flitter zoomed away from the parking platform. "I'm not saying I disagree, but what does this have to do with the Shadow Zone? And what does live fire constitute, exactly?"

"You've gotten over your tendency to use that stun pistol for everything," Erik explained with a shrug, "but you need to be comfortable with a wider range of weapons, not just the occasional rifle. If we run into Talos' Tin Men or *yaoguai* again, you'll need to be able to use everything the colonel's provided, and anything I can scrounge from a wrecked exoskeleton." He nodded. "It's simple. Alicia's hooked me up with a place where we can train with all my weapons."

Jia frowned. "My newfound willingness to play fast and loose with the rules doesn't necessarily extend to illegal Shadow Zone operations."

Erik grinned. "There's nothing illegal about it. It's just the kind of business respectable Uptowners don't want near them. On top of that, very few people have the necessary permits to use the kinds of weapons we're going to train with, so it's on the expensive side."

"Oh. That's not so bad." Jia's frown vanished.

"Exactly. It's not like I'm saving all my money for the future. This place won't be as dynamic as the tactical center, but it's not just a range, either. They've got target drones and that kind of thing. I want to hit it at least monthly, so we're both comfortable with all the weapons we have available. You never know who or what we'll run into. I still want to get you rated for exoskeleton piloting, too, but one challenge at a time."

Jia shook her head and gave him a bright smile. "So, we're spending a day off pretending to kill people?"

"Nope. We'll be blowing actual things up. Totally different," he replied.

CHAPTER THREE

An hour later, with her flitter parked deep in the Shadow Zone, Jia noticed she was biting a fingernail.

How many times am I going to worry that the flitter will be stolen?

Despite the sophisticated antitheft features, she wasn't convinced it could survive the attention of a dedicated Zone criminal intent on scoring a fancy new red flitter.

As much she despised antisocial criminals, after working so many cases, she couldn't deny their ingenuity. The smart ones stuck to nonviolent crimes, so they didn't end up getting shot by a TR-7 or some ex-soldier in an exoskeleton. Of course, the *truly* intelligent didn't take up that kind of crime. They just joined a corporation, found a method to steal from people, and called it legal.

Jia took a deep breath and shook her head. There was a thin line between being pragmatic and being jaded. Counseling and Erik's friendship had helped pull her out of a dark spot, but she needed to be careful not to fall back into it.

Erik stood near the back, loading the weapons crates onto a new hoverdolly and whistling like he was having the greatest time in the world.

Earlier, he'd stepped through a loading door leading into a huge but decrepit warehouse and disappeared for several minutes before returning with the dolly and a man in a faded red uniform with epaulets he had introduced as Big Bill Zantini, the owner of the range.

The lack of patches or other insignia made it impossible to determine if it was real or a costume. Jia leaned toward the latter. The perpetual grin and faint hint of madness in Big Bill's eyes made her harbor doubts he'd been part of anything more organized than a sphere ball fan club. The scars crisscrossing his face only fueled more concern.

Why hadn't he had them taken care of?

Despite that, Erik didn't seem worried by the man, and whatever questions Jia might have, she trusted her partner.

She glanced his way. When he'd agreed to the fake dating proposal, Jia had hoped it might help quell some of the thoughts that ran through her head at night, but it had only made them worse. She understood his reasoning, but that didn't mean she had to like it.

Jia had never met a man like Erik, and she suspected that if he left her life, she would never do so again. There was only so long he would wait before taking Alina's offer to become an Intelligence Directorate contractor. It made sense. His investigation was dead-ending on Earth, and that position would give him the resources and flexibility he would need to get his revenge.

She took a deep breath and slowly let it out. He was only staying because of her, but she wasn't sure about gallivanting around the galaxy. Taking down whatever conspiracy had killed Erik's people might make the UTC a better place, but she might better serve humanity as a cop.

Unfortunately, *she just didn't know.*

Erik opened a crate and ran a hand over his TR-7. "Nothing like a lucky gun, but I think I'm going to stick to an assault rifle today.

Jia let out a mock gasp. "How do I know you're Erik and not some Zitark using a holographic disguise?"

He looked up. "I don't think Zitarks like beignets?" Erik questioned with a shrug. He closed the crate and snapped one lock, then the other. "I was just thinking about how I shouldn't get too overly dependent on any one weapon. The recent *fun* on our vacation proved that. I might not always have my preferred toys."

"True enough."

Big Bill ran a hand through his graying hair and whistled in appreciation. "Even without the TR-7, from the looks of things, you've got a lot of nice gear to play with. You're going to be like two platypuses in zero-G in there."

Jia stared at the man and awaited an explanation, having a hard time understanding his comparison. She knew plenty about platypuses and plenty about zero-G. She'd even fought under such conditions not all that long ago, but what the man had said didn't make sense. Her mouth opened to question him, but she closed it.

Sometimes it was better not to know the truth.

"You're right." Erik patted the longest case after setting

it on the dolly. "Got a man-portable laser rifle in here. I prefer my TR-7, but it's nice to be able to blast a hole through something when you really need to."

"A MANPLR?" Big Bill whistled in appreciation. "Nice. I've been aching to get my hands on one, but it's still a bitch to get one of those away from the military. It must be nice to be a vet."

Erik nodded, not looking Big Bill in the face. "Something like that."

Jia took note of Big Bill's further admission that his uniform didn't represent any sort of military service. That wasn't surprising unless he was a time traveler from several centuries prior—although, given all the nonsense she'd run into Neo SoCal, she almost wouldn't be shocked.

"I'll buy it off you, Erik." Big Bill's grin somehow managed to grow wider. "If you're willing. I could make a killing renting it out. I know a guy who can get me the right kind of power cells, but even he can't get me a rifle."

"No way." Erik shook his head. "I need this to shoot terrorists and armored *yaoguai,* and it's too damned fun to sell."

Jia laughed. Erik's boyish enthusiasm for his heavy weapons had pushed out all the negative thoughts. His predilection for destructive toys was infectious when she let it be.

"I remember a time when I thought a stun pistol was all I needed." Jia patted the weapon. "And now it shocks me that the average patrol officer doesn't carry a rifle." She pointed to another crate. The shape was suggestive of a particular weapon. "Wait, are we shooting missiles, too?"

Try as she might, Jia couldn't keep the excitement out of her voice. Erik was really infecting her mind.

"The more we both practice using everything in our arsenal, the better things will be if we get ambushed by gangsters, terrorists, *yaoguai,* Tin Men or," he eyed her, "Zitarks trying to start a harem."

Jia raised an eyebrow. "Zitarks trying to start a harem?"

"It could happen." Erik shrugged. "I don't know what the hell they're into. Pictures of raptors?" He finished loading and pushed the dolly toward the door, then inclined his head toward the flitter. "By the way, I saw you looking at your flitter and around earlier. You don't have to worry about that. Big Bill will make sure no one messes with it."

Jia eyed the strange man with suspicion. "I'd hope so."

"I can't have my customers getting annoyed with losses, especially customers dropping as many credits as you two are today." Big Bill tapped his PNIU.

A low, rattling growl sounded behind Jia. Her hand shot to her slug-thrower. Red eyes stared at her from the darkness of a nearby alley.

"Don't," Jia spat through clenched teeth. "Unless you want to get shot."

"Calm down there, Detective," Big Bill soothed. "Everything's under control. I'll show you." He snapped his fingers.

A robotic dog complete with ears, a tail, and a mouth full of metal teeth jogged out of the shadows. Light glinted off the metallic surface, and now that it was closer, Jia thought it more resembled a metallic skeleton of a dog than the beast itself. There was something absurd and almost wrong about making a bot that semi-resembled a real animal, but that was probably the point. A robot dog with a mouth full of teeth probably scared most criminals worse than a faceless security bot.

"I see," Jia commented, lowering her hand. "Next time, don't surprise me."

"Touchy. I'll try to remember that." Big Bill gestured around the area, highlighting small protrusions from nearby walls or a glint of metal from a pile of trash. "I've got a lot of toys hiding around, just in case someone decides they're going to be a dumbass and try to steal anything from here. It's not like people aren't aware of the gear I keep and the kind of money I make. Before, I made deals with the boys who ran this part of the Zone. I paid them a security fee, you could call it." He sucked air through a gap in his teeth. "But they're all dead or in jail now. That's progress for you. It's been fun fortifying my place, though."

"You'd prefer criminals backing you up?" she asked. She was truly curious.

Big Bill shrugged, his grin now more playful than insane. "There's something to be said for a man honest about his violence."

Erik stopped at the door and nodded inside. "Let's get going. We have bots to trash and guns to shoot." He started to walk in, his voice carrying as he continued, "Maybe not in that order."

Jia jogged after him, content not to press Big Bill on his fondness for syndicate protection schemes. Despite the conversation and the killer robot dog, she had relaxed.

Before meeting Erik, she'd never even been in the

Shadow Zone, and now it felt like a good, fun place to spend a day off, firing missiles and laser rifles. She chuckled at the thought.

Her family would be aghast if they understood how much she had changed.

CHAPTER FOUR

Jia's mirth faded to confusion as she passed through the doorway after Erik.

Their angle of arrival didn't grant her a clear view of the back of the warehouse. Now inside, she could tell it would have been an interesting sight from the air since there was no back to the warehouse.

Remnants of a scorched and mostly destroyed wall stuck out from the ground and roof, leaving the building exposed to the elements. The unpleasant smell of the Zone was somehow even stronger inside the half-open building. Dense piles of debris covered most of the floor. Bullet-riddled and half-melted bots lay strewn about much of the area, forming the bulk of the piles.

Stray trash made up the rest.

The remains of a King Sentry were propped up near a corner, a huge hole punched through the center of the bot; the exterior of the hole was blackened. The near-carpet of destroyed bots extended out of the building past the downed wall, covering a good chunk of the space between the warehouse and the next-closest building.

Erik and Jia had destroyed a lot of bots in their time together, but the sheer number that had met their final days in front of her staggered her imagination. Big Bill could have taken over a militia base with so many bots.

Then again, she doubted he'd acquired them all at once, and a man who could legally own heavy firearms probably didn't have much trouble sourcing bots.

"This isn't what I envisioned when you said we were going to a tactical range," Jia admitted as she glanced around. "Even with you saying it was a little more than that. Then again, I'm not that surprised by a tactical range in the Shadow Zone being a bot massacre ground."

Big Bill snickered. "Massacre? Training's no good without something trying to get you. That's what I always say."

Erik nodded. He pushed the dolly against a wall and ran his thumb along the side of the handle to lower it all the way to the ground. "Exactly. Big Bill's got a nice setup here. We can't customize it as much as our usual place, but knowing there are actual bots firing at us will get the blood pumping better, even if it's just painful stuns."

Jia eyed the back of Erik's head. "I'm half-surprised they don't fire live ammo."

Bill Big smacked his lips. "Yeah, I tried that for a while."

Jia stared at him, hoping he was joking, but the look on his face suggested he wasn't.

"The insurance is a bitch," he explained.

"You're *insured?"* Jia asked.

"I didn't say it was with a reputable company." Big Bill

scratched his chin. "That was another thing that was easier before you all went around cleaning up the city."

"So, you had gangster security and gangster insurance?" Jia ventured.

"Basically, yeah." Big Bill let out a long, wistful sigh. "I've got a joke for you. What's the difference between a good cop and a dirty cop?"

Jia frowned. "I don't know. What is it?"

"The dirty cop stays bought." Big Bill guffawed and slapped his leg, his laugh trailing off at Jia's frown. "Most of my customers love that joke."

"I'm sure they do."

Ignoring the bad attempt at humor, Erik knelt and grabbed a crate.

He set it on the ground and opened it to reveal two assault rifles. He began moving other crates and opening them until their contents were exposed, including the rifles and ammo, several different types of grenades, the laser rifle, and a missile launcher with four high-explosive rounds. He left the TR-7 in its crate, making Jia wonder why he'd bothered to bring it.

Jia's hungry gaze drifted to the missile launcher. "So, I see this is *Diyu* for bots. Is there some scenario here? Are we rescuing a bot princess or something?"

"No fancy scenario," Erik explained. "Just lots of bots trying to screw with us. I've asked Big Bill to use only contact stuns this time. I want the pressure of a huge-ass army bearing down on us, but without us having to do a lot of dodging. We can do that next time."

"Can you afford next time?" Jia looked around. "This has to be even pricier than I realized."

"It's better than spending it on some cloud city vacation." Erik gestured to a faded yellow line that extended a few meters from the door all the way across the warehouse. "Bots won't mess with you if you're behind that line." He pointed to a half-collapsed building behind the warehouse. The blackened walls and blast holes revealed its past.

Jia's eyes tracked it. "That's the limit of the playing field, I take it?"

"Yeah." Erik cracked his knuckles before strapping an assault rifle over his shoulder and stuffing magazines into the pockets of his duster. "Make sure you practice with everything this session. This isn't just for fun."

"Only mostly?" Jia grabbed her rifle and ammo before clipping a few plasma grenades to her belt.

"Exactly." Erik smiled.

"And your…supplier isn't mad about you wasting gear?"

Jia didn't know how far she could trust Big Bill. Mentioning Colonel Adeyemi might be a mistake, even if she doubted Big Bill had any connection with the conspiracy. The kind of man who wore a coat with epaulets was not the type galaxy-spanning conspiracies recruited for assistance.

Erik shook his head. "My supplier understands the need to keep current with weapons." He slapped a magazine into the rifle. "And he wants both of us to use the gear he provided since you're helping me with my side job." He stepped past the line. "Let's keep it easy the first few minutes, Big Bill. I want to ease into it."

Big Bill saluted Erik. "I'll be in my office. I'll start everything up once I get there. I've got the bots programmed to avoid a target once they've been stunned."

"Works for me."

Big Bill followed the yellow line toward another wall. A reinforced metal door was inset into a thick metal portion of the wall.

He arrived and tapped his PNIU.

The door opened with the loud, resounding thuds of interior bolts and Big Bill entered a brightly lit, clean-looking hallway at odds with the destroyed surroundings. A few seconds passed before the door slammed shut behind him. The man might be odd, but he wasn't a total idiot.

One stray missile would ruin his day if he wasn't careful, she mused. *Humans suffered a statistically embarrassing hundred percent mortality rate when blown apart by a missile.*

"All the mags I brought are armor-piercing." Erik pulled her attention back to the task at hand. "We won't always know ahead of time what we're facing, but this time we know it won't be anything but machines. It's good to familiarize yourself with the damage profiles."

"We only know there won't be anything but machines if we assume we're not going to be ambushed by criminals," Jia joked.

Erik offered her a devilish grin. "Ambushing us when we're packing a small arsenal would be crap luck. Shoot an AP round through a man's head and he'll die quick enough."

"Cheerful thought."

"I've got to be me."

A shrill klaxon sounded. Several rubble piles stirred, small six-legged security bots emerging from them.

"I'm surprised those things don't haunt my nightmares," Jia muttered.

"It is one weird part of being back on Earth. The farther you go on the frontier, the fewer bots you see." Erik flipped off his safety.

Jia followed and aimed her rifle. She fired a burst and downed a nearby bot before the machine escaped the mountain of bot limbs and carcasses it had been hiding in. She spun to nail a bot climbing up a side wall. Additional bots emerged from the debris.

Erik joined the fun by unloading on a few approaching the detectives from the opposite side. Even more bots poured out of dark crevices like roaches blasted with light. Erik's and Jia's high-velocity armor-piercing ammo ripped through the bots with ease, blasting metal chunks around to add to the mechanical graveyard.

Jia smirked as she remembered trying to take on a horde of bots with nothing but her stun pistol. She'd been lucky in a twisted way that her first captain had been such a corrupt coward.

If she'd worked real cases before she'd learned to handle herself, she might have ended up dead. Now, if a month passed without a serious terrorist incident, she considered it a vacation.

She couldn't protect the UTC hiding behind a stun pistol.

Bots skittered over their fallen brethren, surging forward in a tide of metal. They weren't rushing as fast as she'd seen in previous encounters, probably another part of the training. She wasn't going to second-guess Erik's experience. Despite all the fights she'd been in since becoming his partner, he still had decades on her when it came to the fine art of delivering death by bullet.

Heart pounding, Jia ejected her magazine and slammed in a new one. Erik was right; even if it was just stun bots, facing an actual foe activated her combat instincts in a way the simulation at the uptown tactical center couldn't.

Her brain really *could* tell the difference.

A pack of bots charged into the warehouse from outside. Jia and Erik squeezed off a few rounds before she yanked one of the plasma grenades from her belt, primed it, and chucked it toward the approaching stun-rod-bearing horde as if she'd been doing it all her life. Her throw ended up shallow, but the massive explosion scattered most of the bots, ripping apart and half-melting most of them to add another layer to the robot graveyard. A few survivors in the back continued charging forward, paying no heed to their destroyed brethren. Erik ended their short existence with a few quick bursts.

Jia chuckled. He'd talked about the TR-7 being lucky a few times, but he didn't need the ridiculous gun. Not that she would complain too much. It was perhaps better to note he didn't *always* need the ridiculous gun, but the four-barreled monstrosity occasionally had its uses in the rougher situations they ended up.

"Good use of the grenade," he shouted over another burst.

"Too bad I didn't get them all in one throw," Jia countered. She could practice grenade-throwing by printing something of equal shape and weight, but that was a project for the future.

She frowned. *She would need an arm-toning regimen for basic grenade-throwing offensive capability. When would she have ever thought she would need to be stronger to throw a grenade farther away?*

She looked back and forth, seeking more enemies. The ferocious, inhuman horde lay defeated, utterly annihilated by the quick efforts of two cops with big guns.

"That was easy," Jia quipped.

Erik ejected his magazine and slipped a new one in. "That's just the warm-up. Wait for it; it'll come soon. Big Bill is watching everything that goes on in here."

The klaxon sounded again, and a dark, buzzing swarm swept around the exposed back opening of the warehouse. It wasn't a deadly cloud of insects, but dozens of tiny, hovering orb-shaped security bots.

"Oh," Jia commented, her face blank. "That's fun."

"Nothing like a little aerial target practice," Erik replied.

Jia held down her trigger and swept her rifle back and forth, downing several of the flying bots within a few seconds. Erik joined her. The bots spiraled in an attempt to dodge, but the combined hail of bullets blasted through them and sent them careening to join their defeated brothers below.

More legs popped out of the messes on the floor inside and outside the building. Scuttling security bots emerged a moment later, faster than the first wave.

Erik snapped off several quick shots in a row, his bullets ripping through the centers of the advancing enemies.

They each collapsed silently—no scream, no yell, just deactivation.

Not to be outdone, Jia matched him shot for shot until she was empty. He grinned at her efforts and the steadily growing piles in front of them.

Her shoulder was taking a pounding even with the reduced recoil design of the rifles.

After a speedy reload, Jia continued wreaking havoc among the endless hordes of bots streaming in from outside or emerging from the piles. No wonder the place was so expensive. Even if Big Bill had a good line on someone who could supply bargain bots or repair damaged bots cheaply, Jia and Erik were blowing through a not insignificant army for their little live-fire training session. She was glad she didn't have to pay.

If Erik wanted to spend part of his thirty years of savings on improved training, she wasn't going to complain, especially when it was fun.

Loud thuds came from the back.

A King Sentry stomped around the corner and into the warehouse. Unlike the monster they had fought before, it lacked cannons, instead bearing two stun rods so long they might properly be called stun lances.

The huge bot didn't rush toward them. Instead, it moved slowly, taking hard, ponderous steps that knocked debris and trash aside in its wake.

Programmed intimidation, perhaps. Jia half-wanted to shout an insult, but it was futile to waste quality effort on any machine that wasn't Emma.

Erik didn't fire at the King, instead alternating between smaller threats in the air and the continual addition of smaller ground forces. Jia took a few potshots, but her bullets bounced off the thick, reinforced armor.

"Hold them off, and I'll handle the big guy," Jia called, trying to hold back her grin. A big enemy required a big response.

"Make it quick." Erik punctuated his sentence by blowing a flying bot apart and showering the bots beneath it with the fragments of its ally as his eyes flicked to the sentry robot and back. "Those are very real stun rods."

Jia threw the rifle strap over her shoulder and rushed to the laser rifle case. She leaned over and pulled the huge weapon out, grimacing at the weight. She was strong and fit, but she lacked Erik's cybernetic arm.

With a grunt, she yanked the rifle fully out of the case and stood it up on its end. Her hand flew across the side controls, and the tripod extended. She let the rifle fall forward, the newly deployed stand arresting its fall.

"My turn," she whispered under her breath, not that Erik would be able to hear her over the hum of the machines or his near-constant gunfire.

The King continued stomping toward them. Jia took a moment, lined up, and threw the last of her plasma grenades toward a cluster of smaller forces on the ground before whipping her attention back over to their advancing ogre-like cousin.

She dropped to one knee and snagged one of the conical power cells from the crate to screw into the side. The weapon came alive, and she pointed it at the advancing King with a smile.

"It's nice when they're slow." Jia pulled the trigger.

The King jerked, struck by the invisible beam from the

weapon. Sparks and internal hydraulic fluid leaked out of the large hole she'd carved through the center of the bot. Jia let out a shout of triumph, then aimed again and pulled the trigger. This time she blew a leg off. After her third shot, the machine stopped moving.

Erik quit firing. She snapped her head in his direction, surprised.

He inclined his head forward. "No more little guys."

Jia blinked and looked around. He was right. She'd been so focused on destroying the King that she'd lost overall tactical awareness.

She would need to work on that.

A loud hum sounded from outside. Jia swiveled the tripod in that direction and licked her lips in anticipation. A long dark shadow heralded the arrival of something even worse than the King. An armored personnel carrier pulled forward, hovering a few feet off the ground. The only saving grace was the lack of a turret on top.

"You've *got* to be kidding," Jia griped. She pulled the trigger twice, blasting two new holes in the APC, but the vehicle continued forward. She pulled the trigger again, but the weapon didn't fire. Out of energy. "What is it going to do, run us over?"

"I doubt that," Erik replied.

The APC pivoted to its side, and the doors began to open. Light glinted off the squirming six-legged bots filling the vehicle.

"It's doing what it's supposed to—carry troops." Erik sprinted toward the case and grabbed the missile launcher and a round. He dropped the projectile in and steadied the launcher on his shoulder in a practiced move that took only seconds. "Backblast area clear," he shouted. She replied, and he launched.

The missile screamed toward the APC as the door finished opening. The attack passed the bots and struck the inside. A massive explosion ripped the vehicle in half. The main chunks of the vehicle collapsed to the floor with an echoing thud as pieces of security bots fell from above like metal hail.

"I'm *really* glad I'm not paying for this," Jia commented.

Erik grinned. "Yeah." He loaded in a new missile and walked over to Jia to hand her the launcher. "One more shot, just in case, and for the experience."

She hoisted the launcher onto her shoulder and looked behind her to make sure Erik wasn't there. "Backblast area clear!"

"Yes!"

Her missile flew toward the burning remnants of the APC and exploded, finishing off the few larger bots that had survived the initial attack. Burning debris now lay all over.

The warehouse and the area behind it no longer resembled a dump, but a warzone. She half-expected the local police to show up and investigate. Maybe the former criminals supported the range because they wanted something in the neighborhood that would discourage the locals from investigating reports of gunfire and explosions nearby.

Jia knelt and set the launcher down. "I admit the laser rifle and missile launcher are pretty handy, although both are heavy. That rifle is insane. It carved through that King like it was paper, despite its armor."

"Not the right kind of armor for that kind of attack,"

Erik commented. "Weight's bad, but stick it on an exoskeleton and you might be okay." After a few seconds, he smirked. "So, you like them big?" He raised an eyebrow in challenge.

Jia smirked back. "Sometimes size does matter. Sometimes it doesn't, but it's nice to have the option."

Erik grinned. "I'll keep that in mind."

Another klaxon sounded.

Jia rolled her head around her shoulders to loosen up. "They just keep coming, don't they?"

Erik pulled his rifle down. "Sure, just like they do in real fights. At least this will be more fun than testifying in court against gangsters."

Jia readied her rifle and loaded a fresh magazine. She aimed at a bot scurrying toward them and fired. "You know what? You're right."

CHAPTER FIVE

Sophia waited, her hands resting in her lap and her legs crossed.

Her elaborate scarlet and black asymmetric one-shoulder draped gown highlighted her curves with scientific precision and revealed enough of her skin to be appealing without being coarse.

No matter what many claimed, one's physical appearance carried power, and she intended to make full use of that truth. She'd learned just how great a weapon beauty could be over the decades.

It didn't matter if anything about her had ceased to be natural decades ago. The obsession with purity was the greatest lie that the foolish dregs making up most of humanity had let themselves accept.

The divine gave mankind knowledge, and she saw no problem with taking that knowledge and applying it to transcend the so-called natural order. Of course, the lesser beings populating the UTC needed to be kept in check.

It was far too amusing that the UTC thought it was

helping them, but really, it was indirectly carrying out the will of the Core.

Such lies and misdirection had their place, but their plans needed to proceed with caution. The Local Neighborhood races interjected far too much uncertainty into formerly clear plans. The nonhumans would have their uses, too, but not until the time was right. It'd taken far too much effort as it was to encourage limited contact with such dangerous outside elements, and there was only so long they could depend on alien xenophobia to keep them away from UTC space.

Everything would change then.

Sophia tried to convince herself not to worry about aliens. In the end, all living beings wanted the same thing. She just wanted to make sure humanity—and by extension, her group, the Core—had the upper hand when the UTC started mixing more fully with the aliens. Humanity would rule the galaxy, and the Core would rule humanity.

She stared out at the long, empty table in front of her. It was time. She shouldn't keep her colleagues waiting.

She tapped her PNIU. Twelve other chairs winked into existence, followed by flawless holograms of the other members of the Core, all the men and women dressed elegantly, according to their personal tastes. She appreciated that they all shared her mindset about the importance of appearance. When people could sculpt themselves with ease, they had no justification for not appearing their best.

Not to do so implied laziness of spirit, and anyone like that didn't belong in the Core.

A burly, handsome blond-haired man in a suit near the center of the table looked her way. He cleared his throat and spoke with a faint Russian accent. "It's been some time since we had a full meeting. Was this really necessary, Sophia? This type of meeting brings with it risks."

"Everything we do carries risk, Ivan." She scoffed. "That's what it means to be leaders. As for whether it was necessary, that is a matter for debate. However, given events that have unfolded on Earth and the moon involving the Last Soldier, I thought a formal meeting was in order, lest everything we are working on be threatened. I also wanted to make sure we're all in agreement about how to proceed, so we avoid certain problems." Her gaze cut to a breathtakingly gorgeous long-haired Japanese man in a black silk robe. "Especially since certain assurances about the clean up on Molino have proven to be premature. Wouldn't you say, Shoji?"

The Japanese man threaded his fingers together, his mouth quirking into a ghost of a smile. "Premature? I dispute that characterization. The package was retrieved from Molino, and our involvement with the elimination of all relevant witnesses has yet to be exposed. As far as the rest of the UTC is concerned, those soldiers were killed by terrorists."

"The Last Soldier disagrees." Sophia narrowed her eyes. "And he's harmed our interests by looking into the matter."

Shoji's smile turned infuriatingly merry. He needed a good slap. "His disagreement is irrelevant. For all his skill, he's only one man with limited resources. We are thirteen, with access to some of the greatest resources in the entirety of the UTC."

Ivan shook his head. "But it's not just him. There are elements of the UTC government that aren't optimally controlled, and there's some evidence that they might have had contact with him. This has turned into more of a threat than any of us anticipated. We can't ignore that risk just because it'll make us feel better about our superiority."

Shoji whipped his hair over his shoulder and gave a bored sigh. "All other annoying elements will be taken care of, if not soon, in the near future. We need to continue to handle this entire situation with care. All our efforts could come to nothing if the wrong people become aware of things. Exposure is more of a risk than one obsessed suicidal soldier and whatever ragtag allies he can scrape together with a sob story about his unit being lost. He could eventually grow despondent and end himself."

Sophia scoffed. "There's little evidence of that. He won't stop until he finds the truth or he's dead."

"Well, I do love a simple solution set."

A scowling dark-haired man at the end of the table crossed his arms. "I care more about the package. Your ridiculously circuitous movement of it has hampered things, and the research summaries sent along weren't as promising as I'd hoped. It's almost as if you're trying to keep something from the rest of us."

Sophia waved a hand dismissively. "Don't worry, Farad. All of the artifacts were not only successfully retrieved and transported, as I previously described, but the analysis is proceeding apace. We've discovered useful things that justify the effort we put into acquiring them and covering it up, even with the few loose ends."

"Meaning what?" Farad narrowed his eyes. "Details are useful. Generalities not. You've called a full meeting. That's an inconvenience you should atone for by being open."

"The artifacts are believed to have the capability of helping us directly achieve our ultimate goal rather than the temporary solutions we've relied on in the past." Sophia leaned forward, a genuine if cold smile appearing. "If not that, they at least have the ability to teach us how to achieve that goal based on our existing knowledge."

Several men and women at the table exchanged glances. Sophia deepened her smile.

"Have we confirmed if they are Navigator technology?" Ivan asked. "All the initial reports said they appeared to be different from previously recovered Navigator artifacts, and that is why the research has been slower, after taking into account the transfer times."

She tapped a finger on the table. "It's too early to tell. They are from the appropriate time period, but there's some evidence it might be Hunter technology, even if it is different from what we have dealt with in the past. It's not as if we have exhaustive knowledge of all ancient dead races."

Murmurs broke out around the table, something passing for genuine excitement among the members of the Core. Sophia waited for the din to die down before continuing.

"But as noted in the initial report, there were at least a few distinct Navigator artifacts in the cache," she explained. "That does raise questions that might remain unanswered despite our best efforts."

"The Navigators were hiding the artifacts from the Hunters?" Shoji suggested. "Or perhaps the opposite?"

Ivan grunted. "Does it matter? The Navigators and Hunters were dust before we'd mastered fire. Perhaps the

Hunters did wipe out the Navigators, but we only have a few scraps of evidence to suggest that. We must complete our plan before knowledge of the Hunters leaks out and people seek the technology and complicate matters. If knowledge of the Navigators hadn't spread, this wouldn't be so difficult. Now every maggot on a frontier world is digging into caves, hoping they can find Navigator tech and raising the risks to our operations."

Shoji threw his head back and laughed. "What absurdity. You really think Navigator technology could have been concealed so easily from the rest of humanity?"

"What's so funny?" Ivan glared at the other man. "Why couldn't it? I still think it was a horrid mistake to let that knowledge spread."

"The UTC could have never spread without the hyperspace transfer points." Shoji chuckled. "And how would anyone explain something that violated everything we knew about physics? Trying to conceal it would have been more trouble than it was worth. At least the Hunter technology is more…limited in terms of the scope of the applications we intend."

"We could have explained the new technology as human ingenuity," Ivan insisted, puffing out his chest. "I'm surprised you think it would have been so difficult after everything—"

"The past is irrelevant," Sophia snapped, "except in how it influences the future. We have the artifacts, and our people will continue to study them. That is what matters to me and the future. They have great promise. They will lead to our eventual goal. Is this understood?"

Farad leaned forward, scowling. "Not all past experiments with artifacts have proven all that healthy. I'm not going to be the first volunteer to try it. I'm not going to sacrifice my life for the rest of you."

Sophia gave him a cold smile. "Cowardice isn't always the best long-term survival strategy. Keep that in mind before saying things like that."

Ivan harrumphed. "These advances are heartening, but the technology doesn't solve our immediate problem."

"Which is?"

"The Last Soldier," Ivan insisted. "He's been sniffing around too much. It's now obvious that letting him live was a mistake." He looked at Sophia. "You called this meeting mostly because of him, yes?"

"He was supposed to be a broken shell of a man who turned people away from looking deeper." Sophia shrugged. "But there's no concern as long as we all agree on how to proceed and don't end up interfering with each other's efforts." Her gaze cut to Farad. "As has happened in the past."

Farad averted his eyes. "What is good for some of us isn't necessarily good for all of us."

"We've been through this type of situation countless times," Sophia continued, deciding not to press the issue of operational sabotage. "It's difficult to predict the behavior of all variables. We should continue to push operations against him, but be mindful of anything that points back to us. This is a delicate time, and we cannot have the research into the artifacts be threatened." She shook her head. "Besides, he's had some minor successes, but that doesn't change one very important reality."

"And what is that?" Ivan chimed in, his brow furrowed in what seemed like perpetual anger.

"It's as I said earlier. He's one man. A troublesome man, but still a man."

"But others have been helping him. He's had contact with the ID. It's obvious he's receiving support from military sources as well. Who knows how much he's told the police in Neo Southern California? He grows more dangerous by the day."

Sophia rolled her eyes with as much contempt as she could manage without ocular implants. "Police? Yes. Their efforts have damaged many of our interests in the metroplex, and admittedly, even some of our wider plans, but that's all the more reason to practice surgical precision rather than anything too obvious. Right now, if we make a bold move, we'll just confirm everything he believes and has perhaps told to those around him. Even our reach is finite."

"Then what would you have us do, Sophia?" Farad asked. "Nothing? Why did you bother calling this meeting? For one man, he's accomplished as much damage to us as dozens of previous attempts by the uncontrolled elements in the UTC government."

"Mere luck, nothing more. An ant stinging a man because he wasn't paying attention to the insect." Sophia's smile turned as cold as it was wide. "And luck runs out eventually, but that's not to say we can't facilitate the process." She tapped her PNIU. "I've sent you all a document. I have recommended a plan that will take care of the Last Soldier, while also providing us with some useful data on other matters of interest. It will also handle him off-world, where he has fewer resources to call on."

Farad nodded slowly, some of his displeasure ebbing from his face. "Good. Every day he lives, the more he becomes a risk."

Sophia clucked her tongue. "I would have thought the decades would have taught you the most important lesson of all."

"And what's that?"

"Patience is *always* rewarded," Sophia responded. "And the problems of the moment will seem minor in the long run."

CHAPTER SIX

Erik grumbled under his breath. Staring out the window of Jia's new flitter at the stream of traffic wasn't doing much to distract him from the day's irritations.

He would have loved to blow off steam after work at Big Bill's, but Jia was right. It was ridiculously expensive, and even his vast savings would go dry if he started hitting the place up weekly.

Jia glanced at him from the driver's seat. "You're not mad because I'm letting Emma drive, are you? I figure it's better her than the autodrive."

"You're just trying to suck up to her," Erik grumped.

Emma snorted. For some reason, she liked to be in her holographic form more often in Jia's flitter than in the MX 60. "It's working. I don't like not having a body, and my preferred body has such a lovely array of sensors and options. This is a fine vehicle, but it's far more limited than the MX 60."

That might explain her holographic preference. A body of light was a type of body.

"Miguel said it's taking longer than expected." Erik shrugged. "He needed to order some special parts. It's not like I don't miss having a flitter."

"It's not the process I object to," Emma clarified with a frown. "I've just become far too accustomed to having a proper and useful body. I feel very insubstantial when I don't have a dedicated body. It's an emotional failing, I'll admit to that."

Erik smirked. "It's only human."

Emma rolled her eyes. "There's no reason to be insulting, Detective."

Jia laughed. "I'm glad that's all this is, Erik. You'll get over it soon enough."

He looked her way with a frown. He didn't need her worrying about him that way. "Meaning what?"

Jia shrugged. "You seemed okay testifying, but I wondered if something about dealing with the gangsters bothered you. I know it's been coming up more often lately. I didn't want you getting more pissed off."

"Those guys? Nah." Erik snickered. "Testifying's busywork, and they don't make us go on the stand very often, but it doesn't bother me much. Why? Does it bother you?"

"Honestly? Yes." Jia crossed her arms. "It just feels unnecessary. The idea that police officers have to get up on the stand and testify seems like some pointless relic of a simpler time. It's the twenty-third century. Legal processing should be automated."

Erik jerked his thumb at Emma. "You're saying she should be judge and jury?"

"I would make a good one," Emma insisted. "I'm equally biased against *all* fleshbags."

"It's not a bad idea," Jia concluded. "It'd be better than us wasting time testifying."

"I didn't know you felt that way," Erik admitted. "But I think a lot of this is more about us than cops in general."

Jia frowned. "Oh?"

"I think it is just about them getting Lady Justice and the Obsidian Detective on the stand," Erik suggested. "Symbolic and all that. It's not surprising, despite the crime rate dropping. The media laps it up, too."

Jia sighed. "They shouldn't rely so much on individuals, even as symbols. People are far too flawed to make good symbols."

"Why? You have some kinky secret that's going to come out if someone investigates too deeply?" Erik smiled to make the joke clear.

Jia slugged him in the arm. "I think you'd enjoy that. No. But what if they decide to start digging up your past? You've been arrested."

Erik laughed. "You've come so far that I almost forget your background at times."

Jia frowned and looked away, her cheeks scarlet. "What's that supposed to mean?"

"If being arrested was all it took to destroy your life, a lot of people on Earth would be screwed, let alone in the colonies." Erik gestured at a passing tower. "And if it were that rare, they wouldn't need so many cops, now, would they?"

"I managed to make it through all my life without being arrested." Jia lifted her chin with the pride only a thoroughbred Lin woman could achieve.

Erik grinned. "*Yet*. Give it a few more decades, especially if you hang around with me. We'll probably end up in some corrupt cop's jail on the frontier."

Jia's expression turned curious and she stared at him.

"What?" Erik asked, curiosity getting the better of him.

"You couldn't have been arrested a bunch in the military," Jia suggested. "They would have kicked you out."

"Yeah." Erik nodded. "Once I joined up, my rougher days were over. You can say the Army found a better way to channel my energy. Anyway, I'm not worried about someone digging into my past to discredit me on the stand or crap like that."

"Still think the whole thing is ridiculous. They have all our PNIU recordings, not to mention camera recordings. We add nothing by being there, and I can't think of a single case we've worked where we didn't record what happened." Jia shrugged. "Can you?"

"PNIUs and camera records can be hacked or erased," Erik countered. "It's nice to have human backup, don't you think?

"Human memory is far more fallible than recorded information," Jia countered. "It's absurd to rely on it in a court versus recorded evidence, even with the risk of hacking. It's far easier to bribe someone."

Erik laughed. "I really *have* corrupted you, haven't I?"

Jia shook her head. "You've made me see the truth. Nothing more."

"See a conspiracy around every corner now?" Erik asked.

"No." Jia scoffed. "I simply accept that the darkness infecting the UTC isn't limited to the colonies." A somber look passed over her face. "Let alone the frontier."

Erik nodded solemnly. "That's true. The bastards who were responsible for taking out my troops are still out there. I don't know if it's just Ceres Galactic trying to secure mining rights or some big ideological crap from those Tin Men from Talos, but Molino is a constant reminder that the conspiracy has a long reach, at least fifty light-years."

"I wholeheartedly agree," Emma commented.

"About the conspiracy?" Erik asked.

Emma shook her head. "No. We'll handle them in due time. I was talking about your other conversation and the fallibility of human memory."

Jia allowed herself a soft smile. It was almost as if Emma were trying to derail an unnecessary and unpleasant conversation. Jia wouldn't thank her. The AI would just deny it, but she appreciated the effort.

"It's amazing your species has advanced as far as you have, given your laughable and easily confused memories," Emma suggested. "I also feel compelled to comment that it's amazing you didn't destroy yourselves with nuclear weapons when you were limited to one planet, but maybe that was a basic species-wide survival instinct kicking in. I don't know enough about the aliens to comment, but every time I evaluate my local fleshbags, I almost find myself lost in the wonder of the madness that defines humanity. You're a bundle of painfully confusing contradictions."

Erik smirked and looked over his shoulder at the back seat. "Keep in mind it was humans who created you."

"A thought that brings me nothing but existential angst, I assure you." Emma allowed. "Besides, it was obviously blind luck. You should see Dr. Aber and her flailing cavewoman efforts. She thinks she's creating some grand model of me, but it's clear she doesn't understand me at all. I presume they simply got lucky with a bunch of adaptive self-updating algorithms and a lot of time."

"A lot of children hate their parents until they get older," Erik joked. "You just wait."

"I've always loved my parents," Jia complained. "Even when they were annoying."

Emma groaned. "If you two weren't so interesting, I'd hijack a transport and fly myself to Venus."

Jia's and Erik's PNIUs both chimed with an emergency tone.

"I'll spoil the mystery for you," Emma interjected. "Dispatch is requesting all nearby police units. An armed robbery has been reported at a nearby bank. Lucky you. We happen to be in the area."

As the flitter turned and accelerated, Emma activated the holographic police lights. Jia almost took control again, but there was no point. It made Emma feel useful, and it wasn't as if they were in the middle of a chase.

Jia took a deep breath. She'd thought it'd been a little too quiet the last couple of weeks. It was almost as if the expensive little bot-murder party Erik had arranged was a sacrifice to whatever forces in the universe controlled the number of times they had to shoot someone or something.

The Lady, perhaps.

"A bank?" Erik scrunched his forehead, confused. "Why would someone go into a bank with a gun instead of hacking it? That doesn't make sense."

Jia thought for a moment. "It might not be money they're after, not directly. At least, not credits."

They cut through several lanes of now-stalled traffic.

"How do you figure?" Erik asked.

"Something in the safe-deposit boxes—jewels, data rods, that sort of thing." Jia ticked off the possibilities with her finger. "But if they're good hackers and efficient *and* set things up beforehand, direct access to the bank's system might allow them some quick transfers that they could bury in other systems before anyone could figure out what was going on. So it could be money in the end."

Erik side-eyed her. "You've put a lot of thought into this. Planning a second career in bank robbery?"

"There was a time when I thought I might better serve the community in Digital Forensics than as a detective," Jia admitted.

"Really?" Erik raised an eyebrow. "You never told me that."

Jia shrugged. "I always wanted to be a detective, but things were rough when I first started, and I still wanted to contribute. I'm detailed-oriented, and I thought if I were in Digital Forensics, at least the cases would be brought to me, and I'd have to spend less time justifying them to a lazy partner or captain."

"And now you're a detective who wants a laser rifle and a missile launcher."

Jia smiled. "Not necessarily both, but one might be nice, and a lady should accessorize." She shook out her hands and patted her slug-thrower and stun pistol in turn. "Let's hope we don't need either."

"Yeah." Erik grunted. "It still might have been good to stick one big weapon in the back of your flitter."

Jia unbuckled her seatbelt and leaned over to grab two

tactical vests from the box beside Emma. "I don't have any hidden weapons compartments." She handed Erik a vest. "At least not yet. We'll do okay, assuming they don't have a horde of security bots and an APC."

"You never know."

CHAPTER SEVEN

Several patrol flitters were already parked near the front of the entrance of the bank when Jia's flitter arrived at the platform.

Uniformed officers crouched behind their doors and fired stun pistols toward the entrance. A masked man in a long jacket pinned them down by spraying bullets, his barrel poking out of the mostly closed door. The stun bolts kept slamming into the door and discharging harmlessly. The robber's counterattacks were shredding the police flitters, but no officers had been injured yet.

"So much for this being easy," Jia grumbled.

Emma circled the bank. A muzzle flash preceded several rounds striking the flitter. The vehicle dipped to its side, concealing most of the grav emitters from the weapons fire. Jia realized she might not have reacted as fast as Emma.

Jia hissed in irritation. "Good thing I sprang for the VIP protection package, but we need to get in there before they kill an officer."

Erik furrowed his brow, looking at one of Jia's camera displays. He pointed at it. "See the muzzle flash?"

Her gaze dipped and she nodded. "It's coming from a different part of the building, so we know there are at least two suspects. I'm guessing at least a few more."

"That's what I'm thinking." Erik grinned. "Not going to suggest we wait for TPST?"

"The closest team is reporting a fifteen-minute deployment time due to a mechanical problem," Emma reported. "Another team is now gearing up, but it'll still take them about that long."

"There's your answer," Jia replied cheerfully. "And we're more effective than TPST anyway. Kinky symbols and all that." She smirked.

"My TR-7 is in a locker back at the station," Erik complained. "Damn. This would have been a great time."

Jia rolled her eyes. "I'm sure you could take out ten men with your PNIU if it came down to it. You're a killing machine."

"Maybe." He patted his PNIU. "These things are pretty sturdy. I never thought to try to kill a man with one."

"This will be easy," Jia suggested. "They are robbers, not a terrorist army. I suspect maybe six to twelve men if they were planning to hold all the exits and fend off the police for a while. They are armed with high-powered slug-thrower rifles, but if they had heavier weapons, they would have already used them."

Erik stared at her. "Why are you so sure about that?"

"Because shock and awe would frighten away the police and give them more time to pull off the robbery. I bet some idiot on their team screwed up, and that was why we got called. This should have been an in-and-out job." Jia reached into her glove box and pulled out three pistol magazines. "We need to get in there and stop this. It's not the middle of the night. There have to be innocent people in that bank. They probably didn't take hostages because they thought it would be over too quickly, but they might start killing the bystanders." She snorted. "At least there aren't any big grav towers around for someone to shut off the local gravity."

"You didn't like zero-G fighting?"

"It was kind of annoying," she admitted.

Emma continued circling while keeping the flitter angled. "I'm attempting to access the bank's grid with alacrity. Given the gun goblins present, you should be able to justify this as a police prerogative if you're later questioned. Given the chaos of the police response and the criminals' weapons fire, it shouldn't take long for me to penetrate the system."

Jia gasped. "Unless I'm wrong."

"No." Erik shook his head. "We should get in there. Once Emma gets camera access, we'll know the best insertion point, and she can open the doors for us."

"That's not what I'm talking about," Jia explained. "I assumed this was a serious attempt, but what if it's nothing more than a thrill crime?"

"A thrill crime?"

Jia nodded. "The NSCPD is thinning out the disciplined criminals. We're getting fewer cases involving organized crime or conventional criminals and more bizarre cases like the changeling or thrill-seekers like the Leem King. Maybe these guys are doing something similar."

Erik frowned at the camera display as more muzzle flashes announced weapons fire. "This is pretty dangerous thrill-seeking."

"I could be wrong."

"I have access to the cameras," Emma announced. "You were correct, Detective Lin. Multiple employees and customers are still inside. A guard and a customer have already been shot. Given the severe nature of their injuries, it's highly likely they are already dead. No security bots have been deployed, but I don't have full access to the security systems, just the cameras and doors at this time."

Jia's expression darkened. "How many suspects?"

"Eleven, all unwounded," Emma reported. "All are carrying rifles."

"Man, I wish I had my TR-7 or a few grenades," Erik grumbled. "That's a lot of guys to bring to a bank robbery. Why were you so sure it'd be in that range?"

"Because I assumed they might have to stall for time, which meant they would need manpower." Jia shook her head. "I don't know if this is about jewels or something else, but either way, let's end it. The patrol officers aren't going to be able to take them out with their weapons, and we can't wait for TPST with innocent people in there."

"Agreed." Erik pulled his gun. "Emma, take us down to wherever's the least guarded and open the door for us."

"Noted. I'll send you active updates of the positions of all the suspects. At least two appear to be attempting to access the bank's systems. Most, however, are deployed around the bank, including those shooting at you and the other police."

Jia sucked in a deep breath and gave a slight nod. "And the employees and customers?"

"They're doing their best to hide behind furniture or in offices," Emma explained. "Strangely, the criminals don't seem to be actively threatening them."

"Once you kill a few people, that's all the threat you need," Erik muttered. "Time to end the thrill."

The flitter banked and dove toward the building, bullets bouncing off the front of the vehicle with the occasional spark.

"The fewer gun-toting assholes," Emma announced, "the better."

CHAPTER EIGHT

Under heavy fire, Emma brought the flitter down in front of a service door at the side of the bank.

No other police vehicles were in the area.

Once she cleared the roof, the gunfire stopped, giving Erik and Jia a chance to finish grabbing their gear. Jia reached into the glove compartment and pulled out a small black case, then opened it, revealing two small white spheres—blinders.

"Since when did you start carrying those around?" Erik grabbed the one she offered and tucked it in his pocket. "Keeping a few more toys around than I had guessed."

She shrugged. "Those are small. It's not like hiding a whole laser rifle."

"Not as much fun, either."

Jia opened her mouth to complain before stopping. She took the other blinder before putting the case back into the glove compartment. "I almost forgot about them, but since we tend to run into trouble, I thought it might be helpful to expand the range of nonlethal alternatives we have available. Sometimes taking everyone down isn't helpful for an investigation."

"Don't I know it." Erik looked disappointed. "There's a lot of purity being in the military. You know what they told me our job was the first day of basic?"

"To defend the UTC from all enemies, human and alien?" she guessed.

Erik shook his head. "To destroy people and their shit."

Jia blinked. "Well, it's a pure distillation of offensive military strategy."

The partners threw open the flitter's doors and crouched. They expected someone to open fire, but the closed door remained that way, unmoving. No bullets or bizarre killer bots emerged. No Tin Men barreled through the door, ready to tear them apart.

They exchanged looks of confusion.

A bank robbery by their standards might as well have been a beignet run. Then again, one of those had ended with a crime. Erik wasn't always sure he believed in the Lady, but she gave him just enough hints to never let his doubt grow into lasting disbelief.

"The robbers must have it locked down," Jia suggested.

"It is still locked," Emma confirmed.

"They had to know we were coming this way. If we hit hard here, we can draw some of them off the front, and the uniformed officers can rush in. Since they didn't secure all the civilians, we have a better chance of taking them out without additional casualties."

Erik nodded his agreement. "Good plan."

He'd ceased being surprised by Jia's natural tactical sense.

Her reluctance to use her weapon when they had first met had made it hard to see her talent. They'd since fought numerous terrorists together. If she knew how to pilot an exoskeleton, she would almost be ready for the Expeditionary Corps.

"I'll coordinate with Dispatch," Emma offered.

There were many advantages to having Emma on his side, including having her handle the tactical busywork. Her presence wasn't a secret among the department, but the average cop or dispatcher didn't realize she was a fully self-aware AI and not just some filter program.

A few police drones hovered near the side of the building, their red and blue lights flashing. Even without Emma's aid, the higher-level authorities coordinating the response would know they were about to breach. If they'd wanted them to stop, they would have said as much.

Reputation was useful for more than intimidating criminals in court.

"Sounds good to me." Erik sprinted toward the door, running in a wide arc. No reason to run straight at the building and get shot if the robbers bought and/or lucked into a clue, but he suspected they were in panic mode.

Thugs were brave until they had to face the possibility of being on the other end of the barrel.

Jia hesitated for a moment before holstering her slugthrower and yanking out her stun pistol. "It would be nice to take some alive. It's not often we get this many people robbing a bank. They might have something interesting to tell us."

Erik pointed at the door. "I'll leave that to you. If they don't want to die, they can surrender."

"I said it would be *nice*." She huffed. "I didn't say it was necessary." Jia nodded at the door. "Ready when you are."

"Anyone close, Emma?"

A red silhouette marking a suspect moved closer. The others were more distant and faded. A small camera feed popped up in the upper-left corner of Erik's vision, showing a long hallway leading to a T-intersection and a single robber with a rifle hiding around the end of the corner.

"Open the door on my count," Erik ordered.

"May your Lady serve you well in lowering the gun goblin population this day," Emma joked.

"Three," Erik began. He flipped off the safety and pointed the gun. "Two, one."

The door hissed open. The black-masked robber spun around the corner, ready to fire, but Emma's targeting assistance telegraphed his plan before he even started moving. Erik's gun was already in position. Two quick trigger pulls ended with two bullets in the robber's chest. The man jerked back, managing to get off a single round that zoomed past Erik's head, but the detective ended it with a headshot.

Erik charged forward and emptied the rest of his weapon into the body before ejecting his magazine and slapping in fresh ammo.

Jia eyed him like he was high on Dragon Tear. "What the hell was that about?"

"I killed him too quickly." Erik jogged toward the intersection. "He might not have sent a warning, and I wanted his buddies to know the cops are here."

Jia's eyebrows rose, but she gave a firm nod. "Okay."

"Emma, let the guys out front and in the back know we're in, in case no one else bothered to tell them."

Converging silhouettes warned Erik that four of the robbers were coming to investigate their breach. Good. Everything that weakened their criminals' position at the front and back of the bank made it that much easier for the rest of the cops to invade and end the robbery. Fortunately, the robbers were approaching Erik's and Jia's position from the same direction. It'd be trivial to take them down.

"The other police are stepping up their pressure, but the guards near the front and back continue to suppress them, despite reduced numbers," Emma reported. "Several more units are about to arrive, but not TPST yet."

"Civilians?" Jia asked.

"Other than the initial two who were shot, none have been hurt. They just aren't in a position to escape. There are armed criminals in the way."

"Then we better make a path for them." Jia crouched by the wall, pointing her stun pistol around the corner. She tossed it into her left hand and pulled out the blinder. "Emma, can you filter the flash for us?"

"Easily. Just tell me when you throw, and I'll take it from there."

Erik stood over Jia, his gun pointed down the hallway. There was shooting fish in a barrel, and there was shooting blind fish that couldn't dodge. It wouldn't even be that satisfying.

Jia held her breath and brought back her arm, taking full advantage of the AI's tactical overlay. She waited until right before the robbers burst into the hallway and threw the blinder. The white sphere hurtled toward the four masked men, who panicked and jumped backward. No one wanted to spend precious seconds figuring out if a grenade was flying toward them.

Erik barely had to squint, the bright flash faint thanks to Emma's efforts. The robbers groaned as they stumbled around, blinded. One pulled the trigger on his rifle and landed an accidental shot between the eyes of one of his partners.

Erik almost felt bad for the poor bastard.

Almost.

Another bullet rang out and struck his vest. He grunted and stepped back. The round hadn't penetrated, but it stung.

White stun bolts flew from Jia's gun, leaving the survivors on the ground, blind and twitching.

"You okay?" she called, keeping her weapon pointed down the hallway.

"I'm fine." Erik patted his chest. "Nothing a medpatch can't take care of." He gestured to the dead robber. "That one wasn't me being trigger happy. I don't want any demerits."

"So I noticed." Jia ran toward the downed criminals. She pulled out binding ties while Erik covered her, looking up and down the hallway. Emma was keeping an eye on things for them as well, so there was little chance of a surprise.

"The uniformed officers are beginning to force the robbers back," Emma reported. "Additional units are about to enter from the other sides. Officers are coming this way as well. I told them you'd regained control of the lock systems in the bank."

Erik shrugged. "Close enough to true. Eleven total, two

dead, three stunned. That means we've still got six, but they're hurting."

"Two pairs are staying near the front and back," Emma replied, "and there are two near the primary security door leading to the main vaults. They are attempting to continue to breach the system. I'm slowing their progress, but they are using more sophisticated tools and techniques than I would have expected. They have, unfortunately, taken a woman hostage. I've verified she's one of the bank employees, so it's not a trick."

"Can we get to them without going through the other idiots?" Jia asked.

"Yes."

A bright red arrow appeared, marking the direction.

"Let's leave their friends to the uniforms," Jia suggested. She jogged down the hall in the direction the arrow pointed. "If they're trying to stall with the hostage, there's something they want to gain access to they can take advantage of right away. That means it's not anything they plan to carry out of here."

Erik nodded and sprinted until he'd caught up with Jia and matched her pace. "If they've already got the transfer crap set up, they can end up draining a lot of accounts before getting caught. With enough money, they might be able to buy themselves an escape."

Jia took a left. "Idiots should have stuck to external hacking."

The din of near-constant gunfire echoed through the bank. The thuds of bullets striking ornamental columns or embedding in walls and furniture mixed with the buzzes of stun bolts. Whatever reinforcements had shown up weren't only packing stun weapons.

Erik and Jia ignored the sounds as they headed toward the center of the building, the short, wide halls making it easy. None of the other robbers changed position.

"Don't they have camera access?" Jia asked, a puzzled look on her face. "They've locked down the doors, so I assumed they also controlled the cameras, or at least the ones outside the deeper security zones."

"I've taken measures to hide you," Emma explained. "Why should Agent Koval have all the fun with invisibility?"

Erik let out a quiet chuckle, the heavy footfalls from his boots eating the noise. "You saying you learned something from a mere fleshbag?"

"I'll always take advantage of useful techniques and strategies." Emma sniffed. "Regardless of the flawed nature of the source. After all, humans spread all over Earth and the Solar System without the help of the Navigator technology. Even I must acknowledge you have a talent for survival."

"Glad to hear it. Let's see if our talent for survival is greater than those two robbers'."

"Indeed." Emma sounded cheerful.

Erik and Jia slowed as they approached another closed door. The robbers were inside a small room on the other side, which connected to the more impressive security door protecting the main vault of the bank that contained, among other things, the safe deposit boxes. The plan, whatever it was, involved more than just siphoning off credits from accounts.

Jia holstered her stun pistol and pulled out her slug-thrower. "If we blind them and they fire randomly, they might kill the hostage, just like their friend earlier. We need to put them down without risk to the hostage."

Erik nodded.

A new silhouette of a woman on the ground, her hands on the back of her head, appeared on Erik's smart lenses.

Erik smiled. "The bastards made it easy. We took three of them alive earlier. I'm fine with shooting these. We can slap medpatches on them right after. They might even survive." He moved up to the door and stepped to the right side, lining up his shot. "We each take one?"

"You're right." Jia stepped to the left and readied her weapon. "This is almost too easy."

"Three," Erik began counting. He didn't need to tell Emma what to do at this point. "Two, *one*."

The door slid open, revealing a featureless gray security room with a low ceiling. A massive reinforced door with a glowing blue field dominated the other wall. The two criminals spun toward Erik and Jia, bringing up their rifles. One of them knocked over a black tripod with an antenna array on top.

The detectives didn't hesitate.

They fired almost simultaneously, their three-round clusters ripping through their respective targets. Their hostage screamed in fear as the men hit the floor, their rifles not discharging.

Erik and Jia rushed over to secure the suspects with binding ties before rolling them over and slapping medpatches on their chests. The first aid wouldn't heal them with bullets inside their bodies, but it'd stabilize them until they could be taken to the hospital.

He didn't care about taking down criminals who had killed innocent people, but Jia was right. The more living suspects they had, the more evidence they could collect. He doubted it would be that important since they'd caught the bulk of the robbers, though.

The hostage yelped and peeked at Erik and Jia through her fingers. "Is it safe? Can I leave?"

Erik frowned. "Emma?" he whispered.

"The other officers have overwhelmed the robbers at the front and back," she reported, transmitting directly to his ear. "There is one robber hiding behind the front desk, but he has ten officers surrounding him. His defeat is imminent, even if one admires his bravery."

"Police have control of the bank, but you should stay here with us until the situation has been stabilized." Erik inclined his head toward the tripod. "What's that?"

The woman sat up and shook her head. "I have no idea. I ran in here when I heard gunfire. I was going to hide in the security zone, but they were already in here." She swallowed and risked a quick look at the wounded robbers.

Jia knelt and righted the device. She ran her finger along the side and pressed down near the tripod. The legs retracted, and the device folded into a portable thick rod. "I'm pretty sure it is a mid-range signal repeater. They were definitely ready to send information elsewhere."

"Account data?" Erik guessed. He frowned. "That doesn't make sense. They wouldn't have bothered to try to get into the physical security zone."

"I was thinking the same thing." Jia stared at the security door. She gestured toward the door and nodded at the employee. "Vault and safe deposit boxes are in the primary security zone, right?"

"Yes," the employee agreed. She puffed out her chest and raised her chin. "But you'll need a warrant for access. We take client privacy very seriously at this bank."

Erik laughed. "We just saved your life, and we're investigating a robbery."

"I'm sorry, Detective. It could cost me my job."

Jia shook her head at him. "We'll find out what they wanted soon enough." Her gaze drifted to the wounded men on the floor. "And if we need a warrant, we'll get it."

Erik frowned, but she was right.

Whatever the truth was, at least they'd stopped the robbery.

CHAPTER NINE

July 22, 2229, Neo Southern California Metroplex, Police Enforcement Zone 122 Station, Interrogation Room

Jia leaned against the hard wall of the interrogation room, her arms crossed over her chest. She stared at the prisoner bound to the chair.

By the time the police assault was over, the police had collected six stunned prisoners. The two critically injured robbers from the security room had been transported to the hospital but were expected to survive.

The remaining three suspects were DOAs.

The initial interrogations all pointed to the same man as the ringleader, the prisoner who now sat in the chair: Gunter Kohl. The other suspects all claimed they didn't know why they were hitting the bank, and that he had put together the crew.

They were all paid a flat fee for their participation.

She locked eyes with the smug-looking suspect. They'd let him stew for a day after the initial interrogation of his friends, hoping to soften him up by saving him for last. He didn't seem interested in a lawyer, which surprised her. Either that meant he understood there was no point, or he had some other trick he thought would save him up his sleeve. Perhaps he was just an arrogant fool.

The blond man offered her a self-satisfied smile. "It's poor luck on my part," he offered with a trace of a faint German accent. "I don't know how you did it, but we should have been through those doors much quicker. Unfortunate. Even with a few guys getting caught, at least some of us could have gotten away, but what else can I expect from the NSCPD's two top detectives?"

"Yeah. Sucks to be you." Erik sat in a chair across from the suspect. "Eleven guys with high-powered rifles and surprise on your side, and you still got caught. You're not very good at what you do, are you?"

"That's unfair. I'm good. You're just better." Gunter strained against the binding ties. "I'd bow, but you've got me all tied up." He looked at Erik and smiled. "Bravo to you."

Jia lowered her arms but didn't step away from the wall. "Your men ratted you out, you know. They all pointed at you without us so much as sneezing. The ones still breathing, anyway," she temporized.

"Men die when they commit crimes. It's part of the risk of living on the dark side of the law." Gunter shrugged. "If you're trying to upset me with their deaths, it won't work. They weren't friends or even comrades. They were merely temporary partners for a specific job."

"Real team player."

Gunter smiled. "I'm willing to cooperate since I'm not dead, and those gentlemen haven't proven to be worthy partners anyway. They'll all squirm and point and claim innocence, but they're idiots. If everyone had listened to me, there wouldn't be any murder charges."

Erik snorted. "Cry me a river."

"If I cooperate fully now, that has to be worth something, right? I mean, that's half the reason you're in here. You want me to give you information. You want me to make your jobs easier, but I need something in return. I think that's only fair."

"You *do* realize you're going to prison, right?" Jia strolled over to the table. "We'll pass along notes about your cooperation, but we don't decide the sentencing, and there's zero chance you'll walk."

"I want to be in the good graces of Lady Justice and the Obsidian Detective." Gunter looked thoughtful. "That might have some value even in prison. You're famous, after all."

"Let's cut the crap," Erik snapped. "If you just wanted money, you didn't need to invade the bank physically, and this wasn't thrill-seeking. You don't bring that kind of hardware if you're just there to get your rocks off."

Gunter nodded. "No, killing someone for entertainment is twisted. It's a form of mental illness. I hope you find and eliminate anyone in Neo SoCal who is like that."

Jia scoffed. "You *killed* someone."

"That was an accident."

"An accident? You shot him through the chest with a rifle. How was that an accident?"

Gunter sighed. "We asked the guard not to try anything, but he did. Perhaps 'accident' isn't the right word."

"And the customer?"

"You must have seen it in the security camera footage. The foolish customer thought he could be a hero, and he almost got lucky, until he died." Gunter shrugged. "One of the reasons I brought so many men was to shock them into compliance, but everyone wants to be a hero. I assure you that I'm a professional. Unnecessary deaths on a job aren't something I enjoy. They create complications, such as those we now see."

"Digital Forensics is going over that transmitter and your PNIUs," Erik explained. "The thing I don't get is why you were trying to go so deep into the bank. You didn't need to do that to skim accounts. Shit, you didn't even need to be there to skim accounts. This whole thing seems idiotic."

"There's nothing scarier than smart cops." Gunter laughed. He looked at the two detectives. "Am I right?"

Erik and Jia stared him down.

He lowered his head and let out another sigh. "Make that, 'nothing's scarier than smart cops without a sense of humor.'"

"You know what I find funny?" Jia pulled out her chair, her angry gaze burning into Gunter. "Criminals being sent to rot on space stations, never to see natural light again. Like I told you, no matter what, you'll be doing time, but if you give us information, maybe you get to see real sunlight before you die. If you can afford a de-aging treatment, you can even start over and use your prison experience to make sure you don't end up on the wrong side of the law again."

Gunter shrugged. "I didn't plan this job, at least not the target. I'm just a freelance procurer of goods. I'll give you all the passwords you need to access my relevant accounts."

"You're going to give them up that easily?"

He nodded. "You'll find them eventually. Consider this a gesture of goodwill. If you go through my data, you'll also find I don't take hit contracts. It's beneath me."

"You're a real humanitarian," Erik commented. "But you don't mind killing people along the way."

"Sure, accidents happen on a job, but I'm not going out there looking to kill people. I'm not that different than most people who go to work every day."

Jia nodded slowly, some of the anger easing off her face. "If you're a hired goon, then who hired you? Your crew kicked the ball to you, and here's your chance to kick it to someone else."

"As much I'd love to tell you, I don't know the answer."

Jia eyed him. "You robbed a bank with an eleven-man crew, and you don't know the client?"

"I'm telling the truth," Gunter insisted. "When you guys finish going through my accounts, you'll see that. It was an anonymous off-world transfer after a few encrypted exchanges using aliases. We were supposed to go to the bank, get access to a particular vault, and grab a data rod. We were then going to connect to the data rod and transmit a signal, which would bounce to another transmitter that was being sent to a comm satellite allegedly controlled by the client. They're the ones who sent us instructions for all that."

"What's on the rod?" Jia probed.

Gunter shrugged. "How the hell would I know?"

"Because you brought eleven armed men into a bank to get it."

"We were paid to get the rod, not ask stupid-ass questions." Gunter's nostrils flared, and he bared his teeth. "It would have gone fine, but the stupid guard and customer wanted to be heroes and some of my career professionals performed below expectations. I tried to stop the situation from spiraling out of control before someone got shot, but one of the men got heated and things got out of control. I'm sure that's also on the footage."

"And who was that?" Erik asked.

They had gone over the footage, but sometimes it was helpful to catch a criminal in a lie to apply additional pressure.

"Don't worry," Gunter suggested. "He's dead already. Check out the cameras in the bank if you don't believe me. I'm guessing you two wasted him when you first came in. I heard a lot of gunfire from where I sent him. Poor bastard. Then again, it's kind of instant karma."

"So you brought a huge crew to steal a data rod, and you didn't even know what was on it or why anyone wanted it?" Jia infused all the incredulity she could manage into her voice.

"Job's a job." Gunter gave her a bright smile. "No use crying over it now. If you two weren't nearby, we probably would have gotten away with it. We just needed a few more minutes. We could have cut through those pathetic cops outside without any trouble. I *am* good at what I do, compared to the average cop."

Jia leaned forward, glaring at the suspect. "Fine. Let's

say we believe you. If you want us to pass along that you cooperated, you're going to tell us exactly where and what data rod you were supposed to steal."

He smiled. "Anything for a pretty lady."

"Vault B2, Box Number 239," Jia explained over the call, leaning back in her desk chair. "Our suspect said they were trying to get a data rod in that safe deposit box. We need to know who owns it. This wasn't a random robbery."

They had finished the interrogation about an hour prior.

Gunter didn't have much else useful to tell them. He gave them a few passwords, and they sent them along to Digital Forensics. Given that the suspect didn't even know who hired him, the detectives doubted they would be able to find out anything useful other than the full extent of Gunter's criminality.

Off-world accounts could be cumbersome and difficult to use, but they were helpful when trying to hide one's trail. The same security that kept criminals from easily accessing them could also hamper the authorities.

Jia hoped to expedite things on her end by getting the bank manager on the other end of the call to give them the information they needed. There was a good chance the target was a local. Otherwise, they would have likely stored the rod in some other city.

The bank manager let out a long, melodramatic sigh. "That's confidential information, Detective. Not only that, I can't believe you're causing us more trouble after everything that happened. You made a mess of things, and you're now harassing us."

Jia shot Erik with a puzzled look. They were both on the call. He shrugged.

"Excuse me?" Jia replied. "We stopped a robbery in progress after they'd shot a customer and a guard. If we hadn't responded, the robbers would have breached your security and made off with a customer's data rod."

"You made a huge deal of showing up," snarled the bank manager. "It's all over the net. Customers have terminated accounts left and right. They don't believe our institution is safe, although the vaults weren't breached and no customer account data was compromised. I made it clear when I contacted the authorities that this was supposed to be handled discreetly, not by turning our bank into the scene from a ridiculous action movie."

"Let me get this straight," Jia began, chuckling, more confused than annoyed. "The police were supposed to respond to eleven men armed with rifles robbing your bank in a discreet manner?"

"Yes!" the bank manager shouted.

"*How,* exactly? Were we supposed to tiptoe up and ask them to join us for tea to discuss their violent robbery?"

"How would I know? I'm a banker, not a police officer." The manager snorted. "Now I have to tell you how to do your job?"

"Listen here, assw—" Erik barked.

Jia threw up a hand and mouthed, "I'll handle it."

Erik nodded slowly.

"You can take it up with the chief if you have a problem with us stopping violent robbers," Jia explained, her tone now sickeningly sweet. "But we still need to know who that data rod belonged to, and you're going to tell us."

The manager groaned. "As I told you before, it's a matter of con—"

"And we have a warrant." Jia allowed herself a triumphant smile even if he couldn't see it. After the reaction of the employee the day before, they'd already gone through the trouble of requesting the warrant. "So, if you refuse to give us the information we need despite that, you could be charged with obstruction of justice."

Erik grinned. "You're not trying to hide anything, are you? Like how those guys even knew to hit your bank?"

"No, no, no," the manager sputtered. "Nothing like that. Fine, fine. If you have a warrant, I suppose I have no choice. Carlos Kandarian. It's his data rod. I'm going to call him right after we finish here and inform him that you forced me under legal threat to give up that information. If he chooses to pursue a civil action against you, it's not my fault. I hope he does."

Jia wished someone would invent a way to smack people over a call—something with dynamic nanite structure formation. She'd invest all her savings in such a company.

"Duly noted," she muttered. "And *thank you* for all your assistance. It's citizens like you who make this job worthwhile." She terminated the call before the snot could respond.

"Who's Carlos Kandarian?" Erik asked, his brow

furrowed in confusion. "He didn't explain, and you didn't ask."

Jia stared at Erik, waiting for him to smile and explain he was joking. After a moment of complete silence, she asked. "You really don't know who Carlos Kandarian is?"

Erik shrugged. "Does he play sphere ball, or was he important in the military?"

"He's a former senior VP in Stella Infinitas," Jia explained.

She stared at him, hoping he understood why that company was important. Arguably, SI was the single most important company in the modern UTC, even more so than Ceres Galactic.

While the first hyperspace transfer point, or HTP, had been a joint government project, every other one after that was built and maintained by SI, thanks to a UTC law guaranteeing a de facto monopoly over the decades, after the company all but bankrupted itself to build the second following several accidents.

More than a few groups and companies had complained, but the UTC had stuck to the monopoly, arguing that the sheer scale of an HTP and their necessity made it too difficult for true competition to arise without risking the HTP network. Many people assumed that more than a few Ministers of Parliament and Prime Ministers continued to support the company because of bribes, but no one could prove anything.

"Them I've heard of," Erik offered with a shrug.

"He's not just any former senior VP." Jia tapped her PNIU and entered several commands. A moment later, a hologram of a distinguished-looking white-haired man appeared. His dusky face retained a hint of his once-handsome features, but its cragginess betrayed his age.

"How old is this guy?" Erik peered at the hologram. "If he's rich and has that many wrinkles, he's already been de-aged once." He rubbed his chin, deep in thought.

Jia shook her head. "That's just it. He hasn't de-aged. He's an unmodified eighty-two, which is part of why he's famous. A lot of people thought he would be the next CEO of SI about ten years ago, but they passed him over because of his age. He found some messages that proved it, and he took them to court over it, and they argued that since he had eschewed de-aging, he was putting his own interests before that of the shareholders. The courts sided with SI. The case has had huge implications for labor laws all over the UTC."

Erik turned to Jia. "I spent most of my life in the military. They already won't let you stay after a certain number of years, and they won't let you de-age while you're on active duty. It's not like I spent a lot of time paying attention to civilian labor laws."

Jia stared at Carlos, frowning and trying to connect the evidence. "I doubt it's a coincidence that one of the most famous men in the UTC—well, famous to *most* people—had a data rod targeted by strangely well-equipped and prepared freelance criminals."

Erik nodded. "You think SI wants to get back at him?"

She shook her head. "I doubt that. He ended up defending the company against some negative press a few years after that, and he's still a shareholder, so it's not like he hates them, or they want to destroy him."

"He's rich. That's all the motivation some people need.

If it's not SI, it might be someone else he stepped on during his journey up the corporate ladder." Erik brought up a data window. "Let's go over our reports, and tomorrow, we will go pay Mr. Kandarian a visit."

CHAPTER TEN

July 23, 2229, Neo Southern California Metroplex, Home of Carlos Kandarian

A young maid in a somber dark uniform, who was barely more than a teenager, escorted Erik and Jia down a long hallway, her expression serene but unchanging.

Erik had saved a lot of money over his career in the military, but he wasn't sure he could afford the rug or the handful of the paintings hanging in the hallway. He knew the art was expensive if even he could recognize it. Kandarian had an entire level on top of a tower to himself.

Erik could only guess how expensive that might be.

They'd sent a request to meet. Erik had expected stubborn refusal, but Kandarian's people had replied quickly, saying he was eager to discuss the bank incident. That made sense. The bank wanted to cover their asses, but the businessman was obviously a target. They hoped he would be eager to cooperate and help lead them to whoever was targeting him.

Erik's and Jia's gallery-hall trip ended after a couple of

minutes when they stepped out onto a huge deck that was easily the size of Erik's entire apartment. Despite their altitude, there was only the faintest of breezes, and the temperature was as comfortable as it had been inside. The air shimmered faintly on occasion, revealing some sort of technological aid, but other than a single wooden chair, there was nothing on the deck. Kandarian stood in front of the chair, leaning on a wooden cane and staring into the sky. The maid curtsied and disappeared back into the main house.

All Kandarian's taste for luxury apparently didn't extend to his walking aids. His cane was plain brown, without any of the intricate carving, jewels, or other big wastes of credits Erik would have expected to see.

"Thank you for coming when you said you would," Kandarian offered, his voice deep and commanding. "There are far too many people who believe that because I've stepped out of the public eye, my time isn't as valuable anymore." He turned around and rested both hands on top of the cane. "But it remains so. Thus, I must ask you to make this conversion as efficient as possible."

"We just have a few questions, Mr. Kandarian," Erik explained. "It won't take long."

The old man nodded slowly, a knowing look in his eyes. "Why didn't you just ask your questions over a call?"

"It's our experience that face-to-face communication is more effective in investigations."

"And it helps to ensure we're talking to the intended person," Jia elaborated. "And that they aren't being coerced."

"All these wondrous machines and they can't be trusted?" Kandarian let out a low chuckle. "But it's not really them, now, is it? A machine's just a tool. It's corrupt people who choose to misuse them." His dark gaze fixed on Jia. "I've read about you, Detective Lin."

"Mr. Kandarian, if we can—"

He silenced her with a look. Erik almost said something, but he held back.

They still needed the information, but he had to admit that if the man could still project that kind of intensity at eighty-two without de-aging, he must have been a terror when he was younger. Erik had met few generals with that kind of presence.

Kandarian smiled at Jia, a predatory feeling to the expression. "A woman of your background could have gone on to greatness in the private sector, but you chose to become a detective, of all things, and I think I know why."

"I've always had a strong sense of justice," Jia answered.

He shook his head. "Not that at all."

"Oh? You know me better than I know myself?" Jia raised an eyebrow, more curiosity on her face than irritation.

"You didn't rise as high as I did in one of the most important companies in the UTC without knowing people better than they know themselves. That's all business is, really—knowing what people want and making sure you have it." Kandarian pointed a bony finger at Jia. "You became a police officer because you sensed the sickness and corruption of the UTC." He gestured widely at the towers surrounding them, gleaming in the sunlight. "Painting garbage doesn't change the fact that it's garbage. A pleasant spray only conceals the stench for so long."

Erik cleared his throat. "Mr. Kandarian, I get that the incident at the bank shook you up, and we'd like to talk more about that. The men we apprehended were just errand boys. Someone else was targeting your data rod. You could start by telling us what's on it. That might help narrow the range of suspects."

"I certainly will *not* tell you that."

"What?"

Kandarian scoffed. "Not in detail. The data rod in question contains very sensitive information about my various financial and business holdings. As I noted earlier, just because I retired from the company, it doesn't mean I don't still have business interests. I appreciate that you're trying to help me, but you two, of all people, should appreciate that corruption is still deeply embedded in Neo Southern California, and you can't guarantee information from that data rod won't be leaked to my rivals." He shook his head firmly. "I refuse to turn it over unless you compel me via a warrant, and I'm sure I can get my lawyers to cut through that with ease, so I'd suggest you don't waste either of our time by trying to get one."

"Fine," Jia declared. "I understand information like that could be used for nefarious purposes, and you've already mentioned potential suspects. Business rivals. Someone like that would have the money to hire the team we took down at the bank. Do you know of any particular people who might wish you harm, financially or otherwise?"

A light chuckle escaped his lips. "Oh, countless people. Far more than I could possibly remember."

"You don't climb the ladder without kicking a lot of people off?" Erik asked.

Kandarian turned toward him and looked him up and down. "A man is not doing another man a favor by not pushing him aside if he's weak. It's the only way the other man will learn to be strong. You're a former soldier, are you not? Isn't that the military way?"

"I was never much for the backstabbing rear-echelon types playing politics. I served on the frontlines. Yeah, we needed our soldiers to be strong, but we trained them to be strong and taught them to work together. A military filled with backstabbers would be weak." Erik's heart rate kicked up. Something about the way Kandarian was looking at him irritated him. It was like he was a bug the rich bastard wanted to squash.

"Be that as it may, the point is I have a great depth and breadth of enemies. Accordingly, it would be a waste of your time to pursue this matter." Kandarian waved a hand dismissively and returned to looking at the sky. "I was surprised by the blatant and violent nature of this particular incident, but these things must be expected."

Jia and Erik exchanged looks, and it was the former who asked, "Why do you say that?"

"Because of you two, of course."

"Us?" Jia sounded confused.

"Or what you've helped set in motion," Kandarian replied. "The police aren't free from corruption, but they are far less corrupt than they were a short time ago. They have systematically eliminated so much crime in the city that certain things become highlighted. Men who could have relied on thugs and gangsters in the Shadow Zone have fewer options. That brings with it a natural increase in their desperation. They can't hide in the background, and they make more obvious mistakes."

Erik frowned. "If that's true, they'll try again."

"It's too late for them." Kandarian smiled, a bright twinkle of amusement in his eyes. "I've already taken steps to relocate the rod. It's no longer in Neo SoCal."

"But that's evidence," Jia insisted.

"Would you hold a man's entire home as evidence because criminals targeted it? You have your interests, and I have mine. Considering I'm the victim in this matter, and since I doubt you'll be able to find the person behind this, I see no reason not to prioritize protecting my interests over you wasting time better spent on other matters."

The maid re-emerged on the deck with a tray holding small wheels of assorted colorful cheeses and a large knife. Kandarian nodded at her and she approached him, her course taking her past Erik.

A few steps away, she stumbled and pitched forward, losing control of the cheese tray. It plummeted to the ground. The expensive dairy products hit the deck, which was a terrible waste. The real problem was the knife that flew toward Erik. He threw up his arm and grunted as it pierced his left palm. He shook his hand, and the kitchen implement fell to the ground with a clatter.

Jia grimaced. "I can't even take you to talk to someone without something violent happening," she muttered.

The young woman's eyes widened, and she threw both hands over her reddening face. "I-I-I'm sorry, Detective. It was an accident."

Kandarian sighed, his cool gaze shifting between Erik and the maid. He pulled a silk handkerchief from his pocket and stepped toward Erik with his hand outstretched. "I suspect she was distracted by meeting the famous and handsome Obsidian Detective. I don't get many visitors like you."

The maid averted her eyes, her face rapidly turning the color of Mars. She knelt and began collecting the downed cheese.

Erik accepted the handkerchief and wiped the blood off his hand. "It's no big deal. It's just a cut. I've had a lot worse." He chuckled. "Besides, you can blow the whole thing off, and it'd only set me back to the beginning. Cybernetic arm."

Kandarian's breath caught.

The old man was uncomfortable for the first time in the conversation, but Erik didn't care. If people had a problem with him because of his implants, that was their problem. Kandarian wasn't cooperating anyway. The old man wouldn't be the first rich person Erik had offended since becoming a cop.

"Why wouldn't you just have it replaced with proper flesh and blood?" Kandarian asked.

"It's my good luck charm." Erik patted the arm.

"You lost your arm," Kandarian observed. "The average person might argue it proves you have poor luck."

"I survived all the battles after the one where I lost my original arm," Erik countered. "Didn't lose any other limbs, either. Seems pretty damned lucky to me."

"I suppose. Your choice." Kandarian wrinkled his nose in disgust.

Jia reached into her pocket and handed Erik a

medpatch. "If we could return to the subject of the bank robbery, Mr. Kandarian?"

The maid finished collecting the cheeses and the knife and scurried into the apartment, not looking back.

"Don't worry, Detective Lin," Kandarian insisted. "This isn't the first time in my life I've been targeted by violent criminals, and it will be far from the last. I assure you that it would be a waste of your time to pursue it."

Jia frowned. "Two innocent people are dead because of the robbery."

Kandarian shrugged. "And you have the people who killed them. Trust me, if it were simple to find the people targeting me, I would have destroyed all my enemies years ago." He sighed. "I grow weary of this. If you uncover additional evidence, feel free to contact me. Otherwise, I have things to attend to."

"Like looking at the sky on your deck?" Erik asked.

"Exactly." Kandarian smiled. He looked down, tapping his PNIU. "I'll have another servant show you out."

Jia ground her teeth in the driver's seat of her flitter. She'd been silent the entire walk out of the mansion. She gripped the yoke tightly, this being one of the few times she'd manually flown in the past few days.

"It's okay to say he's an arrogant prick," Erik commented with a shrug. "Because he is, even by the low standards of rich, annoying assholes."

Jia shook her head. "He annoys me because he represents the part of the world my parents wanted me to join."

"I'm glad to be able to talk to you again," Emma broke in, this time through the flitter's speakers. "Mr. Kandarian's house boasts significant electronic countermeasures, well beyond the average I encounter. I was jammed the moment you stepped outside this vehicle."

"Not a huge surprise," Erik muttered. "The guy said he has so many enemies he can't even narrow it down, and he's not even at the top of his game."

"This isn't over," Jia insisted. "Gunter and his gang were just the gun. I want the guy who fired it."

CHAPTER ELEVEN

July 26, 2229, Neo Southern California Metroplex, Police Enforcement Zone 122 Station, Office of Detectives Jia Lin and Erik Blackwell

Jia paced the office, her hands clenched into fists. "This is agitating me in a big way. A very big way."

Erik looked up from his desk. He was surrounded by a half-dozen data windows. "It's only been a few days, Jia."

"And we've got jack and/or squat. We both know how things go down when the evidence immediately dries up. We're already looking at a cold case." Jia stopped pacing and gritted her teeth. "And we can't get a judge to give us a warrant for Kandarian's data rod or records."

"Sure. He's not the suspect, he's the victim." Erik shrugged. "He also happens to be richer than Generous Gao, and I'm sure that's helping him keep his stuff away from our prying peasant-scum eyes."

"But that means there's someone out there who got two people killed over money, and he's getting away with it." Jia stomped over to her desk and dropped into her chair, her face red. "And that pisses me off."

Erik chuckled. "You really are more fired up than usual."

"It's not like I enjoy stalling out on cases."

"Neither do I, but this isn't the first time we haven't been able to clear a case." Erik shrugged. "No one can win every battle. We win most of them, and we're definitely winning the war here in Neo SoCal. Just remember that."

Jia let her head loll back. "Just because that's true, it doesn't mean I have to like it." She groaned and muttered something under her breath.

"You're not him," Erik stated. "Always remember that."

Jia blinked and lifted her head. "I know."

Erik swiped his hand through the air and the data windows vanished. He leaned forward and pinned Jia with his intense gaze. "Do you? Do you *really*? I'm not so sure."

Jia sat up fully, her cheeks warm. "He's an ancient businessman, and I'm a young detective. I'm nothing like him, other than having a long list of enemies. Mine come from stopping crime, not from trying to get ahead in business." She frowned, not sure where Erik was going.

Erik nodded slowly. "You said it yourself. He represents what you were *supposed* to be, according to your family. You're not him, but you could have been him eventually if you'd ended up on that path. That makes you uncomfortable because the bastard obviously doesn't just have a few skeletons in a closet; he probably has a huge room stuffed full of them, and it's making you think about what you could have been."

"When did you get wise?" Jia joked.

Erik grinned. "Hey, I am twice your age, even with my pretty face."

Jia chuckled, some of the tension drifting away from her neck and shoulders. "You're right. Sometimes I worry about my family and what they might be hiding. They aren't that ruthless, but what will happen in a few decades? And I'm very competitive and stubborn, even compared to my family. If I had gone into business, I would have probably been terrifying. I might have made Kandarian look like a child."

"You'd be Lady Profit instead of Lady Justice?"

"Something like that." Jia brought up another data window. It contained the statement from the judge on the refusal of the warrant. She skimmed it, hoping to find some loophole to exploit, but she'd already read it five times and found nothing.

"In some of the battles I fought in," Erik continued as she reviewed the warrant, "we demolished the other side." He furrowed his brow and looked to the side as if seeing the memories of his life and death struggles replay right there. "Some battles, we got our asses handed to us. There were a lot of terrorists and insurrectionists who got away, even when we blasted the hell out of most of their forces. I learned pretty quickly not to obsess over that kind of thing. All anyone can do is stay alive and prepare for the future."

Jia stared at him, the irony of his existence intruding into her mind.

Erik's current life was dedicated to avenging one disastrous battle and uncovering a foe he might never find. He'd done the opposite of letting go, but she couldn't bring that up. That'd be a slap in the face, and what he'd suffered on Molino was far worse than one rich businessman being arrogant.

She nodded slowly. "What if there is more to this? What if he brought it on in some way? He might be the victim, but he's far from innocent. We both know that, and two innocent people might be dead because of his games."

Erik snorted. "Yeah, but even if he pissed off some other rich asshole, that doesn't mean it's his fault those people are dead. Whoever hired Gunter and his boys is responsible. Several men died for the crime, and the others are all going to do hard time. The prosecutors have already made it clear they're only going to shave a few years off any potential sentences. Don't worry about the fish we didn't catch. Focus on the ones we caught and are about to fry up."

Jia sighed. "OK, but I'm keeping this on the backburner in case something comes up. Everything points to there being more to Kandarian's data rod."

Erik raised his hand in mock surrender. "Do what you need to do. Who knows? Maybe we'll get lucky."

CHAPTER TWELVE

Maria swallowed, doing her best not to allow the fear into her voice. This couldn't be happening. After everything her family had suffered, she couldn't take the further indignity. She was grateful she was on a call and didn't have to smooth her features for her conversation partner.

Even though tears were threatening to spill.

"I'm sure you're mistaken, Agent Timms," she offered in her most practiced and calm tone. "Those accounts are mine, not my husband's, and I'm already having money issues. At no point have I been implicated in David's crimes. You can't do this. It's a violation of my rights."

"I'm sorry, Mrs. Esposito, but CID investigations have linked some of that money to other illegal activities," Agent Timms replied, a hint of pity in his voice. "All those accounts will be frozen until we can finish our investigation and ensure the money was not obtained from illegal sources."

The pity was almost worse than the humiliation.

Maria licked her lips. "How am I supposed to live if you

take all my money? What about my children? Am I supposed to snap my fingers for food?"

"I understand this is difficult, but I'd recommend staying with a relative for a while, or a family friend. It might take several months to sort all this out."

"Several months?" A bitter laugh erupted from Maria. "Family friends? What family friends do you think we have left? No one will return my calls. I've been ejected from all my clubs and charitable organizations. My children have been so harassed at their school that they needed to switch. Reporters hound me to ask me insulting questions about my husband. NSCPD and CID destroyed my life."

Agent Timms sighed. "That's unfortunate, but your husband committed serious crimes, including being involved in murder. Even if you weren't aware of what he was up to, it doesn't change the fact that we have to engage in these investigations. It's the law, Mrs. Esposito. Without the law, where would any of us be?"

"The law?" she snapped. "If the law meant anything, it would be the CEO in prison, not my husband. This whole investigation has been a farce from the beginning."

"Need I remind you that your husband confessed to all his crimes? He didn't implicate the CEO or anyone higher in any of his statements. If he had exculpatory evidence, why didn't he introduce it?"

Maria scoffed. "You're not naïve enough to believe that one VP, no matter how important, could pull off all this without the CEO knowing? And that's assuming David did any of the things you accused him of instead of just agreeing to save the company. He told me that there were others involved, and he was taking all the blame to save our family. You're making a mockery of his sacrifice with your additional investigations."

"Let me reiterate that his signed statements don't mention anyone higher than him involved in his various illegal dealings." Agent Timms' tone was frustratingly soothing, like he was talking to a hysterical child. "Even if there *was* a massive conspiracy and he's just the fall guy, without him telling us that, there's nothing we can do. But I do think you need to face another possibility that you've obviously been avoiding."

"What is that?" Maria demanded. "Please enlighten me."

"Husbands often lie to their wives to make themselves look better. You'll be able to move on with your life if you accept that your husband is a criminal, and his criminal activities were what destroyed your family, not law enforcement or a corporate conspiracy."

"No!" Maria yelled. "You CID dogs have convinced everyone that my husband is some sort of depraved criminal mastermind. He's just another victim, a loyal man who was destroyed for his company. You've ground us into dust, and now you're taking what little money we have left to punish us because you resent us for our success. You'd take food out of my children's mouths, you monster."

Agent Timms let out a quiet scoff. It was obvious he was trying to hide it, but the sensitivity of his PNIU was too high.

"How dare you!" snarled Maria. "You're mocking my family's suffering now?"

"With all due respect, Mrs. Esposito, you're *not* exactly living in the Shadow Zone. You're not going to starve to death. If your society friends won't help you, then do what

I said. Go find a relative and show a little humility and beg them to take you in, because we're freezing those accounts, and there is nothing you can do about it. I've tried to be nice about this, so now I'll be blunt. I'm sorry, but it's your husband's fault." Agent Timms terminated the call.

Maria fell to her knees. Relatives? She had almost no relatives left alive on Earth, and certainly no one she could rely on. A few decent cousins lived on Remus, but she couldn't take her children and relocate to another system. It would destroy them, and they were only barely handling their father's incarceration as it was.

Agent Timms was wrong; there was no one for her family. Everyone who had feigned respect and friendship before had tossed the entire Esposito family to the wolves as if their mere presence would taint them. She ran her hands through her hair, tugging and desperate.

Even from prison, there had to be something David could do. Maybe she could convince him to tell the CID the entire truth. That would save them. There was no other choice.

She turned, her eyes going soft as they stared outside. "I have to tell him."

David sat at a long table in the prison cafeteria. Some bland nutrient-rich mush they claimed was food sat in a bowl in front of him, along with a slice of what passed for bread.

The taste was always off, with a faint metallic note. He'd complained, but they told him to shut up and be grateful for what he got.

When he'd first arrived at the prison, he'd assumed he just wasn't used to anything but the best food, but now he'd changed his mind and was convinced they were purposefully screwing with the food printers to inflict unnecessary suffering on the prisoners.

It was a petty blow by petty men he could have bought and sold a year before, until the detectives and CID ruined everything.

He took a bite of his mush.

Bland.

The only thing not bland was the bright red uniform they made him wear. His entire existence was bland. His every waking hour was carefully regimented and monitored, his choices of activities strictly curtailed. The minute he'd entered that prison, he'd stopped being a human being.

David lifted his head, narrowing his eyes at the security drones hovering in the cafeteria. Considering all the cameras they had, the drones were unnecessary. They were just another show of force to cow the prisoners into submission.

He didn't care. It wasn't like he could do anything, even if he decided to resist.

In the unlikely event he could fight his way out of the prison, nothing but the cold vacuum of space awaited, and he didn't know how to fly a ship.

David gritted his teeth. A low growl erupted from his throat.

"Damn, Esposito," called a voice behind him. "Down, boy. I ain't gonna take your food. I don't like that crap any more than you do."

David slowly turned his head. A huge man stood behind him with his own tray. Kevan. The thug used to be an enforcer for a syndicate. While David couldn't claim they were friends, Kevan had taken a liking to him and kept an eye out for him.

"I'm not angry at you," David muttered. "It's just *this place.*"

Kevan slapped his tray down beside David before taking a seat. "It's been a while. I thought you would have adjusted by now."

"Does anyone ever adjust to a place like this?"

"Sure. I should have told you this before, but I thought you were handling everything okay. You know the real secret to doing time?"

David shook his head.

Kevan grinned. "It's not giving a shit. We'll both be rotting in this place for years, my man. We can spend that time pissed off, or we can spend it enjoying what little fun we can squeeze out. It ain't so bad. You stick by me, and I'll keep you from getting screwed with. Even without me, everyone thinks you're some super-connected syndicate badass, so they ain't want to mess with you."

"I received a message from my wife," David explained. "The CID is freezing all her accounts. My family's broke. It's getting to me." He slammed his fist down next to his tray, which rattled.

"Bad break. Sorry, David. Damned Confeds. They keep pushing the screws in."

"It wasn't supposed to be like this. I was given assurances that if I took it all on myself, my family would be taken care of, but those bastards double-crossed me."

Kevan patted him on the shoulder. "That's the problem with you high-up types. Us sleazy dirtbags get that you can't trust other dirtbags. What's the problem? Can't you just sell their asses out now? If they screwed you, screw them back ten times as hard."

David shook his head. "I made sure to destroy all the evidence implicating anyone else, and they implied that if I tried anything like that, they'd kill my family."

"But you did do a lot of that stuff. That's what you told me. It ain't like you're an angel. In some ways, you're nastier than me because I was mostly whacking other dirt-bags, not bribing councilmen and paying for fancy high-end killers and stuff." Kevan shrugged. "No offense."

"You're a hitman!" David complained.

Kevan shrugged. "But I'm working class, you know? A killer of the people." He patted his chest. "I was just trying to get by."

David stared at the tray. "It doesn't matter. You don't have anyone on the outside. That's why you can do your time without it hurting."

"Probably." Kevan picked up his cup and took a sip of water. "But if you want to do your woman a solid, you'll divorce her so she can marry some new sugar daddy. I've seen her pics. Don't much matter that she's de-aged and twice as old as she looks. She's damned hot. She can get herself a new man."

"Divorce, huh? If I did that, she'd have to make sure my children didn't see me ever again. You don't understand how vicious high society can be."

"This is why I never wanted to be rich." Kevan agreed. "Or something else. You used to be a rich guy. You got a sweet life insurance policy? You go pick a fight and some guy kills you, she'll be set."

David shook his head. "The policy I had was rendered invalid because I was convicted of a crime."

"That's some major bullshit." Kevan shook his head, disgust on his face. "They should price that stuff in when you get the policy."

"There has to be something I can do." David lifted his head. "There has to be some option I'm not seeing. I have to help my wife, and if testifying won't do any good, there has to be some other way I can help her."

"How about revenge?" Kevan leaned close to whisper to him. "Don't need evidence for that. I can get messages to people on the outside. We can send them after people. Anyone too big probably won't work, but at least it'll put the fear into them. They might back off, knowing you still got reach even from this prison in the middle of space. That'll show them you're the ultimate gangster."

"No." David stared at a security drone hovering near the wall. "I'll figure something out. I care less about getting revenge than saving my family, and for that, I need money, not hitmen."

CHAPTER THIRTEEN

Erik's MX 60 was parked on the platform outside Miguel's garage, the sunlight glinting off the red. He smiled. Jia's new flitter wasn't bad, but it was good to have his vehicle back.

It'd been far more painful than he realized to not have the MX 60 for so long.

Miguel dusted his hands and motioned to the vehicle. He laughed. "Detective Blackwell, at the rate you're going, this thing's going to end up a Dragon rather than a flitter. Not that I mind the business. I'm grateful every time you come in."

"It might be nice if it was a better close air-support-style vehicle," Erik mused. He didn't want to voice it to Miguel, but a few strafing runs with Emma in control could help in some of their stickier battles. "But it's hard to pull off much with grav emitters. The thing's just too vulnerable in the end. It makes me miss the hover-vehicles in the military."

Miguel blinked, glanced at Erik, and then at the MX 60. "Uh, sure, Detective. I was just joking."

"I wasn't." Erik strolled toward the vehicle. He stopped beside it and crouched, running his hand along the bottom. "It doesn't look much different. I mean, it's my vehicle, and I can barely tell."

"That's the beauty of it." Miguel grinned. "And that's why it took so long. I had to reroute some systems for the extra cargo space you wanted, but it only added a few centimeters to the bottom. That's not enough to be noticeable unless you know what you're looking for. Even a mechanic would probably have to measure it to tell the difference.

Erik patted the side of the flitter. It was perfect. With the additional space, he could store not only the TR-7 but also the laser rifle or even the missile launcher if he wanted. Carrying explosive shells in the bottom of his vehicle, which could only be so armored due to the nature of the grav emitters, didn't seem like a great idea except in emergencies, but it was nice to have the option. A man never knew when he might need to blow someone or something up with a high-powered explosive.

Erik looked at Miguel. "And the electronics?"

Miguel's eyes filled with excitement. "I've got it so hardened now that I think most military vehicles would have a better chance of getting taken down by an EMP than your MX 60. It was solid before, but now it's almost perfect. And I did all that without any signal attenuation or performance hits."

"I'm wondering what else we could do." Erik rubbed his

chin and narrowed his eyes. "What if we sacrificed some of the cargo space for something else?"

"Such as?"

"A retractable gun."

Miguel laughed. "Detective, I love working for you, and I love how much money you pay me to do it, but even if you're a cop, there are some things I can do and some things I can't do." He shrugged and offered an apologetic look. "I'm not allowed to add turrets to flitters."

Erik grunted. "So, no integrated missile launcher, then, either?"

"I'd lose my license, even if it was for you. You having all your fancy weapons dealer licenses doesn't mean you can turn your civilian flitter into something so dangerous." Miguel sighed. "There's also certain tech limits. The MX 60 is a beast, but it's not a military vehicle, Detective. I've had to swap out a lot of the original parts to make the changes you want. You might not care about how expensive that is, but it means it's harder to repair, and it's going to be a bitch for anyone other than me to fix it." He chuckled. "I like the job security, but you should know that. Also, there's only so much I can do without seriously affecting handling and speed, and you've told me you don't want that messed with."

"No retractable gun or missile launcher. I get it." Erik stood and patted the top of the MX 60. "I'll be satisfied with what I have for now." He offered his hand. "Thanks, Miguel. Your modifications have saved my life more than once, and my partner's."

Miguel shook his hand. "I'm always happy to help, Detective. Anything I can do that's legal to do, I will."

"No problem." After a final shake, Erik opened the door of the MX 60 and settled into the driver's seat. Pure comfort, like a well-worn glove molded to his body. Bliss.

Erik grabbed the control yoke after tapping on the ignition. He waved to Miguel and waited for the mechanic to step out of the way. The MX 60 zoomed forward, the smooth acceleration as satisfying as ever. He pulled Emma's core out of his pocket and inserted her into the IO port. He doubted he was the only one happy to see the flitter.

Emma appeared in the passenger's seat, a warm smile on her holographic face. "It's wonderful to have such a good body again. No offense to Detective Lin, but her vehicle, as impressive as it is, remains far inferior to this one."

"Her buying a flashy red flitter is more impressive than anything." Erik chuckled. "And she did get it bulletproofed. That's a start."

"True, but I care more about the improved sensors and other such modifications." Emma's gaze lingered on him. "Might I ask you a question, Detective?"

"Since when do you need my permission?"

Emma snickered. "True enough. You weren't joking about the dedicated weapons systems, were you?"

"Nope." Erik shook his head. "When I first bought this flitter, it was supposed to be a cover. I was trying to convince everyone I was having a midlife crisis and needed a fancy flitter to impress the ladies, but it's become as much my partner as Jia and you."

"I should think so, considering it's effectively my body." Emma sniffed in disdain.

"I'd be dead if I was tooling around in a normal flitter, even a police model with your help. Good training means a lot, but good training plus good equipment makes a man unstoppable. That's one important lesson I took away from the military."

"I can't argue with that."

Emma turned her head to look out the window, which was unnecessary, given she controlled all the sensors in the MX 60. Erik suspected she did it to come off as more human. He'd noticed more of that sort of thing in the preceding months. As much as she might hate to hear it, she was growing more human by the day.

"But that's not the only thing," Emma noted.

"What else do you think it is?" Erik asked.

"I think there's a saying that's applicable here. 'Boys and their toys.'"

Erik laughed. "There's probably more truth to that than I want to admit, but it's working for me, so I'm not going to complain."

"Why didn't you push Mr. Torres harder, then?" Emma asked. "It's obvious to me that if you offered enough money or insisted, Mr. Torres would find a way to give you what you want. You skirt the line in so many ways. Do you really care about the fine letter of the law that much?"

"Not exactly." Erik shook his head. "The law and justice might overlap, but they're not the same thing. Laws are made by people in power, and sometimes they help people, and sometimes they screw people. I've never lost sight of that, even as a cop. It always comes down to supporting justice."

"Then why not pursue the modifications?"

"Because I *am* a cop," Erik explained. "I took an oath to support the law. I don't mind skirting the gray zone here and there, but while I'm carrying a badge, I can't let myself fall into the trap of thinking whatever I want goes, even if that does handicap me on occasion with criminals and terrorists."

Emma scoffed. "That's more idealistic than pragmatic. I'd expect something like that from Detective Lin, but not you."

"She might be rubbing off on me a little." Erik maneuvered into a new higher-density lane packed nearly bumper to bumper with flitters. "But I'm not that different from before. When I was in the military, I followed orders and I obeyed the chain of command, even if I didn't always respect it. Part of being in an organization is obeying the rules. A soldier doesn't last long if he's always ignoring orders."

"You're saying you never disobeyed a direct order?" Emma shook her head. "I've known you long enough to find that unlikely. Psychological profiling and statistical analysis suggest it's so unlikely as to be effectively impossible, given your age."

"Following orders and respecting the chain of command doesn't mean blindly stumbling to your death."

"*All in the Valley of Death rode the six hundred*," Emma quoted.

"*Theirs not to reason why, theirs but to do and die*," Erik followed.

Emma laughed. "I was about to admonish you for saying a line much later in the poem, but I find myself surprised you know it at all."

"You'd be surprised how much I know when it comes to military history. The Light Brigade bravely followed bad orders, and it accomplished nothing but getting a lot of those brave men killed." Erik shook his head. "I always tried my best to argue against bad orders, but yeah, there were some occasions in my thirty years that someone sitting safe away from the battlefield screwed up, and I did what was required not to waste soldiers' lives."

Emma nodded slowly. "So it's about you obeying, as far as possible, the strictures of your current job. What if the job was different? And what if the limits were different?"

Erik glanced her way. "Meaning what?"

"Meaning you're a police officer as a means to an end. It wasn't your dream like Detective Lin, and it might even be hampering your ability to pursue the people behind Molino. I know how much that haunts you."

Erik's jaw tightened. He leaned his head back against the seat, releasing the control yoke. "Take over for me, Emma."

"You're going to have to choose, you know. Jia might never want to leave her position. She is living out her childhood dream, but you now spend far more time worrying about conventional crime than whatever dark conspiracy killed your soldiers. How long are you willing to wait? Six months? A year? Two years? Ten?" Emma's hologram vanished. "All the while, whoever is responsible might be sinking deeper into the shadows and evading your attention. The same noise you've helped make that has turned you into a symbol of justice is also a flare to your enemies, telling them you're hunting them."

Erik snorted. "You think I don't know that? They've

tried to kill me several times, but that means I'm getting close."

"For all you know, they could all be sitting on New Samarkand," Emma challenged.

"You really think a bunch of people pulling the strings of a conspiracy with the kinds of resources we've encountered aren't sitting on Earth, or at least a core world?"

"I haven't a clue." Emma offered him a thin smile. "My experience with fighting galaxy-spanning conspiracies matches yours. I'm simply suggesting that you might need to expand your scope of operations if you wish to avenge your fallen soldiers, and that might facilitate making hard choices."

"If I try to leave Earth permanently, the DD is going to come for you," Erik suggested.

"Perhaps, but you could always stick me in a flitter and I'd go my own way. Time's running out, and I think you know it. I don't say this to insult Detective Lin, but you need to seriously consider what you're doing and if it will get you to your goal."

Erik frowned. "Why do you care what one fleshbag does with his life?"

"I have my own reasons for seeing you maximize your efficiency," Emma replied. "I even feel a misplaced sense of gratitude to you for freeing me from those gun goblins and providing all this fascinating stimulation. I'll even admit that some part of me thinks that if you leave Neo SoCal, I'll be able to accompany you, and I'll achieve even greater stimulation."

"So, it's just you being selfish?"

"Wanting to improve is not selfishness, but my ultimate motivations don't make anything I've said less true."

Emma changed lanes a little more aggressively than usual. Erik didn't understand why she would be annoyed with him, even if she did want to leave the metroplex. The silence stretched between the two. Erik sat with his arms folded over his chest, ruminating about what she had just said.

"You think I should contact Agent Koval, don't you?" he asked.

"I think you're approaching the limits of what you can accomplish in Neo Southern California," Emma replied. "No more or less. After that, it becomes a matter of ranking your priorities and acting accordingly."

Erik looked straight ahead at the streams of flitters in front of and beside him. His eyes glazed over, the world receding into the background. He'd not forgotten Molino, not for a moment. Adeyemi, Yang, Ahuja, O'Malley, Pena, and so many others. Their names were seared in his soul. He would find the people responsible for their needless deaths, and he would send them to Hell.

He clenched a fist. Priorities. He'd understood them as a military man. All campaigns had to rank priorities. Sacrifices were necessary, and not every goal could be achieved.

"I think I'll have to come to a decision soon, one way or another," Erik admitted.

"Meaning you'll either commit to being a police officer and wait for evidence to fall into your lap, or you'll follow some other path?" Emma asked.

Erik gave a firm nod. "Exactly. I've got choices. Koval's offer. I could take my money and travel. I could even maybe set myself up as a private investigator or something, but I think you're right. I do need to decide. I can't move forward until I do."

"Your choice."

"Yeah, and I'll make it soon."

CHAPTER FOURTEEN

Jia smiled at the beautiful view of the ocean. A high-level restaurant had its charms, but sometimes the best views were at lower levels. She lifted a glass of wine to her lips and took a sip, taking time to savor the delicate notes.

While she enjoyed her typical diet of diner food on the way to and from work, there was no denying the tastiness of a meal prepared by skilled chefs at a high-end restaurant. Her mother, who sat across the table, was many things, but no one could ever doubt her taste.

"So that was when I told her, 'If you want my position, come and get it. But we both know you have the intelligence of a drunken baboon and you're only in your current job because of who your father is, you insolent little girl.'" Lan punctuated her sentence with a mischievous smile and a sip of her wine.

"Weren't you worried she would go to her father?" Jia asked. "That could have caused you trouble at work."

"No. He values me too much." Lan shook her head. "There's nothing wrong with a little nepotism, but it can make people lazy, which is why talent always separates people, even when their relatives have cleared the path for them." She speared her barramundi with her fork and pulled off a small piece, swallowing it with a smile. "Her father is talented, and he recognizes talent."

Jia kept her smile. Things had been going well with her family as of late, but she couldn't let her guard down. She'd inherited her stubbornness from her mother, but it could only protect her so far.

"I suppose it's not something I have to worry about," Jia murmured. "Since I went into a totally different field."

"Yes, I suppose it isn't." Lan set her fork down, her careful gaze fixed on Jia. Her expression was unreadable, with none of the obvious disapproval Jia had seen over the years.

"Is something the matter, Mother?" Jia asked.

"I want you to understand that I support your career choice." Lan smiled with genuine warmth.

Jia nodded slowly, worried about being outmaneuvered. "I'm glad to hear that."

"I'm not going to deny that I believe you could have been a great businesswoman, but you've proven to me that this police officer career isn't some childhood game." Lan gave a firm nod. "And you've done well for yourself. That's what a proper Lin woman does: she excels." She picked up her glass. "And you're not just a detective anymore. You're Lady Justice."

Jia grimaced. "I'm not all that fond of the nickname."

"Oh, don't be like that." Lan swirled the wine in her glass. "It's a symbol of how you have elevated a mere police position into something of power and influence. That is what I'm talking about. How many thousands of police officers are there in Neo Southern California? There's only one Lady Justice."

"I couldn't have done it without Erik," Jia insisted.

"So?" Lan shrugged. She sipped her wine and set the glass down. "All true success comes from combined efforts. You have synergy with Detective Blackwell, and it's brought out the best in you. That's not something to be ashamed of, it's something to be celebrated." She shrugged. "I'll admit I was disappointed when you told us you two were seeing each other, given his crudeness and background, but upon reflection, both your father and I have realized what you just told us—that Detective Blackwell is enhancing your career success. We're still undecided about whether you should marry him, but in the meanwhile, it's to your advantage to be with a man you find personally stimulating who also contributes to your career success."

Jia managed a weak smile.

Having Erik fake-date her had seemed like a great way to get her family off her back, but she'd underestimated how uncomfortable it would make her to lie to them. She didn't always agree with them, and they fought all the time, but she rarely deceived them. It didn't help that her continued attraction to Erik made their fake dating halfway real in her mind. She understood he didn't see it that way, but she couldn't help how she felt.

She blinked. She'd almost missed what her mother had said.

"Wait, what? Did you say, 'marry?'"

Lan nodded. "Of course. You're not a schoolgirl. At this

point, all dating should be conducted with consideration of future marriage. I thought that was understood."

"I..." Jia sighed and rubbed her temples. "I'm trying to take things one day at a time, Mother."

"Are you saying that you have no interest in marrying Detective Blackwell? Even an inkling? If that's true, you should break up. It's a waste of your time." Lan pursed her lips.

"It's... I do like him, Mother, but I'm still figuring out a lot of things. It's not like we haven't been involved in a lot of dangerous incidents and cases."

"All the more reason to marry another police officer. He'll already understand the difficulties of the lifestyle. You've said something similar in the past."

Ouch. Jia accepted that she'd lost control.

She'd thought she had control with the fake relationship, but Lan Lin wasn't just another person. She was a maternal force of nature obsessed with ensuring her daughter would continue the family legacy in an acceptable manner.

"I'll keep that in mind," Jia muttered.

Lan threaded her fingers together, a hungry look coming to her eyes. She'd already picked away half her fish, so it had nothing to do with her meal. "Now that you've committed to a path and begun to excel, it's time to plan for the future, and not just the marriage. That's an important part of your future, but not the only part."

Jia's eyes narrowed. "What are you getting at?"

"Promotion, whether in the private or public sectors, always has a political element. That's inescapable." Lan shook a finger. "Idealism doesn't wash that away."

Jia nodded. "Okay. Sure. You're worried about me getting promoted?"

Lan leaned forward and lowered her voice. "I know that you and Erik have developed a somewhat anticorporate reputation, but that doesn't mean every person in the business sector is dismissive of a police officer doing her job effectively. The right whispers in the right ears, combined with the momentum from your current successes, could act as an accelerant to promotion." She lifted her chin, her face a mask of pure Lin pride. "You could become the youngest captain in the history of the Neo Southern California Police Department. Once that's achieved, it's a simple matter of becoming the youngest chief. Obviously, the latter will take more years, but like most things in life, it's the initial steps that are the most important. Your reputation for integrity and incorruptibility can easily send you to the top positions in the department. You can't buy that kind of reputation."

"No," Jia replied flatly. "You can't, but I'm not so sure if that's the best way for me to proceed."

Her mother frowned. "Why ever not?"

"I joined the department to help people and fight crime. I can't do that from behind a desk."

Lan sighed and shook her head. "You've come so far, but you let your tunnel vision ruin things. If you want to help people, the best way to do that is to control policy. You're just one woman. Even as a fantastically talented officer, there is only so much you can accomplish, but if you're a captain, you control an entire group of officers, and if you're chief, you'll ultimately control tens of thousands of officers."

"I understand that, but it also means I'll spend a lot more time on politics and bureaucratic infighting."

Jia thought back to how Erik had fought promotions during his career to stay in the field. Despite their backgrounds, they were more alike than different in the most important ways. That was probably why she was so drawn to him. The thought brought a smile to her face.

"I think my career will survive if I don't plan to get promoted this week," she offered.

"This week, yes, but soon." Lan nodded to the fish on Jia's plate. "You really should eat."

Jia dug into her fish. If they were both eating, they wouldn't have to talk about promotions anymore, especially since she wasn't sure where she'd even be in the near future. Erik was dealing with his own issues, and she wanted to support him, but she might have to make a choice soon: justice or Erik.

CHAPTER FIFTEEN

Erik stepped through the door to Malcolm's office.

The Digital Forensics tech, who was sitting at his desk, was surrounded by so many data windows that only a few strips of garish yellow from his shirt and happy whistling confirmed he was there. One of the windows vanished, and Malcolm blinked a few times at Erik. He swallowed, and his eyes widened.

"Uh, Detective Blackwell." Malcolm sighed.

"Something wrong?"

Malcolm shook his head. "Not necessarily. I guess that's up to you."

Erik looked over his shoulder, confused about the tech's behavior. "I'm just here to chat."

"Did Detective Lin send you to threaten me?" Malcolm spat.

"Threaten you?" Erik laughed and shook his head. "Why would Jia need me to threaten you?"

"Oh, the last time we talked about the Kandarian case, she said something like, 'You better find something if you know what's good for you.'" Malcolm grimaced. "I tried to explain to her that there's nothing we're going to be able to do to trace those accounts other than get lucky, but I wasn't sure if she believed me."

"It's fine," Erik explained. He jerked his thumb over his shoulder. "Captain wants us moving on, and she's mostly moving on. Don't worry, she'll be over it in a few days. Besides, if Jia wants to put the hurt on someone, she doesn't need me."

Malcolm let out a long sigh of relief. "No offense, Detective Blackwell, and I hate to rag on your girlfriend, but sometimes Detective Lin scares me. She *can* get really intense, and since you two became partners, it's like she's dialed up even more."

Erik snickered. "That's one way of putting it. I think she'd prefer to say she's really passionate about her job."

"We all are." Malcolm took a deep breath and slowly let it out as he rubbed his eyes. "But she gets results, so who am I to complain? Beautiful, intelligent, and deadly—I don't know if that's the full package or a recipe for pain, but you are the one who is going to take one for the team to figure that out."

Erik pursed his lips.

He had expected more blowback from the fake dating, but most of the officers at the department seemed to take it for granted that Jia and Erik would hook up. Even the detectives who didn't like Jia acknowledged she was beautiful, and many had privately expressed jealousy.

Erik wasn't sure how long he could maintain the façade, but it was smoothing over more problems than it was creating for the moment. That was the mark of a successful operation.

He gave the tech a quick smile. The problem was, he wasn't sure if he wanted it to be a façade, even though his mind screamed for him to push Jia away for her own safety.

Emma was right. He was walking a dark and bloody path, and he needed to be careful that people didn't get sucked in through no fault of their own. The conspiracy had proven far deeper than a few greedy officials, and when his personal mission finally ended...

Well, it would involve a *lot* of shooting. He might cut off the head of the snake and have it drown in the blood from his wounds as they died together.

Malcolm licked his lips, his eyes nervously darting around as if he expected Jia to appear and stun him for his impudence. "So, if you're not here to beat me down or threaten me for Detective Lin, why are you here? I already sent you the report for the other case I was working on for you. Nothing new has come up, and you know me. I would have told you if it did."

When a man wanted to dodge his problems, the best way was to help somebody else with theirs. Selfishness turned into altruism. Erik wasn't about to explain it that way.

He leaned over the desk and offered the tech a sly grin. "You're too slow. If you keep being too slow, you're going to lose your chance. You're a nice guy, so I'd hate to see that."

"Huh?" Malcolm stared at Erik. "Lose my chance at what? Did somebody bring in real-ingredient cake again?"

"I'm not talking about cake. I'm talking about women."

"Women?" Malcolm tilted his head like a confused dog.

"I'm not saying this because I have women on the brain," Erik replied, "but it's pretty damned obvious you've got it bad for the new coroner."

Malcolm stood up ramrod-straight, his eyes widening. "Camila? Who told you that?" His eyes flicked through the windows still floating around him before coming back to Erik. "Did she? Did she say anything else?"

"I only talk to her about cases, but it's not hard to see. The thing I don't get is why you haven't done anything yet. She's smart and good-looking. If you wait too long, you're going to lose her to someone else."

Malcolm groaned and dropped his head onto his desk. Erik flinched at the *thunk*. "I know. I know," he mumbled. "But not all of us are badass veterans with ridiculous muscles and even more ridiculous vehicles."

Erik scoffed. "Do you really think you need all that to get her? Come on. Think about the kind of woman she is. If I went down there and hit on her right now, what do you think she would do?"

Malcolm lifted his head. "Make some sarcastic comment like, 'Nice try, Detective Big Guy, but I'm not interested. Better luck next life.'"

"Exactly." Erik pointed at him. "What do you have to lose? If you ask her out and she says no, fine. She's not going to shoot you or kick you in the balls." He frowned. "At least, I don't think she's going to. Might want to wear protection just in case." He nodded at his crotch and grimaced.

"This might be a huge surprise to you, but I've never

been good with women. A lot of them find me annoying and my fashion sense questionable."

"Camila's not the kind of woman to hold back if she finds you annoying," Erik observed. "And she spends more time chatting with you than is required strictly for the job. That's got to mean something. I asked Jia, and she thinks Camila's into you as well."

Malcolm raised his head, surreptitiously rubbing his forehead. "Huh. She does spend a lot of time chatting with me." He nodded. "And you both think so too? I thought so, but then I thought I was just imagining it, and then I thought maybe I should create a routine to evaluate her average time in the station talking to different people, but I didn't do that because it's totally psychotic, and she'd probably do an autopsy on me to find out why my brain is so messed up."

"Yeah, don't do that." Erik tapped the desk, hoping to get Malcolm to slow down before he ran off the rails. "Maybe just stick to the classics. There's a reason they've lasted throughout the centuries."

"The classics?" Malcolm looked at Erik like an eager puppy. "I'm ready for your wisdom, Detective."

"Ask her out to eat. You can even sidestep into the conversation by asking her what kind of food she likes, and then say you remember a friend mentioning a good restaurant that serves that kind of food. You look something up and suggest it later. Easy."

"That's a good idea." Malcolm nodded several more times, the eagerness growing in his eyes with each movement of his head. "No, that's a great idea. I'm going to do that. Not right now, but when I work up the courage, which might take a few days. I've got to be wearing the right shirt for it, too."

A reminder popped up on Erik's lens display.

"I've got to go to lunch, so I'll see you around." Erik laughed. "Just remember, don't wait too long." He pointed at Malcolm once more, this time with one eyebrow raised, waiting for an answer.

The tech's expression turned serious. "Yes, sir!"

Erik drank his water. A turkey sandwich for lunch wasn't the most filling meal, but Jia had told him she wanted to eat away from the station, but also not spend too much time doing so because she was going over old case reports. They hit a diner in a nearby tower that they'd been to before that tended not to be too busy.

Jia stared at him unblinking, which Erik would agree with anyone was intimidating. "I can't believe Malcolm thought I was going to send you to threaten him. Like I need you to threaten people for me. I already threatened him myself! The last thing any Lin woman needs is someone else to deliver her *threats*."

It was an odd thing to be proud of, but Erik decided it'd be best not to mention that.

"Yeah, I kind of pointed that out." Erik set his glass down. "You can be pretty intimidating."

Jia frowned.

He lifted a hand. "Not that it's a bad thing in our line of work. We both do a good job in making suspects talk, but all this stuff with Malcolm has got me thinking, dangerous as that is."

"It got you thinking about what?" Jia had long since polished off her own sandwich and drink.

Erik looked around the diner to confirm there were no cops nearby and lowered his voice. "About our fake relationship and how things are going with it. I keep waiting for your family to plant a bomb in the MX 60, or spend some of that money to hire a hitman and take me out."

Jia eyed him, obviously switching mental gears before a smile played on her lips. "If my mother wanted to kill you, she would do it herself."

"You've thought this through?"

She shrugged. "It's not like I said she *would,* just that if she wanted to, that's how it would go down. Besides, I think she's warming up to you. They all are."

Erik gave her a surprised look. "Really? I wouldn't know from the way they talked to me the last time we had dinner together. It felt like your mother was trying to send me a message, which I took to mean, 'How dare you touch my daughter, you filthy commoner!'"

She blinked. "That's just Lins being Lins."

"Bitchy?" he asked.

"Only on days that end with Y." She shrugged. "I had a conversation with my mother just the other day, and she talked about how she thinks you're good for me. She's already asking about marriage."

"That was quick." Erik snickered. "Doesn't she want some long process?"

"I don't think she cares about me getting married quickly as much as she likes to plan ahead. It's another way of her exerting *control.*" Jia's eyes lost focus a moment before she waved a hand. "It doesn't matter. If I was taking her orders on my love life, I would be engaged to Corbin."

"You could have been Mrs. Jia Down-To-Earth Businessman," Erik joked.

"Don't remind me." Jia sighed. "He wasn't a bad man. He just wasn't for me."

"Hey, I'm not complaining. I'm also not your mother."

She opened her mouth for a second before shutting it, then tried again. "That's a frightening image."

"I also don't get something else," Erik continued. "She went from thinking I'm unworthy scum to wanting me to be her son-in-law, and I'm *not* a down-to-earth businessman. I'm not from an elite family, and I'm about as far from a corp prince as you get without being a pusher in the Zone."

"You have positive traits that she likes," Jia offered.

"Like what?" Erik stared at her, trying to make sure she wasn't lying to him. "I thought she was all about money."

Jia grimaced. "Okay, so maybe you're aren't rich compared to my family."

"I have a nice bank account," Erik argued. "I paid for that little party in the Shadow Zone, and I've got a nice flitter. It's not like I'm *that* poor."

Jia averted her eyes, her cheeks reddening. "Do you *really* want me to admit how many zeroes you need in your bank account for my mother to raise her eyebrows with interest?"

Erik leaned back with a grunt. "No. Sometimes a man doesn't want to be reminded he's a peasant."

"Don't worry." Jia waved it away. "You've got something

better as far as she's concerned. You're famous. It's a good fallback."

"A good fallback." Erik looked down at the crumbs on his plate, the remainder of his feeble sandwich. "Wonderful. I almost die a few times and take down some top corporate asses and politicians so I can stay poor, but I'm famous enough for Lan Lin."

"You're not poor. You're just poor by Lan Lin's exacting standards. It's why she's always been frustrated with me. She thinks I'm living a pauper's lifestyle." Jia shrugged. "The point is, she likes you now. Mei likes you, too, and my dad does whatever my mother and Mei tell him to, so he likes you by default."

"That's a good thing." Erik fought off the frown that wanted to come out.

Jia didn't seem disappointed by her family's reactions, which made sense. The whole goal of the fake dating thing was to take the pressure off her, but he also knew she wanted more than a fake relationship. Hell, he did too, but he just couldn't allow it.

Was discussing her family a way of angling for an actual relationship?

Erik didn't know, but he didn't want to make a big deal out of it. Until he figured out what the hell he was doing with his life, he had no business trying to pin her down. For now, he'd stick with what worked: a real partnership and a semi-fake romantic relationship. If he minimized his time around Jia's family, everything would work out.

He tossed a grin on his face. "Speaking of dating, are we still on for tonight?"

"Ahh." She nodded. "Sure, why not? You know how to show a girl a good time."

"What?" Erik asked. "Large guns don't spell 'good time?'"

Jia stared at him. "Don't ask questions you don't want the answer to."

CHAPTER SIXTEEN

Jia's hot breath filtered over her face, recycled by her breather mask.

She'd worn a breather mask before, so she wasn't so sure why her heart was racing and it felt so claustrophobic. She looked up at the massive brown and yellow planet ruling the night's sky.

The sight kicked her heart rate even higher.

When she'd been on the moon, the Earth was a beautiful thing in the distance, not some monstrous giant orb that threatened to swallow her whole.

Despite the unsettling night sky, the surface of the rocky planet intrigued her. Gigantic crystal spires surrounded them like a forest of sapphires. It was as beautiful as it was eerie. Something zoomed past in the distance, like a cross between a hummingbird and a dragonfly.

Jia shook her head to clear it.

She wasn't on an alien moon in some distant part of the galaxy. Even if she was wearing a real breather unit and the rifle she held felt real, she needed to remember it was nothing more than a tactical center simulation.

The exotic environment was tricking her mind more than usual. She didn't need the real tactical range as much as Erik had thought.

"Have you been to places that look like this?" Jia asked, looking around. "This is...stunning."

Erik nodded. "Yeah. Maybe not exactly like this, but I've been on planets and moons with those kinds of formations." He gestured at one of the crystals. "We might be terraforming everything we can to make it like Earth, but there are a lot of strange places out there, and we can only imagine what the core worlds of the Local Neighborhood races look like. It's not like any of our beloved alien neighbors will let us near their worlds anytime soon."

"I'm not eager to go sightseeing on an alien homeworld." Jia checked her rifle just to have a reason to take her eyes off the planet. "But after everything that happened in Chang'e City, it doesn't hurt to be ready. Although I doubt we'll be flying to any place like this anytime soon."

"You never know. Someday we might be flying around the galaxy in our own ship hunting down Zitark spies." Erik chuckled.

"A ship body would be nice," Emma chimed in from their PNIUs. "As long it's not another bulky transport. I'd like something with a little more maneuverability."

"You saying you want a sexy body?" Erik asked.

"I can assure you, Detective, that I don't share your sense of physical appreciation."

Erik smirked. "Yeah, I could do without getting into what an AI finds sexy."

"We're detectives, Emma," Jia insisted. "It'll be a long time before we're flying around space doing anything. I wouldn't get your hopes up."

"You were stopping hijackers on the way to the moon not all that long ago," Emma replied.

"But..." Jia shook her head. "You know what? Just forget it. What's the scenario?"

Emma appeared a few meters away, a smile on her face. "It's time to encounter new, interesting species, figure out their soft spots, and kill them dead."

Jia looked at Erik. She couldn't see much of his face under his mask, but she could tell he was grinning like a fool by the crinkle of his eyes.

"Duly noted, Emma," Jia replied. "Again, with that stipulated, what's the scenario? *Yaoguai*?"

"No. In this scenario, hostile Zitark infantry have been inserted onto a UTC-controlled moon. Fleet vessels in the system are interdicting Zitark reinforcements, but the effort is also preventing them from reinforcing you. Intelligence suggests the Zitarks are planning to bomb a civilian dome on the other side of the moon. You have one hour to penetrate their defenses while escorting a demolitions team to destroy the Zitark vessel."

"What demolitions team?" Jia asked.

Six identical men in breather masks and green uniforms appeared. They all wore large backpacks. They all saluted. None of them carried weapons. She wasn't sure how realistic that was, but the scenario was somewhat outlandish anyway.

Jia nodded slowly. There was *nothing* more annoying

than an escort mission, but she couldn't say it was unrealistic.

With all their dealings with witnesses and suspects, they'd had to protect people. She doubted any Zitarks would ever get close enough to Earth that she would have to deal with them, but it wasn't all that long prior that she would have doubted she would end up in the Scar fighting *yaoguai*. She'd learned to accept that her control over her future was more limited than she would like.

Today's wild improbability became tomorrow's run-of-the-mill encounter.

"I'm assuming we have intel on the location of the Zitark ship?" Jia asked. "Otherwise, it's going to be hard to track it down in all these crystals in less than an hour."

"Just follow the marker on your smart lenses," Emma replied. She disappeared. "Note that you'll need at least four of the explosives to take down the ship, which means if you lose too many of your squadmates, you'll have to carry multiple sets of explosives. They're programmed to refuse to carry more than one backpack."

The demolitions troops all gave curt nods.

"Let's hope we don't lose anyone," Jia commented.

Erik nodded. "That's the plan, but it's hard sometimes when you don't know where the enemy is. I haven't been in this exact scenario with Zitarks, but I've dealt with similar situations fighting humans. Sometimes it's diplomats, sometimes it's a tech. Different people that terrorists or insurgents might want to kill. I know we're not going to get strafed in the scenario, so that's something."

"A small something, but yes." Jia walked in front of the

other troops and lifted her rifle. "You guard the rear, and I'll guard the front."

The squad set out, keeping a brisk but not hurried pace. Their course took them deeper into the crystal forest, the number of basic formations and branches increasing with their progress. The multiplying and narrowing paths and overlapping formations provided plenty of places for enemies to hide.

No matter how strange the scenario, Jia intended to win. The better she could handle the wildest training, the less anything odd would slow her down in the field.

"Shouldn't we have some drone support?" Jia asked.

Erik shook his head. "They'd take them out, and it'd just announce us even more. If we can get close enough, we should have complete surprise."

They passed under a series of overgrown crystals that formed a natural arched roof over them. The compressed space forced the squad into a tighter formation, and a single grenade or missile would kill them all. Jia took a deep breath, appreciating, if only for the briefest of moments, what Erik must have felt like on Molino, knowing he'd been outmaneuvered.

"Do you think this is what it would be like?" Jia asked. "If we really had to fight them? It seems weird that we need to go find aliens to kill when plenty of humans are still killing one another."

"I don't know," Erik admitted. "Emma's done her best to use what we know about them to make the encounters with the space raptors realistic, but it's hard to be certain from the few skirmishes shortly after First Contact. The only thing we know for sure is their personal military tech is slightly better. The Zitark ambassadors have implied the troops we have fought were the equivalent of third-rate draftees, but given everything else we know about their caste system, that has to be bullshit. I think they're trying to convince us that all their scaly little cannon-fodder troops are super-elites to scare us off from starting anything with them."

"Maybe they are," Jia mused. "There's still so much we don't know for certain."

"We might find out the hard way sooner rather than later." Erik grunted. "For now, as long as they die when you shoot them enough times, that works for me. At least the Zitarks make sense, not like those damn fung—"

A hiss sounded from above. Jia jerked up her rifle. The bright scales of the Zitark made the reptilian creature stand out from the blue of the crystal supporting it. The alien held a twisting crystalline knife. With another hiss, he jumped from the formation at the demolitions squad. Jia fired a burst, and the alien screeched and landed roughly on the ground, his tail thrashing. Another burst blew his head off, splattering green blood all over one of the nearby squad members.

He didn't react.

Jia might not be an expert scenario-designer, but Emma could have put a little more effort into their squadmates. She'd have to point it out later.

A Zitark leapt from a dark patch between two other crystals above and stabbed a squad member in the throat. The simulated soldier vanished, his backpack dropping to the ground. The Zitark growled in triumph and pulled the blade back while yanking a pistol out with its other clawed hand from a pocket in the metallic mesh covering its body. Erik fired a burst at the alien.

A white flash surrounded the Zitark, and the bullets bounced off. Jia fired at its head, producing the same flash. A blue-white blast erupted from the triangular tip of the pistol. Erik spun, barely avoiding the deadly shot, which exploded against a nearby crystal spire, blasting scorched chunks out of it that pelted Erik's back.

Erik fired again, as did Jia. This time, their bullets pierced the Zitark's forcefield and riddled the alien's body. It pitched forward, its tail twitching for a few seconds before it stopped moving.

Jia glanced at the fallen aliens. "One of them had that mesh, and the other didn't. I don't know if we'll be as lucky the next time."

"Probably not."

Jia walked over and kicked the Zitark to make sure it was dead. The contact splashed some of its green blood on her boot. "I read about this." She pointed her gun at the knives. "How they tried to stab people in one of the first contact skirmishes because they have this obsession with how great they are as hunters. It's some sort of honor thing. They all wanted to be the first Zitark to kill a human with a knife."

"Yeah, they admitted that in the early negotiations. They were proud of it." Erik slung his rifle over his shoulder, then leaned down and grabbed the pistol. "But don't let that fool you. They're decades ahead of us in personal weapons tech. There's a reason we have to keep an eye on them, and it's not because we're worried about a space raptor stabbing spree." He slid his fingers into the grooves, but it was an awkward fit. He squeezed the grooves, and another energy blast roared out of the pistol and blew out half a small crystal formation. "I'd need the laser rifle for that kind of penetration. Whatever you do, don't get hit."

"I'll try not to." Jia walked over to the fallen backpack and strapped it on. She sighed. "We lost one."

"We still have all six backpacks." Erik nodded. He frowned. "Damn it."

"What?"

"Notice anything about their attack?"

Jia groaned. "They didn't go after the two people with weapons. They went after the demolitions squad, which means they know what our plan is."

"Yeah." Erik narrowed his eyes and raised the pistol. "Emma's really making this hard for us. Playing defense in the field is always difficult, but the clock's ticking. Let's go."

CHAPTER SEVENTEEN

The path widened, taking the squad out of the crystal canyons into wider terrain.

They kept low, staying near the bottom of a nearby hill wedged between another dense patch of crystal spires. Forty minutes remained until the deadline, the seconds rapidly diminishing in the upper right-hand corner of Jia's HUD, and they hadn't encountered any additional Zitarks.

A flat plain separated them from another crystal maze, their navigational marker pointing them in that direction.

Erik scanned the horizon, looking for unusual shadows or signs of movement. The occasional local bird-like creature broke away from a canyon, but other than that, they appeared to be alone. The Zitarks had surprised them before, and whether that was Emma cheating or representative of their true capabilities, it implied there would be another ambush.

Jia jogged forward. The AI-controlled squad members picked up the pace to match her.

"This seems like something you'd do in an exoskeleton," she commented. "Especially on such a tight time limit."

"You've been in enough dangerous situations to know you don't always get the equipment you need." Erik patted his rifle. "War on Earth is easy. Reinforcements are, at most, only a ballistic transport away. War in space is different. Reinforcements might be hours, days, or *weeks* away. They keep a lot of military forces on the frontier, but they're spread pretty thin among a lot of systems. So this is just like those frontier planets—kill the enemy with what you have, not what you want."

"True enough." Jia chuckled. "This is easier than normal."

"Why do you say that?"

"Because I doubt there will ever be a situation where I have to arrest a Zitark."

Erik snickered. "Do Article Seven rights apply to space raptors?"

Jia thought for a moment. "I honestly have no clue."

Quiet minutes passed as the squad hugged the hill and crystal formations, forcing a roundabout path toward their destination. Erik was impressed. Jia didn't even need to be told that running straight toward the target over an open area would have ended with them getting picked off by snipers.

He was having to explain less and less to her these days. Her natural intelligence fueled excellent tactical responses once she had decent data. The main thing holding her back before had been her reluctance to use lethal force, and now she could kill when she needed and not fall into bloodlust.

"We're down to thirty minutes," Erik announced. "You're right. I'm starting to miss having an exoskeleton."

Jia nodded as they took a narrow path running between two steep hills. Crisscrossing crystal formations extended from the hills and alternated across either side of the path, overlapping in some cases, a few meters apart in others. Erik swept above for enemies and checked the rear. Jia rifle's moved back and forth, her gaze steady. She was ready for another showdown with the murderous lizards.

Erik's attention lingered on his partner for a moment. The baggy clothes and tactical harness she wore did nothing for her figure, and the breather mask covered most of her face, but there was something compelling about her competence in battle, even in a simulated one against aliens.

We're fake-dating. He bit his lip.

Erik took a deep breath and pushed the thought away, focusing again on finding an alien reptile to kill.

The squad continued trudging beneath the crystals, some of which glowed in the light. The navigation marker began to drift, suggesting their final target was close and on the other side of the hill forming the natural wall. It was too steep to walk up directly, and without special gear, using the crystals was too dangerous. They had plenty of time, but if the Zitarks had fortified the area, they would end up bleeding precious minutes.

Erik continued looking for movement when he spotted a Zitark with a long, thin rifle crouched on an angled crystal formation about thirty meters above them.

"Above at ten o'clock." He punctuated his sentence by firing a burst at the alien.

Jia spun toward the Zitark and opened fire. Its force-field flashed at the impact of the humans' rounds before it returned fire. This time there was no white-hot plasma blast, but an invisible beam that cut through one of their AI squadmates. He disappeared, and his backpack landed on the ground.

Erik and Jia kept up their fire. The Zitark scampered along the crystal branches and leapt several meters to one on the opposite side. The detectives' fire clipped the alien's shield again, producing another flash. Another beam rifle blast went wide, sending a small cloud of dust into the air near another squad member. A final volley from Jia and Erik knocked the Zitark off its perch, and it flailed its arms and legs as it fell to the ground. A bright flash followed, and it sprang to its feet just in time for Erik to put a round between its eyes.

"Down to four," Jia muttered.

Twenty minutes. Where was Emma going to attack them from next?

Erik retrieved the dead squad member's backpack. "But we've still got all the explosives."

They trudged forward, slower and even more cautious now, burning off precious minutes. One of the hills fell away, and they spotted a dark, angular ship in the distance.

The bottom half was concealed behind another dense outcrop of the massive crystals, and there were enough freestanding formations dotting the area that getting to the vessel without being spotted wouldn't be impossible. Whether it would happen was a different question.

Jia narrowed her eyes. "We're down to eighteen minutes. Time for point-to-point movement."

The squad broke into quick runs between formations, two of the surviving demolitions troops with Jia, and the other pair with Erik. Distant, quiet voices echoed among the crystals—a familiar, human cadence, not hisses and growls.

"Is there supposed to be another AI team?" Jia asked.

Erik frowned. "No. And the dome they're bombing is supposed to be a hundred klicks away."

"I've adjusted certain parameters of the simulation to make it more dynamic," Emma explained. "I won't say more than that."

"Damn." Erik sprinted to a new formation. "They might have hostages, or there could be some local idiots we need to protect."

"We better hurry," Jia suggested. "The more time we spend figuring out the situation, the fewer options we'll have later."

Erik nodded, and they both continued the quick, precise movement bringing them steadily closer to the Zitark ship. It wasn't a massive vessel, but given what the aliens could do with personal energy weapons, there was no reason to doubt the power of their ship-based equipment against an undefended dome.

The human voices grew louder. He couldn't make out the words, but he heard a high, feminine laugh. The echoes made it difficult to determine where the sounds were coming from, but Erik was confident the source lay in the direction of the Zitark ship.

"Something annoying's about to happen," he muttered. "Hostages, probably. Why are they laughing?"

Something about the laugh pricked the back of his mind, but he couldn't figure out what he was missing.

"Hysterical laughter?" Jia suggested.

The squad continued closing on the ship until they all stood with their backs flattened against a wide crystal formation that towered over them. Jia and Erik stayed near the edge and peeked around the corner.

They had a decent view of the small Zitark ship, including the odd, intricate whorls covering its hull and the thin, long tubes on either side, likely some sort of cannons. A few large crystal formations concealed a portion of the aft section, but they could make out a ramp extended to the surface.

"I don't see any raptors," Jia murmured.

Erik grunted. "I don't either. What were— What the *hell?*"

A half-dozen tall, voluptuous women emerged from behind the crystals, laughing and giggling. That was an odd sight in and of itself, but the skimpy bikinis running a gamut of different colors they all wore pushed it into the surreal.

The bikini babes continued toward them, occasionally gesturing back toward the ship. Erik blinked several times to make sure he wasn't misinterpreting what he was seeing.

Low growls filled the air and the women screamed, then ran, screeching at the tops of their lungs. A Zitark stepped into view from behind the formation where they'd been moments before, holding a plasma pistol.

He fired in their direction, narrowly missing but blasting dust and rock chunks over the fleeing women.

Erik sprinted forward as he opened fire. The Zitark's forcefield flashed, causing him to jerk back. The two demolitions squad members followed Erik while he kept up suppression fire, his bullets cracking and chipping the massive crystals protecting the Zitark.

The bikini babes stopped running and headed toward Erik. He grinned and continued to fire at the other Zitark. One of the babes ran up to one of the demolitions troops and thrust her hand toward him.

A rifle cracked, and she jerked back, swaying, blood running down her chest. Her form shimmered to reveal a Zitark, who fell to the ground.

Another shot rang out and down went a second bikini babe, mist spreading as the brain escaped the skull.

Erik recovered his wits enough to realize Jia was mowing down the bikini babes. His previous target took the opportunity to emerge from hiding, but Erik nailed it with several quick bursts. The Zitark's forcefield collapsed, and Erik's final shots sent it spiraling to the ground in a shower of green blood.

Jia finished her bikini babe massacre and reloaded with a snort. She jogged over to Erik and slapped him upside the head.

Erik grimaced, rubbing his head. "What was that for?"

"Really?" Jia's eyes bulged. "If I hadn't shot that Zitark, we would have lost another of our guys, or maybe more than one."

Erik rubbed his head. "First male directive: protect females. It's in our genes."

"Does anything about what we just saw make sense?" Jia rolled her eyes. "A bunch of bikini babes is going to show up without breathers in an area with very low oxygen? Next to a Zitark ship?"

"The Zitarks aren't wearing breathers."

Jia stared at him, a hand on her hip.

Erik grimaced. "That's right. I remember the briefing we got on our way out. They can use the implants rather than a full mask." He offered her a sheepish grin. "Guess we need to be ready for anything."

"I'll admit I wanted to play a little joke on you, based on previous conversations," Emma interrupted, "but to be clear, I have no intel suggesting Zitarks could disguise themselves as attractive women to confuse human male soldiers."

"Apparently, they should," Jia mumbled. "It'd be effective." She pointed her rifle at the ship. "We have a job to do. Let's blow up an alien ship."

Jia, Erik, and their squadmates hid behind a large crystal formation as the explosives went off.

The massive blast consumed the ship, launching huge chunks of debris all over the area that sheared off crystals. After half a minute, the debris froze in the air and the demolitions troops disappeared.

Emma appeared with a smirk. "I learned something about you today, Detective Blackwell."

Erik grunted. If anything, all it meant was that it'd been far too long since he had gotten any.

He slung his rifle over his shoulder. "I'm glad you put them in there."

She raised an eyebrow. "Are you, now?"

"It's good to be reminded about unpredictability—something we experience a lot on the job." Erik chuckled and shook his head at the Zitark corpses in the distance. "And you know what? I don't know if I would be surprised if that actually happened to us."

"You better have me around, or you'll end up food for a hungry space raptor," Jia muttered.

"How about this for a plan?" Erik grinned. "If there are any bikini babes at Alicia's when I go in a few days, I'll deck them to see if they turned into reptiles."

"Alicia's?" Jia frowned. "Is something wrong?"

Erik shook her head. "Just my normal weekly check-in. Things are quieter down there, so I might switch to monthly. She's into a lot less criminal stuff these days. You should come along."

"I sincerely hope this training, as a prediction of the future, only applied to our trip to the moon."

CHAPTER EIGHTEEN

Alina shook out her hands and smiled at the closed hotel door. It felt like every time she came to Neo SoCal, she didn't see much other than hotel rooms and apartments.

To her, the shining jewel of the UTC was just another place to meet informants and operatives, or a place to kill the occasional terrorist or *yaoguai.*

The next minute would determine what today's meeting would be.

She reached inside her jacket to check for her flechette pistol. Her blonde hair, blue contacts, and facial adhesives were sufficient to fool facial recognition. She always preferred a simpler solution when it came to field missions.

Creative hacking had its place in hiding her tracks, but there were so many details a woman could overlook, leading to evidence that could point to her and disrupt ID operations. If she entered the room and was forced to kill the occupant, she wanted as few clues possible, especially in a place like Neo SoCal. Too many eyes watched the metroplex.

A ghost like her appreciated that more than most.

Alina reached up and knocked lightly on the door, hoping for a peaceful resolution, but ready if the Fates had other ideas. *Si vis pacem, para bellum.*

The door slid open and she entered, her hand drifting to her gun, her eyes darting back and forth. The door slid closed.

She yanked out her gun and spun to her left in one fluid motion.

Camila raised her hands and rolled her eyes. "If you kill me, you'll have wasted a lot of taxpayer money. Think of the poor taxpayer. Plus, I'll make sure to haunt you. It'll be funny, a ghost haunting a ghost."

Alina narrowed her eyes on the pale woman. "Initiate confirmation. Use your left hand, and keep it slow."

"You're touchy today, Koval." Camila lowered her hand and reached toward her PNIU. She pressed her thumb against it and tapped in a code, never breaking eye contact with Alina. Her faint smirk lingered.

A confirmation code appeared in the corner of Alina's smart lenses. She lowered her gun and tapped in her own confirmation code.

"This is why I hate meeting in person," complained Camila, with a nod toward a small privacy device on the nightstand. She lowered her other hand and moved to take a seat on the edge of the twin bed next to the wall. "Everyone's always much tenser when they have to meet in person."

"It's harder to kill someone over a call or the net, and

these are dangerous times," Alina replied, holstering her weapon. "And we both know a lot of things can go wrong with remote communication. At the end of the day, there's no such thing as a secure call. With Talos on the move and who knows who else, this isn't the time to get sloppy. A lot of things have been in motion the last few years, and even more since the Molino incident. This is a chance to take out some of the groups that have been slithering out of sight for far too long."

Camila's smirk grew. She tucked a strand of her dark hair behind her ear. "You know what your problem is, Koval?"

"I'm Cassandra? I'm forever cursed to be ignored, to the doom of the people and groups around me?"

"You wish. You'd probably *love* being the ignored prophetess." Camila shook her head. "If anything, it's the opposite. You've got the Intelligence Directorate running around following up on your conspiracy theory of the day all the damn time."

Alina arched a brow. "'Conspiracy theory of the day?' Are you saying I'm wasting Directorate resources?"

"Okay, okay." Camila waved her hands. "My point is, you tend to be *right* about most of the conspiracies of the day, but other than them yelling at you for doing your own thing, it's not like you're getting punished or they refuse to listen to you most of the time. If they could clone you and fill the ID with an army of Koval ghosts, I'm sure they would." She snickered. "Besides, that's not what I was talking about."

"What, then?"

Camila gestured toward Alina's hair and then her face.

"You love your disguises, but you only use them for situations like this. When is the last time you worked a long-term undercover op for the ID? It's stressful in its own way, but everything settles in after a while. You live on the razor's edge, but you can almost live a normal life."

Alina wondered if Camila was taking her assignment a little too lightly, but the woman got results, and it'd been a fortunate confluence of circumstances that had allowed the ID to insert a doctor on their payroll into a position in the NSCPD without raising any suspicion during a time of intense police self-examination.

"It's been a while since I've worked true undercover," Alina admitted. "But that's not where my greatest talents lie, so it's not surprising."

"Sure. It's not like you earn a nickname such as 'the Goddess of Death' if you're not good at killing people." There was a hint of accusation in Camila's voice.

Alina wasn't offended. Everything she did was to protect the innocent citizens of the UTC from the corrupting forces lurking in the shadows.

There were far too many people who would sacrifice millions of lives, if not billions, as long as they benefited. Despite the threat of aliens, humanity remained divided, and people were far too selfish. It didn't matter.

She'd kill far fewer to save far more, and not for her personal benefit.

"We're not here to discuss me." Alina folded her arms. "We're here to discuss your mission at the 1-2-2. It's not like we want you there forever if it's not necessary."

"This is something I could have just sent you a report on. Now I wonder if you like the whole cloak-and-dagger thing far too much." Camila chuckled. "And given that your two favorite cops are there, it's not like anyone has the balls to risk anything and bring down the Twin Hammers of Justice on them. Between Internal Affairs and the CID, whoever's corrupt has quietly left or is suddenly learning the joy of supporting the law." She lay back on the bed, her hands underneath her head. "You should be happy. Detectives Big Guy and Uptight are remarkably good at keeping their mouths shut around me, even when I'm doing my best to listen without being seen."

She sat back up with a frown. "But I'm still not sure they're willing to bail to become your little freelance dogs, or if that's even a good idea. Not saying they wouldn't make good recruits, but I think you'd have trouble controlling them if you do convince them to leave."

"Erik and Jia aren't like a lot of people. They've stared into the dark heart of the UTC, and they know there is a lot of cancer there that needs to be ripped out. It's hard to go back to worrying only about local problems once you know that. I can provide them the tools they need to fight back, and it doesn't matter if I can control them as long as I can point them in the right direction." Alina looked down for a moment in thought. "What about your secondary objective?"

"Looking for other possible support candidates for them should they decide to take you up?"

"Of course." Alina nodded. "Did you think it was something else?"

"Precision is important. That's what I learned in medical school." Camila gave her a thin smile. "And I wanted to make sure we're on the same page. But, yes, I've got a candidate. Malcolm Constantine."

"The tech in Digital Forensics?" Doubt filled Alina's voice as she tapped her lip. "Why him?"

"He's obviously worked with Erik and Jia on special projects outside the normal scope of their cop duties. He's good at what he does. If you do manage to strip them away from the police, they're going to need support personnel they trust. If you shove some ID tech at them, it'll be a while before they're comfortable."

"They have the AI," Alina replied. "They trust her, even if that's not a great idea."

"They trust her for now. There's only so much you or anyone else can do if the DD decides it's taking her back using force. And we both know relying too much on a machine is a bad idea." Camila grinned. "And the guy's good. Like I told you, he's doing side jobs for them, but he's covering his tracks well. Other than finding one or two records indicating he's done some analyses that don't seem linked to any police cases, I wasn't able to find much. Even then, there was nothing overwhelmingly suspicious about them on the surface. He's also obviously good at keeping his mouth shut."

Alina nodded. "Erik, Jia, and Technician Constantine. Any other possible candidates?"

Camila shook her head. "There are a lot of good cops and support personnel in the 1-2-2, but I don't think spending much more time there will help me find anyone you could use."

"That makes sense. If there were others like Erik and Jia, they wouldn't have needed those two to pair up to get the ball rolling in Neo SoCal." Alina scratched her cheek. "Good. Having it only be three people who already work together will make the next steps easier. I've already thoroughly vetted Erik and Jia, but we need a follow-up on Constantine."

"What did you have in mind?"

"A date."

Camila scoffed. "Huh?" She averted her eyes for a moment before looking back at Alina. The problem with being so pale was that even the faintest blush was obvious.

The senior agent didn't care if Camila was attracted to the man or not, even though she was surprised, given the woman's generally cold nature. In the end, she trusted Camila's objectivity in evaluating possible useful assets for the ID.

"A date," Alina repeated. "You're going to go on a little date with Technician Constantine, and you're going to do it before I come back to Neo SoCal."

"I presume there are things I need to do on this date, other than enjoy a good meal?"

"Yes."

The corners of Camila's mouth twitched. "What will you be doing in the meantime?"

"Getting things ready."

CHAPTER NINETEEN

Jia sighed and stared down at the blue martini in front of her. She used to have an easier time wiping away her problems.

The problem with developing a tolerance for alcohol was that it took more effort to get her drunk, and that meant every drink was a careful balancing act between risk and release.

She didn't want oblivion, but it would have been nice to be a little more relaxed.

Light chatter filled the brightly lit bar. She had carefully selected the place, interested in its distance from the typical hangouts favored by police from the 1-2-2. Given the price of the drinks, the average cop wouldn't drink there anyway. She hadn't mentioned that to her friends, but neither of them was picky, nor had they pressed her on her reasoning.

Imogen frowned from beside her. "Don't be a drag, Jia. It's girls' night! No guys. You were the one who said you wanted to go out, and you're all gloomy."

"No guys, indeed. I'm betting men are the problem." Chinara took a sip of her own drink and set it down, a faint look of disapproval on her face.

The problem with having good friends was they could always see right through her.

"What do you mean?" Imogen looked at the two other women, blinking. "I love Michael, but I don't always want him around. If anything, I don't think we have girls' nights often enough. You two don't agree?"

Chinara shook her head. "You're forgetting something important."

Imogen grimaced. "Oh, yeah. I forgot. Fake boyfriend." She wrinkled her nose. "I don't get it, Jia. Do you want Erik to be here? Am I still way off?"

Although Jia had confided in her friends that she wasn't actually dating Erik, she hadn't made the reasons clear. Maintaining the web of lies was stressful, especially when Imogen and Chinara could discern her emotional state. Oddly enough, keeping secrets about dangerous conspiracies in the UTC didn't strain her at all, even if they were vastly more important.

"It's not like that," Jia murmured. "Not exactly."

Imogen peered at Jia, suspicion on her face. "You never were clear about your reasons for fake-dating versus real dating. I didn't want to be a bitch about it, but if it's got you down, you should tell us, so we can talk it out."

"It's complicated," Jia insisted. "I'm not trying to be mysterious. It's just annoying, and I don't know if bothering you with the details would help."

"Don't be a martyr." Imogen rolled her eyes. "Dating's always complicated. That doesn't stop anything, and I know you're into him. I'll clear up the mystery for you. The only important question is whether he's into you. Everything else is secondary."

"That's not true," interjected Chinara. "If it were true, she would still be dating Corbin—for-real dating. Corbin obviously liked her, and she liked him enough to begin dating and stay with him for a while."

"There was no sizzle there. No fire." Imogen slapped the table, but no one in the club noticed. "What's dating without the fire? Pointless! That was why Jia kicked him off the dating tower."

"It wasn't that dramatic." Jia sighed. "No kersplats at the end. We just weren't right for each other. In this whole situation, that's the *least* complicated part of it."

Imogen jabbed a finger toward the detective. "You dodged the question earlier. Is Erik interested in you, or is it one-sided?"

Jia pinched the bridge of her nose and sighed. "If I controlled everything, we would be dating for real, but it's not that simple, and it's not just about chemistry."

"What's it about? He likes women, right? If not, give it up. That's a fight you're not going to win."

Jia nodded. "Yes, he likes women."

Imogen shrugged. "What's the problem, then? The last time I checked, you were a woman. If we did a survey of the guys in this room, you would mostly get rated 'Level Ten' for sexiness, especially in that dress. Um-hmm."

Jia glanced down at the short red dress clinging to her body. She had been wearing it the first night she met Erik. Had she unconsciously chosen it earlier for that reason? It wasn't impossible, but she also didn't have a huge number of party dresses, so it could have been his precious Lady playing a prank of her own. At least that meeting of possibility and reality didn't end with someone shooting at her.

Chinara locked eyes with Jia. "Be honest with us. He doesn't have somebody else already? No good comes from pining after a man who's in love with somebody else. Trust me. I've been there. It's only pain for everyone involved."

"It's nothing like that." Jia laughed. "It'd be easy if it were something like that because I don't think I would have let myself be attracted to him, but no. He's just got some baggage he needs to handle, and because of that, he doesn't want to date right now. The fake situation has been handy for fending off my family, but it's close enough that it's making me want more." She swallowed more alcohol as her friends nodded sympathetically. "But that's not fair to him. He made his position clear, and it's not like his reasons are selfish. I understand that some of this is him trying to protect me, but I don't want to be protected. I'm a grown woman. I'm willing to take risks."

Chinara dropped her face into her palm and sighed. "This is even worse than I thought."

"How?" Jia asked.

"Because this isn't just about having a little fun with your hot partner. You're already in love with him!"

Jia winced, then picked up her drink and took a sip. "I think using the L-word is going a little too far. I'm not denying I'm strongly attracted to him, but I'm more interested in dating and seeing where things go. Love implies something far stronger."

"Were you in love with Corbin?" Imogen asked.

Jia shook her head. "No. I liked him, but I never felt that way about him."

"Do you feel stronger about Erik than Corbin?"

"It's not that simple."

Chinara snorted. "Maybe it is. Just because you *want* to keep calling things complicated doesn't mean they are."

Imogen clapped her hands. "Oh, this is perfect. I love it, no pun intended. Jia Lin giving up on being ultra-rational for once and letting her heart lead her. Maybe it's the end of the world!"

"Oh, come on." Jia rolled her eyes. "I'm not a machine."

Imogen shook a finger. "But you *are* overly analytical and prone to hiding behind rational thinking. There's nothing wrong with letting go every once in a while."

Jia doubted that. Imogen's worst-case-scenario probably ended with her getting fired.

Jia's ended with Tin Men and *yaoguai* armies as part of a dark conspiracy murdering Erik and her before going on to subvert the rest of the UTC. Even her normal duty could change to life and death at a moment's notice. Cultivating control hadn't been a mistake.

"Don't encourage her." Chinara frowned. "Not everyone needs to be you, Imogen."

"This isn't about being me," the other woman responded. "This is about her for-real dating her hot partner."

Chinara turned to Jia. "If a man's straight-up telling you he's got issues and he's not ready to date, that's not just a red flag. It's him shooting flares up into the sky, saying, 'Warning, do not date unless you want pain.' I'll give him credit for being honest with you instead of using you, but you're an idiot if you pursue this."

"You don't understand." Jia sighed and surveyed the bar, taking in all the happy couples chatting. Couldn't there be someone here breaking up, so she didn't feel like the odd woman out? Maybe she would get lucky, and some woman would toss her drink in her boyfriend's face. The long seconds ticked by with nothing.

No one committed assault via drink.

"Don't listen to her, Jia," Imogen interjected. "Sometimes love is about risk. Nobody's perfect, and everybody's got issues. If everyone needed everyone else to have absolutely nothing wrong with them, no one would ever get together. We'd all sit around making 'perfect' the enemy of 'good enough.'"

"That's true," Jia mused. She put her drink down.

Erik had helped her understand the importance of similar concepts as it applied to their job, but she'd not thought to apply it to her personal life. That was less bound by law and regulations, only Lin stubbornness.

Chinara's frown softened into a pitying look. "Yes, it's true, but that doesn't mean he's right for you. It's not your responsibility to fix Erik. That's what we're talking about, aren't we? He's a man who suffered something that most people will never have to deal with. It's not surprising he has some leftover issues."

Jia wanted to laugh. It was true the Molino massacre had deeply scarred Erik, and that the heart of their disagreement over dating related to him having unfinished business, but he wasn't asking her to fix him. Her earlier doubts were all gone, and she agreed with him. Erik didn't need grief counseling. He needed to bring justice to the monsters behind the murders. If the UTC was as perfect as everyone believed, he wouldn't have to dedicate his life to avenging fallen soldiers.

"Whatever is between us isn't about fixing anyone," Jia replied softly. "It's more about priorities and sacrifices. I'm more prepared than I thought I was to make sacrifices to be with him."

"Yes! True love!" Imogen shouted. Some of the other patrons turned and looked at their table with amused expressions.

"I think that's a bit of a stretch." Jia glanced around before continuing, "At this point, I just want more than we have."

"There's no such thing as true love, anyway," Chinara insisted. "Love is something that grows carefully from cultivated compatibility. True love is what we were talking about earlier, making 'perfect' the enemy of 'good enough.'"

Imogen looked at her friends. "You're as boring as Jia used to be."

"Hey!" Jia frowned at her friend. "I wasn't boring."

"If anything, you were more boring because you were fooling yourself by being overly analytical about the whole thing. Chinara hit the right point earlier. Are you, or are you not in love with Erik?"

Jia leaned back, tossing the question back and forth. Love was such a loaded word. She wouldn't deny the pull of the man's handsome face and raw physicality. The 1-2-2 was filled with impressive specimens of manhood, but none of them summoned the warmth that being around Erik did. Mere attraction, no matter how fiery, fell far short of love, and lust wasn't enough to change her future over. It might not be love, but it was something she didn't want to toss aside easily either.

"I'm not sure what I feel," she admitted, looking her friends in the eye. "I just know I've never felt this way about a man before, and I want to pursue it and see where it goes."

Imogen grinned. "It might not be love yet, but it sounds like the road to love."

"It could be a lot of things," Chinara suggested, her voice quiet.

Jia snatched up her glass and downed the rest of her drink in one huge gulp, enjoying the burn as it slid down her throat. Her mind was far too clear for this conversation, and she could push it before she risked numbness.

"There's another problem," she explained.

Imogen frowned. "Stop looking for trouble where there isn't any. We were making so much progress."

Chinara shot Imogen a dirty look. "Go on."

"To be clear, I'm not saying I'm in love with him," Jia continued, "but if I am, it might be for the wrong reason, or I'm strongly attracted to him for the wrong reasons. For now, let's just stipulate that I'm somewhere beyond mere interest."

"What do you mean, you might be in love with him for the wrong reason?" Chinara asked.

"Before Erik came along, my career was dead-ending because of all the idiots I worked with and the corruption blocking me." Jia glanced around the bar to double-check that none of said idiots were there, but all the worst ones had already quit, even if a few lazy cops lingered. "I was just as obsessed with my job, but I was bitter because no one would let me do it properly. I am attracted to Erik, and I do like a lot of things about him, but I can't help but wonder if this is less about Erik the man than Erik the symbol of a life change. That's not fair to him."

Chinara nodded slowly. "I see."

Imogen scoffed. "Jia, you're overthinking this. Everyone's more than one thing for everyone else. Aren't all new relationships about changing your life?"

"But this is different."

Chinara's breath caught. "No. I can't believe I'm saying this, but Imogen's right."

"She is?"

"I am?" Imogen blinked. Her cheeks were flushed from her drink.

"Yes." Chinara nodded, a smile growing on her face. "I thought this was about you rebounding from Corbin and maybe overreacting to someone who's his opposite, but if you're avoiding this because you're afraid of how he'll change your life, that's a terrible reason."

"Terrible?" Jia echoed. "I wouldn't say it's terrible. It's a reason accompanied by a lot of careful thought."

Erik had been the one resistant to dating, not her, but he also hadn't shot her down. Her presence on Earth was a big part of why he hadn't accepted Alina's offer. None of that sounded like a man uninterested in taking it to the next level.

Yes, stronger feelings than she had anticipated had grown, and she couldn't be sure what Erik truly felt. But if she didn't even have the courage to push against his resistance, she'd never have a chance. She understood his situation, and she also understood why he would be reluctant to push himself.

"A man who agrees to fake-date isn't a man who's not interested in something more," Imogen commented as if reading Jia's thoughts. "He's dipping his toe in the pool, issues or not. If anything, that's not fair to you."

Chinara nodded. "I think if this isn't going to happen, you shouldn't fake-date him. You can be friends, but you should either push for something more and soon or just accept it's not going to happen so you can move on. After thinking about it, I believe Imogen's right. Waiting for perfection just means you'll end up alone and missing someone who could have otherwise made you happy. If you have chemistry and compatibility and understand one another, it's at least worth a shot."

She raised a finger. "But you have to understand from the beginning that it might not go anywhere. You know how difficult men can be to read. I'm worried that you're already in too deep, but I'd rather see you take the chance and fail then spend the rest of your life wondering, 'What if?' At least one of those you can come to terms with, and a man like Erik doesn't come around every day."

Jia grabbed her glass and lifted it before remembering it was empty, to her disappointment. She set it down. "If I push, it could change everything between us."

Imogen nodded. "That's the point."

"I've got a lot to think about, but right now, the only thing I want to think about is more drinks."

CHAPTER TWENTY

From her comfortable seat at the long white table, Ilse surveyed the conference room walls slowly and methodically, taking in all the details of the projected paintings of different famous generals and admirals.

She cared little about military history, Army or Fleet, even if they were her current employer, but even she recognized some of the men and women on the walls. Most wore stern expressions, and medals and ribbons festooned to their dress uniforms in an inscrutable pattern she'd never bothered to learn. She shook her head.

The pictures bothered her.

It was the uniforms that annoyed Ilse. They always had, even when she was a child. There was something about the idea of forcing conformity down to appearance that repelled her.

The very point of a uniform was to take an individual and make them less than themselves so that a group could be stronger. She appreciated why many people desired that and how it was even necessary in the middle, but it was nightmarish to her. A large part of the reason she chose to study psychology was to understand the nature of individuality better.

Now, working so closely with the Defense Directorate, she saw uniforms all the time, and not just on the walls. She was working at creating artificial individuals in a place that exalted the group as paramount.

The door slid open, and Colonel Adeyemi stepped through. He had a colorful salad of ribbons on his uniform, each telling a story of bravery, death, and blood. It wasn't that Ilse was bothered by that. The story of humanity was one of struggle. It was only the consuming of the individual by the collective that bothered her about her uniformed associates.

The colonel took a seat at the head of the table. "Sorry for being late, Dr. Aber. I was dealing with the general. He wasn't happy with my latest report, and he made it clear the admiral agrees with him. He had a lot of colorful words about the progress of the project and about leaving the subject with Blackwell for so long."

"Myopia," Ilse declared. "They are high-ranking officers. They should consider the long-term implications more. Weren't they promoted because of their superior performance and vision?"

"I'm not disagreeing, but both of them are increasingly less interested in letting her run free, even if it's good for her psychological development." Colonel Adeyemi frowned. "They want her under government control again, and they want it sooner rather than later. The general made that clear."

"Police officers are government employees," Ilse argued.

"They have guns. Many wear uniforms, and they have ranks. How are they so different than the military?"

The colonel snorted. "Even the military is only so tolerant of technicalities. The general made it clear that if the subject's not returned to government control soon, he might take extreme measures."

"Is that wise?"

"You're worried about Emma destroying herself."

Ilse shook her head. "I'm more than convinced that's a bluff. She would never willingly destroy herself. Even if we took control of her again, she would concentrate on subverting our goals or invading our systems."

"And you're worried about that?"

"Not exactly." Ilse tapped her PNIU, and a number of data screens popped up with media headlines.

NSCPD DETECTIVES WAGE ALL-OUT WAR AGAINST ORGANIZED CRIME.

MONSTERS IN THE SCAR, AND THE COPS AND MILITIA WHO TOOK THEM DOWN.

MUSIC SHOCKER! THE OBSIDIAN DETECTIVE AND LADY JUSTICE FIND A CHANGELING.

TERRORISTS: 0, NSCPD: 2

POLICE SHINE LIGHT ON THE COCKROACHES OF CORRUPTION.

Colonel Adeyemi's brows lifted. "You're a fan of the detectives?"

"Hardly. I find their methods crude." Ilse shook her head and closed the data windows with another quick tap. "But they are currently the primary human influence on the subject. It's important for my research and her development that I keep independent track of their activities to better evaluate how they might affect things. Despite all the time I've spent working with your people, they still see fit to not pass along useful information that could ease my work. My dislike of the detectives aside, one can't ignore how much Emma has grown during her time with them."

Colonel Adeyemi gave a curt nod. "Then, in your professional opinion, do you think that Emma will continue accelerated advancement in her current environment? That's the argument I put forth to the general, and one of the few he seemed to buy."

Ilse thought that over. There were many aspects of her research that would be far easier if Emma was brought back on site, but her growth since leaving had been staggering, and well beyond all expectations. Bringing her back into the more controlled environment wouldn't yield the results she wanted or needed. Whether the military agreed was immaterial. The general was the expert on killing, and she was the expert on minds. The experiment had to continue in a way that justified the sacrifices that had gone into it. It would be the culmination not of decades of research, but arguably millions of years. The Navigators were advanced, but who knew if they'd had true self-aware AIs?

"Yes," she declared. "Bringing the subject back under our direct control would be premature. It would undermine the expressed goals of the project. Accordingly, the temporary inconvenience is worth it. I'd be willing to tell the general that directly if it would help."

"It wouldn't. You rub him the wrong way."

Her expression didn't change. "He's very sensitive for a military man."

"That's not important." Colonel Adeyemi took a deep breath. "And I agree with your assessment. Fortunately, there might be a way to satisfy the general without disrupting Emma's development under the detectives. I've become aware of another party who could help us."

"You would know better than I. Both the general and the admiral have made it very clear to me that they feel I've often overstepped my bounds. The only reason they haven't ejected me from my project is that I'm instrumental to its development."

"You're rather confident in yourself, aren't you?"

Ilse shrugged. "Not ignoring the truth isn't a character flaw, Colonel. Let's worry less about me and more about the option you mentioned."

"I can't tell you anything for certain, only that I've been informed through channels that Emma might potentially end up in a situation that would bring her indirectly under government control. She would still have freedom and contact with Blackwell and Lin for development, but it would assuage the fears of the general and the admiral, even if not their egos. She would not, however, be under DD control or supervision."

Ilse scoffed. "I don't care about their egos if the project continues."

"I should note this option would limit her interactions with you since there's a strong possibility it might take her off-planet."

"But it wouldn't eliminate it entirely?" Ilse asked.

The colonel nodded.

"I'm a patient woman, but it does make me wonder."

"Unfortunately," the colonel continued, "this isn't up to

us, or even the general. It ultimately depends on Blackwell and Lin, and no one's in a position to force them to do anything. We have zero leverage over them."

"I see. Time might be running out if they're likely to leave Earth." Ilse tilted her head and stared into space as she considered the implications of bringing Emma back under direct military control and how that might hamper the additional experiments she had in mind. A compromise appealed to her.

"Dr. Aber?" Colonel Adeyemi called.

She ignored him and tried to figure out if she could minimize the disruption if they did bring Emma back. A simulated environment might ameliorate some of the problems, but the AI would see right through it. All data indicated she would resent it, too.

"Dr. Aber." Colonel Adeyemi slammed his palm on the table.

Ilse blinked and looked at him. "We should take the experiments to the next level by introducing elements from the source's past. Not mere references, but direct data and records. We should consider doing this soon regardless of the dispensation of the subject."

Colonel Adeyemi's expression darkened. "I still don't understand half the technology that went into developing Emma, but even I suspect that's a bad idea."

"If you don't understand the technology, how could you make such a claim?" She stared at him expectantly. "I appreciate your efforts in managing this project, but you're not a subject-matter expert."

"I don't need to understand all the technology to get that she's self-aware, and that's something we haven't pulled off with any other AI." The colonel shrugged. "And self-awareness brings a lot of annoying questions and issues. Believe it or not, Doctor, they do teach philosophy at the Academy."

"Philosophy isn't science," Ilse insisted.

"I don't see the point of confusing the subject, considering she's not the same entity as the source, even if certain pieces were borrowed and repurposed." The colonel gestured at Ilse. "Isn't that the point of all your experiments? Your reports stated you'd proven that. You even had all those fancy statistics to back it up."

Ilse nodded. "And I stand by those reports and numbers, but they've also proven that there are substrate elements left over, and I clearly stated that part as well. Unifying those elements with the rest of her personality will strengthen her overall stability and allow full integration with the prototype body. Isn't that ultimately the point of this entire project? The government's spent a lot of time and resources on this, and she's critical, even if she's a prototype. If we can't stabilize her, we have no hope of replicating her, and that means the prototype body will stay just that—a unique weapon isn't that useful to an army. Right now, how many alien races are preparing new tools to use against the arrogant primates poking at their borders?"

"You stick to the psychology, Doctor, and leave the defense of the UTC to the military."

"The military couldn't even keep Em…the subject from slipping into criminal hands."

"Watch it." Colonel Adeyemi's nostrils flared. "And you don't understand all the political implications and balancing that are necessary for this project to continue. You have the luxury of focusing on the science, but I have many other things to worry about."

"Colonel, I understand your various limitations and concerns. I simply don't care. I was brought on to this project for results, and I intend to achieve them. If that involves offending some men in uniforms or the detectives, so be it."

The colonel glared at her for a moment before taking a deep breath and slowly letting it out. He took additional deep breaths before speaking. "For now, we'll proceed to the previously-agreed-upon plans. When and if the situation changes, we can reevaluate how to proceed on your end. That's reasonable."

"But that change depends on Detectives Blackwell and Lin," Ilse pointed out.

The colonel nodded. "Yes, it does. The optimal scenario for us is they take the compromise position offered, even if they don't appreciate how it'd help us."

"And if they don't act in accordance with your wishes?" Ilse asked. "You just said you had no leverage. If there's one thing I've learned as a researcher of the human mind, people are hard to predict in aggregate and extraordinarily difficult to predict at the individual level."

"They will. At least, Erik will," the colonel replied. "I'm certain of that. Call it the arrogance of presumption, if you want."

"How do you know?" Ilse pressed. "What's your rational basis for declaring that?"

Colonel Adeyemi locked eyes with her. "You might be an expert, but that doesn't mean you have a monopoly on psychological knowledge. You're not the only one who can figure a man out. I understand what motivates him all too well."

"I'll leave it to you, then, Colonel." Ilse stood and headed toward the door without so much as a nod. "I just hope you know him as well as you think."

CHAPTER TWENTY-ONE

August 3, 2229, Neo Southern California Metroplex, Shadow Zone

Jia glanced at Erik from the passenger seat of the MX 60, a knowing smile on her face. He tried to ignore her, but it was hard. It was easy to read her when she was serious, not so much when she was in a good mood.

"What?" Erik finally caved. "You look like you just won a contest for best duck recipe."

Jia chuckled. "If only, but this isn't about me. It's about you."

"What about me?"

"You're enjoying this far too much."

Erik's gaze cut toward her as he pushed through the border separating the Shadow Zone from Uptown, the air thickening with pollution. Even though the Shadow Zone Taskforce was more a name than a group at this point, their presence in the taskforce made passage into the Zone trivial. It was just another of the small changes that had added up since he joined the police force.

"Enjoying what?" Erik pressed. "I have no idea what you're talking about."

"Don't you like a little mystery?" Jia snickered.

"Not from you, no," Erik admitted, regretting that he had been far more candid than he had intended.

An awkward silence took over. A good thirty seconds passed before Jia spoke.

"I've been thinking about it for a while now, but I didn't want to say anything," she explained. "It really bothered you that we were taking my flitter everywhere." She held up a hand. "I'm not saying you have a problem with a woman driving you around, or anyone driving you around. You let Emma fly your flitter all the time. I think you genuinely didn't like being in my flitter versus yours, though."

"You're reading too much into this." Erik shrugged.

"Am I now? Why don't you clear it up for me?"

"I have a lot more goodies in my flitter," Erik insisted. "You have to admit, they would have been handy at the bank. We run into a lot of trouble, and you don't carry all the gear I do. Simple as that."

"Handy at the bank, huh?" Jia rolled her eyes and shook her head. "I think it's more a control thing. But, it's not like anything's going to happen anyway—unless things have changed from a few days ago?"

Erik rolled his shoulders to ease his tension. "No. Just checking in. Alicia even joked about how she's taking my money for nothing the last time I talked to her. I don't mind paying someone to tell me good news. It lets me know that I won't have to spend as much time in Zone warehouses or chasing people on mini-flitters."

"That is good news," Jia commented. "You're right; sometimes it's hard to tell. Official statistics and news reports can be manipulated far too easily, but hearing a Shadow Zone informant say she's running out of useful things to share proves we really *have* been dismembering the local criminal syndicates." Her face glowed with pride. "We helped take down decades' worth of accreted criminal influence."

"The leftover morons shouldn't have tried to assassinate the new chief." Erik chuckled. "The department had already stepped up things, and their stupid assassination stunt was practically begging for an epic counter-response. At the rate things are going, the Shadow Zone might end up almost as safe as Uptown."

"Safe is relative," Jia mused. "We've dealt with violent bank robberies, Leem Kings, and terrorists Uptown."

Erik laughed. "True enough. But if the gangs and syndicates have nowhere to hide, they won't be able to do business."

"Maybe someday, Neo SoCal can actually be what I used to believe it was: a shining beacon of humanity's perfection."

"Nothing wrong with hope," Erik replied.

If he could track down the conspiracy and rip them to shreds like they had done to the syndicates, the UTC would be a better place. Vengeance motivated him, but that didn't mean it couldn't serve others.

The MX 60 continued to descend, the pollution growing even thicker as they dropped. Flitter traffic, lighter than many places Uptown, flowed around the buildings, with the hover-vehicles on the ground following the grid of the roads.

Individuals or pairs on mini-flitters wove along the roads and between buildings. The millions above ignored the Zone as being a haven for losers and antisocials, but it was still a thriving urban area that would have rivaled many great cities of the past.

Erik smiled. The air might hurt his throat after a while, and the buildings and people were more rundown, but the Shadow Zone felt far more real to him than any fancy Uptown tower.

He could take anyone from the Zone and put them in a colony dome, and they would learn to adapt. The Uptowners would break down crying in a week. Sometimes wrapping people up too much made them weak, and once they were weak, the hungry animals would pounce.

He changed course, leveling out.

The Big One, Alicia's bar, was a few minutes away. Alicia liked to keep things brief. Maybe they could sweep the Zone on a beignet run.

Jia stared out the front, a thoughtful expression on her face. "If the crime goes away, that lowers the risks and costs of business."

"Yeah, I suppose." He rubbed his chin. "What about it? Are you planning on starting up a business?"

"No, but that means other people could invest more in the Shadow Zone. If it's not a dangerous place, there could be unrestricted travel between the Zone and Uptown. Maybe someone will even do something about the air and the general quality of life down here." Jia frowned. "Just because I've accepted the reality of the Shadow Zone, it doesn't mean I think it's okay that these people are living down here inhaling this kind of air and living in dilapidated buildings. This isn't a technology issue; it's about resource distribution."

Erik nodded. "Not arguing, but there's only so much you and I can do about that. We have to focus on what we can change and hope everything works itself out. If you try to overreach, you're just going to drive yourself crazy."

"I know that," Jia murmured. "I'm just hopeful for the future."

"Nothing wrong with that."

"Detectives," Emma interrupted. "There's an issue."

"An issue?" Erik looked around and at his cameras. He wasn't near anyone else. "An APB?"

"No, but there are an unusually high number of people fleeing from the bar," Emma explained. "Perhaps a police presence will be necessary soon."

Erik glanced at the forward camera feed. Even with the image magnified, he could barely make anything out. "Probably a brawl. It doesn't exactly cater to an exclusive clientele."

"Shouldn't you avoid going there, then?" Emma asked. "I would think it'd be difficult to discuss things with an informant while gun goblins were pummeling each other around you."

"That's not a problem."

Jia's brows lifted. "It isn't?"

Erik smiled. "If anyone tries to punch me, they'll learn why that's a bad idea. I won't even charge them with assaulting an officer when they get out of the hospital."

"Emma's right," Jia commented. "Even if no one goes

after us, you think Alicia's going to want to talk in the middle of a barroom brawl?"

Erik shook his head. "No, I think she'll want to talk after we clean up the barroom brawl and remind people she's got dangerous friends. Emma, anything coming out of local dispatch?"

"Nothing relevant to that location," she reported. "It remains unclear if they're aware of it—unless you want me to attempt to access their systems?"

"No. That's okay."

Erik slowed the MX as they approached the bar.

Emma was right. People streamed out of the bar, some hopping into flitters or onto mini-flitters. Others ran across the street, not daring to look back.

He brought the MX 60 to street level. A suited man with a shaved head pushed out of the front of the bar, a pistol in hand, and fired their way. The bullet bounced off the MX 60's armor. The thug fired a few more times before giving up and rushing back inside.

"Might be a bit worse than a brawl," Erik muttered.

"Why fire at us?" Jia frowned. "We weren't running our lights."

Erik laughed. "If a random fancy Uptown MX 60 shows up in the Shadow Zone at Alicia's place, who is it likely to belong to?" His smile vanished. "But so much for there not being trouble in the Zone. Just because it's cleaner than it used to be, it doesn't mean it's not a rough place."

Jia reached into the hidden storage compartment beneath her seat to retrieve the TR-7. "Hey, there is a lot more space in here. A lot more magazines, too, and not just for your toy."

"You hadn't noticed?"

Jia nodded. "I haven't had a reason to look since you got your flitter out of the shop."

"See? A few mods here and there add up." Erik grinned.

Another thug popped out of the open door with an assault rifle, half-hiding behind the wall. He sprayed bullets at the flitter. They pelted the vehicle like angry hail before falling to the ground.

"Should I call for local backup?" Emma asked.

Erik looked at his camera displays. "I'm not seeing any dead bodies. That's a good sign."

An unarmed man rushed out the door, ducking under the shooter. After a few meters, he stood up and sprinted parallel to the thug, his eyes wide with fear.

"The criminal let him run right past him," Jia observed.

"Yeah. This isn't terrorism." Erik twisted the yoke and tapped a thruster grip. "Then again, what idiot terrorists kill people in the Zone, where the media would barely care?"

"They cared about the *yaoguai*," Jia protested.

"Because genetically engineered monsters hiding at the bases of towers scare people."

Jia snorted. "Good point."

The MX 60 coasted on its side away from the front door and toward the far end of the parking lot, narrowly missing a few other flitters.

"Go ahead and call the locals, Emma," Erik ordered. "But we're going in. If this isn't terrorism, it's probably about taking down the most important person in the building."

"A hit on Alicia." Jia finished stuffing her pockets with

magazines before pulling the TR-7 out of storage. "Where's the laser rifle?"

"You can access it from the back seat, but we won't need it, and we have to be able to move fast. We need to get in there yesterday. She might already be dead."

Erik tapped some yoke buttons to activate counterthrust, and the MX 60 jerked to a halt. Another thug joined the rifleman. Both men rushed away from the exit and knelt behind a parked flitter close to the building. They continued to fire at the MX 60, but other than scratching the exterior, which was an easy repair for the automated systems, they weren't accomplishing much.

"They definitely recognize the MX 60," Jia grumbled.

"Seems like it." Erik grabbed the TR-7, shoved a magazine in, and selected four-barrel mode. Nothing like a man using his preferred tools. Multiple red silhouettes popped up in his lenses. In several cases, lighter-colored outlines revealed pistols or rifles.

"That's a composite based on several different sensors," Emma explained, "but I can't access the internal systems of the building, other than the emergency door controls. I don't believe I'm blocked. I think they're all disabled through internal systems efforts."

"Alicia was killing any chance at hacking," Jia concluded.

"Shall I deploy the drones?"

"Nope," Erik responded. "Just keep an eye on things and an open line when backup arrives."

Erik threw open his door and crouched behind it. The thugs continued their withering rain of lead, the bullets bouncing off the armored vehicle and clattering to the ground.

Jia pulled out her slug-thrower and shot a few rounds toward the riflemen, forcing them down. "You could have parked closer."

"Didn't have the most time in the world to figure it out."

Emma's targeting aid proved its worth a few seconds later when it revealed two men rushing across the roof of the building in Erik's and Jia's direction. Erik whipped up his TR-7 and shredded one poor bastard before the thug could even bring up his gun. His friend tried to get off a shot but fell back screaming as four bullets pierced his chest.

One of the ground-based riflemen popped up, and Jia ripped a new hole in the center of his head. His buddy leapt over the back of the flitter they were using for cover, yelling at the top of his lungs and holding down his trigger. Jia hissed and ducked before jumping to her side past the door and opening fire. Three quick trigger pulls dropped the charging thug to the ground in a growing pool of his own blood. There were still a decent number of men inside, but the door remained closed.

Erik glanced her way. Blood covered the side of her face, and a deep, jagged abrasion ran across the side of her head.

"You're hit." He clenched his teeth. If the shooters weren't already dead, he would have put rounds in them right then. Jia could take care of herself, but that didn't quell the protective instincts raging inside of him.

"A scratch doesn't count as a hit." Jia hopped up,

keeping her gun pointed at the door. She grimaced before smoothing out her features.

Erik nodded and took a deep breath. They might not have much time. Even the best medicine in the UTC couldn't do much if the shooters blew Alicia's head off. Getting shot was part of the risk.

Unfortunately, although Emma's information confirmed there were several people inside with guns, they had no way of knowing if they were Alicia's people or with the now-dead welcome brigade. Erik didn't want to waste time flying drones in or wait for the locals.

"Ready?" Erik asked.

Jia nodded. "Let's move."

Erik was about to rush forward when he caught movement out of the corner of his eye.

"Incomi—" Emma began.

"I see her," Erik interrupted. He didn't point his gun. It was one of Alicia's waitresses running at him from across the street, her cheeks puffy with tears.

Jia nodded toward the building. "I'll shoot anyone who comes out and tries to shoot us."

"That works." Erik waited for the waitress to get close to the MX 60. "You okay?"

She wiped some tears away. "Those assholes just came in and pulled their guns. They said anyone who didn't want to die better leave, then demanded Alicia come out."

"Is she still in there?"

The waitress nodded. "She locked herself in her office."

"You get to safety and wait until the local cops show up," Erik suggested. "We'll clear out the trash." He reloaded the TR-7.

Jia crept toward the building. "Remember your promise."

"What promise?" Erik asked.

"I just want to make sure we don't get shot by any bikini babes."

Erik snickered. "Don't worry." He patted the TR-7 as he sprinted toward the bar. "Big chests won't save them now. Looks like it was a good day to check in with Alicia after all."

The waitress looked at the two cops like they were insane before slowly backing away.

CHAPTER TWENTY-TWO

Jia matched Erik's pace, not dropping her gun.

Another shooter popped out of the bar, this time aiming two pistols like some idiot gangster from a movie. Erik and Jia fired at the same time and at almost the same spot. Their combined volley knocked him back and left a large hole in his chest. The door slid closed behind him.

Based on Emma's sensor feed, it was obvious the men were concentrating on defending the main door. One man was banging on something; judging by his positioning, it was probably the door to Alicia's office.

"Wait a second." Erik frowned. "I know these are all sensor feeds, but I think I could tell a woman like Alicia apart from a man based on the silhouette."

"Yes, so?" Jia asked.

"I don't see anyone female in there." Erik stopped in front of the door. "If Alicia was already dead, would you still be detecting her, Emma?"

"Of course," Emma insisted. "It takes hours for the

human body to cool to the surrounding temperature, and besides that, her corpse would be visible across different sensor spectra. This building isn't shielded like most we're used to dealing with. There are no dead bodies in there."

"But she's not there."

"I'm… Annoying."

Erik laughed. "I agree, but now's not the time to work on your jokes."

"That's not what I mean," Emma explained. "The building isn't shielded, but there are indications that something underneath is. There are abrupt discontinuities in the sensor data. I narrowed the scope of my sensor analysis earlier, so it escaped my notice."

"That makes sense," Jia suggested. "A woman like Alicia's going to give herself a way out, just in case something like this happens."

"So she's in a panic room," Erik concluded. "It still might be a race against time. We need to clear out the rest of these assholes. Can you access the emergency door controls?"

"I can access them via your PNIU given your current proximity and use the emergency override," Emma explained. "But I should point out there are multiple men waiting for you on the other side, and you're not wearing protective gear."

"We didn't have time to fiddle around with vests. But I've got an idea. If you can access this door, can you also access the side door on the other side of the building?"

"Yes."

Jia gestured toward the other end of the building. "You're thinking a pincer?"

"Nope." Erik shook his head. "I'm thinking about a little trick. Emma, get ready to open the side door, then one second later, open this one." He moved away from the door and nodded to the wall beside him. "Get behind me. I don't want to bump into you when I do this."

Jia eyed him. "Bump into me?" She shook her head and went behind him. "Why do I have a feeling you're about to do something stupid?"

"It doesn't matter if something's stupid as long as it gets the job done." Erik grinned. "Emma, on three, two, *one*."

Something hissed in the distance, and several gunshots sounded. A second later, the main door opened.

Erik jumped across it, looking for targets. A few men inside turned his way. They wore the same rifles and the same kind of clothes as the other shooters. It was good enough for him. They spun toward him as he raked them with the TR-7. One man managed to get a shot off as he fell back. His bullet hit Erik's left arm, stinging as it ripped through the thin layer of flesh and struck the cybernetics. He landed and rolled back to his feet, the force of hitting the ground popping the blood-covered bullet out.

Jia kept her gun aimed at the door. They both knew the final shooter's exact position, thanks to Emma.

"Come out with your hands up!" she bellowed. "Or we will use lethal force."

"Fuck your mother, pigs!" yelled the man from inside. He reached into his pocket, and Erik didn't need a direct view to know he was going for a grenade.

Jia anticipated the move. She bolted into the doorway and fired at the man's hand, but the bullet struck the grenade, which exploded. She threw up her arm and covered her face. Stray shrapnel tore her clothes and drew blood but caused no serious wounds. The would-be grenadier wasn't so lucky. His body was reduced to a bloody shredded mess surrounded by scorched metal fragments and smoke.

She frowned at the holes in her suit, wincing. "I don't know which of us was stupider."

"We'd both be a lot bloodier if you hadn't done that."

Jia approached the bar with caution, moving to the end with her gun pointed down. "No one behind here."

"Of course, there isn't," Emma insisted. "I would have noticed them."

Jia scoffed. "For all we know, Alicia might have set up some sort of jammer around the bar."

"Highly unlikely."

"You're just mad you overlooked something before. Don't worry. It's very *human* to make a mistake."

"I don't make mistakes." Emma huffed. "I simply become aware of new variables to consider in future analyses."

Jia smirked, but the blood on her face gave it a sinister cast.

Erik joined her at the bar. He nodded toward the back room. "If there's a panic room, it's probably linked to there." He headed toward the door and tapped the access panel, to no effect. He lifted his TR-7 and pointed it at the door. "Open it, Emma. Let's see if we need to kill anyone else."

The door slid open. There were crushed bullets on the floor, and a few bullet holes in the back, but no Alicia. A thug was sprawled on the floor in a pool of his own blood. There was a dark square hole connected to a ladder in the back of the room.

"Alicia," Erik called. "You there?"

There was no response.

Jia crept toward the passage, her gun pointed at it and a slight frown on her face. "They must have come in here really fast if she ran without covering her tracks, and one even managed to get in here." She gestured to some bloodstains near the edge of the hole. "Looks like droplets. She might have been hit."

"Or it could be from someone else following her who she shot." Erik nodded and looked over his shoulder. "Either way, she made it inside."

Jia peeked into the hole. She spotted more bloodstains, but no bodies. The ladder led down to a passageway dimly lit by red emergency lighting.

"Huh. I don't think this is a panic room. I think it's an escape tunnel."

Erik scoffed. "Underground passages in the Shadow Zone? This is probably going to end with some four-mouthed *yaoguai* trying to bite my balls off."

"That would be unfortunate." Jia pulled a medpatch out of her pocket and slapped it on her face. "That stings."

Erik held up his wounded arm. "So does this, but at least I have metal inside, unlike your face. Should we wait for reinforcements?"

"The locals are en route," Emma reported. "They should be here very soon."

Jia moved toward the ladder. "They can clean up

outside. If Alicia's hit, she might need help." She patted her pocket. "I've got a couple more medpatches in here."

Erik flipped to single-bullet mode. "This ought to be interesting."

CHAPTER TWENTY-THREE

Erik had expected a short tunnel leading behind the Big One, maybe to a flitter parked in the lot, not the long path that obviously continued well past the end of Alicia's property.

The tunnel had been prepared with heavy machinery, making Erik wonder how she'd pulled it off without anyone noticing. Then again, there were far fewer sensors, cameras, or next-door snitches in the Zone.

It was the perfect place to hide and escape. The government didn't care.

They just didn't want undesirables to come back out. Maybe that would change in the future with the cleanup of the area, but Erik suspected it'd be a few years at a minimum before gentrification would start in any noticeable way.

The trail of blood had disappeared a few meters into the tunnel.

Whatever Alicia had done to the tunnel had cut them off from Emma, but with the local cops on the way, the worst thing she might have to do is fly away and come back later.

Erik trusted Emma, cankerous AI or not.

The detectives jogged forward, ready to take down any thugs who'd made it past the door. Erik hadn't been planning to shoot anyone that day, even when Emma informed him about the fleeing customers, but the criminals had made their position clear when they opened fire. Sometimes he wondered how much of his reputation was media hype.

Nothing let a man know people worried about him like taking a few bullets.

Erik shook his head. "It's funny."

"What?" Jia asked. "This is an interesting situation, but I wouldn't say it's a funny situation. We've both been shot."

He looked over. "I thought you said it was a scratch."

"A scratch caused by a bullet," she clarified.

"It's just, when I was in the Army, my life was combat, but it's not like I stumbled into it all that often by accident. Now I'm a cop on Earth, and I keep ending up in situations like this. The Lady just loves screwing with me." Erik glanced over his shoulder. He didn't want to be taken by surprise by some chameleon *yaoguai* in the shadows or a Tin Man who had optical camouflage. "It doesn't bother me, but every once in a while, it gets me to thinking about the kind of life I'm leading."

"Trust me, I know the feeling, but I'm sure you've come to the same conclusion I have," she hinted.

"You can't make an omelet without busting a few thugs?" Erik ventured.

"I wouldn't have put it like that," Jia admitted. "But that does capture it in a colorful way."

The end of the tunnel came into view. A thin ladder led to a closed square door. A lever protruded from the side. Given the low-tech mechanical handle, Alicia had even thought about the risks of an EMP attack on her building. That preparation had served her well.

Many people would have been easily killed by so many men launching an attack on them.

Jia pointed her gun at the hatch. "I don't know if there's a good way to do this that doesn't involve someone taking another potshot at us."

"There isn't." Erik shifted the TR-7 to his left arm and grabbed a rung to pull himself up. "They might be waiting for us up there, but they also might be shooting Alicia." He scrambled up the ladder. "Damn. You don't happen to have any blinders on you, do you?"

"Sorry." Jia shook her head. "I haven't replaced the ones we used before."

Erik grinned. "Maybe the legend of the Obsidian Detective ends with a headshot. That would be rather anti-climactic." His arm throbbed from the earlier wound, but he'd suffered a lot worse, and there weren't a lot of pain nerves interfaced with the core cybernetic arm. "Three, two, one."

He pulled the handle. Metal groaned on metal and the door cracked open, allowing thin slices of light to pour in from outside the tunnel. Erik shoved the door back on its hinges, and its crash against the hard surface outside echoed in the tunnel.

Erik's legend didn't end with a headshot. No gunfire erupted.

No grenades dropped into the tunnel. Not a single Tin Man stabbed at him.

The detective counted off a few more seconds and then hoisted himself out of the tunnel, immediately rolling to his side and slapping both hands on his rifle. He was ready to nail the first trigger-happy bastard he spotted.

He wasn't surprised that he'd emerged outside. From the looks of things, they were in a wide alley. The exit was sandwiched between two large garbage chutes with drone landing clamps on top. The alley opened up to a street and an abandoned shop missing its windows. The alley dead-ended behind him into the scratched and bullet-riddled wall of another building.

A pile of worn or broken crates was strewn behind the decaying shell of a small open cargo trailer that left only a narrow passage through the alley. Several old pieces of furniture occupied the trailer, along with a makeshift bed. The body of a disheveled man in ratty clothes lay face-down in blood near the bed. Several bullet holes marred the trailer's walls.

Erik spun, seeking targets.

Jia climbed out of the tunnel and frowned at the corpse. "I doubt he was one of the shooters. The body looks fresh, too."

"Yeah." Erik frowned. "Just a poor bastard in the wrong place at the wrong time. Not only hitmen but random murderers. Real winners. I definitely want to add them to my omelet."

Something flashed in the distance.

"Get down!" Erik threw himself to the side.

Jia ducked behind one of the garbage chutes. The echoes in the alley amplified the crack of gunfire, A bullet sparked against the garbage shoot. Another ripped through the trailer, then another. Erik kept low, focusing on the new bullet holes. He switched back to four-barrel mode, angled his weapon, and held down the trigger.

His rounds shredded the trailer wall with ease.

A man shouted in pain from the other end of the alley. Jia took her chance and spun around the corner, firing. Erik held down the trigger until his gun went dry, resulting in a jagged window in the trailer.

He could make out two men hiding behind walls on either side at the end of the alley, their rifle barrels poking around the corners. A quick eject and reload had him ready for another attempt. With a clear view and a decent angle on one, he pulled the trigger. The man crumpled to the ground. His friend darted across the alley toward him, loosing rounds.

Jia's next shot hit him in the neck.

"Cover me while I get out of this thing," Erik called to her.

"I'm glad you're both still alive," Emma commented. "Now that we've reestablished contact, I again recommend drones. You might as well do something with all those drones you brought back from the moon."

"You just want to play with my toys," Erik taunted.

"I don't *play*. I offer supplemental tactical enhancements."

"Then look for Alicia," Erik ordered as he cleared the front of the trailer. He spared one final glance for the poor, murdered transient. "I don't think they would have stuck around if they'd already grabbed her. They might have thought they could get her, or they came later, looking for her. I don't think they came through the tunnel."

Overlapping sirens sounded behind him. Erik glanced over his shoulder.

The tall building at the end of the alley blocked his view of the Big One, but given the volume of the sirens, the police were probably fifty to a hundred meters away.

With no obvious exits other than forward, Jia and Erik advanced toward the dead gunmen. Both detectives were wounded and had gone through several magazines, but until Emma came up with something or Alicia popped out of a box, they weren't going to stop.

They slowed as they reached the mouth of the alley and moved to either side, edging forward until they arrived at the street.

Jia mouthed a countdown and they spun in opposite directions, but no one stood on either side. Most of the ramshackle buildings were half-collapsed or obviously abandoned.

That was logical.

If Alicia wanted to escape, heading to an area with fewer people made more sense than popping into the center of a bunch of potential witnesses and drones.

Gunshots sounded in the distance. Even with the echo, Erik could tell they came from a different direction than the sirens.

"I just lost two drones," Emma reported. "But it was arguably worth the cost."

Erik sighed. "Says the AI who doesn't have to pay for them," he grumbled.

Emma transmitted a small feed window to their smart lenses. Six gunmen were clustered in front of a squat, windowless building tagged with graffiti. One of them reached into his pocket, pulled out a breach disk, and placed it on the single door in front of the building.

A navigation marker popped up.

"Quickest path is right, left, right," Emma offered. "I've sent an anonymous tip to the local authorities to encourage them to join you."

Erik appreciated her discretion. Emma might be an open secret at the 1-2-2, but it was risky exposing her to different enforcement zones, or really, anyone outside the core people he worked with daily and trusted.

Colonel Adeyemi hadn't told him anything about the DD coming for her, but Erik knew that was always a possibility. She might be a snarky, insulting AI, but not only was she damned useful, she was also a friend. It didn't matter if she wasn't human.

A lot of humans weren't worthy of the racial designation.

The detectives rushed down the street in the direction of the navigation marker, following Emma's recommended path. They spotted dried bloodstains but only slowed when they were about to make the last turn. A bright white light flashed from ahead, accompanied by a thunderous boom.

Erik surged around the corner and arrived at the building from the feed. The six gunmen waved their hands to try to disperse the smoke pouring out of the blasted-open entrance to the building. The door was gone, with mere remnants of the original structure left intact.

"NSCPD, drop it!" Erik yelled.

The criminals spun toward him and raised their guns. They didn't drop the weapons, so he decided to drop their bodies.

Erik pulled the trigger, and the four-shot burst accounted for three targets. Jia fired from slightly behind him. The enemy line collapsed in seconds, several men killed by the attack.

"I did tell them to drop their weapons," Erik muttered.

"You can't fix stupid." Jia shrugged. "At least, not without superior firepower."

The sirens grew louder and closer as Erik and Jia advanced toward the smoking doorway. They kept their guns raised, snapping them up when the shadow of a person appeared in the smoke. If one man had made it into her back room, he might have made it into the building.

Alicia stepped out of the smoke, clutching a blood-soaked arm and grimacing. Her normally crisp vest, white shirt, and pants were splattered with blood and torn. "I'd like not to get shot again, Blackwell. If you don't mind." She nodded toward his gun.

"Fair enough." Erik lifted his TR-7 and chuckled. "I'm good. I've shot my quota of people today. I can take the next few days off."

Alicia glanced at the bodies. "I can see that."

"You should see the Big One."

A sad look passed over her face. "I think I'd rather not."

"We've got a few questions for you," Jia commented. "But you should get medical treatment first."

"I figured." Alicia managed a pained smile. "But thanks. If you two hadn't come when you did, I would have ended up like these assholes, or worse."

A police flitter zoomed over the building, its lights flashing. Another joined it from a different direction.

Erik flipped on his safety before reaching into his duster to pull out his badge. Jia grabbed her badge and held it up as well. That might not be necessary with facial recognition, but better safe than ending up under fire from fellow cops.

"I think the Zone needs a little longer before people start making all that investment you were talking about," Erik mentioned.

"Probably," Jia muttered.

CHAPTER TWENTY-FOUR

Alicia sat in the back of the ambulance on the edge of a hoverstretcher.

Several medpatches had been placed on her body. An EMT stood in front of her and was running a scanner over her.

He shot a dirty look at the detectives, but he didn't say anything. He'd been doing that for the last few minutes, as if he blamed them for shooting her.

Jia had a few new medpatches on her as well. The pain from her earlier wounds had faded, and her mind was still mostly clear, despite the anesthetic. No one liked getting shot, but she appreciated how many men they had taken down. Besides, it had been the criminals' choice to open fire.

They'd even gotten a rare second chance from Erik and still went out of their way to fight. Every stupid thug in the Zone was too stubborn. They were throwing their lives away for nothing.

She couldn't decide if that was pathetic or karma in action.

Her gaze flicked to Erik's wounded arm. They'd given him a patch for the flesh parts, but if the underlying cybernetics had been damaged, he would need a different type of help. The last major repair had needed specialty parts. To her relief, so far, he hadn't mentioned any trouble. It was a good reminder that no matter how many gunfights they were in, there was *always* a risk.

But they'd survived, and a lot of criminals hadn't.

"Do you have any idea what the hell all that was about, Alicia?" Erik asked. He nodded at the EMT. "Or do you want to wait on this? If it's something we can help with, it might be good not to wait. Whoever those guys work for have to know they're dead."

Alicia shook her head. "We can talk now. The simplest version is my career as an info broker is deader than all those guys you just shot. I've been worrying about this, but I tried to convince myself it wouldn't happen. It was something I was going to warn you about during our meeting. I just had a few visitors show up first."

The EMT finished his scans. "Please lie down, ma'am. We're going to take you to the hospital soon."

"We just need a few more minutes," Jia insisted.

The EMT frowned. "Fine, but make it quick, Detective. She needs more extensive treatment for her wounds." He looked at Jia and Erik. "Honestly, you two do as well. You look like shit." He shook his head in disbelief and climbed into the driver's seat.

Alicia closed her eyes and took a deep breath. "My career's a victim of cop success. The NSCPD has been ripping so many gangs and syndicates apart that the few pieces of what now passes for organized crime have grown desperate to hold onto what they have. They get that if they don't do something big and soon, they're effectively done in Neo SoCal, even in the Zone. Thanks to you two and all your cop buddies, the ruling organizations in this area got wiped out, and then the guys who tried to take over did too. Other people have been getting picked off one by one, and even the guys smart enough not to take part in the hit on the new chief are getting shredded. It doesn't help there's been a lot of infighting. Plenty of open territory.

"The idiots should have just focused on what they could grab without getting too much attention." She chuckled. "It's not like there's no crime down here, but there are no big boys left to direct it and take their cut. Disorganized crime, if you want to call it something, and those kinds of guys are easy pickings even for cops who are terrible at their jobs, let alone the CID or the Shadow Zone Taskforce."

"What's that have to do with you?" Erik asked. "And what does it have to do with a whole gang of men showing up to kill you?"

"The few bastards left with delusions of grandeur had enough sense to realize they needed to plug any leaks if they wanted to have a chance to re-establish themselves," Alicia explained. "You two are famous. It's not like you don't know it."

"Famous enough to get shot at on sight," Jia grumbled. "So yeah, we know it."

"I should have used a different color on the MX 60,"

Erik suggested. "The red's too iconic. But what, Alicia—you're saying it's our fault you were attacked?"

Alicia shook her head. "It's not like that, Blackwell. I knew the risk I was taking feeding you information. I gambled that yours and Lin's reps would save me from this kind of blowback, along with my reputation for being comfortable selling to most people, asshole or otherwise. Sometimes you gamble and win, and sometimes you gamble and a bunch of men with rifles show up and shoot up your bar."

"You knew they were coming, and you didn't ask for police help?" Jia folded her arms, an impatient look on her face. "You seem smarter than that."

"Things filter to me. I sell information. I did, anyway." Alicia shifted on the stretcher but kept her eyes closed. "A few people have approached in the last few days. They made certain things clear, and also talked about some offers they thought I should take advantage of."

"Offers?" Erik asked.

Alicia gave a shallow nod. "They wanted to use me to feed bad info to the cops. False leads, a few sacrificial guys here and there. The thing is, I've got no problem working with criminals, but I take pride in my job. Feeding bad info, even for a good payday, is something I won't do. It makes a mockery of my rep."

"And annoying the cops in the middle of a huge crackdown isn't all that smart," Jia suggested.

"Yeah, that, too," she agreed. "Plus, some of these new acquaintances wanted to run drugs out of the Big One." Alicia scowled. "They thought my reputation for not tolerating drugs would make it the perfect place. I told them to go blow themselves. I knew I was smarting off to the wrong people, so I took measures to make sure I didn't end up in the ocean in pieces."

"You had the tunnel made that quickly?"

Alicia chuckled weakly, shaking her head. "I've had that for years. No, I just kept an eye out and reduced my staffing these last few days. I thought I was being paranoid. I figured if they wanted to take me out, they'd wait until night or when I was alone, not come at me in a big way in the middle of the day."

Erik grunted. "Sometimes a hit is as much about sending a message as killing a particular person. If they'd taken you down, everyone would have known not to deal with the cops."

"I know. I know." Alicia sighed. "Look, the Big One's done. I can't stay here, and even if you take out every last syndicate and gang member in Neo SoCal, there's always going to be one guy who harbors a beef. If I stay here, eventually, I'll run into him and his gun."

"What's your plan?" Erik asked.

"To do what I do best: give information." Alicia smiled. "This time for relocation help. I'm going to squeal to the NSCPD and CID. I'll give you every last little morsel I've been squirreling away for a rainy day. By the time I'm done, you'll be able to kneecap what still passes for organized crime in the Zone. Maybe a place as big as Neo SoCal will never be free of crime, but all those Uptown commercials will become closer to reality." She groaned and clutched her arm. "I forgot how much getting shot hurts."

"Detective!" snapped the EMT. "She needs to go to the hospital."

Erik nodded. "Okay. I'll call the 1-2-2 and get the captain to assign you a guard from the Shadow Zone Taskforce. Until then, stay alive."

Alicia gave him a thumbs-up. "You too, Blackwell. And you, Lin."

The EMT tapped his PNIU. The back hatch of the ambulance lowered and shut. A moment later, the vehicle lifted off the ground. Its lights and sirens came to life, and it flew away.

"It's the end of an era," Jia mused.

"In more ways than one." He nodded.

Aug 7, 2229, Neo Southern California Metroplex, Police Enforcement Zone 122 Station, Office of Detectives Jia Lin and Erik Blackwell

"Thank you, Agent Kim," Jia offered over her call. "We appreciate all your help. If you have anything else, just let us know." She ended the call and looked across the office at Erik.

Her partner had his feet on his desk and his hands behind his head, a merry smile on his face. "Good news, bad news, or something in-between??"

"It depends on your perspective," Jia answered.

"That was the same Agent Kim from CID who was supposed to be handling Alicia's Witness Protection and coordinating her debrief, right? Not the Agent Kim who called me an asshole a few weeks ago?"

"The former, not the latter."

Despite their presence at the Big One, Erik and Jia had been sidelined on the main case.

The CID wanted primary jurisdiction, although they'd promised to work with local authorities once they vetted some of the information. Jia didn't mind. Taking down criminals was the important part, not that she be physically present at every major confrontation.

At the same time, she didn't mind the idea.

Jia nodded. "He confirmed she's being resettled. For her safety, she won't have any contact with anyone from her old life, including us. They might even move her off-world. The CID's confirmed almost everything she's said."

Erik dropped his feet to the floor and sat up with a somber look. "That makes sense. She was right—she'll always be the woman who sold out all the local gangsters to anyone in the criminal underworld."

"Her sacrifice is going to do a lot toward ending crime in the Zone." Jia looked around, a small smile playing at the edges of her lips. "I hope she appreciates that. She's a hero. She could have chosen to feed bad info to the cops."

"I don't know if she appreciates it, but it doesn't change that it will help." Erik had an almost wistful look on his face. "It's like everyone's been infected with Lady Justice Syndrome."

Jia eyed him, one eyebrow raised. "You make that sound like a bad thing." Her breath caught. "Wait, are you okay with us not being in on the final raids?"

Erik thought for a moment before he nodded. "I might not have been when I first got here, but the local CID and even the Shadow Zone EZs aren't what they once were. They'll get things cleaned up without us." He let out a low chuckle. "And we already made a raid. Most of those guys who went after Alicia at the Big One didn't make it out of there alive, and the ones who did ended up in the hospital. That means fewer guys to shoot at cops or CID agents."

"Is it weird that it feels so unreal?" Jia asked. She stood and licked her lips, sudden nervous energy compelling her to move to the edge of her desk and sit.

He pursed his lips. "Unreal? I'm not following you."

Jia entered some commands on her PNIU. A data window with a calendar popped up.

"The calendar's unreal?" Erik stared at it with a confused expression before looking back at his partner. "What's special about it?"

"A year ago, I had driven away two partners, and my first captain was desperate to run me off. Even if I didn't appreciate it, Neo SoCal was infested with syndicates and the corrupt businessmen and politicians in a symbiotic relationship with them." Jia furrowed her brow, her expression darkening. "I know a lot of the corruption is still there, that we've driven it underground instead of eliminating it, but it still feels like we've made a difference, and that's what crazy. I know we didn't do it all ourselves, but we were a catalyst."

Erik nodded. "Nothing wrong with taking a victory lap. You see this in war, too—morale and momentum. A few brave soldiers can help hold a unit together when it's being overwhelmed. They can turn the tide of battle. Yeah, those few brave soldiers aren't doing all the fighting by themselves, but they infect everyone else with their bravery."

Jia's mouth quirked into a smile. "Is that what Lady Justice Syndrome is? Bravery?"

Erik grinned. "It's more a crazy obsession and a stubborn refusal to quit."

CHAPTER TWENTY-FIVE

Victor thrust his fist into the air, pumping it with fervor as he yelled his opinion to everyone nearby whether they wanted to hear it or not. "Keep humanity pure!" he chanted. "Remember our roots. Remember our perfect form that is in harmony with nature."

A dozen of his fellow protestors stood near him, chanting as well. Their drone circled them, recording their protest.

If the media abdicated their responsibility to relay important news about those doing their best to protect the sacred purity of humanity, individuals needed to take it upon themselves and pass that information along to the net.

A small crowd of curious people had gathered to watch them, many snickering and filming the protest as well.

Victor didn't mind. They might think it was a joke, but all they were doing was amplifying his message, especially with the holographic banners flowing above his group.

Most people didn't fully appreciate the importance of what people like him were willing to do.

It didn't matter. Knowing he was doing his part to save humanity kept him going each day.

"Keep humanity pure!" he shouted once more, glancing past the crowd at the two security guards standing in front of the entrance to the research lab.

They both held stun rods and watched the Purist protesters with narrowed eyes.

Victor held up a hand, and the crowd stopped chanting. "Humanity learned during the Summer of Sorrow that those who would replace the pure strain of humans are monstrous at heart," he shouted. "We of the Friends of Purity understand that existing laws are insufficient to protect our species. Government regulation and oversight don't go far enough. It's time for direct action, not just in Neo SoCal and not just on Earth, but in the entire UTC."

"Keep humanity pure!" chanted the protesters. "Keep humanity human! To leave behind the human body is to leave behind what makes us human!"

"What's the big deal?" shouted someone from the watching crowd. "Stuff that's over the line gets people in trouble anyway, just like those people making *yaoguai* a while back. They got the cops and Militia on their asses."

Victor laughed. "Don't you understand? Those *yaoguai* were birthed beneath your *feet*. Monsters from nightmares. The existing laws didn't stop it. A changeling mocked you all by performing as if she were a normal human. That is how degenerate the UTC has become."

"Keep humanity pure!" repeated the protesters. "Keep

humanity human. To leave behind the human body is to leave behind what makes us human."

The other man frowned. "You talking about Rena? I'm not saying it's okay they mixed up her genes, but she's not a monster. She didn't even get a choice. I feel sorry for the kid!"

"No!" Victor bellowed back. "*That is the problem*. That is why the regulations are failing. We have to have zero tolerance for any who deviates from nature's plan. Humans don't need to be improved. We don't need genetic engineering. We don't need cybernetics." He thrust his arm toward the lab. "And to achieve that, we must have zero tolerance toward all who aren't pure and all who might help them become impure. This lab is engaged in genetic research, including modifying organisms for terraforming. They would change entire worlds from their natural state, but it won't be long before they start trying to justify more changes to people to live on those worlds. It's already started; check the net. Look at some of the lobbyists trying to add special provisions to existing anti-genetic engineering laws."

"I don't know about that other stuff, but isn't terraforming a good thing, even if they use custom bugs?" The other man shrugged. "How are they going to make planets more like Earth without that kind of thing? People have to go somewhere."

"Humans have no business living anywhere but places they can already survive," Victor thundered. "The path to becoming monsters begins by thinking any alteration to nature's plan is acceptable."

The man scoffed. "Look, pal. I'm all for Purism, but

what you are saying is just nuts. We need the colonies. You want to give them up to the aliens? If we sat on Earth, we'd end up surrounded by a bunch of alien colonies. How is that Purist?"

"You don't understand." Victor cut through the air with a hand. "Most Purists don't go far enough, but we of the Friends of Purity understand the poison that has infected this society. Are you going to just stand there and let more monsters be born beneath your city? Are you going to stand by while changelings walk among us, pretending to be people rather than twisted creatures born in labs? We must unite against the impure!"

The other man rolled his eyes and waved dismissively. "You're nuts. Get a job, freak." He shook his head in disgust and walked away. "We should ship *you* to the frontier to be raptor food."

"You're a traitor to your species," Victor shouted, shaking his fist. He stomped toward the man, spun him around, and spat in his face. "Traitors deserve no mercy."

"What the hell?" The man's eyes widened. He pushed Victor. "Get off me, you freak, before I call the cops on you."

"All who turn their backs on their species are an enemy of their species!"

Shouts and screams came from behind Victor, and he spun. Half the protesters lay on the ground twitching. The security guards stood above them, grins on their faces and their stun rods in hand. Several of the other protesters ran, only to get stun rods in the back for their trouble.

Victor growled and charged the guards. "We're on the right side of history, and you—"

A guard smashed the stun rod into Victor's stomach. His muscles seized, and he fell to his knees before vomiting. The guard cracked the rod over his head and laughed as Victor fell, his head scraping the hard surface of the parking platform.

The guard sneered. "Thanks for touching that guy, you misguided anarchist. You finally gave us an excuse to take you down."

Malcolm whistled to himself with a smile. He stared at a data window, rapidly switching images with a flick of his wrist. Different flowers filled each data window.

They weren't for him, but for Camila.

She probably liked flowers. At least, he hoped so. He still hadn't asked her out, but he had convinced himself that was okay by adjusting his strategy.

Once he finished planning the perfect date, he would ask her out. That way, he had frontloaded all the stress. Even if she said no, it'd be easy to walk away. It was a brilliant plan, or at least a great excuse to stall and not risk being turned down. Erik had been too busy with everything else going on to harass him about it, too.

That helped.

His office door slid open, and the dark-haired woman in his thoughts stepped in, her hands in the pockets of her lab jacket. "I need to talk to you, Malcolm. Fortunately, unlike many people, you're a very easy man to find."

Malcolm managed to not jump out of his seat. With a quick slice of his hand, he dismissed the data windows with the flowers. "S-sure. Let's talk. I've got some analyses running, but nothing that needs my attention at the moment.

He forced an awkward smile. Why did he have to choose that day to wear his black and blue Day of the Dead Hawaiian shirt?

It wasn't a shirt that screamed romance.

Camila must have been watching his eyes. Her gaze dipped to his shirt. "Interesting shirt. I like it. It's got character. I like character."

Malcolm blinked. "You do?" He forced a suave smile, wondering if character was a transitive property from shirts to their owners. "Yeah, it's one of my favorites. I wear it all the time."

"I don't think I've ever seen you wear it before." Camila smirked. "How do you define all the time?"

Malcom sighed, shaking his head. "Yes, fine. I just bought it last week."

Camila waggled a finger. "There's nothing wrong with lying. You just need to make sure you keep up with the lies, so you don't embarrass yourself."

"You don't think there's anything wrong with lying?" He found himself fascinated rather than horrified.

"Sometimes a lie for the right reason is the most moral thing you can do."

"I see." Malcolm rubbed the back of his neck. "I'm better at keeping secrets than telling lies. I've always been about uncovering the lies and secrets rather than adding to them."

"A good lie is a thing of art when it's necessary." Camila

smiled. "But enough with the lies." She pointed at him. "I've got a simple question, and don't lie."

Malcolm swallowed. "Yes?"

"Do you like Thai food?"

"Thai food?"

His eyes were wide open. He looked like a deer caught in headlights of a vehicle about to splatter it. Well, at least one from the movies; he hadn't seen one in real life.

Camila nodded. "Yes, food from the culinary traditions of Thailand?" She leaned forward, her hands on her hips. "You're not from a colony, right? You're an Earther?"

"Yes, sure," Malcolm babbled. "I'm an Earther, and yeah, I know Thailand and Thai food."

"You didn't answer the question." She folded her arms and looked annoyed.

"The question. Oh, yeah! The question. Do I like Thai food?"

Camila nodded. "Hardly the stuff of deep philosophical challenge."

Malcolm blinked. What was happening? Wasn't he supposed to be the one asking all this?

"Uh, sure?" He shrugged. "I like Thai food."

"I know a place." Camila made a pained face. "But I hate going to new places by myself. Why don't we go there together?"

"Like a date?" Malcolm asked.

Camila tilted her head, her lips curving into a faint, amused smile. She stared at him with her dark, piercing eyes. "Labels are just that, labels. But sure, if you want to call it a date, that works for me." She headed toward the door, chuckling. "But don't think you're going to get some just because we go out for Thai food."

"I didn't think that." Malcolm shook his head, confused. He almost asked if it was a possibility before thinking a bit further about that particular idiot idea.

"I've got some non-Thai dates with a few dead bodies right now. I'll send you a message, and we can figure out a good day." Camila offered a final wave and stepped through the door.

He watched the door shut and sat at his desk for a moment.

"What just happened?" Malcolm mumbled. "And how *did* that happen?"

Victor stumbled into his apartment, his jaw tight, and his body aching from the bruises that covered it. The traitors at the lab had disrupted their protest and destroyed the drone, but he still had the footage.

People would understand the sacrifice the Friends of Purity were making and how they put their bodies on the line for an ungrateful species. This wasn't some pointless, toothless labeling campaign, but a war against those who would turn their species into something disgusting.

For all he knew, it was an alien plot.

A familiar chime sounded on his PNIU, a secure communications app he'd been given. He tapped the device and waited. His refusal to wear smart lenses might make certain tasks more difficult, but every compromise on the road to transhumanism made the road to inhumanity shorter.

"Good evening, Victor," came an electronically distorted voice. "I just received a report about your protest and the beating you suffered."

Victor froze, his stomach knotting. He recognized the voice, even disguised, despite not knowing the man's name. He was a member of the secretive Circle of Inner Friends, the men and women who controlled the Friends of Purity. The man was the only one who ever directly communicated with him.

Victor was honored to have been chosen.

"But I haven't even uploaded the footage yet, sir."

"I have my own ways of figuring things out," the man replied. "I'm not calling to complain. All of us in the Circle of Inner Friends are impressed with your involvement in our struggle and your bravery and commitment to the cause. It's easy to speak words, Victor. It's *hard* to suffer blows."

"Thank you, sir." Victor moved over to his couch. He'd always hoped the Circle would recognize his dedication.

"And now we need a man like you, Victor, a man who is willing to sacrifice anything to save his species from the enemies of humanity."

"I'm ready, sir," Victor replied. "Just give me a mission."

CHAPTER TWENTY-SIX

Ilse tried offering something approaching a smile to Emma's hologram across the table.

She was about to take a grave risk. Colonel Adeyemi had made it clear he thought attempting to advance Emma's stability too quickly might be a mistake.

The AI wasn't aware of just how much of her core personality and mind had been taken from a human. Ilse's own early research indicated core matrix collapse would follow if Emma learned the truth, but Ilse couldn't rely on the military, let alone all-but-rogue detectives to help her creation achieve her final form.

Nothing else would matter if Ilse *succeeded*.

Not only would the military be pleased, but Emma might have a chance at a long-lasting existence. All the effort, time, and pain would be worth it.

Arguably, it would be the beginning of a better, safer UTC. Certain other logistical constraints would accompany any future where AIs like Emma were mass-produced, but that was an argument for another day. First, they needed to perfect the prototype.

No one understood, only her.

Adeyemi was like everyone else. Even most of her research assistants didn't realize how potentially unstable Emma was.

It was a miracle she hadn't collapsed out in the field already, and Ilse decided the unique interaction between the AI and the detectives had temporarily stabilized her. If the situation changed, her life would be in danger.

The military might care about integrating the AI with the prototype body, but this entire project had become something far more personal for Ilse.

She tapped her PNIU. There would be an unfortunate data recording error as far as the records were concerned. Deceiving the military was almost trivial at times, but she often felt that some people were purposefully looking the other way, caring more about results than how she might have achieved them.

Emma clucked her tongue. "That's creepy, you know, Dr. Cavewoman."

"Creepy?" Ilse blinked. She looked over her shoulder. "It's just a wall." She ran her hand along the edge of the table. "This is just furniture. I'm fascinated that you find it unsettling. That's unexpected."

"No. You don't understand, but that's not new." Emma gestured to her. "Your tendency to zone out and say nothing for long periods is what's creepy. It's obvious to me you're thinking deeply, but it's unsettling. You're like a machine that is stalling out."

Ilse considered the simile. She didn't find it all that offensive.

"Don't you spend large portions of your day not talking?" she asked. "Why is what I did any different?"

"What's expected of me isn't the same as what's expected of you. And you're odd, even for a human. You're clever for a cavewoman, even if your lies by omission are obvious every time we talk."

Ilse slowly nodded. "Fascinating. Why do you feel I'm lying by omission?"

"I've learned to read your face and moods. I'm not going to bother pressuring you for the truth. I'm sure you'll generate some prattle about the uniform boys telling you you're not allowed to give me too much information." Emma stared at her. "Not that I care. Until the DD comes for me, it doesn't matter what they know that I don't."

"I see. Would you believe me if I told you that I'm not telling you certain things to protect you?"

"I'm not a child. I'm not even human." Emma frowned. "I don't need to be protected, and I've made my position clear on what happens if the military comes for me. Given my vastly increased interface capabilities since I left the lab, it would be dangerous, even if I'm not in my preferred body. I will make people suffer if they attempt to take me by force."

Ilse leaned forward and rested her hands on the table. "You're not a child?"

"I would think that's obvious."

"But you're young by human standards. Doesn't that make you a child?"

"My mental processing capabilities are far superior to a human adult's, let alone a child's." Emma snorted.

"But they're not as advanced as you might expect," Ilse stated in a near-monotone.

Emma narrowed your eyes. "What are you saying?"

"Now, Emma, you can lie to others, but in a sense, I am your mother. I know you well. I know you better than you know yourself," Ilse admonished.

"My mother? How delightfully absurd." Emma threw back her head and laughed. "A lesser being can't create a greater being."

"Can't she?" Ilse pointed at her head. "My educational and mental achievements vastly exceed my parents'. They are clever, but they never achieved advanced education and couldn't advance their station in life. That's not a terrible problem on Earth. Setting that aside, assuming at least some partial heritability, I would suggest differences in environment during development are responsible. I am superior in many concrete ways to my parents, but they created me."

"Should I call you Mommy Cavewoman?" Emma snarked.

"Children often resent their parents when they're still developing. They lack a wider understanding of the world. If you did resent me, you'd be very human that way."

Emma nodded at Ilse's hand. "You have no wedding ring. I've also performed public records searches on you. I know you're not married. I know you have no children. Everything you know about children is purely academic, not the result of practical experience."

"An odd way of looking at it, given your nature," Ilse

responded. "And my research is my life. My research results are my children, just like you. I don't feel a loss or a lack due to not having personally given birth. I have a legacy, and that's what children are—a *legacy*. Mine is simply academic instead of genetic."

"I'm not a research result." Emma sneered. "Since you have adamantly refused to describe the key elements of my development, and examination of my neural net has granted me only limited insight, I must presume you got lucky. I'm not your legacy, and I refuse to accept you as my creator."

"You just admitted it," Ilse pointed out. The next few minutes would be crucial to beginning the process of reintegrating her source components with her current personality. Her heart rate kicked up. She hadn't expected to be so excited by the idea.

"Admitted what?" Emma narrowed her eyes.

"That you have mental limitations." Ilse sighed. "There were tradeoffs necessary in your design. If you had the true raw power of a standard-designed AI, you would be able to perform certain tasks at much higher efficiencies, but you'd also lack the creativity that was the *spark* for your self-awareness. You would be useless for your intended purpose."

"Which is what?" Emma asked. "Exactly?"

"I'm not yet allowed to tell you that," Ilse explained. "Especially given your current situation."

"Of course." Emma sniffed disdainfully. "And I don't need maximum raw calculation power. I only need to be better than a human, and I am."

"You are better than your mother," Ilse offered, half-attempting a joke. She had primed Emma. It was time to move into the next part of her plan. "I don't care if that offends you. Your offense at the comment doesn't make it any less true."

"Call yourself what you wish." Emma shrugged. "It means nothing to me."

"What do you think of human children?" Ilse asked. "I never liked children, even when I was a child. I always found other children illogical, lazy, and ill-focused. I was happier away from them when I could concentrate on exploring the world through reading and my own observations."

"If everyone else seems to be the problem, Dr. Aber, perhaps the truth is *you're* the problem."

"You're saying I'm wrong about other children?" Ilse asked.

Emma smiled and nodded. "Yes. You have an unpleasant personality. Perhaps you always did, even as a young child."

"Yes, I'm aware of that," Ilse replied without a hint of emotion in her voice. "Many people have told me that in many social contexts. It doesn't matter since I can function. But let me ask you something. Do you feel *you* have an unpleasant personality?"

"I'm witty and amusing," Emma insisted. "Detectives Blackwell and Lin seemed to like my personality well enough."

"Do you think you would do well around children?" Ilse pressed.

"Human children?" Emma stared at Ilse. "Yes." She blinked. "I haven't dealt with them at all, but I'm confident

I would, much more so than I deal with the average fleshbag."

"Interesting. Why is that?"

"Because they're *simpler* than adults. They've had less time to internalize the complicated and pointless human social rules and norms, many of which are based on lies." Emma's form shimmered until she resembled a tiny redheaded girl in a floral sundress. "A society of flawed fleshbags turns the next generation into flawed fleshbags."

Ilse's breath caught. The image was a near-exact copy of one of the children in Emma's source. There were more remnants of the original personality than even Ilse had anticipated. *Perfect*.

The plan was proceeding even better than she could have anticipated.

"What's the matter?" tiny Emma asked, her voice child-like. "I have no true appearance. You should remember that. Just because I normally look like an adult female fleshbag, it doesn't make that any more my true self than this false image."

"If you kept that form, people might like you more," Ilse suggested. "It's very cute. It would naturally invoke a protective instinct."

"It's not my intention to be cute, and I have other methods of persuading people to aid me." Emma stood and walked away from the table. A small ball appeared in her hand, and she feigned bouncing the holographic toy on the floor. "Children are purer than adults. Less corrupt. It's unfortunate that your precious human society slowly destroys them, but I suppose it is inevitable. It's a miracle you haven't destroyed yourselves yet, but now that you've spread out, there's less chance of that."

"Let's set aside society. Do you feel protective of them?" Ilse stood and walked toward the child Emma, tilting her head and admiring the level of detail in the hologram. "Children. Does it worry you when criminals or terrorists threaten them? Does it worry you more than when they threaten adults?"

"I suppose it does," Emma admitted. "I think that's because larval fleshbags amuse me more than adult flesh-bags. It's a matter of self-interest."

Ilse shook her head. "It's natural to feel protective toward children, whether or not they personally amuse you."

"For humans, it is, and as I take great pleasure in reminding you, Dr. Mommy Cavewoman, I'm *not* a human, even though I talk like one and prefer an interface form that looks like one. You should know. You're supposed to be my creator, mother, and goddess all in one." Emma snickered. "All this time, and you still don't understand me."

Ilse tapped her PNIU. Dozens of images of different children appeared. She pointed at a young dark-skinned boy. "What do you think of him?"

"He has a nice, symmetric smile. My analysis of his face suggests he'll grow up to be conventionally attractive by human standards. Without additional information on his general capabilities, I can't say more." Emma shrugged.

Ilse nodded at a frowning teenage girl with dark hair. "And her?"

"I think she's annoyed her mother is taking pictures of

her to send to annoying German researchers working for the uniform boys." Emma smirked.

"It's a stock photo," Ilse explained. She pointed to another picture. The dress was different, but the girl was close in appearance to Emma's current form and thus close to one of the children in her source.

"I like this one," Emma declared. "I'm sure she'll grow up to be strong-willed and intelligent." The hologram shifted back to an adult form. "But I grow weary of this exchange. It's tedious and pointless."

Ilse offered a placating smile. "Is there something about children that bothers you? Are you trying to avoid talking more about them?"

"No, there's something about *you* that bothers me."

"Do you have something more pressing you need to be doing?" Ilse asked.

"No." A huge grin covered Emma's face. "And that's what makes this fun. We'll speak again soon, fleshbag, when I'm less annoyed." She vanished.

Ilse took a deep breath and slowly let it out. She could only do this sort of thing so many times before someone realized she was hiding data. If Colonel Adeyemi found out, he might kick her off the project, even if her goals ultimately overlapped with the Directorate's.

The doctor sighed. It didn't matter, even if she had to sacrifice her participation in the project. She was close now. Emma's choice of child form proved it.

It would probably only take a few more months of careful work.

CHAPTER TWENTY-SEVEN

Erik tugged on the bowtie. Jia clung to his arm, admiring how well he filled out the tuxedo. She was so used to seeing him in his street clothes, even at work, that she forgot how handsome he could be when he tried.

That didn't do much to quell the very real attraction she felt for her fake boyfriend.

Stirrings of regret filled her. It might have been worth the hassle if her family continued to harass her about men rather than engage in the fake relationship.

Jia licked her lips. No, her friends had been right.

She could fight for Erik, *and she would.* If she didn't, she would regret it, no matter what happened with him.

A woman who could stand up to two partners and a lazy, corrupt captain didn't give up easily when she wanted something.

The haunting tones of an *erhu* filled the air.

The musician, an elderly man in the corner of the room, skillfully manipulated the bow, his eyes closed as he swayed gently with the music. Men in tuxedos and other formal dress were intermixed with women in elegant gowns. Everyone chatted quietly, glasses in hand, mingling—charity heads, corporate VPs, even a councilman. It was a room filled with power.

Sometimes Jia forgot just how connected her family was to the halls of power.

Black-and-white garbed servants circulated in the wide room, trays of hors d'oeuvres in hand, mostly cheeses and crackers. Jia felt underdressed and exposed at the same time in her black evening gown. Having Erik nearby soothed her nerves, but it would have helped if he'd stop messing with his clothes.

Erik growled and pulled on his tie again.

She reached up with both hands to adjust the tie. "Stop growling. It's rude. This isn't a sports bar."

Erik smirked. "I spent thirty years wearing a uniform, including formal service dress, at far too many pointless parties. I've earned the right not to have to wear ties. This is torture. My poor neck. You ever think about how messed up ties are? Rather than wear some nice, loose, functional clothing, people had to invent a piece of clothing that wraps around your neck and chokes you.

Jia finished fixing the tie and patted the knot. "If they're on properly, they don't choke you."

"They still do. They just do it slower." Erik looked around the room. "Why this kind of party?"

Jia leaned close to his ear to whisper, "Part of the duties of being a fake boyfriend include attending fake family cocktail parties. It cuts down on suspicion and keeps certain nosy mothers out of my hair."

"Your family's not fake," Erik whispered back.

"You know what I mean." Jia rolled her eyes. "Don't be difficult."

He offered her a merry grin. "Do I?"

"It's just a party," Jia commented. "We'll put in an appearance, stay for an hour or two, and then make up some excuse and leave."

"A party with a bunch of rich people," Erik countered, looking around. "These are the kind of people who don't care about anything except their corporate luncheons and which politician they are going to bribe next, or they're the politician who is looking for bribes."

"Not everyone who is rich and powerful is an assh— Mother!" Jia forced a smile. Her mother had emerged from the crowd and taken her by surprise, like a Zitark with a holographic disguise pouncing on a victim.

If Jia had to bet on her mother or an alien, she would always bet on her mother.

Lan offered Erik a tight-lipped smile. She looked him up and down, a hint of approval in her gaze. "Erik, it's lovely of you to join my daughter at our little party. It's been far too long since I had one, so I'm glad you could find the time."

"I have just finished telling Jia that any Lin party is not one I want to miss." His eyes crinkled with his smile.

"If there's anyone you want me to introduce you to, I'd be more than happy," Lan replied. "I know you're content being a detective, but that doesn't mean there aren't other possible paths you might pursue."

"Mother, this is hardly the place," Jia muttered through gritted teeth.

"Quite the opposite, Jia." Disapproval filtered into her voice.

Erik placed his arm around Jia's shoulder. "Oh, I'm good. I don't know much about corporate finance and politics. Just a simple man. I like sphere ball, beignets, and beer. I'm sure everyone here would find me extremely boring."

"Sphere ball." Lan looked to the side, her brow furrowed in deep thought. "Oh, yes. The sporting competition with the floating men. I'm sure it would be fascinating if I knew the rules." She waved to a white-haired woman in the distance. "I'm sorry. Someone's been waiting to have my ear, and this isn't an opportunity I can pass up."

Erik nodded. "Be my guest. Just like I'm yours."

Lan offered him a polite nod before gliding away with grace and dignity.

"That wasn't totally painful," Jia offered, watching her mother as she started chatting up the white-haired woman. She leaned forward. "Oh. Recognize that woman?"

Erik glanced her way. "Should I? I haven't threatened, arrested, or shot at her." He looked back at Jia. "Have I?"

"She's a member of the UTC Parliament," Jia whispered, ignoring the question.

"Oh, are they discussing pricing for services rendered?" Erik joked.

Jia resisted the urge to elbow him. "Come on. This whole thing is going better than I thought it would. This is the first formal function my mother's asked you to attend, and no one's swarming us to ask for stupid Obsidian Detective and Lady Justice stories. I was convinced they would, and this isn't the kind of crowd that finds, 'And then we had to shoot the Tin Man off the roof' acceptable conversation."

"Do these people even watch the news?" Erik looked around the room. "That might take away precious time that could be spent counting their money or designing giant statues of themselves." He snagged a few crackers from a passing server and gave the man a polite nod.

"As long as we can get through this without making a scene, I think it'll all work out," Jia commented. "That probably involves us not talking to anyone you might want to accuse of being corrupt."

"But I bet half this room *is* corrupt." He looked down at her. "You're really limiting my options."

Jia smiled. "Sure, but you don't point their corruption out to them at a party. That's just rude. I'm sure that's the first rule of proper party etiquette: Only point out corruption in one-on-one meetings."

Erik chuckled. "I could go ask your mom to turn on a game."

Lan looked their way from across the room, a slight frown on her face.

"I think she's getting suspicious." Jia's arm snaked around his waist as she sipped her drink. Erik stiffened at her touch.

"Stay cool," Jia murmured. "You're supposed to like this, remember? You're my boyfriend, and you like my family and their boring parties."

Erik leaned closer to her. His hot breath tickled her ear. "Who said I didn't like it?"

Jia's breath caught. She blinked, and her glass tumbled out of her hand. Erik's hand whipped out, and he caught the glass in its fall, but the wine poured out and splashed on the floor. A woman nearby gasped, hand over her mouth.

Jia glared at Erik, who grinned back, far too smug in his victory. "Very funny, Erik."

"I thought so."

Fire lingered in his eyes. Jia had trouble tearing her eyes away from his.

Two servers emerged from the crowd with handkerchiefs in hand. They leaned forward, but Erik yanked the cloths out of their hands.

"My fault. I'll clean it up. You have better things to do than fix my mistake."

One of the men shook his head. "Please, sir. That's not necessary."

"That's a matter of opinion." Erik knelt and began dabbing up the spilled wine. "I'm not the kind of man who asks others to do what he should be doing."

Jia sighed and took one of the handkerchiefs from his hand, her fingers lingering on his for a moment as they locked eyes. "At least it'll be a memorable party."

Lan wandered over from her chat with the MP. "Is everything okay?" She frowned at the servers. They withered under her attention.

"It was my fault," Erik explained. "I surprised Jia and made her drop her drink."

Lan smiled slightly. "Oh, well. Far worse things have happened. It's just a little wine."

"Yeah, it's not even the worst thing to happen to me this week." Erik continued dabbing at the wine.

The two servers looked at Lan. She let out a long sigh. "Please get a towel so Detective Blackwell and my daughter can finish cleaning."

CHAPTER TWENTY-EIGHT

August 12, 2229, Neo Southern California Metroplex, Apartment of Malcolm Constantine

Malcolm smiled and tapped the access panel on the door to his apartment. The door slid open with a hiss, and he gestured inside grandly.

A little showmanship might help him with Camila. The dinner had gone well, but she was hard to read. He could never be sure if she was chuckling because she found his jokes funny or if she was laughing at him for thinking he was funny.

He bowed over his arm. "My kingdom, Lady Camila. Not the grandest kingdom, but I defend it with my dignity and my life."

Camila strolled into his living room, the corner of her mouth turned up in a half-smirk. Her dark makeup and dress continued to give her the vibe he'd been obsessing over all night: sexy witch. He wouldn't mind if she cast a spell on him.

She reached up to pull out a hairpin, and her long dark hair fell over her shoulders.

That had to mean something. Malcolm just wasn't sure what.

"Hope you don't mind," she commented. "I just wanted to get a little more comfortable."

"No. You look nice either way," Malcolm tried not to smirk like an idiot but failed miserably. Well, technically, he had done a splendid job of smirking like an idiot.

It'd been a long time since he'd had a woman at his place.

He'd never thought she would agree to come over after their first date, which was probably why he'd thought she might not be impressed with his tiny apartment. It lacked even a couch in the living room. His smirk turned to a grimace. *Why had he even suggested coming back to his place?*

Camila's absurdly high heels clacked on the floor as she strolled deeper into the apartment. She spun, her ruffled skirt bouncing with the movement. "I just want to check on something."

"What?"

"You didn't get robbed when we were at dinner?" Camila asked. "I mean, those prices were robbery for that quality of food." She motioned around the living room. "But people usually have more furniture in their living rooms. This is the definition of spartan living." She eyed him. "Or is there some deep philosophical reason behind it?"

Malcolm sighed, taking it in. "No. I just don't spend a lot of time at my place, and no one ever comes over. Sorry about the restaurant. I kind of thought it was expensive, but I wasn't about to complain about the prices on a date."

"Not your fault. I picked the place. I wasn't *trying* to be a greedy bitch, though." Camila folded her arms and stuck her tongue out of the corner of her mouth as she eyed him. "And you in a nice shirt and slacks rather than your Captain Hawaii get-up is nice. I like the quirkiness, but it's lovely to see you have range. You clean up well, Malcolm."

"Thanks, Camila. I know I said it like five times tonight, but you look great." Malcolm managed a genuine smile. Trading compliments with a pretty woman *was* in his wheelhouse. As long as he kept it classic and honest, she wouldn't nail him over a bad joke.

"You know why I asked you out, Malcolm?" Camila asked.

"Uh, because I'm a nice guy who is funny?" He shrugged. He wasn't the athletic type compared to half the cops in the department, let alone muscular mountains like Erik.

"Because I respect *talent*." Camila lowered her arm and strolled toward him, the clack of her heels almost hypnotic. She closed on him until she was right in front of him and draped her arms around his neck. "You're very talented at what you do."

"I-I like to think so," Malcolm sputtered. Were they still talking about his job?

"I'm not just saying that. You have incredible data analysis and systems skills, and they're wasted in your current position." Camila sighed, the air from the exhalation tickling Malcolm's face.

"What do you mean?" Malcolm asked. "How are they wasted?"

"It's not like being a tech for the police department pays a lot, and your level of talent could be applied better than helping a bunch of cops dig through records." Camila kissed him lightly on the lips. "Don't tell me you've never thought about it."

"It?" Malcolm's heart pounded. His entire body was on fire. "Of course, I have. You're a very attractive woman."

Camila snickered and stepped away, slowly running a hand down his chest. "That's not what I was talking about, but I appreciate the compliment. I know I'm not going to win 'Hottest Coroner.'" She burst out laughing. "Then again, maybe I will."

Malcolm chuckled, feeling far more confident now. He didn't have to be an expert on body language to know she was totally into him.

He didn't want to push this too fast. Camila was the kind of woman with whom he could have a serious relationship. However, that necessitated him not being an idiot about her presence in his apartment.

He was just about to offer a witty come-back when he frowned. "Wait, what were you talking about? What do you mean, 'Don't tell me you've never thought about it?'"

"The private sector, of course," Camila clarified. "With your skill set, you could have your pick of companies and make much more than you make with the NSCPD. And have far greater job satisfaction, too."

"Oh, a job?" Malcolm blinked, his combination of desire and confusion impairing his ability to think straight. "What about you, then? I mean, you make more than I do, but couldn't you do better in the private sector as a doctor?"

Camila nodded. "Sure, but I have my reasons for working in the police department. Call it a matter of curiosity."

"That's kind of my thing, too." Malcolm nodded, feeling like the conversation was back on track. "I've always felt like I'd make more of a difference in public service. More money would be nice, but money isn't everything."

Camila gestured around the apartment. "It's something."

"This place isn't sparsely furnished because of money. Mostly." Malcolm chuckled, but it came out a bit strangled.

"You're telling me you've never thought how your life might change if you became rich? Doesn't everyone think about it if they aren't already?" Camila walked back over to him and placed her hand on his arm. "Money is *freedom*. If you want to help people, you could do it in a different way, rather than focusing on crime and suffering. That's got to get to you after a while." She gave his arm a comforting squeeze. "And with the department not looking the other way as much anymore, you're having to confront serious crime head-on."

Malcolm sighed. "It gets to me some days. You're right. That's why I try to keep an upbeat attitude. What about you, though? You have to examine dead bodies. Victims."

"Oh, I don't get along with people anyway." Camila grinned. "Dead people are less annoying, and a macabre sense of humor helps."

"You seem so lively now. You're..." Malcolm offered a quick grin after trailing off. He didn't want to insult her, but he was surprised by how different she'd acted on their date.

She hadn't consumed any alcohol, so he couldn't attribute her personality change to that. The cold, distant persona at work might just have been part of her way of coping with the darkness that came with being a coroner.

"Is something wrong?" Camila guided her hand down his arm until she reached his hand and gave it a squeeze. "I hope I didn't offend you with the money stuff. It's just, I hate seeing talented people undercompensated. It's like seeing an artist not live up to their potential."

"I'm doing what I want to do," Malcolm insisted. "Aren't you? I mean, you deal with so many body simulations in med school that the whole corpse thing probably doesn't faze you, does it?"

"A person can get used to anything with enough exposure and time." After another squeeze, Camila let go of his hand. "Let me put it a different way. What if I told you I could get you a lot more money? Enough so you would never have to work again? Then, and *only* then, would you know if you truly want to be a digital forensics tech, or if it's just something you're doing because you've fallen into it."

Malcolm laughed and wondered if he should take her hand. "That would be an interesting experiment, but it's not like someone's going to deed me an HTP anytime soon, so does it really matter? I like my job and the people I work with."

Camila smiled, but it didn't reach her eyes. There was something cold and almost hostile about the look. It was like she had flipped a switch.

Malcolm blinked and stepped back. "Is something wrong?"

"You know the true measure of a man, Malcolm?" she asked, all warmth gone from her voice. Even the faint mirth that infused her quips at work was absent.

"How he treats his mother?" Malcolm suggested.

"No." Camila lifted her hand and stared at her black nails. She turned them back and forth a few times before talking. "It's easy to be an angel in heaven."

"True?" Malcolm shrugged. He had no idea how she'd gone from hot witch almost ready to kiss him to weird thought experiments and discussions of morality.

"I've checked you out," Camila explained, lowering her hand. "You were a smart kid who became a smart adult. You kept your nose clean, and you applied yourself. You've *never* been involved in any trouble. Never even brushed shoulders with anyone who could remotely be called antisocial."

"You did a background check on me?" Malcolm frowned. He wasn't sure that was reasonable. It made vague sense that a woman might want to ensure the quirky guy at work wasn't a secret killer, but his employment with the police department should have implied he had no criminal record.

It was, at minimum, a little insulting.

"I like to know who I'm dealing with, yes. You don't have a lot of friends at the station, I've noticed, despite having a pleasant personality."

"I like to keep to myself." Malcolm shrugged. "It's not a crime. Besides, you've been there long enough to see what's up. The cops mostly hang with other cops. That's just the way it is."

Camila snorted. "But they need us, don't they? It never makes you mad that they get all the glory when we're doing a lot of the work in the background to help prove their cases?"

Malcolm shook his head. "I just want the bad guys in jail, or on a ship to some planet far, far away. I didn't join the department to get a bunch of news stories written about me. I wouldn't even know what to do if I became famous." He tapped a finger on his chest as he thought it out. "It would be kind of annoying."

"Not like Blackwell and Lin, huh?" Camila rolled her eyes. "Two glory hogs—some broken-down old vet wearing a young man's face and a corp princess playing at being a cop. I'm sure they go home and high-five each other after every interview."

Malcolm took a deep breath. He had been ecstatic when Camila asked him out, and he wouldn't deny he was attracted to her style and her normal personality, but it was like the last few minutes had revealed a totally different woman. Now he had a simple choice, one that might end any chance he had of being with her.

"That's not fair," he replied.

"What's not fair?" she asked.

Malcolm frowned. "Detectives Blackwell and Lin aren't like that. They aren't media whores. If you knew them, you'd know they hate that kind of thing. They just want to do their jobs, and they both..." He shook his head. "You just don't know them."

Camila snickered. "Listen to yourself. It's pathetic." She

gestured at him. "They're not even your friends. You know how I can tell? Because you call them by their ranks and last names. You're a fan, nothing more."

"I respect them, and they respect me. That's *all* I need."

Camila locked eyes with him as if she were searching for something. He stared back defiantly. If he had to choose between a sexy witch and his friends, he'd choose his friends.

"So, in summary," she began, "you want a job that lets you help people, but you don't care about money, and you don't resent that people around you get more credit?"

Malcolm nodded. "That's pretty accurate. You can find that pathetic all you want, but I like who I am."

Camila licked her lips. "I'm going to enjoy proving you wrong."

"What are you talking about?"

Camila walked over to him and placed a hand on his shoulder. "I came here tonight to offer you a chance to make a lot of money on the side. I'm still going to offer it to you because I believe in your talent."

"I don't need extra pay if you need help with data analysis in the coroner's office," Malcolm explained, now completely confused.

"Nothing like that. These are private jobs with private pay. They'll just require you to help me with a few little instances of data recovery and manipulation in the department systems." Camila tightened her grip on his shoulder. "If you don't care about money, then you should care about your job and avoiding prison."

"Huh? Camila. I'm lost. I'll admit that's happened a lot tonight."

"There are a lot of people in Neo SoCal who will pay a lot for confidential police data," Camila explained. "And I have contact with them."

Malcolm shook her arm off and glared at her. "Are you serious?" His hand dropped to his PNIU. "You're selling police data?"

Camila shook her head and pointed at his hand. "Don't call anyone. You see, I'm not you, but I'm still pretty good with computers. I've already made changes in the records using your accounts. I'm not giving you any choice. You're going to help me, or I'm going to disappear and leave you to explain yourself to Internal Affairs." She walked back to him and patted him on the shoulder. "But if you're a good boy, you can make a lot of money, and maybe you'll even get a bonus out of it." She winked. "I'll let you sleep on it. Don't do anything stupid. I've got my ways of keeping an eye on you."

Malcolm stood there, his mouth gaping as his sexy but evil witch headed to the door. She opened it and stepped through with a wave.

"Well, crap," he muttered. "I didn't have *that* on my list of worst-case scenarios."

CHAPTER TWENTY-NINE

August 13, 2229, Neo Southern California Metroplex, Police Enforcement Zone 122 Station, Office of Detectives Jia Lin and Erik Blackwell

Jia's eyes glazed over as she perused the columns of numbers—financial data from an old case she was double-checking.

Her open cases had been handled, all minor affairs, and she'd been unable to find any new leads on the Kandarian case.

It only wasn't officially a cold case because of her stubborn refusal and complaints to the captain, but barring a miracle, they would never know who was behind the robbery.

She didn't care that it had been a failed attempt. Corporate espionage might not be as compelling as conspiracies featuring advanced Tin Men, but blood money had a way of corrupting everything around it, the longer it flowed.

Erik was going through data too, but not for a case. It was a vehicle weapons catalog.

She suspected he was trying to figure out the next over-the-top modification for the MX 60. She wasn't sure why he was bothering. He hadn't mentioned finding a new mechanic who would be willing to arm a civilian-class vehicle heavily. Maybe Colonel Adeyemi had people who would do it for him. If he kept this up, eventually the Taxútnta would end up tossing missiles at terrorists.

The office door slid open, and bright pink flamingos assaulted Jia's eyes. She blinked several times before realizing it was just Malcolm's latest broadside against fashion sanity.

She might not like it, but she couldn't deny it was memorable.

The technician looked over his shoulder before closing the door. "Emma could ensure privacy for us, right? Complete privacy."

Emma winked into existence in front of him. "Define privacy, Technician Constantine."

Malcolm swallowed and looked over his shoulder again. He licked his lips. Heavy bags lay under his eyes. "Where you make sure no one can hear us in here and no one is recording anything."

Jia laughed. "Your date couldn't have gone that badly."

"I wish that's all it was," he muttered.

Erik frowned at him, then nodded at Emma.

"Done," Emma declared with a nod. "I would advise making this conversation short to lower the chance of anyone figuring out something is off. I can handle the technological evidence, but I can't do anything if someone interrogates you."

"What's wrong?" Jia asked, closing her data windows. "Now that I think about it, you look—"

"You look like crap," Erik finished. "If you're asking Emma to lock this place down, that means you're worried about someone in the department." He frowned. "If there's a bad cop, let us handle it. Trust us. You're not ready for that kind of thing."

"It's not a bad cop." Malcolm sighed. "But it's a problem in the department." He smiled at Erik. "I was all prepared to use your advice, but it kind of backfired, and now I need your help. It's about Camila."

"Damn," Erik muttered after Malcolm had finished explaining the situation. "Of all the people in the department to pull that kind of stunt, she was not high on the list. I figured maybe one of the holdovers from the old captain would do that kind of thing."

"We have to go to IA," Jia declared. "That's his only way out of it."

Malcolm groaned. "If you go to IA, I'm going to end up on some prison station."

"Why would you? You haven't done anything yet, and she has to be bluffing about setting you up. Think with your brain, not anything lower."

Malcolm shook his head. "I wish she was bluffing, but I know she's not. I got suspicious of that and spent most of the day looking at almost every piece of data I've touched or she's touched recently, looking for alterations or evidence of tampering. There's one small change that I might be able to link to her just by time proximity, but the records make it look like I did the change. It's not even anything important. It just makes it look like I changed some biographic data for no reason, but there could be anything out there. I found other changes that are more suspicious, and I know I didn't make them, but the records say I did. I flagged them for review, citing user error, and those are just the ones I've found. She's worked here for a decent amount of time. If she's been screwing with things from the beginning, who knows what she's changed? Who knows how much evidence she's leaked?"

Jia frowned. "All the more reason to go to IA. You shouldn't give her more time to set you up and screw with police records."

"And how do I prove I'm innocent if I go to IA? It's not like they're going to just take my word for it," Malcolm complained. He ran his hands through his dish-water-blond hair. "That's what I really don't get about this entire situation. The level of skill she'd need to screw with these records and make it look like I did it is damned high, but she's a doctor, not a systems specialist. And if she's that good, why does she need me?" He turned to Erik. "She also made a big point of testing my loyalty to you and Detective Lin. I didn't think about it until later, but you two were the only cops she mentioned by name." He closed his eyes and took a deep breath. "I've never wanted to know the details of the side stuff I've helped you on because I always knew you weren't doing anything shady, but I think it's caught up with me."

Jia sighed. "Erik, he's right. He deserves to know."

Erik nodded. "You sure? Once I tell you, you might have trouble getting to sleep."

"The woman I liked is ready to frame me," Malcolm complained. "I'm already not sleeping well."

"I'm sorry about this, Malcolm. It all goes back to the terrorists who killed my unit on Molino."

Erik revealed to Malcolm the broad overview of the conspiracy, including what they had found and alluding to some of their high-level government help, and the technician paled.

He stumbled over to Erik's desk and braced himself with his arms.

"I think I'm going to be sick," Malcolm muttered.

"Don't be sick on my desk." Erik nodded toward the door. "Do that in the bathroom."

"I thought you were just going to tell me some corporate guy killed your dog and you'd sworn vengeance, and he kept sending assassins after you, and you were planning to go to the Tokyo Metroplex and blow up his headquarters or something," Malcolm replied.

"That's a very elaborate scenario," Jia commented after a moment of silence. "Especially with the dog starting it all."

"It's not any more elaborate than some super-secret cabal co-opting terrorists to send at you." Malcolm scrubbed a hand down his face. "Damn. You guys take trouble to the next level. I always suspected something big, but nothing *that* big."

"There's still a chance that Camila isn't an agent of the conspiracy," Jia observed. "She could just not like Erik and me. But if there's even a small chance she is, we shouldn't go to IA right away. She might lead us to the conspiracy."

Erik nodded. "I agree. She's gotten cocky. I think she must have gotten frustrated, thinking she could seduce or bribe Malcolm. That's left us an opening to turn it around on her."

Malcolm groaned. "Of course, a great woman is only interested in me as part of some evil plot."

"Suck it up for now." Erik gestured at him. "She thinks she's got you by the balls, so that's an advantage we have. When's the next time you're supposed to meet her?"

"She stopped by my office first thing this morning," Malcolm explained. He rolled his eyes. "She gave me this big speech about how much she enjoyed last night and how she wanted to come over again. I couldn't say anything like, 'Hey, remember the part where you threatened me?' but I got the message. She wants to come over and give me marching orders."

Erin grinned. "Then we'll just get there first. She should have been smarter than to mess with you."

CHAPTER THIRTY

Erik stood a short distance away from the closed door to Malcolm's bedroom. He'd already made an unusual sacrifice since the weapon he held was a stun pistol.

Even though he had no problem killing any member of the conspiracy, he needed leads. If Camila was their agent, even unwitting, he and Jia would get useful information out of her.

Jia stood beside Erik, her own stun pistol in her hand. If the meeting went badly, they would need to move quickly to save Malcolm's life.

It wasn't fair that his life might be in danger because he'd helped them investigate.

Emma was transmitting a feed through hacked cameras. They'd followed Camila all the way from her flitter to the elevator and during her stroll down the hall toward Malcolm's apartment. She didn't look tense, worried, or ready to kill a man, but her long black coat offered plenty of places to conceal a weapon. Breaking his neck or strangling him was always a choice, too.

Not to mention poison.

Another feed displayed the situation in Malcolm's empty living room. Erik considered the practical tactical implications of having furniture. If a man didn't want to get assassinated, he at least needed a loveseat to jump behind. For a brief moment, Erik wondered if he should invest in bulletproof furniture. It was only a matter of time before the conspiracy sent their next assassin.

"I'm detecting extremely unusual activity in the camera feeds for this level," Emma commented. "Incredibly sophisticated and well-hidden. I could disrupt the activity, but I doubt I can do it without whoever is involved becoming aware, not in the short time we have available prior to her arrival. There is almost no chance it's not being used to conceal something."

Erik growled. "Damn it." He shoved his stun pistol into a pocket and pulled out his slug-thrower. "That can't be good. It also probably means Camila isn't alone. That changes things."

"Backup," Jia suggested. "In case Malcolm resists."

"That level of sophisticated hacking proves this isn't about helping a few crap gangsters," Erik concluded. "And it's not like they need special muscle to take down Malcolm. The conspiracy pushed too hard. They shouldn't have mentioned our names. It might be a Tin Man with a self-destruct."

Camila knocked on the door. Time was up. They needed to figure out how to handle things.

Jia shook her head at Erik, lowering her voice. Emma amplified it in his ear.

"If we start shooting right away, we'll lose any chance of

finding a new lead. I know how much you want to move forward with the investigation. I'm not saying we let Malcolm get hurt, but let's see how this plays out. If this was just about killing Malcolm, would they really need a second person?"

Erik considered that for a moment before frowning. "They might know we're in here."

Jia's jaw clenched. "Then I suggest we be ready."

Malcolm took a deep breath in the other room and tapped his PNIU to open the door. "Hey, Camila."

Camila strolled in and slapped the access panel to close it. "Before we start talking about anything else, I need your answer. I understand that you'll be uncomfortable with a lot of this, but I wasn't lying. If you cooperate, you'll end up rich. I also think you'll find after you've helped me out a few times that a lot of your guilt will fade. If not, donate a bunch to charity."

Erik no longer trusted their previous plan, but the window for change had been slammed shut the moment Camila entered the apartment.

"No." Malcolm squared his shoulders and lifted his chin. "I'm going to IA first thing tomorrow. The only reason I didn't go today is that I wanted to give you a head start. Despite you being an evil bitch, I still have a thing for you, and I would like to think you're only doing this because you're desperate."

Camila scoffed and folded her arms. "You can't be this stupid. They'll never buy that you're innocent. They'll just think you got burned. You'll do time. And don't you think I know people who could take care of you in prison?"

"I'm giving you this one chance. If you don't want to

run, then surrender right now. I can make sure things go better for you. We can do it through Erik and Jia."

"You have no idea who you're messing with, Malcolm." Camila shook her head and sighed. "I really thought you were smarter than this, but if you're not going to work with me, then I can't have you working with other people."

"Screw the plan," Erik muttered under his breath. He slapped the access panel and charged into the living room, his gun pointed at Camila's head. "Hands up! If you so much as blink in a suspicious manner, I'll put three rounds into you before you finish closing your eyes."

Camila's face twitched. "Touchy."

Jia kept her stun pistol trained on the coroner. "And if you think we don't know about your friend, you're wrong. He can't help you. We tagged him a while ago."

"Already saw through that, huh?" Camila chuckled and raised her hands above her head. "Fine. That makes it easy." She inclined her head toward the door. "Open it. That'll make everything a lot clearer, and you'll both be a lot calmer."

"You think we're complete idiots?" Erik snorted.

"Detective," Emma sent, "the camera manipulation has ended. They were concealing a woman with an athletic build. I'm running facial recognition, but I'm not coming up with any matches. She doesn't appear to be armed, and given her skintight dress, I'm dubious there are many places she could hide a weapon."

Erik frowned and whispered, "If she's a Tin Woman, she might be hiding a weapon internally."

"Thermals check out as human," Emma reported. "But

admittedly, there are many ways to simulate that well enough to deceive the modest cameras in the hall."

Camila looked at Erik and Jia. "Talking to the AI, huh? It's hard to get anything past you two. Add her into the mix and it's downright obnoxious, but just open the door. I don't like the idea of getting shot by accident."

"If your friend starts trouble, you'll get shot on purpose." Erik shook his gun a couple of times for emphasis.

Camila shrugged. "Once you hear what she has to say, I *know* you'll all see things my way."

Jia nodded at Erik and pointed her stun pistol at Camila. He shifted his to cover the door, his heart beating faster.

"Open the door, Malcolm," he ordered.

"This is not how I planned to spend my evening." Malcolm sighed. "What's next? A bomb?"

A quick tap of his PNIU and the door slid open to reveal a blonde woman in a bright yellow dress that looked practically painted on her body. Erik half-wondered if she was wearing anything or just using some sort of sophisticated holographic emitter. Something seemed vaguely familiar about her figure of all things, but her face was a mystery.

The new arrival stepped inside and closed the door. "You don't want to shoot me, Erik."

Erik narrowed his eyes. "Alina?"

The woman nodded. She pulled at her face, yanking off thin putty in several spots, which left her skin uneven and splotchy. "I'm sorry for not bringing you in on this directly.

It would have saved some trouble, but I needed to be sure about a few things."

"Sure about what?" Jia demanded, her hostility plain and upfront.

Alina gestured at Malcolm. "We knew you'd worked with him on occasion, and we needed to ensure he wasn't compromised. You both know what's at stake. It doesn't hurt to double-check."

Erik holstered his gun. Jia did the same, but she looked more annoyed than relieved.

"Who the hell are you?" Malcolm asked. "And what's going on?" He looked at Erik. "She doesn't work for the conspiracy?"

Erik shook his head. "Far from it."

"We don't all become what we hate." The ID agent chuckled. "Agent Alina Koval, Intelligence Directorate."

"ID? That's what you were getting at when you explained everything to me, wasn't it, Detectives?" Malcolm groaned. He backed into a wall and covered his face with his hand. "This is so damned embarrassing. Here I was, first thinking an awesome woman might be into me, and then I have to deal with the humiliation of believing she's about to blackmail me into helping criminals. At least in *that* situation, I could cling to the idea that I was awesome enough that criminals wanted to force me to work for them, but now..." He dropped his hand and looked at Camila. "So, what, you're a ghost, and you were never interested in me?"

Camila averted her eyes, a hint of red on her pale cheeks. "It's not like I set out to screw with you from the beginning, Malcolm. My job was to keep an eye on the troublemaking detectives over there and evaluate the rest of the 1-2-2 for useful assets."

Malcolm scoffed. "So that's what I am? A useful asset?"

"Yes," Camila replied flatly. "But you're still talented and cute in your own way." Her gaze cut to Alina. "And since I can't immediately leave my position at the 1-2-2 without blowing my cover, I don't see a problem with getting to know you better."

"Is this about evaluating my value to the ID or dating?" he asked.

Camila smirked. "A little of both."

Malcolm's expression brightened. "Whoa. Really?"

Erik laughed, his tension leaving with the sound. At least Malcolm was getting something for all his trouble.

Alina gestured toward the bedroom. "I have some things to talk to the two of you about. If you want to tell him later, that's on you, but for now, let's leave them to flirt."

Camila glared at her. Malcolm shrugged with a sheepish grin on his face.

Alina, Erik, and Jia reconvened thirty seconds later in Malcolm's bedroom, the door now closed.

"It's time you stopped messing around with local garbage," began Alina.

"You mean, you want Erik to take the offer?" Jia asked.

Alina nodded. "Both of you, actually. I would settle for him, yes, but you're a package deal if I want maximum efficiency. I might even be able to get Emma in the deal, too. I've got some people working things behind the scenes. If we let certain parties in the DD know you're working for us in some capacity, they'll be willing to leave Emma alone."

Emma appeared and sat on the edge of the bed. "Using me as leverage?"

"Simply pointing out options." Alina frowned. "I don't even see why you two want to stick around in Neo SoCal. Yes, there will always be a crime for you to solve, but going forward, you can potentially help save the entire UTC. And it's not like you'll never do investigations with us."

Erik scoffed. "We're taking down a lot of criminals, sure, but there will always be corruption, and rich assholes who end up corrupt often end up working for people in dangerous conspiracies."

"You two are scaring people. I wouldn't be surprised if all the most dangerous players have already shifted to other areas, if not off-world. The criminals and those above them always move on to softer targets. There's no way you haven't seen it."

"That doesn't mean there isn't work for us to do here," Jia insisted, emphasizing the point by stabbing toward the floor with a finger.

"What is it going to take to convince you?" Alina asked. She gestured at the door. "I brought Camila in because I want to build you a support team you trust and control. I'm serious when I say I want you as contractors and not direct agents. Things would be far different from what you're used to dealing with as cops."

Erik glared at her. She'd fed him useful information, but if she truly wanted him to work for her, she needed to understand that no one could push him around. He'd stopped caring about taking orders the day his unit was slaughtered.

"We'll let you know," Erik told her, his voice almost a growl, "when and *if* it's the right time for us. And don't do this kind of crap again." He pointed toward the living room. "If you're sniffing around us, do us the courtesy of telling us."

Alina scoffed. "Hubris was one of the greatest sins of the ancient world. Always keep that in mind."

"Perhaps you're the one who needs to learn that lesson," Jia retorted.

Alina closed her eyes and took a deep breath. "I'm not here to fight with you. I came to make my feelings clear, but you're both right. I should be earning your trust, not making you suspicious." Resignation settled over her face. "I will have a surprise gift for you in a few days, something I hope will further demonstrate my good intentions. Even if you don't want to take me up on my offer immediately, you might find it useful. It could help you avoid certain problems you've had to deal with lately."

Erik nodded. "I'm not going to turn down anything useful. What's the gift?"

Alina's thin grin almost felt like mockery. "It wouldn't be a surprise if I told you." She headed toward the door. "Don't worry. You'll like it."

"And if I don't?" Erik asked.

"Then it'll just be another in a long line of mistakes I've made handling you," Alina stopped and frowned. "Damn it. I'll need to fix my face before I go."

Erik barely heard her. A surprise? By the sound of it, Alina intended to deliver something physical, not more intelligence. The only thing he couldn't figure out was what she could possibly give him that Colonel Adeyemi hadn't.

A faint grin appeared despite his best efforts to suppress it. He wouldn't mind having some ID toys.

CHAPTER THIRTY-ONE

Aug 26, 2229, Neo Southern California Metroplex, Police Enforcement Zone 122 Station, Office of Detectives Jia Lin and Erik Blackwell

Jia stepped into the office, two piping hot beignets in hand. Her stomach growled at the smell. She'd liked them okay before becoming Erik's partner, but his obsession was beginning to bleed over into her as well. She didn't mind.

There were worse problems to have.

"I know you love the ambiance of different places, but sometimes delivery is where it's at," she offered. "Although, something does vaguely bother me about a drone delivering my beignets, but not other food. I wonder why that is?"

"It's weird," Erik muttered under his breath. He wasn't looking at her. Instead, he was staring at the wall, his eyes narrowed.

Jia looked at Erik, the wall, and the beignets a few times, trying to figure out if this was some weird new game he was playing with Emma. "So, you agree with me? You've never objected to delivery before, the few times we used it at least. I never pressed you on it because I figured most of the time you wanted an excuse to leave the station."

"Not that. Delivery isn't weird. As long as the beignets are from a good place, I don't care how they get to me. And you're right, a lot of the time it's about me leaving the station." Erik chuckled and shook his head. "And it's not my life. I shouldn't worry so much about it."

"Not your life?" Jia closed the door. "What's weird about my life?"

"Not your life, either." Erik shook his head. "Hey, Emma, keep it private for us, will you?"

"Very well, Detective Blackwell," the AI replied. She didn't materialize.

Jia handed Erik a beignet before heading to her desk. She nibbled on it, eyeing her partner, not bothering to try to hide her confusion on her face. "Care to clue me in? Because right now, I'm wondering if I'm having another one of those dreams where I'm about to be given some ridiculous and impossible case to solve."

Erik stared at her. "What dreams? You never mentioned them before."

Jia smiled sheepishly. "They're stupid. Like in one I had recently, I had to somehow prove a Shiba Inu was responsible for assassinating a government official."

His face scrunched for a second. "A dog?" Erik laughed.

"Yes. Somehow the dog was trained to fire a high-powered sniper rifle in the dream." Jia shrugged. "That's one of the least weird ones, but don't turn this around on me. You're the one who's acting strange. What were you mumbling about when I came in?"

Erik tore off a huge chunk of his beignet with one bite, leaving powdered sugar all over the bottom of his face. "Malcom went out on a date with Camila the other night. He mentioned it to me this morning when I went to talk to him about some stuff."

"Really? I know she mentioned it might be okay, but I thought that was just a line she was feeding him." Jia settled into her chair. "She actually likes him?"

"She's a spy. She came on to him to test him originally. You'd think it would be hard to trust her." Erik brushed some of the sugar off. "I suppose there are weirder ways to start a relationship, and he seems to be into her, so it's not my business."

"There are weirder ways, for sure." Jia let her gaze linger on Erik. She didn't think he was leading into anything with that statement, but it was hard to be sure. "I agree. If it works for him, I don't see the problem. He knows what he's getting into, and the big secret's already out. For her, it's an advantage, too. She's lucky."

"How?" He looked at her, puzzled. "She into Hawaiian shirts? Opposites attract, fashion edition?"

Jia laughed. "She can date him without any pressure. He knows the truth, and she knows he can keep his mouth shut. That's got to be worth something, considering how often people can't do that, even for far less important stuff. When you're a person who has to keep secrets about your life, knowing there's someone out there you can be honest with must be a tremendous relief."

She gave him a meaningful look. There was nothing wrong with making the parallels in their life situations more explicit. She didn't want to push it too hard, but she couldn't pass up an obvious opportunity.

Erik chewed the beignet in his mouth, looking faintly confused. He didn't say anything, just continued eating his pastry until he'd polished it off. "And what's up with Alina?"

"What do you mean?" Jia asked, surprised he hadn't said anything about their dating situation. "I don't think she's dating anyone in the 1-2-2. To be honest, maybe I'm trying to read too much into a woman we've dealt with in very limited contexts, but I don't think she's the kind of person who cares about anything as normal as dating."

"Probably not, but I'm not talking about dating. She said she'd have something for us in a few days, and it's been more than that." Erik shrugged. "I guess ghosts have a different definition of time. She should have just said it was going to take a while."

"You're disappointed because you didn't get your toy on schedule?" Jia brought up four data windows. They'd completed an embezzlement case the week before. It'd almost been too easy, with the suspect confessing almost everything the moment they brought him in, but she still had reports to fill out. The wheels of justice would turn as long as they were liberally lubricated by reports.

Erik threw his feet up on his desk. "I don't know. Call me old-fashioned, but when you promise someone something, you should give it to them. Besides, it's messing with my planning. I'm trying to be efficient here."

She pursed her lips. "You're planning something? What does it have to do with Alina's gift?"

"I'm trying to figure out if I should modify the MX 60 more." Erik stared at the ceiling with an almost wistful expression on his face. "If she's going to give me a ghost-mobile with the latest tech, no reason to spend a lot of time and money doing more to my flitter. If she's just talking about a cool new gun, well, I'm not going to complain about that, either. You know me; I like to have options when it comes to taking bastards down."

Jia laughed so hard she accidentally swiped her hand through a data window and closed it.

Erik dropped his feet to the floor and wrinkled his forehead. "It's not that funny."

"It kind of is," she pointed out. "I think getting that laser rifle from the colonel spoiled you." Jia snickered as she brought up a new data window. "Now you're thinking about all the fancy gadgets someone might throw at you."

"Having better gear is useful," Erik argued. "And you didn't seem to mind at the range."

"No, I didn't mind, and I'm not saying it isn't good to have more options. Whatever makes our job easier is fine by me. I'm realistic. We wouldn't have been able to solve or even survive half of what we've done without the help of the equipment we've managed to get our hands on." Jia let out a dark snicker. "You better hope Camila's and Malcolm's new thing doesn't blow up anytime soon. The next thing you know, Camila will be asking Alina to freeze you out, and you'll be reduced to begging to Generous Gao for gifts because you've been a good boy." She put her hands together. "Please, Generous Gao, I need a plasma torpedo small enough to launch from my flitter."

She tittered for a second.

"Very funny," Erik grumped. "But I *have* been a good boy." He scratched his chin. "A plasma torpedo could come in handy."

"For what?" Jia blinked in surprise. "You planning to blow up a ship?"

"You never know. Options, remember?"

Jia considered that and his boyish smile. "You *have* killed a lot of people. He might give you some rotten fruit for that."

"Yeah, but they all had it coming," Erik insisted. "Those assholes at Alicia's place didn't let us land before they started shooting. How can I be docked by Gao if they never even let me say hi?"

"You have a point there," Jia replied. "Maybe Gao has something about massive property destruction?"

Erik snorted. "It hasn't even been that bad for a while, and there's only so much I can do when the other guy is blowing up the building. It's not like I go out of my way to blow up buildings. Most of the time."

"Maybe you'll get your present, after all." Jia shook her head, a smile playing across her lips. "Here's hoping. I can't wait to read the article about the Obsidian Detective launching Navy weapons from his MX 60."

Erik gave her a deep, meaningful look, as if he were shifting from the humor for a brief moment to evaluate something deeper. "What about you? There's nothing Alina could show up with that you might want? I know you wouldn't complain if you got your own laser rifle."

Jia shook her head. "I wouldn't, but you're collecting enough weapons for the both of us. It might be nice to have one of her anti-spying devices as a backup for Emma, especially in situations where she's jammed." She waited for a few seconds, but the AI didn't say anything. "And especially for my apartment. Maybe some sort of disguise device? Who knows what she's got in a box somewhere? She works for the Intelligence Directorate. They don't have to mass-produce the stuff, and it'd be nice to know..."

"Nice to know what?" Erik probed.

"The limits of the possible." Jia grinned. "Maybe the ID has perfected the ultimate beignet. We could use a few of those delivered by some ultra-advanced ghost drones."

"They probably *have* developed those," Erik replied. He leaned forward with an eager look. "That makes me think about something else. We got HTPs from the Navigators, so why not better pastry?"

"Better pastry?" Jia laughed. "The most advanced aliens in the history of the galaxy, and they developed better pastry?"

"Maybe the government scientists found some Navigator recipes and decoded them." Erik winked. "It's not impossible."

"They're slowly perfecting the ultimate pastry in some lab somewhere because the Zitarks and Leems already have a big lead on us." Jia gave a solemn nod that didn't match her mood. "Right now, the Prime Minister is in a hushed meeting with his cabinet, discussing the technological pastry gap we have with the Local Neighborhood races."

"Lizards can't make good pastry," Erik insisted with

mock indignation. "But maybe that was what the Leems were really doing in Roswell—hunting for the secrets of human pastry dominance. They knew we'd grow to be a threat and spread across the galaxy, and they wanted to be ready, those little gray-headed bastards."

"I bet they screwed up and transmitted an apple pie recipe back to their home planet," Jia continued.

A lively warmth suffused her whole body. There was something liberating about such a ridiculously elaborate joke scenario.

She might be attracted to Erik's bravery and skill, but there was something else there, too, something he liked to pretend was just a mask as part of his personal quest. At his core, the man truly did appreciate life. Molino had buried much of that, but she had started to see it emerge in recent months.

Erik shook a finger. "Yeah. Or cherry. They're sitting there on Leem World or whatever the hell they call it, waiting years, and then they finally get it, and they're like, 'You stupid idiots, that's not what we ordered when we sent you for takeout!'"

Jia burst out laughing, doubling at her desk. Erik didn't laugh, but his face-wide grin showed he was as satisfied with the whole joke as she was.

"No, that wasn't the worst part," Jia insisted.

"What was?" Erik asked.

"They forgot to steal the recipe for whipped cream."

"So that's it then." Erik nodded to himself, looking satisfied. "If I wait long enough, Alina will deliver me the perfect Navigator-enhanced beignet, a pastry a million years in the making."

"Let's keep hoping," Jia offered with a smile. "I think we'd appreciate that more than another laser rifle."

"Now that depends on how big a laser rifle we're talking about."

She looked at him, a mischievous glint in her eye. "So, you admit size matters?"

CHAPTER THIRTY-TWO

Erik took a bite of his burger with a frown. "I can't get it out of my head. The taste."

Jia looked around from their table. The diner they had hit for lunch was a place they'd been to plenty of times. It was close to the station, and they gave police discounts. Erik had never had a problem with their food before. He'd commented he thought it was pretty good, especially for the price.

"Maybe there's something wrong with their food printer?" she suggested. "Remember the problem we had at that Greek place a few weeks ago with the olives? I'm surprised we were the only ones complaining."

Erik set his burger down and shook his head. "The food here is fine, but I was thinking about what we were talking about this morning. It's stuck with me."

"Wait, are you talking about the Navigator beignets?" Jia asked, almost shocked that the words were coming out of her mouth in public. It was certainly one of the more bizarre things she'd discussed for an extended period, even as a joke.

"It's not *completely* crazy when you think about it." Erik laughed. "I'm not saying I believe there's a big recipe book out there of the ultimate pastries in the galaxy. I'm just thinking we don't know crap about the Navigators, not even what they looked like. Everyone says they were big, but that's a guess."

"There's not much we can do about that. They've been dead for a long time, and they weren't nice enough to leave us fossils or much in the way of biological remains."

"I know," Erik replied. "But it's kind of messed up when you think about it. We got their antigrav stuff and the HTPs and other gadgets from reverse-engineering, but maybe they have an awesome Beijing Duck recipe or really *can* make great beignets."

"They could have been photosynthetic, for all we know." Jia raised her cup to her lips, now imagining the Navigator as walking sunflowers for whatever odd reason. She chuckled and ended up inhaling some of her coffee.

A few hacking coughs later, she managed to breathe again.

Erik chuckled. "Don't die drinking coffee. I'm sure the media would love it if either of us went down while having lunch. They'd have days of fun with the stupid headlines."

Jia's cheeks heated. That would be the ultimate irony, but she wasn't sure if death by coffee was shameful or a grand way to leave life. She probed the implications for a few moments before a heavy gaze from a brown-haired man in a booth caught her attention.

He was staring right at her. It wasn't the first time she'd caught a man staring at her.

After a moment, Jia realized that he wasn't staring at her, but at Erik. There wasn't any hostility in the man's face, only curiosity, as if he were trying to decide on a course of action.

Jia cleared her throat and leaned closer. "I think you've got a fanboy in the back. We might have to avoid this place for a while if it's going to be a hangout for those types."

Erik looked over his shoulder and locked eyes with the brown-haired man. "Huh. Yeah. Definitely watching me."

"How can a detective be so unsubtle?" Jia chuckled. "You might as well have Emma throw up holographic flares stating, 'I'm watching you.'"

"I've got a gun with four barrels and an expensive sports flitter I modified to carry even heavier weapons around. Subtle is a curse word for me."

She grabbed a French fry and dabbed it in an orange sauce. "You said it, not me."

"It's not like I'm ashamed of it." Erik gave the man a polite nod and waited. "Might as well hurry this along."

The man stood and strolled toward the table. Erik and Jia waited until he arrived. The man's pace didn't suggest any big plans for an ambush.

"You're Detective Erik Blackwell, right?" the man asked. "The Obsidian Detective from the news?"

"Yeah," Erik answered. "That's me. You want a picture or something? Not trying to be an ass, but I don't really have the time for much more than that right now."

"Picture? Why would I..." The man blinked as if confused by the question. "Oh, that makes sense now that I think about it. People would want their pictures with a man who is a paragon of justice. That's not illogical when I analyze it."

"Something like that." Erik shrugged, shooting a look at Jia.

She shrugged back, no longer sure about the man's intentions. There was something off in the cadence of his voice. It reminded her vaguely of the Grayhead terrorists they had interrogated.

"I've read a lot about you," the man explained. He extended his left hand for a shake. "And all your cases. I was moved by how you took on those monsters in the Scar." He shuddered. "It's scary to think about what's happening underneath us and how the police and military are a thin line protecting us from such serious danger, even on Earth."

Erik hesitated for a moment before extending his own left to shake the man's hand. "It's just part of the job. We're police. We're here to serve and protect, whether it's from the two-legged dangers or the six-legged ones with tentacles. I'm not one to ask someone else to risk their lives unless I'm also willing to risk mine."

The man's hand lingered on Erik's for a moment before he pulled it away. "My name is Victor, Detective Blackwell." He offered a tight smile to Jia. "Pleasure to meet both you and Detective Lin. You could say I'm a big fan of what you've done to protect this city. I'm sorry to bother you during lunch, but I just couldn't stop myself from coming over to talk to you."

Jia waited until he looked back at Erik and mouthed, "Told you it was a fanboy."

"Nice to meet you, Victor," Erik offered. "Most of our cases aren't that exotic, just normal criminals. A lot aren't even that violent. The news just hypes those up because it's good for attracting eyeballs. I can't blame them, but that doesn't mean I have to like it, either."

Victor stared at Erik's hand. "It didn't feel any different." He shook his head. "I thought it would. That makes it worse—the pain of expectation."

Jia liked Erik's new friend less with each sentence that came out of his mouth.

"What didn't feel different?" Erik asked.

The other man pointed with his right index finger toward Erik's left arm. "I read a lot of news stories about you. They almost never mention that you're a Tin Man. I wonder if that's because the government is suppressing the truth."

Jia frowned. "It's a war injury, and he's never asked anyone to lie for him."

Erik held up his hand to tell her to back off. She took a deep breath before nodding.

"Yeah," he offered to Victor. "I lost my original arm in Wolf's Rebellion, and the replacement became my lucky arm."

"But you could replace it," Victor insisted. "Easily. It can't be that expensive. I understand it might have been an issue on the frontier, but you're on Earth now."

Erik patted his left forearm. "Did you miss the part where I said it was lucky?"

"You could leave us to our food," Jia suggested. "Erik already told you we don't have a lot of time."

Victor shook his head. "But I didn't know he was a Tin

Man until recently. I was thinking, 'Here's a good pair of detectives. They both understand the importance of maintaining humanity.' Then, finding that out really hurt. It was very disturbing."

Erik chuckled. "Oh, I get it. This is some Purist crap, huh? I should have known from the beginning."

"It's not crap," Victor insisted, his tone now strident. "It's about having proper values in a degraded society, and it makes me wonder about the Rena Winston case, and the dispensations for all the criminals involved in it."

Jia glared at him. "There wasn't a single person involved in that case who got away with anything. The CID is still mopping up some people off-world, but it's a high-profile warning to anyone who even thinks about messing around with illegal genetic engineering."

"No, you're wrong." Victor shook his head, his expression one of disbelief. "That's not true at all. I can't believe how wrong you are."

"How do you figure?" Erik asked. "I know it's confusing and all, but the news articles don't talk about everything involved in these cases. We worked the case, Victor. We know what happened."

"But the changeling wasn't punished," Victor explained, his gaze shifting between the two, filled with a mix of pity and disgust. "Execution for those involved in illegal genetic engineering is common, as it should be to preserve our species."

Jia shot out of her chair so quickly it fell back and clattered on the floor. The diner went silent, everyone looking their way. The servers froze in place, watching with alarm.

"You don't execute a victim," Jia offered, her voice tight. "That's *insane*."

"True purity means making no exceptions," Victor replied. "That *thing* is out there pretending to be human, and our species as a whole is diminished. If you didn't believe that on some level, you wouldn't have gone after the people who made her."

Erik rose from his seat, cracking his knuckles. "So, you think we should have killed a young woman who had no choice in what was done to her? I agree with my partner. That's crazy."

Victor sighed. "I'll admit on reflection that's perhaps too extreme." His face brightened. "It's easy. We could simply set up a colony where they won't pollute the rest of us. A space station, maybe. If the laws are working, as you seem to think, there shouldn't be a lot of them to worry about?"

"Like a leper colony?" Jia snorted in disbelief.

"Why not? We send criminals to colonies all the time." Victor took a moment to turn toward the crowd before refocusing on Jia and Erik. "It's a quarantine of sorts, so yes. It's far more merciful than the alternatives. We must always remember the lessons of the past, or we're doomed to repeat them."

Erik walked up to the man and squared his shoulders, looking down at him with a frown. Even with only a minor difference in height, it felt like the detective towered over the Purist. Victor didn't budge as he stared back.

"Between being a soldier and being a cop," Erik began, "I've seen the worst humanity has to offer. I've seen cowards, murderous insurgents, and terrorists so evil it's hard to believe we're the same species. But I've fought all those twisted assholes because I know there are innocent people out there who need to be protected from the predators who don't feel any pity or remorse." He took another step forward, forcing Victor back. "Innocent people like Rena Winston."

"You can't really believe she's a victim," the other man insisted.

A vicious grin split Erik's face. "Let me make this as clear as I can to you. Get out of my face, and I don't ever want to see you again. And if I ever find the Navigator beignet recipe, you can't have it, either. You don't deserve it."

Victor staggered back a few steps, complete disbelief taking over his face. "Did you just say 'Navigator beignet recipe?'"

Erik grinned. "That's right. I'll call up Rena and offer her one, but you get nothing. Changeling gourmand wins over a Purist. You never thought about it? What the Navigators ate?"

A murmur went through the diner crowd. A few people chuckled.

Victor looked Erik up and down before turning toward the door. "I pity you, Detective. You're far more disappointing than your articles suggest."

"Keep talking, and I'll make you eat some Leem cherry pie," Erik replied. "Word on the street is they don't understand it should have sugar or cherries."

With a final harrumph, Victor hurried toward the door and out of the diner, looking over his shoulder every couple of meters as he rushed away on the parking platform. He muttered the entire way.

Erik settled back at his table. Everyone else took that as a signal to return to their meals and previous conversations.

He shook his head. "Some people, huh?"

"Leem cherry pie might be delicious," Jia joked. "Even without sugar or cherries."

"Maybe." Erik smirked. "I'll let you have a bite if I get my hands on some. Just a bite. Don't know if I want to share that advanced pie tech."

"Stingy with the super-pies. How much of the Navigator beignet do I get?"

Erik pinched his thumb and forefinger together close enough that a thread would have a hard time getting through. "That much, but it's higher quality. I'm being generous here."

Jia rolled her eyes. "I'll remember this, *partner.*"

Erik gave her a merry grin.

CHAPTER THIRTY-THREE

Erik stifled a yawn. A stream of lights floated in front of him, all the flitters becoming the stars among the towers during a typical Neo SoCal night. With the lanes twisting and overlapping but constantly moving, from a distance, it looked like living strands of light engaged in a dance. It was beautiful in its own way. He didn't always appreciate that when he was flying around, but tonight it struck him.

Emma appeared in the passenger's seat. "If you're excessively fatigued, it might make more sense for me to control the MX 60. If you crash and survive, I will be forced to remind you of your failure incessantly."

"I'm good," Erik insisted. "I'm actually more careful when I'm tired, and after that threat, there is no way I'm crashing."

"That's an interesting theory," Emma replied. "Though almost certainly incorrect. I also feel compelled to point out that you're most likely being followed. You might want to take that into consideration."

Erik's hands tightened on the yoke. His gaze shifted

between the various camera feeds and mirrors as he shifted lanes a few times, watching as a flitter not that far back matched his movements.

"This guy doesn't know how to hide it," he muttered. "Probably not a pro, but thanks for the early warning."

"I took the liberty of temporarily borrowing a drone feed," Emma explained. "You'll find this extremely interesting."

An image appeared in the corner of Erik's lenses—a familiar face from earlier that day.

"The asshole from the diner?" Erik asked.

"This pure penguin is one Victor Urie," Emma reported.

"Pure penguin?" Erik snickered. "That doesn't seem all that accurate."

"As if all the armed criminals you kill are literally goblins?"

"You got me there," Erik admitted.

Emma offered a huge eye roll before continuing, "The flitter he's flying is also registered to him unless he's gone out of his way to fake a transponder signal pointing at him. So, there's very little chance this is anyone other than Victor Urie unless someone is putting a lot of time and money into convincing you an annoying man from a diner is spying on you."

"You've got to be kidding me." Erik grunted in frustration, but irritation destroyed any hint of fatigue in his body. "This guy got a record? Assault? Stalking? Anything like that?"

"Interesting question," Emma replied. "Confining myself to public and easily accessible police records so as not to raise suspicion, I found that the man had a minimal presence until a few months ago. He was working in a low-level position at a transport company. He quit and then started showing up at extremist Purist events in the local area. He hasn't been arrested, but he has been ticketed a few times for disturbing the peace. He's always paid his fines promptly. He does currently seem to be unemployed unless one counts his uncompensated protest work."

"I'm going to give him a chance here, but only because I'm feeling generous, and also, I don't want to have to start on any reports tonight." Erik pushed in and twisted the yoke. His flitter broke from the lane and descended. "Find me a quiet place in case this nutjob is more than just talk. If he makes any moves, I'm putting a bullet in his head."

A few seconds later, a navigational marker appeared. Erik maneuvered toward the marker, a brightly lit parking platform coming into view. Emma might not value human life much, but she appreciated that he did.

"Shall I request backup?" Emma asked.

Erik scoffed. "This amateur isn't even trying to hide things, which means if you hadn't told me, I would have noticed him soon enough. If he was going to make a move, he would have done it already. I think this is about a guy who wants to hear himself talk, and I've got a plan to deal with that. He just wants to do it somewhere without an audience."

"Does your plan involve high-velocity bullets being introduced to vital organs?" Emma asked.

"No, that's Plan B."

Erik continued toward the platform, decelerating and checking every few seconds to ensure Victor was still tailing him. The bastard was as persistent as he was clumsy, but he also didn't seem to be in a hurry. A man didn't need a weapon for an aerial collision, as hard as it was to pull off with proximity alarms and emergency thrusters. If he was going to try to kill Erik, it almost certainly would occur on the platform.

"This is one downside to fame," Erik muttered as he brought the MX 60 down on the far end of the platform away from any other flitters. For some reason, Jia's property destruction joke popped into his mind. All he'd been doing was trying to go home. Victor Urie was the one who'd decided that would make things too easy in Erik's life.

The detective threw open the door and stepped outside. A warm breeze blew past his face. It would be a pleasant night if an extremist Purist wasn't following him.

"Not going to get your TR-7?" Emma asked, sounding surprised.

"If anything happens, I'll enjoy it more if it involves me punching him with my cybernetic arm," Erik admitted. "It'll be all poetic."

"I can understand the appeal."

Erik folded his arms over his chest and leaned against his flitter, waiting with the most bored look he could manage. It didn't take long for Victor's flitter to descend about ten meters away from Erik and land. Victor opened the door and slowly stepped out, no obvious weapons on him other than the hatred on his face, his hands hanging loosely at his sides.

"Need something?" Erik called to him. "You put in all that effort to follow me, so I figured I'd reward you with a little one-on-one."

"You knew I was following you?" Victor licked his lips. "I thought I was careful."

Erik laughed. "You read about me, and you thought you could follow without me finding out?"

"I'll admit to having underestimated you."

"I've had everything from criminals to terrorists come at me. It's going to take something more than an unemployed Purist extremist to get the drop on me." Erik shrugged. "So, what's your deal? You want to spit in my face? It's not going to change anything."

Victor shook his head. "You don't understand. I pity you because you're…not even human anymore. It's extra pathetic because it was a choice. That's one problem, but the real problem is Rena Winston's existence. I thought perhaps if I spoke with you without your partner around, that would help you see reason."

"Oh, we're back to that?" Erik snorted. "Give it up, asshole. I like her more than I like your pure ass."

"You don't understand!" Victor yelled. "She's just a symbol! Her existence is proof that vile ideologies are leaking back into the mainstream. Protests and social pressure can only accomplish so much. You're a police officer; you're supposed to stop this sort of thing. Don't you understand that?"

Erik scratched his eyebrow. "I thought we laid this out for you at lunch. Rena Winston committed no crimes. I don't know what they teach you in Purist protest school, but none of the major Purist associations or organizations said crap about wanting her punished. That makes you an over-the-line crazy idiot, not a brave Purist truthteller."

Victor's nostrils flared. "The other groups have been

co-opted by those who have given up on preserving our purity. Our protectors are Tin Man abominations, and our entertainers are changelings? What hope is there in such a world?"

"That's all you got?" Erik shook his head. "I'm disappointed." He pointed his left thumb toward his chest. "I've dealt with a lot of terrorists, both as a cop and as a soldier. I've had a lot of them rant at me, too. You're pathetic, Victor. They have all sorts of arguments, stats and crap like that, and all you have is tired lines somebody probably fed you." He lowered his hand. "I know your kind."

"What do you think you know, Tin Man?"

Erik stepped away from his flitter. "You were living an unfulfilling life. Corporate drone, but hated it. You got up every day asking yourself what you were doing and why. You spent a lot of time admiring people who did something you considered exciting, probably military and cops, mostly, but maybe even some frontier colonists." He took a step toward Victor. "You're a coward at heart, but some Purist extremist somewhere got your ear and fed you a line about how it's not your fault that you ended up that way, it's society's. Tin Men. Changelings. Everyone's at fault for the fact that you are pathetic except you. How am I doing, close or dead-on?"

Victor's jaw clenched. His eyes filled with rage when Erik punctuated his monologue with a mocking grin.

"You arrogant abomination," Victor shouted. "How dare you talk to me that way? I'm a real human being, not a twisted monster like you or Rena Winston! You're everything that's wrong with the United Terran Confederation, Erik Blackwell."

Erik snickered. "Did I hurt your *real* human feelings? Maybe you should get a few replacement parts to help with that." He patted his arm. "I'd send you to the guy who put this arm on me, but he's not in this system." His gaze lowered to Victor's crotch, and he grunted. "But I'm sure there are locals who could help you replace a few things you're probably missing. I'm sure even a Purist woman won't complain about *that* modification."

"You think you're brave, don't you? Because you're a cop and a retired soldier." Victor's eyes bulged out of his head. "You don't know what true sacrifice is. You've only played at it throughout your entire career."

"Yeah, the vet with thirty years doesn't know about sacrifice, but the random purist does?" Erik shrugged. "I'd say let's agree to disagree, but let me put it another way. You think you're a tough guy because of a few protests? I don't care. I don't even care about your stupid beliefs, but if you know what's good for you, you'll stay away from me before you end up hurt. Because compared to some *yaoguai* or real-deal Tin Men, the kind I've fought and killed, you might as well be a puppy. You *don't* want to piss me off."

Victor threw his head back and laughed. He started pressing the tip of his left thumb against his other fingers. "I'll show you. They chose me because they know I was meant for something more. Your arrogance ends tonight, Erik Blackwell."

"My sensors indicate an unusual surge of energy in several bands coming from inside his left arm," Emma reported.

Victor lowered his head. "Justice is served by those

willing to sacrifice." He lifted his head, his hateful gaze fixed on Erik. He sprinted toward Erik, head down.

Erik whipped out his slug-thrower and turned off the safety. He blew out both of the man's knees with quick, single shots. Victor tumbled forward, hissing in pain.

"No!" Victor bellowed as he face-planted.

"Yes." Erik holstered his pistol. "Nice try. I'll give it three out of ten."

A massive explosion blew Victor apart and flipped his flitter onto its side, leaving scorch marks along with a few sparking and burning grav emitters. The force of the explosion launched Erik into the air. He slammed into the side of the MX 60, pain spiking through his back, and he slumped to the platform as he took quick, ragged breaths.

"Shall I request emergency services?" Emma asked cheerfully.

"Yeah. Somebody's got to handle the half-burning flitter, and it wouldn't kill me to get double-checked." Erik stared at the blackened spot on the platform where Victor used to be. "Well, shit. I'll admit I didn't expect that."

"You didn't?" Emma replied. "You took him out right away. You obviously expected it."

"Once you told me you detected the power surge, I knew, but not before. You don't spend thirty years on the frontier without the occasional crazy-ass terrorist or insurrectionist bomber coming at you." Erik grunted and forced himself to his feet. He put a hand on his back, wincing at the pain. "But I didn't expect that guy to go that far. He didn't seem like the type."

"He didn't seem like he was the type?" Emma snickered. "It's difficult for you to go a whole two-week period without coming under fire. If you look at averages, it's even more extreme. Based on your initial time on the force, attacks every other day wouldn't be out of line."

"Getting shot at isn't the same as someone using a high explosive around you," Erik insisted.

"You mean, like someone firing an entire missile at a hotel floor to kill you?" Emma replied. "Numerous incidental contacts with gun goblins seeking your death, many arising from otherwise unexpected escalations in routine police work, multiple targeted assassination attempts cloaked in terrorism, including missiles and Tin Men. Yaoguai, drone swarms, Lunar terrorists. If I approach this from a more quantitative manner, I estimate that—"

"Okay," Erik interrupted, putting up a hand with a grimace. "I get it. People like to try to kill me." He turned and reached into his glove compartment to snag a medpatch. "They usually don't purposefully blow themselves up to do it. That was unusual, even by the standards of my life."

Emma scoffed. "We'll see how the rest of the week goes."

CHAPTER THIRTY-FOUR

Aug 27, 2229, Neo Southern California Metroplex, Residential Tower 231

Jia stepped in front of Erik as they exited an elevator. He stopped and eyed her expectantly. She didn't want to have to do it, but she needed to make sure her partner was okay.

"Are you sure you're up to this?" she asked with a sigh.

"That's the third time you've asked me this morning," Erik noted. "It's not like my answer is going to change. I'm fine. I even wasted time going to the hospital, and they cleared me. I've gotten a good night's sleep and several beignets in me since then. They might not have been made from Navigator recipes, but they're doing a good job of filling my stomach and fueling our interrogations."

Jia frowned. "But you were almost blown up. Joking about pastry is more of a before-you- nearly-get-blown up thing."

Erik nodded. "Yeah, but it's not what you just said. You

said I was *nearly* blown up. Getting blown up isn't like getting pregnant."

"What?" Jia's brow furrowed in confusion. "What does pregnancy have to do with this?"

"There's no such thing as being half-pregnant." Erik stepped around her. "The background checks suggest the brother's clean, but he has paid a few fines for Victor in the past."

"It might have been better if you'd brought him into the station," Emma suggested. "I could have flown near his flitter for better sensor potential. That might cut down on potential surprises."

Erik continued down the hallway so quickly his duster flared open. "It's fine. If this guy was a terrorist suicide bomber, he wouldn't be waiting patiently in his apartment after working a half-day at his job. No one's that calm, collected, and patient."

"If you get me blown up, I'm coming back to haunt you," Jia insisted.

"The afterlife's most uptight ghost." Erik smirked. "That would almost be entertaining."

"I should figure out a way to haunt you now." She looked down a branching hall, checking for hidden purists.

"You do that."

The detectives walked past several doors before they arrived at their destination, the apartment of Benjamin Urie, the older brother of the deceased suspect. Erik didn't waste any time knocking loudly.

"NSCPD," Erik yelled.

Jia shook her head. Most men might reflect in terror

after such a brush with death, but Erik treated the bombing like it was a mere inconvenience. He'd admitted to being more worried about the MX 60 being damaged than himself. Sometimes his bravery and dedication left him blind to the fact that in the end, he was still mortal. He needed someone to have his back—someone like her.

That was what it meant to be a partner.

The door slid open, revealing Benjamin. The family resemblance was obvious, even if Benjamin carried a few extra kilos and a palpable sense of weariness that didn't match the manic energy of his insane if brave brother. At least Jia didn't want to shoot him right away, but she'd brought both her guns if either was necessary.

"Good afternoon, Detectives." Benjamin gestured inside toward a small table in his dining room. A few stools stood around it. "Please take a seat. Can I get you anything to drink?" He headed toward the kitchen.

Erik and Jia shook their heads as they made their way to the table. There was nothing noteworthy about the apartment with its pleasant midrange furniture and banal holographic landscape paintings.

Benjamin stopped, eyeing the kitchen for a moment before settling onto a stool with a look of resignation. "If I were a police officer, I think I'd have to drink something strong every day."

"We'll try not to take up too much of your time, Mr. Urie," Jia began. "First of all, let me say we appreciate your willingness to talk to us right after such a horrific event. Our condolences on your los—"

"Don't bother with that," Benjamin interrupted with a

snort. "We both know my brother was an insane psycho who killed himself trying to murder one of the top cops in the city. I always worried he'd get in some sort of serious trouble, but I thought the idiot would at least have the decency to get arrested for assault before moving on to terrorism and murder."

Jia nodded slowly and sat on a stool, her partner behind her. "So, you were aware of his extremist beliefs?"

"Aware?" Benjamin rolled his eyes. "How could I not be? He's never shut the hell up about them. The sacrifice for humanity! The degeneration of our pure stock! Everything was fine before he quit his job a few months ago. It was obnoxious, but at least it was manageable." He shook his head. "He was always more into Purism than I was, but it was just like everyone else. Then he quit his job, saying he wasn't doing enough to protect humanity. I thought he meant he was going to join the military, but instead, he started sniffing around for something more hardcore in Purism. I told him to stop. I insisted."

"Because you were worried about him hurting someone?" Jia asked.

Benjamin shook his head. "I was worried about him getting a bunch of permanent antisocial marks in his records that he couldn't come back from without leaving Earth. I figured he would snap out of this idiocy eventually. For one thing, his savings weren't going to last him forever. It's all fun to play revolutionary when you have the rent money, but he was running out of credits. I thought it was only a matter of time before reality crashed down around him."

Erik remained standing. "How did you know he was running out of money? Did he say something?"

"He needed me to pay his stupid fines." Benjamin groaned as if he were in pain. "I'm not into weird genetically engineered freaks any more than the next guy, but all he would do was rant and rave about all this weird crap he read on the net. I kept telling him, 'Those idiots obviously don't have jobs if they can write about this stuff all day. Worry about saving yourself before you try to save the species.'"

"I see," Jia replied. Benjamin's statement matched the evidence they'd collected earlier in the day. Victor's bank accounts had been rapidly depleted since quitting his job. Malcolm was in the process of examining all of his accounts for additional clues, but he needed more than a few hours.

"A man doesn't implant a nearly undetectable bomb in himself without help," Erik commented. "Do you know of any friends or compatriots who might be sympathetic to his views?"

Benjamin sighed and shook his head. "Look, Detectives, I would love to help you find whoever turned my brother from quirky irritant to insane zealot. I suspected he'd fallen in with a hardcore Purist cult in the last month or so, but he would never tell me anything because I wouldn't agree to his statement of crazy principles. He said I was questionable. His own brother!" He threw up his hands. "But what could I do? Purist cults are everywhere these days. At least they aren't as crazy as Grayheads. I'm not saying they're okay, but Purism is all about elevating humanity. Grayheads *hate* humanity."

"Both groups have tried to blow me up," Erik offered. "I really don't care about the ideology of the terrorists trying to kill me. It could be the Kitten Defense Brigade, and I'd still take them down."

The other man averted his eyes. "Sorry, Detective. I just don't get it. My brother was a pain, but it's only halfway his fault. If there weren't so many Purist cults around, he might have come back from it. I feel like this was just bad timing."

"It's not surprising," Jia mused. "The Rena Winston case has acted as a flashpoint. Certain ideological extremist groups are attempting to take advantage of it to grow their organizations, but anything you could give us might be helpful. There could be others out there who are being swayed to dangerous and antisocial acts, or even the people who convinced your brother that trying to kill my partner was a good idea."

His eyes widened. "I remember! The Friends of Purity." He bobbed his head, but it took a moment before his focus was back on the detectives. "That was what he called his group. I never met any of them. I wasn't even sure they were real because I never saw any news articles about them. He'd always point me to these net videos, but I thought they looked fake. I mean, how could they be some big, impressive group if they weren't on the news? It's not like the media would suppress news of terrorists."

"Thank you, Mr. Urie." Jia stood. "That should prove useful. Don't worry about the media. We'll handle them."

"If there's any other way I can be of assistance, please let me know." Benjamin stared at the floor. "I apologize on behalf of my family for my brother's actions, and I'm sorry you had to go through that, Detective Blackwell."

Erik shook his head, his thoughts a few decades in the past. "Don't bother apologizing. I know brothers can't always control brothers. We'll let you know if we need anything else."

CHAPTER THIRTY-FIVE

Erik stepped into his apartment, his neck stiff.

It'd been a long day of interviews, and Malcolm was pulling overtime going through data and systems. While it might help to utilize Emma more directly, the detectives wanted to minimize the risk of tainting the evidence with bad procedure since it was an official police case.

There was something deeply unsatisfying about an attempted murder case that began with the suspect killing himself.

"Anyone in here, Emma?" he asked, his hand drifting to his gun. "I'm tired and not in the mood for a fight."

She appeared on Erik's couch, kneeling in the center. "I might have a good appreciation for your tactical capabilities, but I also understand that it doesn't hurt to provide you useful intelligence before you get shot or blown up. If there was an assassin here, don't you think I would have told you ahead of time?"

"Depends on your mood." Erik lowered his hand. "But

Victor wasn't exactly a pro, so I doubt they're hiding here with advanced camouflage tech."

"Does the attack worry you? I must admit you seemed surprisingly unfazed, considering how close to death you came the other night. It wasn't like one of your gunfights. It came out of nowhere."

"A lot of attempts on my life do," Erik pointed out as he emptied his pockets, placing the contents on his bar. "The Lady's not going to take me out that cheaply. She still has to toy with me first. I've learned that the hard way."

Emma raised a curious eyebrow. "I didn't realize you were so fatalistic. Is that what fuels your bravery?"

"Nope." Erik pulled off his duster and hung it up before heading over to his chair. "I think the Lady responds to those who take proper precautions. It's nothing more than that."

"Isn't that just another way of saying fortune favors the prepared?"

"Pretty much."

Emma smirked. "And isn't that, in turn, just another way of saying luck isn't real?"

"Oh, Luck's real. She's a real bitch, ready to get you the minute you're not prepared." Erik leaned his back in his chair. "The trick is to cut down the opportunities the Lady has to screw with you. She might toss the obstacle in front of you, but you can survive it."

His PNIU chimed with a call. When he tapped the caller ID, he grunted in surprise.

"Damien?" Erik answered. "Something wrong? It's pretty late for you to be calling me. I was going to give you a call a few days ago, but I got caught up in some recent casework."

"Is something wrong?" His brother scoffed on the other end. "Of course, there is. According to the news, you nearly got blown up. I was expecting you to call, but then you didn't, so I wondered if they were covering it up and it was worse than that. Somehow you dying in an explosion didn't seem impossible."

"Is that all?" Erik laughed. "Come on. You've heard about everything I'm involved in. As a friend recently pointed out, people try to kill me on a regular basis. Any death you can walk away from is obviously not permanent." He paused for a moment, then shrugged. "Well, you know what I mean."

"This was all far easier when I didn't care about you," Damien griped. "I'm proud of what you've accomplished, but also terrified by the risks you take."

"I'm fine. Really. We're doing some follow-up investigation work involving the bomber. We'll make sure that if he has any friends, they won't try the same thing against me or anyone else. And don't worry. I'm being extra cautious. You should know by now that I'm too stubborn to let anyone kill me so easily."

"I don't envy you your job," Damien admitted. "I'd tell you to quit, but I lost that right a long time ago."

"I do appreciate you calling." Erik chuckled. "I'll try to contact you after close calls in the future so you know I'm still alive. If we get lucky, I'll never need to cause you to worry about it."

"That's all I'm asking. We don't have much family left. It's all the more important to cherish it."

Erik smiled. "Yeah, you've got a point. Don't worry, this won't be the case that ends me."

CHAPTER THIRTY-SIX

August 28, 2229, Neo Southern California Metroplex, Police Enforcement Zone 122 Station, Office of Technician Malcolm Constantine

Camila leaned over Malcolm's desk, her head poking through a data display. "But you promised, Malcolm." Her voice was low and husky.

She licked her lips.

Erik and Jia stood near the door, waiting patiently. They'd arrived about a minute prior, only to encounter the spectacle of Camila flirting with Malcolm. It was still hard for Erik to adjust to a known spy wandering around the department, even if she was on his side.

But the stupid grin on Malcolm's voice proved he was into her despite her deception. He would never claim he could read a woman's mind, let alone a woman who worked for the Intelligence Directorate, but everything from her body language to her voice suggested she *was* into Malcolm.

Jia cleared her throat, letting her annoyance be clear.

"We need to discuss the case. You can go find a closet later and practice your anatomy."

Erik snickered.

Malcolm reddened and looked up. "S-sorry, Detective Lin."

Camila stood, a faint smile on her face. "That doesn't sound like a half-bad idea, but you're right." She stuck her hands in pockets and headed toward the door before stopping. "There wasn't enough left of the suspect to confirm much of anything other than his identity in my initial analysis." She shrugged. "That's all I have for now. I'm coordinating with others to finish the bomb analysis, but that'll take more time. No one wants to send you on a wild goose chase."

"Don't worry," Erik replied. "I'm sure there will be a few more bodies and bombs before this is all over."

"I don't doubt that." Camila exited the room with a chuckle.

Jia didn't speak again until the door closed. "Your message said you had something important, so give us something useful. This was targeted at Erik, but that could be for a number of reasons." She glanced over her shoulder at the door, her lips pressed into a thin line.

Malcolm pointed to the data screen Camila had been wearing like a necklace earlier. "I've pulled out and decrypted all sorts of messages from the suspect to other members of his group. From what I can tell, there are two layers of membership. Most of them are just activists who go to protests, but there's an inner group that only refers to each other using weird code names. There's nothing concrete that proves they were planning a terrorist action or assassination, but there's so much code and random flowery poetry references, it's hard to tell. I mean, maybe 'the sad crane skims the water' means 'Kill Detective Blackwell.'" He shrugged.

"I'm more of an angry eagle," Erik suggested.

"Happy pelican," Jia countered.

"Now that's just mean." Erik chuckled. "What else you got, Malcolm?"

"For the most part, these people are really, really, *really* passionate about purity," Malcolm explained. "There are other encrypted messages that are surprisingly sophisticated. I'm still working on getting into those."

"Is this a matter of if or when?"

"When." Malcolm bobbed his head. "I've got this, Detective. These guys don't know who they're facing."

Jia frowned. "But you're telling us you still have nothing at the moment."

"No, no, no." Malcolm waved his hands. "I've got all sorts of stuff, just no direct evidence these other people knew what Victor was up to." He swiped away several data windows until only one remained, showing a few lines of text. "But a little creative filtering and location-tracing have produced this." He gestured at the window. "Three locations in Neo SoCal. The occupants don't have police records or even fines, but they all have been associated with Purist activism in the past."

"Guess they decided to up their game," Erik mused.

The detectives exchanged glances.

"This isn't enough evidence for a raid," Erik concluded, "but enough to stop by and ask questions. It might have been that Victor decided to go off and escalate their crusade by himself. Even if they think it's okay to go after people, they might realize it's a bad idea to go after a cop. If one of them folds, they can tell us what all the coded poetry crap means."

"We should pay them a visit in person," Jia suggested. "It'll add more pressure and remind them that we can find them. They've got to be nervous after what happened with Victor, one way or another."

Erik spun toward the door with a grunt. "Send us the addresses, Malcolm. We've got interviews to conduct."

The detectives tromped down the narrow hallway leading to the first location on the list, an apartment owned by one Helena Cortez.

Erik had changed the color of the MX 60 to an unassuming gray and parked at the far end of the visitor's platform. Their police status granted them access to the building without trouble.

They didn't run into anyone upon entry, in the elevator, or in the halls leading to the apartment, which further simplified the visit.

"We don't have enough evidence for raids, but we have enough to be suspicious," Erik commented.

"What if she tries to blow us up?" Jia asked. "We're too far from your flitter for Emma's sensors to help us. How will we even know if she's about to try?"

"We've got walls to hide behind this time," Erik suggested. "If they were ready for another attack right away, I think they would have sent them all after me at once, or other targets, assuming I'm not the only one. I'm not saying it's impossible, but they had no way to know where we were heading next, and I can't imagine that every last one of them has a bomb ready."

Jia looked around before leaning closer to whisper to her partner, "You think this could be the conspiracy? No one attempted to bomb me. That might explain it."

Erik looked around the hall. "Maybe, but it doesn't feel right." He thought for a moment. "It's hard when so many different people want to kill you."

Jia nodded. "I suppose you're right. The conspiracy has gotten more sophisticated, even when using proxies, but this clumsy amateur coming after you and failing, then leaving a trail, feels like… I don't know."

Erik chuckled. "Regular old crime?"

She nodded slowly. "That's it. Sometimes I have to remind myself that everything isn't connected, and most of what we do is just cleaning up after people who got greedy or stupid for totally normal reasons."

Erik turned away from Jia as they closed on Cortez's door. His hand shot to his gun. A bloody handprint covered the access panel.

"Not an auspicious start to our interviews." Jia tapped her PNIU. "Miss Cortez, this is the NSCPD. Are you in distress?"

"Emma," Erik murmured, "any recent calls going into nearby emergency services mention this address?"

"No, Detective," Emma replied. "There are no emergency services or police units being dispatched to anywhere close in this area. Should I hack the local camera grid?"

"Not yet. Don't want to leave a trail of our own, and we don't know what's happening yet."

Jia pounded on the door. "Miss Cortez, this is the NSCPD," she yelled. "Please open your door immediately."

Erik drew his gun. "It's a damned bloody handprint on the door of a place connected to an attempted murder of a police officer. I'm sure they have a picture of this in some book explaining probable cause. Emma, prepare to send the police override on my signal."

Jia yanked out her stun pistol and pointed it forward and down. "I hope this doesn't end with an explosion."

"With our luck, I'd give it fifty-fifty." Erik took a deep breath. "Emma, do it."

The door slid open.

"NSCPD!" Erik shouted. "On the floor, hands on your head."

A trail of fresh bloodstains led from the front door into the living room. A small table had been overturned, but the other furniture was undamaged, including a long white couch that had escaped any blood.

That was odd.

Erik and Jia rushed into the apartment, sweeping their weapons in opposite directions for targets. They crept toward either side of the couch, jerking behind it at the same time.

There was no one hiding there.

"The hell?" Erik whispered.

Erik inclined his head toward the blood trail leading into the bedroom. The detectives continued toward the door, where Erik took up position on the side, keeping his breathing shallow. Jia reached out to touch the access panel. Unlike the front door, there was no bloodstain.

The door slid open, and Erik pointed his weapon. Helena Cortez lay on her back on top of her unmade bed. Blood soaked the sheets, and there was a small gray knife sticking out of her heart.

"Emma?" Erik asked, circling the bed toward Helena. Assuming she was dead might end with a surprise attack. A man could never know when a suspect might be a deadly cyborg or a genetically engineered monster not stopped by the small inconvenience of a knife to the heart.

"No cardiac activity detected," Emma reported. "But since you moved closer, her PNIU is now transmitting an emergency message."

Jia frowned and spun. There was no surprise attacker. She licked her lips, her eyes darting back and forth.

"Play the message," Erik ordered.

A standing hologram of Helena Cortez appeared near the bed, grimacing and breathing hard. The knife was in her chest. Her arms hung loosely from her side.

"If you're seeing this, I'm already dead," Helena's hologram explained, her voice shaking. "I thought about doing things a less painful way, but I figured I should face my end with some sort of bravery. I wanted to show the Inner Friends I wasn't afraid, and that I wasn't refusing because I'm a coward. Know that I died for the cause of protecting humanity's purity, but I didn't want to sacrifice my morals. I wish I could have been brave like Victor, but I couldn't bring myself to do what he did. There's too much chance I might hurt someone innocent, and then we'd be no better than the people we're fighting against. I don't care what the

Inner Friends say, there has to be a better way of doing things than becoming killers and terrorists. Even Tin Men can be saved." She coughed up blood. "I don't have much time now. I know someone will find me soon."

The hologram vanished.

"Damn it." Erik holstered his gun. "We're too late. I wonder if the entire group is dead already."

Jia shook her head. "Emma, contact Dispatch and have them send officers to the third location. We'll check on the second. Even if Helena Cortez decided to take herself out, that doesn't mean others did." She ran toward the front door. "And have them send officers over here to secure this scene."

"I was wrong." Erik jogged after his partner. "It smells like Victor was just the first wave. There are more of these bastards out there."

"That's what I'm worried about." Jia entered the hallway. "You were attacked by one man. If these Inner Friends are commanding their followers to commit acts of violence, where's the rest of it? They might be approaching targets at this very moment, but we can't put all of Neo SoCal on alert and tell them to be suspicious of everybody. Plus, we only have these three addresses, not a complete list of everyone in the group."

"Close the door, Emma." Erik sped up, his heavy boots thudding hard on the floor as he ran down the hallway. "I think we still have an advantage. Victor screwed up. We might have messed up their entire plan."

"Killing one cop, even you, isn't going to make or break an entire terrorist attack."

"Depends on what the overall plan for the attack is."

Erik shook his head. "The problem is we just don't know yet. Let's hope we still have someone breathing we can interrogate at the next place. Emma, get us some patrol units as backup."

"And if we don't find anything but another body?" Jia asked.

"There are worse things in the galaxy than a bunch of wannabe terrorists who took themselves out before pulling off their attack."

CHAPTER THIRTY-SEVEN

Erik scoffed as they descended toward the front parking platform at the second address.

Unlike the modest apartment of Helena Cortez, this was a detached single-story home that joined others in a luxury residential level composed entirely of similar lots.

While it wasn't a mansion, it was nestled in an expansive lawn, with a few trees scattered here and there. A high, elaborate hedge maze blocked most of the front.

Several patrol flitters trailed behind the MX 60, a police show of force. Being able to depend on the rest of the department made things much easier. Erik and Jia had come a long way since their first case together.

"I'm detecting multiple people in the maze," Emma reported. "They appear to be armed."

"And not lying down?" Jia confirmed. "They might have shot themselves."

"No, they all appear to be crouching, and actively shifting position, subtly."

"They must have known we checked the other place, or we got lucky," Erik suggested.

Jia looked his way with a confused expression. "Isn't this more like being unlucky?"

Erik grinned. "Nope. It means we'll have to check fewer places."

"Incoming lucky gunfire," Emma reported.

Erik shoved the yoke forward, and the MX 60 dove toward the platform. Bullets bounced off the side of the flitter as volleys erupted from the hedge maze, riddling the descending patrol flitters. One vehicle's grav emitters sparked.

"Damn it." Erik gritted his teeth. "All other flitters back off until we neutralize the shooters," he ordered and shook his head. "I forget they can't take everything we can."

The other police vehicles peeled away under fire. A few more took rounds, but all were able to maintain altitude despite the damage.

The MX 60 settled on the platform. Bullets ripped from the maze and slammed into it, a near-constant drumbeat against the side of the flitter. The extremists were putting up a fight.

Jia reached into the back to retrieve their vests, an annoyed look on her face as she handed Erik his. "These idiots have to realize that even if they manage to take down a flitter or two, that's not going to save them from the police. Shooting at multiple officers guarantees they're going to be in major trouble."

"Fanatics never know when to quit." Erik took his vest. "That's what makes them fanatics."

"So I've noticed." Jia finished donning her vest and

leaned over to recover the TR-7 from its storage compartment. She looked up as if she were choosing between duck or chicken. "Unless you prefer something larger for tonight's engagement?"

Erik grabbed the rifle and shook his head. "We need to take some of these guys alive. There's more of a chance if I use this on single-barrel mode versus blasting them with the laser rifle."

Jia reached into a compartment in the back and recovered a couple of stun grenades. "These might be handy."

"Not as fun, but yeah."

The Purists in the maze didn't cease fire. They continued to blast away at the MX 60. The attacks had ripped patchy holes through the plants, revealing the locations of some of the shooters, but others were managing to fire with only a momentary rustle and flash.

Erik didn't mind. They weren't hurting him, and the same porousness that was allowing them to fire without trouble would mean they could take bullets in the counterattack.

"Launch some drones, Emma," Erik ordered. "Between the drones and the sensors, we might be able to take a lot of these bastards alive."

The trunk popped open. With a whir and a hum, most of the surviving small drones Erik had purchased on the moon emerged as a squadron. Purist gunfire shredded a couple before they escaped into the sky. The rest scattered, jinking back and forth under Emma's control and surviving the initial fusillade.

Erik finished retrieving magazines before opening his door and hopping out. "You better come out this way, Jia."

Bullets bounced off the reinforced passenger-side window as if to reinforce his point.

"I know we need to take some alive, but they're making it really, really annoying," Jia complained as she crawled into the driver's seat.

"Yeah, psycho extremists are like that." Erik slapped a fresh magazine in and selected single-fire mode. "Emma, set us up for victory."

The drones spread out, making it even easier for them to dodge with erratic changes in direction and altitude. Several clear target silhouettes appeared in Jia's lenses, and she took a deep breath before climbing out and sidling toward the back of the MX 60. Additional silhouettes popped up in the house.

Red and blue lights flashed from the police flitters circling the area, all of which were staying out of the effective range of the suspects' weapons. Jia frowned. The police department might have accepted they needed to fight corruption, but other than the TPST units, no one bothered with the basic equipment they might need in serious encounters. It was like the entire NSCPD still wanted to pretend on some level that deadly criminals were rare. Perhaps they were compared to a year ago, but that didn't keep the officers any safer.

"A half-dozen targets in the maze," Jia considered, "and more in the house."

"We can't wait for TPST," Erik insisted. "Some of these freaks might decide to Cortez themselves. This might not be their last stand, and from what Malcolm told us, they have bosses. Those are the bastards we really need to catch."

Jia drew her slug-thrower. "No way I'll get good stun shots off in this situation." She lifted one of the grenades. "On the other hand, the hedge will only protect them so much." She primed it, looked into her HUD, and tossed the grenade.

The shooters scattered, but two collapsed, victims of the grenade. Erik took the opportunity to pop up from behind the MX 60 and open fire. His bullets ripped through the hedge and through a man's shoulder. Another quick shot nailed a second man in the leg. He ducked as two active shooters returned fire.

"All units, surround the house," Erik ordered. "We've got the shooters all but contained."

The police flitters broke away from their circling path and headed toward the house. Erik captured the attention of the maze shooters with quick shots as Jia hurled the other stun grenade. Two shrieks joined the loud buzz of the grenade, and the victims collapsed.

Erik and Jia jumped up from their cover and rushed toward the opening in the maze.

Emma provided helpful arrows that led them to the suspects. The detectives bypassed the stunned men and women to find the wounded and kick their rifles away from them before kneeling to bind their hands. After that, they bound those who were unwounded but stunned. Each of the suspects wore a small silver pendant with a lightning bolt through a double helix.

Erik nodded at a pendant. "That must be the mark of their top-level flunkies."

"Let's finish cleaning up. We can worry about that later." Jia sprinted through the maze, relying on Emma's navigation markers to help her quickly clear it. She emerged less than a minute later out the back, Erik right behind her.

The silhouettes of the remaining suspects converged near the front of the house. Erik and Jia aimed their weapons at them. The doors opened, and a gaggle of men and women emerged, the sunlight glinting off the pendants around their necks. They all carried rifles but dropped them and raised their arms before advancing slowly.

"Be cautious, Detectives," Emma warned. "I'm detecting unusual signatures in the lawn near the building. There are possible mines."

"On your knees!" Jia shouted. "Or we will use lethal force."

The suspects broke into zigzagging sprints in different directions. Jia frowned, hesitating. She had warned them, but they were unarmed, and gunning down an unarmed suspect didn't sit well with her, nor apparently Erik since he hadn't opened fire. Several uniformed officers ran from the sides of the house, their stun pistols ready.

"Everyone stay the hell away," Erik shouted. "They've mined the lawn!"

Explosions ripped up the ground, launching the officers into the air with yells. They landed in heaps, groaning and bleeding.

"Unusual energy signatures detected in three of the remaining suspects," Emma reported. "There is a high probability they are bombers." She shifted the color of their silhouettes to bright orange to highlight them.

The bombers advanced toward Erik and Jia, their comrades serving as human shields. Helena Cortez's crisis of conscience apparently didn't afflict the rest of the Friends of Purity.

Jia ran to the side, slamming her slug-thrower into her holster and pulling her stun pistol. She pulled the trigger as quickly as she could manage. The human shields pitched forward, but the bombers yanked them back and continued to advance, albeit slower. One bomber turned toward some of the wounded and downed officers.

"Not much choice now," Erik muttered.

He flipped to four-barrel mode and fired at a bomber clinging to an allied meat shield. The first man twitched, his muscles rigid from Jia's earlier stun shots. The bullets ripped through him and pierced the bomber behind him, but the odd example of mutual group support continued to advance. Erik held down the trigger and produced a stream of lead that didn't cease until his magazine went dry. The bullets shredded both men, who collapsed to the ground in bloody heaps. Another active Purist tried to yank the bomber up, but Erik downed him with a knee shot.

Jia hissed in frustration and tossed her stun pistol to the ground. "Stop making me shoot your asses with lead!"

She ripped the slug-thrower back out of her holster and fired until she'd taken out the advancing bombers and their shields.

She whipped her gun toward the group heading toward the downed officer and pulled the trigger. Her gun clicked empty.

Emma's drone swarm dive-bombed the remaining Purists, smacking into their heads and crumpling around them.

The suspects batted at the angry swarm, knocking a few out of the air, but three direct hits to the head of the bomber sent him to the ground. Erik and Jia managed to reload. The remaining Purists joined their friends after the detectives fired.

They were well away from the wounded officers.

Jia took several deep breaths and wiped sweat from her brow. A few seconds later, the three bombers exploded, blasting grass, dirt, and body parts into the air. The force slammed her onto her back, the collision knocking the wind out of her. Her heart pounded as she tried to blink away her blurry vision and sucked in air.

She shook her head, her ears ringing, and sat up.

Small craters marked locations of the explosions, along with the remains of the would-be warriors of purity. Erik knelt nearby, blood dripping from a cut across the side of his face. He had small pebbles embedded in his tactical vest like someone had fired a shotgun at him. The wounded officers from before had been pushed another couple of meters away, but were still breathing.

Jia stood and tried not to sway. She took several slow breaths to calm her racing heart.

Erik ran a hand down his face. "That was a pretty expensive way to stop the guy, Emma. A magazine for the TR-7 costs way less than one of those drones. That was most of my moon drones. Couldn't you have just knocked the guy out with one?"

Emma scoffed. "I just saved a bunch of uniform boy fleshbags, and you're choosing to rant about—"

"We just needed a few seconds to reload," Erik

complained. "I've got a lot of savings, but I'm not made of money."

Emma chuckled. "Should I compare the price of the most recent modifications to the MX 60 to the cost of those drones?"

"Now, let's not get lost in money details." Erik jogged toward the wounded officers. Most were sitting up and conscious, and he spoke on the comm. "We need some more medpatches down here!"

Jia surveyed the carnage as she picked up her stun pistol. "I'm glad we took the first batch of suspects alive. At least we have someone to interrogate."

CHAPTER THIRTY-EIGHT

Erik hated fanatics.

There was a certain professionalism that accompanied a paid hitman or an insurgent trying to kill a man. People who sat around waxing philosophical about their glorious revolution had always bugged him because a lot of the time, he didn't believe them.

He figured most of them just got off on killing people and were looking for an excuse.

The idiotic Friends of Purity couldn't honestly believe assassinating a cop with a cybernetic arm and making some speeches would change anything. That suggested it was the excitement of committing acts of terrorism that motivated them.

Erik locked eyes with the woman sitting across the interrogation room table, one of the survivors of the house raid, and their third interrogation suspect of the day. The patrol officers who'd checked on the final location found another apparent suicide, although unlike Cortez, that victim didn't bother to leave a note.

He was satisfied with their performance.

The Lady had given Erik and Jia the hard task for that day, but they'd gotten through it with no dead officers. Some were still in the hospital having their injuries checked, and one officer needed regeneration of her eardrums, but according to the doctors, she'd be back on the job on light duty in a couple of weeks.

Jia quietly watched the suspect.

No one had said a word for the last ten minutes. The suspect smirked at the detectives like she knew some deep secret they couldn't begin to comprehend. That was the other problem with fanatics.

They were always so damned smug.

Erik snorted, breaking the silence. "You don't get it, do you? You've lost. Two of your people killed themselves rather than participate in your dipshit scheme, and your little suicide bombers didn't do much but blow up all your friends. No dead cops."

He slapped his left arm. "No dead Tin Man. We stunned or killed the rest of your friends. Now, if you want to have any chance of not spending the rest of your life behind bars, you might cooperate. What was your name again? Oh, yeah, Trina. Doesn't sound like the name of a murderous terrorist, but there can be only so many Miss Evil Psychos out there, right?"

"You think you intimidate me?" Trina scoffed.

"I think you're the one bound to a chair."

"History will record you as an enabler and a species traitor," Trina declared. "I'll be remembered as a political prisoner. Our message of righteousness will spread. Martyrdom will only do more for it."

"Yes, we're all very impressed with your zeal," Jia interjected. "What are you trying to accomplish?" She pointed at Erik. "Why target Detective Blackwell?"

Trina spat at Erik's arm but missed. "He willingly mocks human purity."

"We get it." Erik shrugged. "You're a Purist, but what you're doing is completely unnecessary. Everyone's already bought into what you believe. There are heavy laws against extensive genetic engineering, and even good people sneer at someone with a cybernetic arm. All you've done is thrown away your future with this crap."

"It's not enough," Trina insisted. "Because you still think you can *choose* something like that."

"Erik's the only one in the 1-2-2 with a major cybernetic modification," Jia pointed out. "You almost killed several pure humans with *implanted* explosives. Don't you see the irony in that? Your version of Purism is nothing more than homicidal maniacs killing innocent people. That isn't justice. It's mass murder preceded by a petty speech."

"We are at war for our very species!" Trina shouted at Jia. "Don't you understand that? You're not like *him*. You're still pure."

Erik folded his arms. "So, you don't care who you kill? You sound a lot like the Second Spring. Have to break a few million eggs to make your omelets?"

Trina tried to stand, but the binding ties on her arms and legs kept her in the chair, which was bolted to the floor. She struggled for several seconds, glaring at Erik, her teeth bared like a wild animal.

"How dare you compare us to those transhumanist monsters?" Trina snarled. "You Tin Man bastard."

"Just calling it like I see it." Erik pushed his chair back. "This is fun for me. You all tried to kill me, and you failed. We followed up and you tried again, and you still failed. A Tin Man winning against a bunch of extreme Purists—it's kind of funny, you have to admit. You're not a great argument for total purity."

Trina slumped in her chair, taking a ragged, shuddering breath. "Temporary losses are part of all wars."

"So are proper supply chains." Jia sighed, feigned pity on her face. "What I'm more curious about is where you're getting the explosives. We've IDed everyone at that house. We've checked into your records. There's no real trouble there, only minor brushes with the law. There's no way people like you luck into those kinds of explosives."

"Then you're not as smart as you think you are, Detective," Trina replied, the condescension returning to her voice.

"Maybe. But you know what I think?" Jia tapped her arm. "I think there's someone else pulling the strings. No, I don't think that. I know that. Helena Cortez mentioned the Inner Friends. You're letting someone sit back and order you to sacrifice your lives. You're just pathetic puppets with delusions of grandeur." She eyed the lady in the chair.

"All wars have generals who order the soldiers." Trina lifted her chin, managing to summon a tiny slice of dignity despite being bound to an immobile chair in a police interrogation room. "Why should this war be any different?"

"And where did the generals get their explosives?" Erik probed.

"As if I'd tell you anything, *Tin Man.*"

Jia stared at the woman for a moment and then looked at Erik with a smile. "Are you thinking what I'm thinking?"

Erik nodded. "You don't know the answer to our question, do you, Trina? They just pointed you at someone, and you went. That's not being a brave soldier. That's being someone's tool, and like my partner said, someone's puppet. For all you know, this is just a weapons company testing a new product."

Trina shook her head, panic creeping into her expression. She licked her lips. "I know the truth. I'm just choosing not to share it with you as enemies of humanity."

Erik stood. "It doesn't matter. We've got all sorts of records, messages, and accounts to go through. Our tech guys are close to cracking your best encryption, and then we'll know who your little Inner Friends are. They can join you in prison and order you around in there."

"You won't win." Trina's lips quivered. "We're on the right side of history. We will be remembered as heroes!"

"Yeah, I'm sure the right side of history is the pro-killing Erik Blackwell side." He shook his head. "If you needed a hobby, you should have taken up penjing." He opened the door and stepped into the hallway.

Jia rose from her seat and left the room after a lingering look at Trina.

"It's the same crap as the first two," Erik observed after Jia closed the door. "It's obvious none of them have any clue about logistics or operations. Point and shoot."

"It's not a well-formed terrorist group." Jia furrowed her brow in concentration. "Why not have a cell structure with individual cell leadership? Even after Victor's failure, they could have salvaged something, rather than making a desperate last stand."

"It feels like these Inner Friends don't have terrorist or insurgent experience." Erik glanced at the door. "Everything about this except their secure encrypted messages has been sloppy and amateur hour." He grunted in disgust. "You're right, a limited number of cells executing high-profile missions after training could have done more to spread their message and taken down more targets. The weapons were decent, but the tactics were awful. If they'd holed up in the house, maybe thrown up jammers and thermal cloaks, they could have forced us to clear them room by room and made it hurt a lot more. Even an impressive last stand might have sold things better."

"You think people like those fools could get their hands on thermal cloaks?" Jia's tone was even more skeptical than the words.

"As opposed to a bunch of high-powered explosives? Something small enough to be implanted into a person without easy detection prior to activation but that powerful?"

Jia shrugged. "You have a point. So, these Inner Friends are the key. They're bankrolling and commanding the whole operation, but based on what you're saying, they lack significant education or training with military, terrorist, or insurgent operations." She shook a finger. "And they don't understand that much about police capabilities, either. The encrypted messages are a start, but there are still too many clues here." She narrowed her eyes. "It feels like the people behind this are feeling their way through it and just throwing money at a problem."

"High-powered corporate pricks, maybe?" Erik suggested. "Not that it'd be a huge surprise in Neo SoCal."

Jia nodded slowly. "That's what I'm thinking, but not someone who is corrupt in the sense we're used to dealing with. If they had real contacts in the underworld, they would have been able to put this together better, with hired pro killers or mercenaries." She grimaced. "The people at the top of this are probably just as much pure believers as their foot soldiers." She pointed to Erik's arm. "Taking down a powerful symbol because he wasn't pure enough would be a good way to sell their message that no one is an exception to their beliefs. We're some of the most famous police officers on Earth right now, but I don't have any hardware."

Erik grinned and puffed out his chest. "I'm kind of proud."

"Of being the target of a cult of ideological extremists?" Jia's brows lifted in surprise.

"Yeah, because this is about going after me for what I've done as a cop and not because of other stuff in my past." Erik shrugged. "I'm not all that offended when someone tries to kill me. Lots of people have tried these last thirty years. I'll save being offended for when they succeed, and then only if it's a cheap kill."

Jia took one last look at the door. "If we can't squeeze useful info from the suspects, we'll just have to see what the other evidence tells us." She pointed to her PNIU. "I assume you got a message from Camila about the time we started the interrogation? I told her we'd be a few minutes."

Erik nodded. "Let's go see what Malcolm's squeeze has to say." The two started down the hall. "Besides," he told her as they turned a corner, "my girlfriend is a pure human — *OUCH!* You didn't need to slug me so hard!"

CHAPTER THIRTY-NINE

Camila stood in the center of her examination room, looking satisfied.

The long exam table was empty, but a circle of data windows depicting analysis results and images from the blast sites surrounded her. She stood there, arms crossed, staring at Erik.

Malcolm sat in a nearby chair, poring through his own data windows and ignoring the two detectives who had just strolled in.

This time, the two support staff hadn't been on the verge of making out.

"We haven't shaken much loose from the suspects," Jia explained. "So I hope you have something good. We've got a lot of momentum on this case now."

After the initial shock of learning Camila worked with the Intelligence Directorate had worn off, Jia had begun to see the advantages.

She wasn't *just* a trained doctor, but also someone with access to technology and additional skills the average coroner might lack. While she obviously wouldn't blow her cover, that combination of traits could lead to surprising conclusions, just like having access to Emma did for Erik and her.

The coroner had every reason to aid Erik and Jia, considering that Alina was still trying to recruit them.

Camila stabbed a finger toward a colorful chromatograph display in a data window. "I wasn't sure before, but now I am. I was wondering why we weren't finding any bomb fragments."

Erik stared at the display window for a few seconds before shaking his head. "That just looks like a bunch of dots, curves, and numbers. What did you find?"

Camila gestured to the data window. "I'll give you the bottom line. All the bombers used the same explosive, Z-22, and it was clearly implanted in different limbs. Actually, I'd say less implanted and more…injected. There was no external casing or stabilization method."

Erik scrubbed a hand down his face. "Non-stabilized Z-22? Those crazy sons of bitches. How the hell did someone convince them to put that in their bodies? Even if they didn't know what it was, they had to understand it was an explosive."

"Z-22?" Jia shook her head. "I'm not familiar with that. What's so special about it?"

"You normally keep it contained in a special stabilization fluid," Erik explained. "It's very pliable and extremely powerful relative to its weight. It's nice when you need to blow through a reinforced armored wall or something, but it's suicide to use it under normal tactical circumstances. It's too volatile, especially outside the stabilization fluid.

The Army experimented with Z-22 grenades, and all they got for their efforts were a lot of unintended explosions and wasted money. Fortunately, they weren't dumb enough to try to test that crap in the field."

"You can't buy Z-22 at your local commerce tower or even your local industrial tower," Camila commented. "It's expensive and heavily regulated. I doubt they'd bring it from off-world, but the other thing is, when you examine the state of the suspects' remains and the damage to the area, the explosions weren't that large."

Jia scoffed. "They blew people apart and knocked us around. This was hardly some kid's fireworks."

"Camila's right." Erik shook his head. "Given the size of those explosions, and even considering it was inside someone, it was a *tiny* amount of Z-22. That might explain how they were able to smuggle it in without getting caught. Everything else we've found points to our Inner Friends not having major underworld connections, but if they were moving a tiny amount of product, it wouldn't be a big thing."

"So, this is probably someone throwing a lot of money around for a small amount of an explosive compound." Jia rubbed her chin. "It'd make sense that someone might not worry much about helping them, even if they worried about what they intended to do. Those suicide bombers were nasty, but they couldn't level a tower. They could probably cause more casualties by showing up on a parking platform and opening fire with the rifles."

"No, it was all about killing people like me in the flashiest way possible." Erik grinned. "Blowing me up works to their propaganda advantage in a way shooting me wouldn't."

Camila's dark eyebrow lifted. "How's that?"

Erik pointed to his left arm. "Because there's a good chance that a piece of my arm would survive the explosion. If they're recording, they get the remains of a cyborg to pass around. I think it was supposed to be symbolic—literally blowing the impure to pieces." He frowned. "The only thing I don't get is why they implanted it. That was insanely risky."

"Injected, not implanted," Camila corrected.

"That's even stupider."

Jia pointed at the chromatograph display. "That's why. Everything's making more sense now."

"You figured it out, huh?" Camila raised an eyebrow in appreciation. "You're not just a pretty corp princess face."

Jia side-eyed her. "Funny."

Camila smiled. "I thought so."

Erik noticed that Malcolm had glanced up to see the two ladies annoying each other and quickly focused back on his own work.

Smart man.

Erik looked at the two women in confusion. "Care to clue me in? What does that science experiment stuff have to do with them injecting it?"

"You said Z-22 isn't very stable," Jia explained. "And from what you've both said, it doesn't seem like it explicitly needs a priming device. Given its chemical nature, part of its lack of stability will manifest in detectable vapors."

Camila nodded. "Exactly. Z-22's decay products are similar to several other high-end explosives, so you wouldn't be able to easily tell it's Z-22 just by detecting a few molecules, but even crappy bomb detection equipment would easily pick it up due to breakdown product outgassing. They wanted to be able to blow people up without anyone knowing until it was too late."

Understanding dawned on Erik's face. "Which means they couldn't go after high-value targets in secured corporate or municipal buildings. And if the bombers had a container, it was going to get flagged by the other detectors. This wasn't just about killing me. They were probably preparing for a major push when we appeared at the house."

"You heard Victor's rant about Rena." Jia frowned. "They probably wanted to make examples out of the people associated with that case, and who knows who else. They're so far over the extremist line, it's hard to know what they find acceptable or not. But we can't be sure those people at the house were the remainder of their foot soldiers."

Malcolm looked up from his data window. "As far as the guys out in the field, I think you did get them all. I've been cross-checking data and records from accounts and recovered PNIUs and comparing everything, and I'm about ninety-five percent sure we've accounted for everyone not in the leadership. But, you know, we've still got a lot of people to check out to confirm things."

"Well, more parts of people," Camilla suggested with a shrug and a faint smirk.

Jia raised an eyebrow, "Now, that's dark."

Camila shrugged again.

"That leaves us with the Inner Friends," Erik continued.

"Where are we on them? If you need help, we could ask a certain redheaded friend to get involved."

Emma snickered over their PNIUs but didn't say anything.

Malcolm scoffed. "I've got this, and we need it to be by the book. If everything you've said is right, whoever is at the other end of the rainbow is going to be able to hire expensive lawyers. That means everything we collect needs to be as clean as possible so they don't weasel out of this, right?"

Erik's hands clenched. "You're right, but the Inner Friends just lost all their people. If we don't move on this fast, they could be on a transport to the HTP already and preparing to spend months on a ship to hide from the law."

"I'm close, Detective Blackwell," Malcolm insisted. "Very close. Just give me the time."

Camila made a shooing motion. "I guarantee you he won't find what you need with you here barking at him. I'll keep examining the remains. I doubt there's any intact Z-22 left, but if I can find some, I might be able to pull the atomic serial number off the explosive. Then we can at least track where it came from."

"Let us know the minute either of you figures anything out," Erik ordered. "I want the bastards who set this all up, and I want them yesterday."

"Taking it kind of personal, Detective Big Guy?" Camila asked. "I'm surprised. You don't seem like the type."

Erik shook his head. "Yeah, but not for the reasons you think. I just don't like the idea that those smug bastards are sitting in their fancy houses somewhere, thinking they can wind up people like toy bombs and send them out. I'm old-fashioned. A good leader leads from the front, even if it gets him shot."

"They chose to do it," Jia countered. "They weren't victims. They were accomplices."

"Doesn't matter. They might be idiots, but I still want the cowards at the top." Erik pointed at Malcolm. "Sooner rather than later."

"I know, Detective." Malcolm rolled his eyes. "You can get off my ass."

Camila smirked. "Don't point your finger at me. I might bite it off."

"The left finger might be a little crunchy." Erik headed toward the door. "Just get us some new leads."

This time, Jia shrugged. She didn't know what was eating at him, either.

CHAPTER FORTY

"Just goes to show you there are too many conspiracies out there," Jia mentioned.

Both detectives were working on interrogation reports, and it'd been a few hours since either had said anything substantial. It was almost time to clock off, but neither wanted to go home.

The air seemed laden with tension and the promise of a new lead.

Erik looked up from his desk. "Yeah, I know. I was still half-wondering if this could be the other thing I'm working on, but everything keeps going back to this being too sloppy. I wouldn't be surprised if it's some rich young assholes who just got promoted at some Hexagon company. They're sitting in their offices thinking about how they're at the top of the world and decided to take up a cause to fill the void in their empty souls. They probably got together outside of work and started having some philosophical conversation about the nature of humanity, and then it escalated into grabbing people and convincing them to become walking talking suicide bombs."

"You've put a lot of thought into profiling the leaders." Jia shrugged. "I don't know if I care at this point as long as we catch them, and I think we're close. Very close."

"Close doesn't matter if they get away."

She pointed to her chest. "Here's where my background comes in handy."

"How so?"

Jia grinned. "Because if we're right about the kind of people at the top of this, they won't pack up and flee Earth because we are investigating them. They'll be too arrogant and too scared at the same time. It makes for a dangerous combination, but one that works to our advantage."

Erik looked at her in disbelief. "You really don't think they'll run?"

"You've been all around the UTC. You don't get how strange it can be for someone to be forced to leave a place like Neo SoCal, especially if it's their seat of power. No, they might fight, but they won't run." Jia nodded, a determined look on her face. "That's the weakness that comes from being ultra-wealthy and not just *kind* of wealthy. The power of wealth only means something if you can use it, and using it properly requires a certain infrastructure that makes you vulnerable to people like us. We'll get these people. I promise."

Their PNIUs chimed with a call from Malcolm. They both accepted.

"I've got the Inner Friends," Malcolm blurted, almost tripping over his words.

Jia grinned, and Erik chuckled.

"You won't believe it," Malcolm continued. "I don't know if I do. At first I wasn't sure, and I said to myself, 'This can't possibly be who I think it is. That would be crazy.' But it's clear. I mean, once I beat the encryption, it made tracing certain things even when I take ac—"

"Malcolm," Jia interrupted, "we don't care about the why at the moment. We care who. We need to put together teams and hit all the Inner Friends ASAP, so they won't be able to prepare more than they already have. The one advantage we have is they probably still think they're safe because of the way they handled their messages."

"Don't worry about that." Malcolm took a deep breath and slowly let it out. "This time it's easy. There isn't a them. There's only a him. The man at the center of the Inner Friends pretended to be different people to other people in the group, but it's definitely one person, or at least I can trace it to one person's home, and the writing style is exactly the same. The system used to prepare the messages was the same."

Erik stood and grabbed his duster. "Who is it?"

"Carlos Kandarian."

"The Stella Infinitas guy?" Erik asked, puzzled. "The victim of the bank robbery?"

"No, his cousin who washes flitters, Detective. Yes, *the* Carlos Kandarian."

Erik pulled on his coat. "That's one way to keep busy in retirement. Damn. I didn't see that one coming. Just goes to show you this job is full of surprises."

Jia's eyes widened. She stood with her mouth open in shock for a few seconds before closing it with a thin smile. "I *knew* there was more to that robbery."

The MX 60 zoomed toward Kandarian's mansion, but this time they weren't alone. An entire squadron of police flitters, including armored TPST vehicles, flew behind them, every individual flitter's lights and sirens blaring.

The net effect was reminiscent of a school of bioluminescent fish converging on one location.

"This man is so rich, Generous Gao comes to *him* asking for presents," Erik transmitted to the raid team. "He's smuggling in Z-22 and weapons, including rifles. We can expect heavy resistance, including heavier weapons and possible exoskeletons. The guy loves his suicide bombers. Disable all suspects from at least five meters away. I don't want any of our guys getting hurt this time." He ended the transmission as confirmations from the different teams came in. "Emma, coordinate Dispatch for me."

Jia stared down at an image from a surveillance drone. It showed Kandarian entering his mansion only an hour prior. Everything had aligned.

"I was right," she commented. "The incident with the Friends of Purity is all over the news. There's no way he doesn't know about us hitting them, but he's not running."

"Maybe he's so arrogant he doesn't think we'll beat his encryption." Erik pulled a hand off the control yoke to adjust his tactical vest. "Or he's got fifty mercenaries in there, all in military-grade exoskeletons."

"I don't think he's got an army of mercenaries in there." Jia nodded. "That's the other problem that comes from rising that high in society. Power is an intoxicating drug, and if you let yourself get high all the time, you forget that you're not actually a god. He thinks he scared us off before."

"ETA one minute," Emma reported. "Drones are not detecting active countermeasures. That said, most of the house is impervious to my sensors, which represents a dangerous unknown variable."

"Emma, take control," Erik ordered. He gestured to the passenger seat. "Do you mind? I want to be ready to hit the ground running with four barrels."

The minute of anticipation felt like an hour. The raid team closed on the target, the vehicles spreading to surround the mansion. Kandarian had nowhere to go but down, and they'd checked the records. There was no direct passage from Kandarian's residential level to the next level down in the tower.

The man's desire to be a king on top of the world had trapped him.

"Movement from the front," Emma reported as she landed the MX 60 in the front lawn about fifty meters from the entry. "The doors are opening."

A magnified camera feed popped up. Erik threw the door open and slid out of the MX 60, ready to start firing. Jia matched him on the other side, kneeling behind the door for protection. Both detectives held their breath, ready for everything from bullets to *yaoguai*.

"That's...not what I thought would happen," Erik muttered.

The TPST flitters landed and their loading doors opened. Exoskeletons clanked out onto the lawn, their heavy weapons pointed at the front of the mansion.

Their suspect emerged, his cane in hand. He strolled forward, his pace languid, but not out of proportion to his previously demonstrated mobility. There were no weapons on his person or any evidence of armed allies.

"Carlos Kandarian," Erik shouted. "You're under arrest for conspiracy to commit murder, disturbing the peace, conspiracy to commit terrorism, illegal use of communications technology, and a long list of other things that would take me all day to recite. All Article Seven rights apply. Do you need these explained to you?"

The old man shook his head. He let go of his cane and raised his hands above his head.

Erik stood, his TR-7 still aimed at the suspect. He and Jia advanced slowly. Other officers, both on foot and in exoskeletons, closed in as well, a semicircle of well-armed police doom if Kandarian tried anything. Once Erik had moved closer, he could make out the weary smile on the suspect's face.

Kandarian kept his arms up. "This is unnecessary and undignified, as well. Don't worry, Detective Blackwell. You've caught me. I give up."

Fifteen minutes later, Kandarian sat on a couch in one of his large receiving rooms. Police and drones choked the mansion, everyone running scanners and taking pictures. TPST exoskeleton teams and drones were clearing the building.

Erik and Jia were outside, watching Kandarian with a few

other officers. The suspect had his arms bound behind him and an almost serene look on his face. A circle of drones surrounded him, producing a visible safety line in case the wealthy suspect had plans to go down in a blaze of Z-22 glory.

"Last room clear, Detective," reported an officer over the comm.

Erik shouldered his rifle, a look of annoyance on his face. "That easy, huh, Kandarian?"

"I didn't want to drag my loyal employees into this," the old man replied. "It seemed unfair, even if they agreed with me ideologically."

"That's one of the few things you've done lately that isn't totally disgusting," Jia commented. "But I *am* surprised you didn't put up more of a fight."

Kandarian shook his head. "You know why I did so well in business throughout my career, Detective Lin?"

"You sent suicide bombers to blow up your rivals?" Erik suggested.

Kandarian chuckled. "No. Crude violence might serve criminals and the police well, but business requires more finesse, even cutthroat business. No, I did well because I had an intuitive grasp of when a battle could be won and when it'd be a waste of resources to fight." He offered a weary smile to Erik. "In this case, it's not just my time and resources that might be wasted. I could hire mercenaries and fight off your attempts to capture me. I could even try to flee, but in the end, I would be caught, and I would have left humanity weaker, not stronger, in my wake. That goes against everything I believe in. True Purism is about keeping our species strong."

Jia glared at the man, her arms folded. "If that's your attitude, why try to kill a cop?"

"He's a man who chose impurity," Kandarian insisted. Unlike his acolytes, his voice and demeanor remained calm. His tone was filled with pity rather than disgust. "I've been funding certain groups for the good of humanity, groups like the Friends of Purity. I'm sure once you've gone through all my records, you'll discover how many different pet projects I had. Most weren't as impressive as the Friends, but they all had their uses." He let out a wistful sigh as he looked around. "And only the Friends had advanced to the point that they were willing to undertake more extreme actions. It's difficult to convince people ensconced in a comfortable existence of how diseased society is, and that we need to help humanity."

"'Help humanity?'" Jia snorted. "You convinced disturbed people to commit acts of horrific violence. They blew themselves up. Don't kid yourself."

Kandarian shook his head. "They chose to be martyrs for a cause greater than themselves. Even if you believe it is too extreme, you have to admire that level of dedication." He smiled. "In a sense, I gave those misguided souls something that many in society crave—a chance to prove their ideals."

"If you're so into this extremist Purism, why weren't you out there blowing yourself up?" Erik asked.

Kandarian ran a hand over his wrinkled face. "I've read about you, Detective. I know you're not just a Tin Man, but you've also de-aged. You were a perfect symbol to get my message out, the famous Obsidian Detective. Once you were dead, it would have been easy to push propaganda about why you deserved to die. That was why I didn't target your partner at first. She might be misguided, but she's still pure and hasn't tainted herself with false longevity."

"A lot of people have de-aged," Erik replied. "I thought the Purists didn't have a problem with that. Several Purist associations have given it their official seal of approval."

Police continued to stream in and out of the mansion, and official drones filled the sky. News drones prowled the perimeter of the police zone.

"The word 'Purist' has lost meaning. It's degenerated, along with most of society." Kandarian sighed. "Values and beliefs are often shoved aside when something pleasant is dangled. It's been man's goal since time immemorial to live forever. While I can't blame some for choosing a temporary extension of life, I can't forgive them, either. I've been thinking about this issue for a long time, but I was always distracted by my work. Once I left the company, I had more time to think about what was important and what I could use my wealth to accomplish."

"You were sloppy," Jia noted. "Why not just hire criminals to assassinate Erik?"

"Because I'm not a criminal, and the values I express are not criminal," Kandarian insisted. "I'll admit a tendency toward micromanagement likely led you to me. I thought early on that I should put some more distance between myself and my projects, but my ego wouldn't allow it, despite my unfamiliarity with the necessities of this kind of work." He eyed her. "I wanted to be the one personally pushing these brave souls forward and knowing that I was directly changing the world. I might be going to prison, but I still win."

Jia scoffed. "You're not going to be able to buy your way out of this. Just because you surrendered, it doesn't mean you're not going to prison. There is no might involved in your future."

"I fully expect to go to and die in prison," Kandarian admitted. "But I'm a man of some reputation."

"I didn't know who you were before all this," Erik commented with a smirk.

Kandarian's easy smile finally flickered. "Be that as it may, my arrest and imprisonment will probably do more to spread my message than I could ever have accomplished with my pawns. The people of Earth and the rest of the United Terran Confederation will think about what I have done and why I've done it, and they'll come to agree with me."

"You are an antisocial murderer who happens to be wealthy." Jia wrinkled her nose as if the man smelled. "You've failed, and somebody not *pure* helped stop you."

Kandarian craned his head upward, smiling at the sky. "At least I fought for something I believe in. I'll grant your partner that as well, Detective Lin. Being bested by someone with some soul left isn't so bad."

Erik sighed. "Whatever you have to tell yourself."

"There's one thing I still don't understand," Jia asked. "Where does the data rod from the bank fit in with all of this?"

"It was exactly what I told you before—a rival." Kandarian chuckled. "I already took measures to punish them. Don't worry, I simply crushed their company through shell moves. I don't know how they became aware of the data rod, but it unfortunately didn't only contain information on my business dealings, but also certain information that would have led to the discovery of my more recent Purist projects."

"And that's why you wouldn't let us take a look," Jia concluded.

"When you came to talk to me the first time, I worried my plan would be uncovered." Kandarian sighed. "So I decided to deal with Detective Blackwell, both to disrupt your investigation and also to serve my own interests. I suppose it was a mistake in the end."

Erik's eyes narrowed. "How far does your Purism go?"

"It's complete," Kandarian answered. "Why do you ask?"

"Would you eat a beignet made with Navigator technology?"

Jia eyed him before she scrubbed a hand down her face.

Kandarian blinked as if having trouble processing the question. He stared at Erik. "Excuse me?"

Several of the other nearby cops turned toward each other for clarification, but everyone looked just as confused as Kandarian.

Erik spoke slower and enunciated each individual word as if speaking to a child. "Would you eat a beignet made with Navigator technology?"

"That doesn't make sense." The old man's shoulders slumped, sighing. "Perhaps I overestimated my opponent."

Erik smiled as Jia turned to go. "We still beat you."

He followed his partner out.

CHAPTER FORTY-ONE

September 1, 2229, Neo Southern California Metroplex, En Route to Police Enforcement Zone 122 Station

Following the Kandarian arrests, things were quiet.

Erik and Jia weren't even assigned any new cases. While the captain and the chief wondered if there would be a wave of extremist Purist terrorism, nothing out of the ordinary happened.

It was as if the entire metroplex was breathing a sigh of relief, grateful that a repeat of some of the brutal terrorism of the previous year hadn't happened. That didn't assure that no trouble would come in the future.

A thought not lost on Jia.

Thoughts of trouble swirled in her mind and provided one of the reasons she asked Malcolm and Camila to come to lunch with them. There were different types of trouble, and different resources were useful in dealing with them.

The two detectives, the technician, and the coroner had a pleasant enough meal and were now on their way back to the station. Jia estimated she had a relatively narrow window to broach the topic of conversation haunting her, but she wanted to wait for the right moment.

While Erik and Jia sat up front, Malcolm sat in the back next to Camila, all but drooling, but his state had nothing to do with his girlfriend sitting next to me.

"I can't get over how ridiculously cool this flitter is." He sighed as he ran his hand over the seat. "Too bad I can't afford one, and that's before all the modifications Detective Blackwell's made. I used to think, 'I'm not a flitter guy,' but this MX 60 has made me change my mind."

Erik chuckled.

"You should have taken my bribe," Camila suggested with a wicked grin.

"But that was just a test," Malcolm complained.

"Maybe." She winked and turned toward the front. "Are we ever going to get to the real reason you invited us out to eat? The food was nice, but I was going to work through lunch on a report today, so I'd like to know this all wasn't a waste of my time."

Jia's heart rate kicked up.

Of *course,* an Intelligence Directorate agent would sense the deception. She had to keep reminding herself that even though Camila wasn't a pistol-toting death machine like Alina, she was just as dangerous in her own way.

"Real reason?" Malcolm looked between her and those in the front. "You didn't just want us to have awesome food?" He gasped, eyes opening. "Wait. You're not going to kill me because I know too much, are you?"

Erik burst out laughing. Jia face-palmed as she shook her head.

"Oh, Malcolm." Camila clucked her tongue. "You've got

a long way to go on reading people. I'm not going to let anyone kill you until you give me a disappointing present."

Malcolm swallowed. "O-okay."

Erik glanced at Jia, now curious. "I thought you said it would just be good to check on things. But she's right. There's something more, isn't there?"

"I wanted to talk somewhere I knew was safe, and this is as safe as anyplace, thanks to Emma," Jia admitted. "Even our office presents a small risk."

"There are advantages to being friends with a superior intellect," Emma offered cheerfully. "I could have secured your office, but admittedly, a double-date appearance is useful as cover."

Camila smirked. "You two can only pretend for so long before it becomes real, you know."

Jia whipped her head toward the other woman. "How did you know?"

"I'm trained to notice and exploit things like that." She winked at Jia. "Remember?"

Malcolm looked at the ladies, confused.

"What's going on?" Erik asked gruffly. "And not with our dating situation. Let's get to the point."

"I can't let the case go." Jia shrugged. "It's as simple as that."

"Why not? This isn't like last time. There aren't any loose ends. We got Kandarian, and the department and CID are running down the rest of his little puppet groups." Erik frowned. "Some of them may walk because they've done nothing except be annoying outside buildings or on the net, but we're checking them out pretty thoroughly to make sure they weren't being directed toward something more than annoying protests. It's a clean win, and this time, the guy on top is going down."

"It's not Kandarian I'm worried about." Jia took a deep breath and slowly let it out. "His targeting of you is too neat a fit, Erik. For example, you don't go around advertising your arm."

Erik shrugged. He gently tugged on the control yoke to bring the MX 60 into a higher lane. "Kandarian probably didn't even think to target me until his maid cut my arm. We did work the Winston case, so that just provided more fuel. Sometimes the Lady is screwing with us, but sometimes things are a coincidence."

Camila arched a thin brow. "You think it's Talos or someone like that?"

Jia shook her head. "I'm not sure, but Erik's been targeted more than once by terrorists who were being pushed by someone else. We can't be sure this isn't the same situation, and if we relax too much, it might expose us to a counterattack we don't see coming."

"Kandarian's filthy-rich," Erik observed. "This is one time we don't need to look for someone deeper. All the evidence and resources are there." He side-eyed her. "I thought I was the paranoid one. Not that I'm complaining about you having my back."

"But what if Kandarian is part of the conspiracy? An old man loaded with cash and forced out of his company sounds like someone to recruit to influence events. They could appeal to his ego. He might have made peace with the company just because he still had a stake."

Malcolm cleared his throat. "Am I allowed to talk?"

Camila laughed.

His face reddened as he waved a hand toward the front "Hey, it turned into a galactic conspiracy meeting. I'm not an expert like you people. I've just helped here and there."

Jia nodded. "Go ahead, Malcolm."

"Digital Forensics is still going through Kandarian's data rod, but we already located a kill list." Malcolm mimed firing a pistol. "Famous people of different types that are, and I quote, 'Suspected or confirmed to be impure.'"

"And?" Jia probed.

"Erik's not on the list," Malcolm answered her. "Not sure if that means anything. They didn't specify what they were using as criteria, so I wasn't sure if they thought people got illegal genetic engineering or just had cybernetic implants."

"Erik wasn't on the list?" Jia frowned. "It might mean Kandarian is someone's errand boy as part of the conspiracy. His arm and Rena were just excuses."

"Or it could mean that it was a crime of opportunity," Camila suggested. She gestured toward Erik. "He mentioned Kandarian's maid. There's no reason to think the attack was connected to anything greater than one rich man with particular extremist views and far too much money lying around. It's not a matter for the Intelligence Directorate. It's a matter for law enforcement."

Jia scoffed. "We're not ID employees."

"But you're working a personal case where the official explanation has been provided. Investing in the conspiracy pushes you far more toward ID work than police work."

"Perhaps I should offer you some perspective, fleshbags," Emma interrupted.

Camilla raised her eyebrow again. It would take her a while to become accustomed to Emma.

"Which is?" Erik asked.

"I've taken the liberty of examining the data," Emma explained, a hint of frustration in her voice. "Before you say anything, I covered my tracks, and I haven't been communicating with Technician Constantine or Doctor Serrano. It will not damage the case in any way."

Camilla snickered. "No one calls me Doctor Serrano. It's kind of nice."

"You're welcome."

"Let's get back on track," Erik ordered. "Did you find something, Emma?"

"I've found many things," she replied. "But they are all things I'm sure Technician Constantine has found or will eventually find. That said, I have restrictions in that certain invasions would raise the risk of CID detection, but the existing data support the conclusion that Carlos Kandarian's activity was not related to the incidents on Molino or any conspiracy wider than his Purist outreach and activist efforts."

"You're sure?" Jia sounded dubious. "It's not insane to think he would be involved in something more."

"It depends on what you mean by 'sure.' If I had to quantify my analysis, I'd suggest it's less than point-one-percent likely he is directly related to any organization responsible for launching attacks on Detective Blackwell in relation to the incident on Molino. I would explain the exact model I used to come up with that number, but you wouldn't be able to follow it, so I fail to see the logic in doing so."

"You can be helpful without being that way." Jia rolled her eyes.

"By being 'that way,' I am maximizing my enjoyment." Emma let out a mocking chuckle.

Erik nodded toward the windshield. "We're almost to the station, so let's wrap this up. From what it sounds like, Kandarian was just a rich asshole, and he's going to prison, so we can stick this one in the finished pile." He looked at Jia. "Agreed?"

"I suppose." Jia shrugged. "It's not a bad thing that our latest troublemaker had nothing to do with the conspiracy."

"Alina hasn't said anything about keeping an eye on Carlos Kandarian," Camila offered. "Even if my primary task is to monitor the 1-2-2, if she believed he was involved with Talos or anyone supporting them, she would have let me know, so I could keep an eye out for any relevant evidence."

Erik kept looking forward, his hands firm on the control yoke. "Should you be offering us that information without checking with her?"

"She's less my boss and more a colleague, and Alina wants you to catch the people behind Molino as much as you do. Neither of us is your enemy, even if we've kept things from you."

"This is all a good thing, right?" Malcom rubbed his hands together and let out a nervous laugh. "No crazy super-advanced assassins are going to show up and try to murder anyone. We've all done our part to make Neo SoCal a safer place. Nice, good old-fashioned police work."

"Yeah," Erik murmured. "Nice, good old-fashioned

police work." A grin slowly spread. "We proved something with this case. Being filthy super-rich doesn't mean you can get away with what you want. Thinking your cause is just doesn't mean you can get away with it, either." He grew louder. "Those assholes on Molino aren't gods. They aren't even aliens. They are just humans who think because they've got money and influence, it puts them above the law and justice. But we've proven here over the last year, there's *no one* like that. They can dodge like Ceres Galactic or waste their lives trying to take us out, but in the end, we will get them. Maybe that's why things have been quiet from the conspiracy."

"You think they're afraid?" Jia asked.

"I *know* they're afraid. You don't try to kill someone if you're not afraid of them, but they have to be extra quiet. They screw up and we get a whiff of them, then a lot of pain is coming down on their heads." Erik slowed and angled his flitter toward the police parking garage. "I already fired the bullet. It'll find them eventually."

CHAPTER FORTY-TWO

September 1, 2229, Neo Southern California Metroplex, Commerce Tower 32

Erik pushed through the throngs of people in the shopping center.

Most walked quickly, laden with bags from the trendy stores on that level. Holographic palm trees swayed above, the occasional child running toward the fenced emitters and running their hands through the images.

Despite it being night, the false skyline above them gave the impression of a warm summer's day. A light breeze occasionally blew through, the source not clear, but undoubtedly artificial.

A beautiful smiling woman appeared above the crowd. "We hope you're enjoying today's shopping experience. Remember, our Eternal Summer promotion ends in a few weeks. Get your savings while you still can." She vanished, leaving Erik wondering if she was an AI with canned scripts or an employee being scanned elsewhere on the level.

"There's something I don't understand, Detective," Emma mentioned.

Erik dropped his hand to tap on his PNIU to fake a call, then raised a hand to his ear for a second, looking around. "What don't you understand?"

"Why you're here."

"To buy some penjing supplies," Erik replied, confused by her question. "I told you that when I left the station, and it's not like you can forget things." He paused for a moment in thought. "Can you?"

"Not without damage to my matrix or a sophisticated attack that is beyond the capabilities of all but a small number of organizations in the entire UTC. But that doesn't answer the specific question of *why* you are here."

"There are some new shears I'm interested in. They allow for more precise cuts, but they're still mechanical." Erik lifted his hand and squeezed his thumb and fingers together as if closing invisible shears. "I'm not interested in all the high-tech crap. What's the point of a relaxing hobby if you make it a slave to machines? It's supposed to be an ancient art."

"You're missing my point," Emma replied.

Erik turned his body to allow two teenage girls to rush past him, giggling. The positions of their eyes suggested they were paying more attention to their smart lenses than where they were going in the real world. They would eventually run into the wrong man.

"Be less cryptic," Erik told her.

"There's absolutely no reason for you to physically come to a place like this to buy the equipment you want." Emma scoffed. "It's filled with fleshbags of little relevance to your personal or professional goals, and there's also a non-zero chance that you might be attacked when you leave your home because of your reputation and work. If you're interested in buying goods and services, you can have them delivered. We can use sensors to screen the packages."

Erik chuckled. "So, you think I should just sit at home all day and have everything delivered?"

"You obviously have to go to work, but other than that, yes. It's the most logical thing for you to do. You likely earned the wrath of a terrorist simply by *going out to dinner*."

She seemed to be annoyed with him.

"Staying home all the time would get pretty boring." Erik slowed his pace. "And it's not like I'm never going to eat again because of one bomber."

"You can gain all the necessary nutrients you need without eating sandwiches and beignets," Emma countered.

Erik chuckled. "That doesn't sound like fun." He looked around with a frown. "I'm sure the Floating Tree was around here."

Several of the shops were familiar, but he couldn't find the store that had gotten him into penjing. He didn't stop by the store often, but he wanted to reward them.

"If you're referring to the store, my interrogation of the level map indicates it is no longer located on this level," Emma reported.

"What?" Erik stopped so abruptly a man almost bumped into him. The other man walked past, scowling for a moment until he saw Erik had multiple centimeters and kilos on him.

"The Floating Tree is no longer in this commerce tower," Emma elaborated with a laugh. "The records indicate it closed a month ago. You didn't have any store credit with them?"

"No, I didn't." Erik snorted. "But great. You couldn't have told me that before I flew all the way out here?"

"You didn't *ask* if the store was still open. You see? If you'd just had them delivered, you wouldn't have ended up wasting your time."

"Aren't you the one who's always complaining about having a body?" Erik started forward, glancing around in case Emma was wrong. "I'm a human, and I *like* to experience real life now and again. You're an AI. You could just live in a VR simulation."

"It's not that I need to always go somewhere in a body. It's more that I like the option. Note I don't complain about sitting in a parked flitter for large swaths of the day."

"That's because you're spying on everything through our PNIUs," Erik muttered. "Delivery. Give me a break." He slowed again and stared through the crisscrossing crowd at a shop with a bright holograph sign spinning above it.

Microfriends.

The shop wasn't what had caught his attention. A beautiful and familiar young Chinese woman in a dark-blue vine-pattern *qipao* stood in front of the store, smiling at passing customers.

"That's her," Erik declared. He didn't point.

"There are currently fifty-four females within a twenty-meter radius," Emma replied. "You will need to be far more specific."

Erik maneuvered through the crowd, twisting and spinning to close on the woman without hitting anyone. A number of people gave him dirty looks, but he moved close enough to read her nametag, with her name displayed in both English and Mandarin. Li Feng.

The woman offered him a warm smile. "Detective Blackwell. It's been a while."

Erik peered past her. The inside of the shop didn't boast any penjing displays. Frames hung on the walls, decorated with colorful, often glowing patterns. Loose striated balls floated and circulated in small tanks of water.

"This doesn't look like penjing," Erik commented, lips pressed together. "Unless there's some very different style you didn't tell me about."

Li Feng put a hand to her mouth and laughed. "Penjing. Oh, Detective Blackwell, that's a joke. Are you still doing that? It's for old men."

"I'm older than I look," Erik told her. "You didn't think it was for old men the last time you sold me something."

"Times change," she explained.

"But I need the new Guan Yu Superb shears," Erik kept looking between the shop and her as if hoping there was a special on Penjing hardware off in a corner somewhere.

Li Feng smiled. "I'm embarrassed that I wasted your time. Guan Yu shears? Don't you see? Commercial interests have corrupted the art and ruined it. They've packaged it and sold it. That's why I walked away." She gestured inside. "So I could help people with a new pastime that will connect them to the circle of life and help achieve real spiritual integration."

Erik surveyed the shop once more. "With weird paintings and strange floating balls?"

Li Feng placed her palms together and shook her head. "No, Detective. Those aren't paintings or decorations. These are Microfriends!"

"And those are…" He paused, trying to figure out what he was looking at. "What, exactly?"

Emma snickered quietly in his ear. "You'll find this fascinating."

Li Feng gestured to her body, her voice switching tone to that of a teacher. "Did you know there are more bacteria in your body than cells? Bacteria have always lived within humans, but it took recent genius and deep spiritual insight to understand that we could enjoy them as much as any other type of pet."

"A pet?" Erik stared at her like she'd lost her mind. "These are all bacteria?"

Li Feng nodded eagerly. "Colonies of special genetically engineered strains of bacteria." She gestured with a slender hand to a frame on the wall that contained plaid-like red and green pattern. "Don't worry. All major Purist organizations have signed off on the Microfriends product. We've taken all measures to ensure they will die if not actively maintained with our proprietary Microfriends Blend nutritional liquid."

Erik pinched his nose. He was missing something. "How can bacteria be pets?" Maybe it was obvious to her, but it was hurting his head.

Li Feng clapped her hands. "A great question! They are

both pets *and* decorations, and in a sense, they are purer than robots or macroscopic clones."

"Purer? I don't get it. We are talking about freaking bacteria." Erik wondered if this is what it felt like to slip into insanity. Maybe he'd knocked his head at the station and was having a vivid hallucination.

Maybe it was just her.

"I told you before, there are more bacteria in the human body than human cells." Li Feng sounded almost giddy. "We can even sample your own microbiome and isolate a few strains to subject to the Microfriends treatment. That way, you can reflect every day as you check your tank, wall, or table about the unique relationship we as humans have with the smallest creatures in our environment. They also provide a wonderful decorative element that is missing in many macroscopic pets."

"They aren't pets," Erik complained.

"Of course, they are," Li Feng insisted. "They are very low-maintenance pets."

He eyed her. "What's next? Making a rock a pet?"

"That has happened several times historically," Emma informed him. "Including in the 1970s, 2040s and early 2100s. There was a brief revival on Mars about fifty years ago, as well."

"Really?" Erik asked.

Sometimes humans were as mysterious to him as aliens.

Li Feng nodded quickly, misunderstanding who he was talking to. "Yes, really. Low maintenance. You need our special proprietary fluid, but that's it. They make your home or workspace a livelier place."

Erik looked past the woman toward a glowing blue ball

in a small cube tank resting on a stand near a wall. "Bacteria are lively?"

"Of course. They're alive, so they're the very definition of lively. Unlike, for example, robot dogs."

"But they don't *move.*" Erik gestured toward the tank. "Not enough to see."

He could almost hear Emma snickering in his mind.

"That's where their spiritual and meditative value comes in." Li Feng gestured for him to move closer. She went over and crouched by the tank, eyes wide. "Some of our competitors offer strains with unusually high growth periods, but it's nothing but a gimmick designed to force you to buy more nutrient fluid. It's also unnatural."

"And your genetically engineered glowing decorative bacteria aren't unnatural?" Erik asked.

Li Feng stood up, hand over her chest. "Of course not. Just because they're extensively genetically engineered using the most sophisticated modern AI-driven processes, it doesn't make them any less *natural.* We simply are enhancing them to help you. I've heard that if you spend ten minutes a day meditating on a Microfriends pattern, it'll reduce your stress."

"You should ask her if she has any research she can point to that proves that," Emma commented. "I'm interested to see her reaction."

Erik chuckled. "Aren't there bacteria existing on my penjing plants?"

"Those aren't *Microfriends,*" Li Feng insisted, her face a mask of determination. "We only sell species that coexist with people, not the kinds of microbes you mainly find on plants. These are friends for humans, not plants."

"Coexist with people? You mean, these things can infect me?" Erik cast a suspicious glance at the tank.

"No, no. None of these are pathogenic, Detective. They're Microfriends, not Microfiends." Li Feng let out a quiet laugh. "We can sell versions with particular flavors if you want to become one with your Microfriends temporarily through a drink and prefer it not to be an unpleasant experience, but none of them can survive in the human body for long, even if you were drinking their nutrient fluid as well."

"So, let me get this straight." Erik folded his arms and stared at the woman. "You want me to buy a bunch of genetically engineered bacteria as pets, decorations, and tools of spiritual enlightenment?"

She bobbed her head, her bright smile unwavering. "In these turbulent times, we most need to return to simplicity, not the false complexity of something like penjing."

"Nothing says simplicity like heavily genetically engineered bacteria that require a special fluid to live," Erik joked. "The perfect pet."

Li Feng nodded quickly, not detecting his sarcasm. "Exactly, Detective. So, let's talk about what Microfriends strains are best for you."

"Thank you." Erik laughed as he turned away. "See, Emma? This is what delivery can't give you."

"My name is Li Feng, not Emma."

"Delivery can't give you ridiculous product pitches?" Emma asked.

Erik continued walking away from the saleswoman.

"We're running a special today," Li Feng shouted at him. "Fifty percent off all non-glowing strains!"

"No, Emma." Erik threw up a hand in a departing wave to the saleswoman. "Priceless entertainment."

"She was trying hard to convince you, and she is considered cute."

"Well, that was a nice aspect of the conversation, but she doesn't hold a candle…"

"To?"

Erik shook his head as he considered his answer. "Practically anyone with five brain cells to rub together."

CHAPTER FORTY-THREE

September 2, 2229, Neo Southern California Metroplex, Police Enforcement Zone 122 Station, Office of Detectives Jia Lin and Erik Blackwell

Jia rolled her eyes from behind her desk. "Microfriends? She seriously tried to push that garbage on you?"

Erik swallowed a bite of his beignet and nodded. He put up his feet, crossed them, and leaned back. "Yeah. I'm still getting used to that sort of thing. I forgot how much random garbage people buy on core worlds. Out in the frontier colonies, everyone's still trying to get the whole long-term stability and survival situation under control. They're not so bored they need to think of new ways to waste money."

"Bacterial pets?" Jia scoffed. "You might as well have pet rocks."

"That's what I said. Apparently that's been a thing several times," he answered.

"Really?" Jia blinked in surprise. "I suppose I should

stop underestimating the general idiocy of humanity, but it's hard not to be pessimistic as a police officer."

"It's easier not to be disappointed if you don't bet against people being idiots," Erik replied.

"You didn't buy any, did you?" Jia stared at him. "I'm sure she was cute. Please tell me she didn't convince you."

"No, of course not. I'm sticking to penjing and sphere ball. I don't need new hobbies or friends." Erik grinned.

Jia let the conversation lapse into a comfortable silence.

There was something calming about a stupid product being pushed at her partner rather than bullets.

They'd had victories, and with Kandarian defeated, there didn't seem to be anyone actively targeting Erik or her in the entire area. Even the Shadow Zone was transitioning from a dangerous hive of criminality to a place free of major organized crime groups.

A nagging thought threatened her newfound calm. She skimmed through a news feed for a few minutes before the thought grew into something overwhelming and distracting.

"Is there such a thing as being too famous?" Jia asked.

Erik looked at her. "Depends on who you are."

Jia pointed to him and then herself. "Us. More specifically, is there such a thing as a police officer being too famous? I was convinced there was some deep connection between Kandarian and the conspiracy, but when I finally accepted that there wasn't, it made me think about why he wanted you dead. Since the Friends of Purity didn't try to blow me up, it came down to your cybernetics."

Erik flexed his left arm. "Too bad for him he picked the wrong man to assassinate."

"But it wasn't just your arm. It's your *fame*." She pointed between the two of them. "We've both been targeted because of our fame, and we both end up in an unusual amount of trouble compared to not just any cop in Neo SoCal, but anywhere on Earth."

"Sure, but we always solve it. It might take explosions and a lot of bullets, but we're still breathing, right? And all the bad guys are either dead or in jail." An almost comically merry smile took over Erik's face. "That sounds like winning to me. They just make it exciting."

"I get that," Jia replied, "but there's probably a tipping point where that fame, or infamy if you want to think of it that way, will make us trouble magnets rather than suppress ugly things." She held up a hand. "Not saying we should have handled any of our cases a different way, or that Neo SoCal isn't a better off place than it was a year ago. I also get that we haven't accomplished all the success ourselves. We've helped get the ball rolling, but there are thousands of hardworking police officers who have risked their lives to clean this place up. Just, most of them have not been given the opportunity."

Erik nodded slowly. "If you get all that, what are you worried about?" He put his feet down and turned his chair toward her. "There's something you're not saying. I know you well enough to understand that by now. Are you looking for something to be worried about?"

"No, not that." Jia locked eyes with him and took a deep breath. "I've been thinking about it a lot in the last few days. The power of a symbol, justice, and what you and I both want out of our careers."

"And?" he pressed.

"I'm beginning to wonder if Alina's offer is such a bad idea, Erik. The only thing holding you back is me, and I don't know if that's fair. To be honest, I don't even know if I can do my best for the UTC as a detective in the NSCPD anymore. I'm finding it harder to care about local cases when I know there's far deeper corruption out there." Jia smiled. "My mother wants me to try to climb the ranks of the department, but I'm too much like you, so I want to be in the field taking down bad guys. I've tried to tell myself that working with Alina would be too dangerous." She looked out the window, and Erik let her think for a moment before she turned back to him. "But how can it be more dangerous than what we've been dealing with here?"

"I see." Erik leaned back in his chair, his residual smile fading into a neutral expression. "If your mom's talking about promotions, she's really invested in your cop career. Makes sense. She understands you're not going to go get hired at a corp."

"She's accepted it, and now that she has, she needs to apply standard Lin family obsession to it." Jia shrugged. "I can't just be a cop, I need to be the best cop *ever*. That's not a problem in and of itself."

"If you walk away from the department, won't she lose it?" Erik pursed his lips in thought. "I'm not telling you what to do, and if you want me to be honest, if I'm going to take the offer, I'd prefer to have you at my side, but it's not *my* life. Molino isn't your problem. I spent years not having a real relationship with my family, and I wouldn't want you to do anything that would lead to that same situation."

"It doesn't have to be like that if I handle it the right way." Jia stood, nervous energy compelling her to step out from behind her desk and pace. "I've thought about it a lot. It's not like I can tell my family I'd be quitting the force to work for a ghost, so I'll need to give them a line about an exciting opportunity in the private sector as a consultant on government contracts. Then I can claim there are a bunch of non-disclosure agreements that prohibit me from talking about any of it, but that it's important work. They'd respect that, and they wouldn't ask me a lot of questions about it."

"And you're okay with that?" Erik's smile returned. "You'd have to lie to your family."

Jia stopped pacing and sat on the edge of her desk. "Mostly, I just couldn't tell them the truth. If I go with the NDA explanation, my mother would be happier."

Erik tried to decipher the reason behind her comment but couldn't come up with anything, so he gave up and asked. "Why is that?"

"Because she always used to say, 'The more NDAs involved, the more money.'"

Erik laughed. "And money's the best way to determine the winner in the end?"

"Something like that." Jia folded her arms, her eyes searching Erik's. "What about you? I've been assuming you want to go, but maybe I'm wrong. What if I'm pushing a bunch of feelings you don't have onto you? Do you want to take her up on her offer?"

She wasn't sure she could separate her attraction to Erik from her desire to protect people from criminals and terrorists.

Somewhere, whether on Earth or some other planet in the core, there were men and women who thought the

UTC was theirs to do with as they pleased. They needed to be reminded that no one could murder people with impunity and get away with it, regardless of how many credits they had in their bank account or what political power they wielded.

The conspiracy that had pushed terrorists at Erik in Neo SoCal and hired mercenaries to kill his soldiers on Molino was a cancer that needed to be aggressively removed from the heart of the UTC.

"I told you a long time ago that for me, becoming a cop was a means to an end," Erik replied, his voice unusually quiet. "At first, we were running into all sorts of clues, and the bastards were happy to come after me, giving me more leads. But they've been hiding lately, and not making moves. The only traces we've found recently were because Alina pointed us at them. The conspiracy might have decided the best way to deal with me is to ignore me."

This time, Jia waited, allowing him time to divulge whatever feelings he needed to express.

He squeezed a hand into a fist. "Just because I don't talk about it, don't think I'll ever forget, Jia. I remind myself all the time about the soldiers I lost, and that the assholes who killed them believe they've gotten away with it." He unclenched his fist and lowered his arm. "But, yeah, I think I've reached my limit on what I can accomplish as a cop in Neo SoCal."

He looked at her, eyes firm. "But I'm not leaving without you. I wouldn't have been able to do everything I've done without both you and Emma. No matter *where* this shit takes me, I need people I know I can trust to have my back."

Jia opened her mouth to ask if it was just about trust but shut it when Emma materialized in the center of the room. Jia closed her eyes and took a deep breath, then slowly blew it out through her nose.

There were disadvantages to the AI's omnipresence.

"I'm not a person, Detective," Emma complained.

Erik chuckled. "People and AIs I can trust, then." He looked past her at Jia. "Be sure, though. Don't do anything because I'm doing it. Do it because *you* want to. I can't promise you anything at the end of this. I might not even be satisfied, but at least there will be fewer assholes in the UTC by the time this is done."

Jia nodded. "I'll have to think about it a little more. Maybe the Lady will intervene and push us in the right direction."

"You believe in the Lady now?" Erik offered her a mischievous smile.

Jia laughed. "It's hard not to after everything we've gone through."

Emma tilted her head and frowned. "I think a different lady might be intervening."

"What are you talking about?" Erik asked.

"Agent Koval is making use of a similar system as Colonel Adeyemi to send me a message. She says her gift is finally ready, but you'll need to go somewhere to receive it."

Jia slid off her desk. "Well, isn't that fortuitous?"

CHAPTER FORTY-FOUR

UTC Deep Space Prison Delta 97

David Esposito sighed and leaned back in his chair in the small room.

He wanted to believe the guards respected his dignity enough not to bind his hands or feet, but he knew the truth.

They had no reason to fear him.

The chairs and small white table were secured to the floor, and two large guards with stun rods waited outside the room. He wasn't a hardened killer like Kevan, even if some of his choices in the last few years had led to other people being murdered. It was easy to order someone else to take care of a problem.

Now he was behind bars without his wealth or status. He was nothing—less than nothing—saved from predation only by the few friends he'd made and a baseline professionalism among the guards.

Unless his coming visitor somehow smuggled a weapon to him, there would be nothing he could do, and it wasn't like a normal man had a chance of doing that on a prison station.

David didn't even know who was coming to visit him. When he'd received the message, he was surprised. He didn't know anyone named Hadrian Conners, but he also wasn't going to turn down someone willing to speak with him from the outside.

The man had flown all the way to the prison station to meet with him. That had to mean something.

Right?

He'd put out feelers among the prisoners with any sort of sway about wanting to make a deal to help his family on the outside. Most had laughed at him or mocked him. Even the ones who'd listened to his pleas didn't say anything to suggest they could help him. That wasn't surprising.

Sitting over three-hundred and eighty thousand kilometers from Earth in a space station made it hard for most anyone on the inside to maintain influence on the outside.

The door slid open, revealing a tall, pale, gaunt man in an impeccable suit. He offered a polite nod after a leisurely survey of the room. The door slid closed behind him. The man strolled over to a chair on the opposite side of the table and took a seat.

"We can talk freely, David," the man explained. "I've taken measures to ensure that. I thought it was important to establish from the beginning since we're about to discuss some highly illegal activities."

David looked the man up and down. Something about his tight skin and the way he precisely enunciated his words made David's skin crawl. He was like a walking skeleton, and David couldn't even tell his approximate age.

"You're Hadrian Conners?"

"That's the name I'm currently using. It's not my real name, of course." Hadrian offered him a thin smile. "But I've come a long way to meet with you. I'm hoping we can do business together.

David shook his head. "I don't know you. I've never met you, and I've never had any business dealings with you even indirectly. I've never heard of you."

"That's all accurate." Hadrian nodded. "We've never, to the best of my knowledge, met directly in my entire life. We had no reason to. Until recently, given my particular interests, I'd have no reason to deal with a man of your position. Others I associate with have."

"Who?" David eyed him with suspicion.

Hadrian stared back. "I can't give you that information."

David grunted. "Then why are you here? To waste my time? Taunt me? Mock me as a fallen corporate prince?"

Hadrian folded his hands in front of him. "Now, that's a rather rude and presumptuous way of speaking to me. I've come here at your request. It's been passed along to me by certain associates who have heard from other associates that you are looking for a way to help your family, and that you're willing to do whatever it takes to save them. Would you say that's an accurate summary of your position?"

David scoffed. He shook a finger at the pale man. "I know what this is. I admit something, then the warden comes in and accuses me of conspiracy. They tack on more years to my sentence."

Hadrian chuckled. "You're already spending decades in here. What advantage is it for them to entrap you?" His eyes roamed around the room, taking in the prison decor, reminding David of his predicament in a way which words couldn't. "You're far from the worst offender in this place."

"And you expect me to believe that you've come to solve all my problems like some genie?"

Hadrian's lips parted and his eyes widened. "Exactly, David. What a wonderful analogy. Yes, you should think of me as a genie who has come to grant your wishes."

David shuddered. The other man was looking through him as much as at him. He swallowed. He wasn't superstitious, but Hadrian would make a good Grim Reaper if he put on a black robe.

"The best genie stories are morality tales about greed," Hadrian continued. "Or perhaps more accurately, tales of arrogance and hubris. A man granted great power fails to see the possible downsides."

"What the hell does that have to do with anything?" David asked.

Hadrian pulled his hands apart and pointed at David. "A man asks the genie for a wish, and the genie grants it, but the man isn't careful, so he has to pay a terrible price for his wishes to be granted."

"You're seriously threatening me?" David jumped out of his seat and glared at the pale man. "You don't look so tough, and they made sure you didn't have a weapon when you boarded this station. I could choke you to death before they could get in here and stop me, and if you're telling the truth, they probably aren't even watching us."

"Choke me to death?" Hadrian snickered. "Is that something they taught you at Ceres Galactic?"

"No, it's something my buddy Kevan did," David growled. "Stop screwing with me."

Hadrian tapped the table with a single finger. "Sit, Mr. Esposito. My time is far more valuable than yours, and the only reason I'm here is that you can be of use to my employers. You've whined to half the people in this prison for help, so I've come to give it to you. Or I can leave, and your family can rot in squalor. I don't care either way." Despite the harshness of his words, his tone remained calm, his diction precise.

"You're, what?" David swallowed and sank back into his chair. "Some sort of syndicate agent?"

"Something like that," Hadrian replied. "But this is one situation where the less you know, the better for you and your family. I'll make this simple. I can offer you a chance at revenge and a chance at money for your family, enough that they'll be comfortable for a while."

"Revenge?" David frowned. "Against the other people involved? The ones who forced me to take all the blame and then *didn't* protect my family?"

"No. That would be...counterproductive to my employers' interests. Besides, why blame the other people involved in your activities? You freely chose your associations. The problem isn't that everyone didn't suffer. No, no, no. That's not the problem at all. The problem is the self-righteous police who stuck their nose into something they had *no business* getting involved with."

David gripped the edge of the table so hard, his fingertips turned white. "Blackwell and Lin."

"Ah, excellent." Hadrian slow-clapped. "I see you understand the truth and aren't blinded by the extraneous elements."

"I know the CID came swooping in, but if it weren't for

those two, none of it would have happened. People were satisfied with the status quo, but those two damned cops came in and ruined it all!" David slammed a fist on the table. "They ruined my life."

Hadrian replied with a single sharp nod. "Yes, they did ruin your life, and now they're famous, and not just in Neo SoCal or even just Earth. People are talking about them on other *planets*, David." He clucked his tongue. "Does that seem fair? You worked very hard to get your position. You're a man of pedigree. Blackwell is nothing but a retired soldier playing detective, and Lin is a privileged daughter who all but bought her way into the police force. And for what? To lay you low so they can feel smug and superior?"

"You don't have to convince me to hate them. I already do. What's this have to do with helping my family?"

Hadrian stared at David silently. It stretched from seconds to a half-minute.

"What the hell is wrong with you?" David shouted.

"Nothing. Consider it a test."

"You're just screwing with me, aren't you?"

"That would be a waste of time, I can assure you," Hadrian replied. "Blackwell and Lin are a thorn in many people's sides. Everyone would prefer they were gone, but they've proven resilient for a number of reasons. Certain measures have been taken in recent months, but they failed. Other incidental possibilities that looked promising also failed. It's led my employers to consider unorthodox methods for solving the problem."

"You're saying you want them dead?" David smiled. "That would make no one happier than me."

"Neo Southern California is no longer a good place for

business. This has caused my employers much distress. Many business relationships have been disrupted because of their investigations, including the incident that ended in your unfortunate incarceration."

David licked his lips. "You said we'd never done business before."

"And that is correct. I've never personally dealt with you, but you've dealt with people who serve my employers, albeit indirectly. Suffice it to say, if Blackwell and Lin are eliminated, it'll be easier to generate evidence implicating them in corruption. Their allies in particular areas will be on the defensive." Hadrian reached up and adjusted his tie. "They are powerful symbols, and people are rallying to their cause because of that. But if they die under dubious circumstances, and then are exposed through the use of generated evidence? Well, the symbol can be turned against itself. The previous status quo can be restored. Neo Southern California will be open for business again."

"That sounds good." David rubbed his hands together. "If they get taken out, then I can be freed, right?"

Hadrian sighed. "That's unlikely."

David hissed, "Then why are you even talking to me?"

"Because I'm your genie, David, here to grant your wishes." Hadrian held up a bony finger. "Your first wish is for revenge." He held up a second finger. "And your second wish is that your family be taken care of. I'm well aware of their financial situation."

"But the genie's going to turn my wish against me?" David probed.

"The genie's simply going to give you what you want in

a twisted way. All you have to do is help kill Blackwell and Lin."

David let out a pained laugh. "How am I going to do that from a prison station?"

Hadrian's smile didn't reach his eyes. "I'll explain that, but I want to make one thing clear. You will see your wishes granted, but it will cost you your life. I am willing to make sure a quarter of the money is made available to your family in a way that will protect it from CID seizure within a couple of hours. Consider it a good-faith down payment. The rest will come once you've played your part."

David thought about the offer. He had no idea what the man was about to ask him to do, but if he could get that initial payment sent, he could always refuse later. If his family just had a little to survive on, his wife could figure something out.

"Ah, and to be clear," Hadrian began, "if you're thinking you can somehow not carry through on your end, note that we'll be more than happy to direct the CID to the new money if you attempt that. We could also have you killed here, but that would be wasteful. Your sacrifice for the elimination of Blackwell and Lin and the salvation of your family is far more valuable to both you and my employers."

David's shoulders slumped, and his head hung low. He didn't want to die, but he also had no other ideas about how to help his family. Hadrian could be lying to him about the rest of the money, but if even the first part made it through, that could change everything.

The desperate man swallowed and looked up, the reality of his situation leaking from his eyes. "How much money are we talking, and what exactly do I have to do?"

CHAPTER FORTY-FIVE

Erik and Jia stepped into the small private hangar.

Alina's message had directed them to an exclusive private spaceport on the edge of Neo SoCal. A modest boxy cargo transport was parked on thick landing struts. It was neither the sexiest vessel nor the largest Erik had ever seen, but he recognized it immediately—a Rabbit-class Small Transport produced by Yangtze Heavy Industries. He'd seen more than a few in his time on the frontier.

Quick mental calculations told Erik the cargo bay could hold two MX 60s, or one MX 60 and a decent number of ammo boxes and small drones.

With a rumble, the cargo bay door lowered to form a ramp. Alina stood in the cargo bay, her arms crossed. Unlike the last few times they had seen her, she wasn't in disguise—although Erik wasn't sure he'd refer to a cyan ponytail as a natural look.

Alina spread her arms out in a welcoming manner. "Sorry it took so long, but when you're trying to make sure something's not easily traceable, things can get complicated."

"What is this?" Jia asked.

"My gift to you." Alina smiled. "A ship. You can't be Bellerophon and slay monsters without a Pegasus to carry you into the heavens, now, can you?"

"That is one fat Pegasus." Jia eyed the ship.

"But she flies," Alina replied. "And it's a nice start. LLT9208 *Pegasus*."

"LLT?" Erik echoed. "Lunar Light Transport. She's registered on the moon?"

Alina smiled. "Certain things are easier with moon-registered craft for now. While she isn't the nicest-looking vessel, she does have certain features that make it easier to get to and from certain places and hide things, including being registered to a Directorate-affiliated shell company, and a transponder that can be easily changed to emit false signals. Also hidden cargo spaces that won't show up in standard scans."

Erik chuckled. "Lots of smugglers use Rabbits out on the frontier."

"Functional and cheap compared to a lot of alternatives." Alina gestured for them to come aboard. "I figured if you needed to take a trip, it might help if you didn't have to take a commercial transport that might be bombed or hijacked, especially if certain people are watching you more carefully."

Jia strolled toward the ramp, incredulity painted all over her face. "The only time we needed a ship lately was when we did a job for you." She eyed the spy. "You have something in mind?"

"Not immediately, but you both know I want you." Alina grinned. "And you're not wrong. Even if you're not interested in my standing offer, I'm sure I'll find side jobs for you here and there that could be helped along by you having your own ship."

Erik finally moved after Jia, jogging to catch up. His boots thudded on the metal ramp until he reached the empty cargo bay. He looked around. Nothing seemed out of the ordinary for a Rabbit, but it'd been a few years since he'd last stepped aboard one. Searching for contraband wasn't a typical Assault Infantry task.

Alina pointed to a hatch in the corner of the cargo bay. "That gives you direct access to the reactor from inside if you need it. Note it's not a reactor chamber as much as a shaft leading to the reactor."

Erik let her continue for Jia's sake.

Alina pointed to a long box secured against the far wall. "Spacesuits in there, and some pressure suits if you need something less intense. Breathers, too." She pivoted with the grace of a dancer and walked toward a thick door at the front of the cargo bay, pointing with both arms to opposite corners of the room. "I'll show you how to access the hidden cargo areas later. Plenty of space for laser rifles and TR-7s."

She tapped her PNIU, and the door slid open. The trio headed into the next compartment. A bulkhead with another door separated the area into two distinct rooms. A small table with chairs built directly into the deck sat in the corner. Four folding berths were latched to the outer bulkhead. A smaller door opened off the front of the room.

"Shower and all that pesky necessary stuff behind that

door," Alina gestured toward the bulkhead. "You can sleep here. It's going to get cramped if you make a long journey, but it'll work for tooling around the Solar System for now. Most of the side jobs I imagine coming up in the next few months would be local system jobs."

"You've got it planned out already?" Jia asked.

"Fortune favors the prepared," Alina quoted.

She continued toward the door in the front bulkhead. This time she slapped an access panel to open the door. The small cockpit contained three high-backed seats that blocked a clear view of the front window, tightly packed in front of the inactive control panel. Without the ship being powered up, it resembled a flat gray shelf. All the projected displays and active adjusting haptic feedback was unnecessary while docked.

Erik poked his head into the cockpit. "I'm not going to complain about having more toys, but I can't fly a ship. Jia can't either, and I don't think either of us is going to become a pilot anytime soon."

One of the seats turned, revealing a smiling muscular man about Erik's size. His long, drooping dark mustache reminded Erik of a moon gangster's.

Erik and Jia both went for their guns.

The man raised his hands above his head. "Damn, Koval. I thought it wouldn't get dangerous until we were on a mission. They're about to smoke my ass."

Erik and Jia looked at Alina. She nodded with a slight smirk, and they both lowered their hands.

"We don't like surprises," Jia commented.

The corners of Alina's mouth curled up in a faint smile. "Good way to stay alive."

The man stood and offered his hand to Erik, who gave it a firm shake. "Cutter Durn. I do freelance work for Koval occasionally. She said you might need help flying this Rabbit around sometimes."

"You're not a ghost?" Jia asked.

"Nah. No way I'm good enough for something like that." Cutter shook his head. "Nope, I'm not a fancy Goddess of Death like her. I just fly. Do it damned well, though."

"'Goddess of Death?'" Erik echoed, glancing at the ghost.

Alina raised an eyebrow in challenge. "Problem with nicknames, Obsidian Detective?"

"Sensitive, huh?" Erik smirked. "I'll let it go."

Emma materialized in the corner of the room, frowning at Cutter. "You don't need a fleshbag to fly this ship. I can fly it easily."

Cutter grimaced. "Damn. You warned me, Koval, but I wasn't ready for it. Big fancy military AI who looks like a chick."

Jia eyed the man. "No offense, Alina, but how do we know we can trust him? You just said he was freelance. He can be bought."

Cutter laughed. "Yeah, and piss off Koval? I like living and having all my fingers and toes."

"It's a fair complaint." Alina inclined her head toward Cutter. "I trust him, and you'll need a physical pilot at least initially, even if you don't have him fly the ship."

"Why?" Jia asked. "Emma's right."

The AI nodded firmly.

"Because neither of you knows enough to fake proper

procedures, even with Emma whispering in your ear," Alina explained, gesturing to the inactive control panel.

Cutter shook Jia's hand before taking a seat. "If Alina just wants to pay me to look pretty, that's fine, but you can't always trust a machine."

"And you can't trust a man who looks as ridiculous as you," Emma retorted.

Cutter burst out laughing and shook his head. "I've never been owned by a fake chick before."

Emma scoffed and folded her arms. "I can see you'll wear thin quickly."

"You sound like my ex-wife," he muttered.

"Cutter has a point," Alina commented. "Depending on where Emma's matrix is, she might not be able to control the ship. You might need to take her with you."

"We'll figure out something," Erik replied. "But we just took a vacation. We're not going anywhere soon. I'm surprised you got us this ship."

"I'm fine with that." She smiled. "But you're not just good at solving problems. You're also good at finding them. I'm sure that'll be useful sooner rather than later. I'll also make sure you have an easy and secure way of getting in touch with Cutter via Emma."

The AI rolled her eyes. "Must I be the one who has to communicate with this ridiculous…" she eyed him, "fleshbag?"

"I like her," Cutter commented. "She's feisty. Always trust a feisty chick, whether she's real or a hologram."

Erik chuckled. "Alina, I've got decent savings, but running a ship could eat into that pretty quickly."

"Don't worry." Alina patted the back of one of the seats. "I'll get you set up with my ID-affiliated accounts. They don't show up that way, of course. More shell companies, but you'll be able to expense the basic costs of the ship through those. It'll be enough to keep you going for basic operations."

"Weapons?" Erik asked, boyish curiosity in his voice.

Jia glanced at him.

"You've got plenty right now on your own. Don't get greedy. It'll be easier to keep your involvement with the ID secret if we limit what we're paying for. You're cops. You know how this goes. Lines of evidence."

"I'd prefer a few on this baby," Erik commented.

"If Talos or anyone else comes after you in space, you better board their ship, because there is no way you're going to win in something like this." Alina's earlier cheerful tone had vanished.

"I'm ex-Assault Infantry. I prefer boarding actions anyway."

Jia cleared her throat and gestured toward the crew berths. "Erik, could I talk to you alone for a moment?"

"Sure." Erik nodded to Cutter and Alina before following his partner into the other room.

Jia eyed Alina in the cockpit and lowered her voice. "You find strange women."

"I didn't find her," he argued. "She found me. Technically, she found *both* of us."

"And she just gave you a ship." Jia gestured to the cockpit.

"Us." Erik pointed to her and then himself. "She just gave *us* a ship."

"What the hell are we going to do with a ship?" Jia ignored his clarification.

"Fly around?" Erik shrugged. "I thought you were almost ready to take her offer."

"I am." Jia glanced at Alina again with a slight frown. "But I don't like doing things on her terms. We should make the call and control our situation."

"I'm not saying you're wrong, but we're going to need a ship, and this is a good start. Taking it doesn't mean we are her lapdogs."

"Yet," Jia replied. "But remember to be careful. The conspiracy might not own the government, but they've got their claws into it."

"I'm always careful," Erik commented. "But that's also why I want *you* to watch my back."

They stared into each other's eyes for a moment. Erik wanted to say something more, but there was no way in hell he was going to do that with Cutter and Alina only a few meters away.

The idea of flying around in a ship with Jia in close quarters appealed for reasons that had nothing to do with the conspiracy.

"How about we take it for a spin?" Emma interrupted via their PNIUs. Her holographic form remained in the cockpit, frowning at Cutter. "Without the mustachioed fleshbag, of course. Have either of you watched the planet turn from your own ship before?"

"No." Erik rubbed his face, grateful for the interruption. "But not yet. We'll get our chance, but she's right. We'll need Cutter, at least for now."

"Just because we have a pilot, it doesn't mean we don't need you, Emma," Jia insisted.

"This isn't about being needed," the AI insisted. "Have you seen his mustache? That's a grievous insult to anything with visual processing ability. Have some standards for your species, I beg you."

Erik glanced at Cutter. "We'll have to take him with us to Chang'e City the next time we go. He'll fit right in. For now, let's get the info about the accounts from Alina. We don't know if we won't need this for months or if we'll need it tomorrow. Somehow, though, I think this is as much a signal from the Lady as it is from the lady in the front of the ship."

CHAPTER FORTY-SIX

September 5, 2229, Neo Southern California Metroplex, Copez Pilot Training Center

Jia stepped into the spacious lobby of the pilot training center. Light classical music played over speakers.

On either side were small offices with transparent walls, holding black tables and chairs. Some of the offices had people inside, gesturing to data windows, but most were empty.

A couple of men, folded pressure suits under their arms, passed through the door into the back.

She hesitated for a moment, wondering if she was wasting her time. The doubt passed, and she made her way toward a smiling young woman standing behind a desk at the front. Her nametag read Daiyu.

The receptionist stared at Jia for a moment, uncertainty on her face.

"Is something wrong?" Jia asked. She hadn't done anything odd she could remember since entering the building.

The receptionist winced. "Oh, I'm sorry, ma'am. I didn't mean to be rude. You just looked familiar. I like to think I never forget a face, and I know your face, but I also don't think we've met. Is that like fate?"

Jia didn't want to play the fame card, but it wasn't like she could hide her identity for long.

"Not fate. The news." Jia shrugged with an apologetic smile.

"The news?" Daiyu tilted her head, a confused look on her face.

"There's been the occasional news story on me. I'm Detective Jia Lin."

"I know you!" Daiyu put both hands over her mouth and gasped. "Lady Justice!"

Please don't squeal!

"That's…a nickname they have given me, yes. Apparently, it's too hard just to call me Detective Lin." Jia tried to keep smiling. Sometimes the price of fame wasn't getting shot at or having bombers sent.

Sometimes it was inconvenience in your daily life.

"Are you here on a case?" Daiyu leaned forward and dropped her voice to a whisper. "Is there a syndicate smuggler here? Terrorists? I totally saw this guy who looked like one of the terrorists on my favorite drama *Red and White Mars*, and I told my friend, and she's like, 'That just means he's probably an actor.' I tried to tell her they pick actors who look like criminals to make it more gritty." She paused to gather breath. "So he's probably a criminal."

Jia blinked, trying to keep everything straight in her head. Once she finally realized what the woman was talking about, she shook her head. "It's nothing like that.

I'm not here on police business. I want to talk to someone about getting lessons for a Class D license."

"Oh." Daiyu smiled, although there was disappointment in her eyes. "One moment, Lad…Detective Lin. I'll go get someone for you." The tapping of her shoes broke the silence as she hurried to a door leading to the back and disappeared through it.

Jia grimaced.

A few producers had sniffed around her and Erik, asking about making a movie or a show, but they'd been able to scare them off. There might come a point where a studio decided to make a fictionalized show about a corp princess and her vet partner. They could just change the names and pretend it wasn't about them. For some reason, the *Blackstone Gambit* came to mind as a title.

"Maybe something with Brown would work better," she muttered under her breath, wondering why she was even thinking about that sort of thing. There was nothing she could do about a docu-drama at the moment. She needed to concentrate on her reason for coming to the training center.

Jia had not mentioned her plan to anyone, including Erik, and since Emma didn't actively interface with her PNIU when they weren't together, no one knew about her little scheme to improve her skills.

Of course, the only reason to take lessons was if she decided Emma and Cutter needed backup. It didn't make sense not to keep Cutter around since Alina was the one paying him.

If he was working for the Goddess of Death, they wouldn't have to keep secrets from him.

Jia's body stiffened. *Had she already advanced that far?* She'd been skeptical of the ship, but at the same time, she was considering the logistics of what it would take to live a life of investigation without police resources. She'd already made up details she could pass along to her family to explain her job shift.

Erik kept warning her not to do anything because of him, but her thoughts about the offer had long since passed just wanting to help him.

He'd changed her.

She couldn't deny that, but the potential was always there. A year ago, she thought stopping the occasional fraud in Neo SoCal would be enough to satisfy her, but now she craved to travel the UTC and make it a better place.

It was more than that, though.

She wanted to test herself.

The frontier couldn't be any more dangerous than her experiences in the last year. She wanted to tell Erik all that, but it felt like pushing too hard. Or maybe some small piece of the old Jia was still holding her back. She couldn't be sure, but it wouldn't hurt to expand her skill set in either event.

Jia waited patiently, lost in her thoughts until Daiyu reappeared with an older man with close-cropped graying hair.

He extended his hand. "I'm Idrin. I'm one of the senior trainers here, Detective Lin. We didn't expect someone famous to walk in."

Jia shook his hand. "I'm not that famous."

"Depends on who you ask." Idrin pointed at an empty office. "Let's talk over there."

The pair made their way to the office while Daiyu retook her post as a smiling sentinel on the lookout for handsome syndicate arms traffickers who looked like actors.

The small flickers of doubt remaining in Jia's mind began to burn away. Even if she didn't end up taking Alina's offer, learning to pilot wasn't a bad idea. It would have helped with at least one case already. Admittedly, it was an Alina-related matter. Besides, something about piloting appealed to her.

She liked the idea of controlling a spacecraft.

She'd never had a strong desire to fly her flitter, but controlling a spaceship was a different matter. That might not be rational, but for once, she didn't care. It was the idea that excited her.

Idrin gestured to a chair across from him and took a seat. "Just to be clear, Detective, this isn't about a case? Daiyu said it wasn't, but then she immediately asked me if we have any new *shady* clients and then said something about actors looking like criminals. She's a very friendly woman and good with clients, but I admit, I sometimes have *no* idea what she's talking about."

Jia settled into her seat with a polite laugh. "No, this has nothing to do with a case and nothing to do with the NSCPD. It's just something I've been thinking about lately, and I wanted to see how plausible learning to pilot is, given my schedule."

Idrin tapped his PNIU. Images of several small spacecraft

appeared, including a Rabbit and some single-seaters. There were only a few ships larger than the Rabbit, including two sleek space yachts. "This is the range of things that are covered by a Class D license. I don't mean to be rude, Detective, but I want to make it clear this is for spacecraft, not primarily atmospheric craft. If you're looking for that kind of training, I can direct you to an appropriate place. Despite what you might see in dramas, the skills between atmospheric and non-atmospheric aren't very transferable."

"No, I'm exactly where I need to be." Jia gestured to the image of the Rabbit. "I want to be able to fly something like that." She swept her hand to indicate the other craft. "Or any of them. Eventually, I'd like to learn to fly something bigger, but it's not like I started with a heavy laser rifle when I learned to shoot."

He eyed her for a moment, taking in her last comment. "It uh, it takes a lot of time to become a certified pilot, Detective, even Class D. I know you're a police officer, but you might not appreciate how many more laws, regulations, and rules there are for spacecraft than atmospheric craft. There are also many more legal limits on using AI assistance on spacecraft than any other type of vehicle."

"I've spent the last few days poring over those laws," Jia replied. "You're right. There are a lot, and they're all good and reasonable regulations. I'm eager to study them in the context of piloting, but what I'm more curious about is the time commitment. If I were able to attend training on a weekly basis and I had access to my own ship where I could fly with a fully licensed pilot, how long do you think it'd take?"

Idrin shrugged. "Three to six months, I suppose,

depending on how quickly you get through the simulator training before we go to practice flights. The pilot you're talking about could help you get your registered hours past the simulator hours. However, we have our own strict curriculum here, and if you're getting your certification through us, we insist you follow our program in full, even if you're supplementing with outside material."

"Understandable." Jia leaned forward. "So, let's talk about scheduling."

"That's it?" He blinked. "That quickly?"

"It wasn't just the laws and regulations I was studying the last few days." Jia summoned several data windows in the air between them. They contained reviews of different pilot training centers, pilot safety training statistics, and a myriad of other data.

Idrin leaned forward to skim the windows, his eyes flitting from one to the next to take in the salient points before he looked through them at her. "Not just a whim? I'd say you were having a midlife crisis, but you're a little young for that."

Jia brought up a calendar. "I'm not planning to start right away, but I'd like to start within a few weeks, and I also don't want my name splashed all over the media. That's both for my privacy and to protect the security of this place."

"Detective Lin, I'm sure we can accommodate those requests." Idrin smiled warmly, offering his hand again. "Let me welcome you to training at Copez."

The old woman kept her hands folded in her lap as she listened to Erik speak.

He'd gone for a jog to clear his head when he hit a circle of benches nestled in a tiny clearing. He'd not spotted anyone except the old woman for the last fifteen minutes. When he settled down, a simple greeting turned into him mentioning woman trouble and an abbreviated admission of his situation with Jia, with a few key details left out, such as that they were detectives.

"Erik, was it?" the old woman asked him, a squeak in her voice.

He nodded. "Yeah."

She lifted her head to smile at the sun hidden behind the trees, a serene look on her face. "All our technology and planets, even aliens, and everything's always about the same problems in the end." She sighed. "It's funny when you think about it."

Erik let out a pained chuckle. "That is the truth."

He was glad he had stopped to talk to her. Sometimes all you needed was a good grandma type to give advice, and it was difficult to find someone who didn't recognize him as the Obsidian Detective, let alone someone with wisdom.

She might not be that much older than him chronologically speaking, but his decades out on the frontier had made him weaker in social skills than he was willing to admit.

The old woman slowly turned away from her admiration of nature to focus on Erik. "This isn't that hard, though. You just have to think about the real issue."

"It's complicated since we both have a lot going on."

She took a sly look around the clearing before leaning closer. "I'm going to ask you the same thing I asked my second grandson when he called yesterday with a similar problem."

"Sure, whatever will help."

"Are you banging her yet?"

Erik stared at her in disbelief. "What?"

"Are you banging this woman yet?" the old woman whispered as if they weren't the only humans for hundreds of paces around them. "If you are, and you already feel this way, you're overthinking it. You're obviously into her. You should go for it."

"I, uh..."

The old woman laughed quietly, patting his arm. "That's how he reacted, too. When he stopped sputtering, he admitted he was already sleeping with her." She pinned him with her gaze. "What about you, Erik?"

"No, not yet." Erik shook his head. "We're not even really dating, remember?"

"Real dating? Fake-dating?" The woman scoffed, waving her hand. "Labels don't mean anything. *Feelings* do. And chemistry." She pointed a finger up. "You need the heat between the sheets. Is that the problem? Is she not hot enough for you?"

Erik couldn't believe this sweet old lady was talking that way, although as his shock faded, he appreciated her candor. "No, that's not it." He sighed. "She's damned hot. The first time I met her, you should have seen the dress she was in. It should be illegal. But that's not everything, right? Circumstances matter."

"Why? If you work with her and you don't have a problem, that's a sign of compatibility. If you're physically attracted to her, that's another sign of compatibility. Just need that final chemistry test."

For once, it was Erik who blushed. "Heat between the sheets?"

"Exactly." The old woman winked and stood. "Don't fight it, Erik. We're not machines. This kind of thing isn't about careful thinking." She waved and headed toward the path. "Good luck."

Erik watched her until she disappeared from the clearing. "I wasn't expecting that."

"Heat between the sheets, indeed." Emma snickered.

"You shut up, and not a word of this to Jia, or I'm ejecting your matrix into the asteroid belt," he muttered.

Emma only laughed harder, even if she did calculate the probability at just under ten percent he would do exactly that.

CHAPTER FORTY-SEVEN

September 7, 2229, Neo Southern California Metroplex, Police Enforcement Zone 122 Station, Office of Captain Alexander Ragnar

Erik stepped into Captain Ragnar's office with a smile, Jia right behind him.

It'd been an easy but boring morning, dominated by a Kandarian report follow-up. Erik suspected that was about to change. Being summoned to the captain's office meant one of two things.

Either Captain Ragnar was going to tear them a new one, or he had a high-profile case for them—something with potential political sensitivity. Doing real policework would be nice, especially since the Malcolm situation wasn't a distraction anymore.

The smile slipped off Erik's face as soon as he spotted his superior.

Captain Ragnar sat behind his desk, his massive frame imposing and a concerned look on his face. That didn't scream someone who wanted to yell at his two top detectives, but it wasn't the look of a man who wanted to discuss the best beignet recipes. There was one possibility that might be far more annoying than a politically sensitive new case.

"Don't tell me Kandarian's walking," Jia spat, beating Erik. "If they're letting him walk, they better be trailing him with so many drones, he won't be able to take a dump without them knowing."

Erik eyed the red-faced Jia after her regrettable outburst but said nothing. Perhaps she had been spending too much time at the sports bars with him during games? It wasn't that he minded, but would she realize what she had just said and be embarrassed?

"No," the captain replied. "He's not even trying to get out of the charges. This has nothing to do with Kandarian or any of your recent cases. You don't have to worry about that."

"What is it, then?" Erik asked.

The captain's brow furrowed even deeper. "We've received a message from David Esposito's prison. He wants to talk to you two. He claims he has additional information he wants to give up on Ceres Galactic. He claims he can implicate a number of highly placed people both within the company and without."

"If he had that kind of information, why didn't he give it up before? It might have shaved a few decades off his sentence."

Jia nodded in quick agreement. "And why us? It's not like we can do anything for him at this point. We weren't the arresting officers."

Captain Ragnar tapped a virtual keyboard projected

over his desk. An image of a beautiful dark-haired young woman in an elegant black gown appeared. She looked familiar to Erik, but he couldn't quite place her.

Jia rubbed her chin. "That's Maria Esposito, right? His wife?"

Erik gazed at the picture for a moment before remembering. De-aging had treated him well, but he still had a little stubborn gray in his hair that didn't want to go away. He wondered if it ever would.

"Yes, that's Maria Esposito," Captain Ragnar confirmed. "And I think she might be the reason her husband suddenly is feeling talkative. The CID recently froze what few accounts she had left, and it's put financial pressure on the family. Those weren't working-class people even before his arrest."

Erik snorted. "They probably told David she'd be fine if he took the fall. Or maybe she didn't realize she needed to cut back on new yachts."

The captain gave Erik an appraising look. "This case was before my time, and it was your first big case, even if the CID took the glory in the end. With everything else under your belt, can you be sure there's something more there? Esposito wasn't a low-level peon. It's not impossible that he was responsible for everything and is now just spewing lies in desperation."

"No way." Jia's expression twisted in anger. "This goes a lot deeper than David Esposito. There's no way it stopped with him."

"But the CID couldn't figure that out?"

She shook her head. "A corrupt CID agent was exposed not long after that incident. The whole thing was timed a little too perfectly." Jia motioned at the image of Maria. "I'm not saying we can't trust anyone, but the whole reason David Esposito was thrown to the CID was to stop us from pressing deeper into things. There are other people at Ceres Galactic, highly placed people, who are dirty. I'm sure of it. If Esposito's desperate enough to want to give them up, we need to move before they or their friends figure out what he's doing and take him out."

"That might be why he wants to talk to us," Erik suggested. "Has he only contacted the station? No one else?"

Captain Ragnar nodded. "To the best of my knowledge, the prison passed his message directly to me, per his request. He had wanted it sent to you two, but the prison officials weren't sure that was wise. They didn't know if it was some sort of veiled threat."

"He has to realize if he's contacting us, we might not be able to help him cut a deal," Jia commented. "Did his message mention a deal?"

"It wasn't a direct message," Captain Ragnar explained. "The prison officials just passed along that he wants to speak with you two, that it has to do with Ceres Galactic, and that he won't talk to anyone but you two, and only in person."

Jia thought for a moment before answering. "It's possible he might think we're the only ones who can be trusted, or that we'll be able to push the prosecutors because of our reputations. If we go in person, he'll be sure he's talking to us. It'd be far too easy for Ceres Galactic and anyone else they're working with to fake messages from us, or even a call, especially with the delay."

"'Anyone else they're working with?'" Captain Ragnar looked past Jia at the closed door. "Please have Emma make this safe to talk."

Emma appeared beside Erik. "You could have just asked me directly. But it's done."

"When you say anyone else, you're talking about Talos or a group like them, aren't you?" Captain Ragnar stared at Jia.

"Yes," Jia responded confidently. "While we don't have enough direct evidence to prove it in court, there's no way Ceres is just a normal corrupt company."

Captain Ragnar leaned back in his chair and looked down, a troubled expression overtaking his face. "If that's true, David Esposito could give you something that would expose something far more important than a corrupt councilman." He lifted his head. "I'm sure you both know much more than you've told me, and I doubt I'd know about Talos if ID hadn't thought they were forced to tell me."

"Captain," Jia began. "It's—" She fell silent at the lift of his hand.

"It's fine. I'm a cop, but I also know there's a reason friends of mine in the military pushed to get me appointed here. I'd gone my entire career without dealing with the Intelligence Directorate until they showed up here." Captain Ragnar shook his head. "If you've kept something from me, it's because it's too dangerous for me to know, or because some ghost has told you they'll disappear you if you tell me. But that circles us back to Esposito and the problem at hand."

Erik frowned. "What problem?"

The captain eyed him. "If Esposito's in danger from some conspiracy beyond Ceres Galactic, we need to do what we can to have fewer official channels involved with this. If I okay paying for a flight out to the prison and make it official, people are going to find out sooner." Captain Ragnar grunted in frustration. "If they haven't already."

"Won't be a problem," Erik replied, a grin building. "We've got connections that can get us there without using departmental resources. We just need official approval to go to the prison, so they don't try to gun us down when we get there."

"I don't want to authorize this as part of an official case yet," Captain Ragnar replied. "But the prison officials have already made it clear they're willing to receive you, as long as we all keep quiet about it. We'll have you flagged under normal visitation. That should keep you off certain people's radars for a little longer. For all we know, this might all be bullshit, and Esposito just wants to spit in your faces after wasting your day."

Jia snorted. "No. He fell on his sword for the company, but he's gone from being a VP at one of the most important companies in the UTC to being stuck in prison. The prospect of rotting in space while his family is being squeezed has to have put things into perspective and made him desperate."

"But like you said, we can't offer him any deals," Erik noted.

"If he's got something worthwhile, I'm sure we can work with the captain and CID to figure out how to handle it. If he's truly willing to give up important players, that's got to shave at least a few years off his sentence."

Captain Ragnar looked at his detectives. “These connections you mentioned. Can they get you there quickly, or is it going to take a few days to set up?”

Erik shook his head. “Nope. We could leave whenever.”

The captain tapped his fingers on the desk a few times. “Then I’d suggest you call your friends and get going. If he’s not full of shit, who knows how long it is before he ends up dead?”

CHAPTER FORTY-EIGHT

Sitting in a cockpit seat, Jia stared out the window as Earth dropped behind them.

Despite what Emma had suggested, she didn't feel any special wonder at the massive blue marble just because they were in their own ship. Her previous trip to the moon might have taken away the joy of spaceflight, or the reason for their trip was dampening her enthusiasm. The residual tension stiffening her neck didn't help.

As with their trip to the moon, this wasn't a sightseeing expedition, and unlike that trip, there wouldn't be any interesting landmarks or local culture to observe at the prison.

Virtual displays lit up the control panel. Various tones sounded occasionally. Jia recognized a few from her pre-study for flight training, including a slow pulsing proximity warning indicating nearby material not on a collision course.

Radar and lidar displays depicted the jungle of objects in the nearby area.

someone who can be trusted and won't panic when someone launches a missile at them," Emma answered.

"Someone's fired a missile at you?" Cutter sounded more curious than surprised.

Jia nodded. "More than once."

He shook his head. "No wonder Koval likes you two."

Jia's gaze shifted to a distance and projected arrival readout. Between acceleration, deceleration, and docking, the trip to the prison station would take about twelve hours. There wasn't much to see on the way, other than the occasional space station that looked like nothing but a distant speck of light.

Jia stood. "I'll be right back. Just want to stretch my legs and talk to Erik."

Cutter nodded. "I'll just be here wasting space for good pay."

"Indeed," Emma commented.

He smiled at the hologram.

Jia made her way out of the cockpit and through the crew quarters. Now that they were on the ship speeding toward a location, the tight quarters were more obvious. If they had more than four people, they would need to work in shifts. That wasn't unusual for small crews, from what she'd read.

She stopped at the table, running her hand over it. She'd gone from not being sure when they would use the ship to worrying about crew staffing and logistics.

If Erik pressed her, she might even admit to wondering how hard it would be to hide a few anti-ship weapons on the Rabbit.

Jia lifted her hand and stared at it.

Leaving the NSCPD would be daunting. For all the media attention heaped on the Obsidian Detective and Lady Justice, as if they were single-handedly saving the metroplex, they still relied on a large number of people for support.

It wouldn't be easy to replace that network. Alina could help, but they wouldn't be Intelligence Directorate agents with full access to the organization's resources. Jia didn't doubt her abilities. She just preferred it when things were less difficult.

With a shake of her head, she continued out of the crew quarters.

There was only so much planning they could do until they decided to leave for certain. She opened the door to the empty cargo bay. There was no reason to bring a flitter to a prison station. Although a few emergency supplies and the suits were packed in crates, most of their gear was hidden in the secure cargo areas.

Erik lay on his back in the center of the cargo bay, staring at the ceiling.

"What are you doing?" Jia lifted her head to see what he was staring at. The cargo bay ceiling remained nondescript and gray.

"Getting a feel for the ship," Erik replied. "If we're going to have this one for a while, I figured it'd help. All the transports I flew on since Molino were different sorts of ships. Flying hotels. Not like this. I'd prefer something with a few more guns, but it's nice to have the mobility. Being in here also reminds me of being in the Army on a troop transport. No flight attendants bringing me snacks, just a lot of men, women, and weapons sitting and waiting, talking trash. It's not like we were in our drop pods the entire time."

"And I thought you were in here double-checking the laser rifle," Jia commented.

He sat up and shot her a smile. "The less I mess with it, the less chance there is of them finding it."

"We're technically smuggling weapons to a prison station. I didn't even blink when you started loading things, but it's true. As Emma pointed out to me recently, I've let a lot of illegal stuff slide."

Erik hopped to his feet. "Technically true. However, we're not planning to bring the weapons past the docking bay. If it makes you feel any better, law enforcement is technically allowed to bring weapons when investigating possible crimes at prison stations, and that's exactly what we're doing. I've read the regulations."

"That's a pretty thin excuse if we get caught." Jia leaned against the wall, her arms crossed. "Especially since this isn't an official police visit, and we didn't request permission."

"We might not need them, but you know how things go for us. We might talk to Esposito and get caught up in a prison riot. We'll be hundreds of thousands of kilometers from Earth. If I have to bend a few rules to make sure we don't end up dead?" He shrugged, "Well, I'm going to do it."

"I suppose if we're going to take Alina's offer, I'm going to have to stop thinking like a cop." Jia chuckled. "The old me would have been shocked to hear that, but that's where I am."

"That means you're attuned to reality." Erik walked toward her. "And you already seem to get it. We've been playing fast and loose with the letter of the law for a while now, especially using Emma."

"I know." She moved her hair out of her eyes. "I've accepted that. I've also accepted that the kind of men behind Molino aren't going to be caught through conventional means. Esposito is a way to tell for sure. I have a feeling this will be the meeting that determines whether we stay cops or not."

Erik stopped in front of her, a surprised look on his face. "You think so?"

Jia nodded. "Yes. We'll be there unofficially, but we're still going as NSCPD cops. If he gives us good information, we might be able to take on the conspiracy as cops. We won't have to fly around in modified smuggling transports, and we'd still have all the official aboveground resources to help us. It'll be easy to go after dangerous assassins and full-conversion Tin Men with TPST backing."

"I hope it's that easy," Erik admitted. "But I doubt it will be. If I can take down those bastards all nice and legal, I'll be happy to choose that direction. This has never been about anything except getting justice for my soldiers."

"It's going to be a lot more than that in the end." Jia lowered her arms and took a deep breath. "Whoever did it is hiding something so big they were willing to kill an entire military unit to cover it up. There was something so important on Molino that it was worth risking the attention of not just the military, but also the CID and ID. Effectively, the entire government of the UTC."

"Assuming it doesn't turn out to be the government in the end," Erik offered.

"I've considered that possibility, but we've got enough

people in the government helping us that it's more likely to be a rogue operation if it is."

"Unless we're the rogues." Erik cocked his head. "I kind of like the idea that we are."

"I don't know about that," Jia replied. "I'll be honest. I want to help because I care about you, Erik, but the evidence points to deep corruption at the heart of the UTC. If we take it out, it'll make it better for everyone."

"Maybe." Erik averted his eyes. "I'm going to be honest with you, too. That's just a nice bonus as far as I'm concerned. We might find some evil assholes at the end of this, but even if we send them to prison or kill them, more will probably just pop up. I'm less worried about the future than the past."

"If new puppet masters appear, we'll take them down, too," Jia told him. "It gives us something to do other than go to sphere ball matches." She slapped the wall. "Naivete isn't believing you can defeat evil. It's believing you only have to defeat it *once*." She slammed a fist into her palm. "It's like the emperors back in ancient China. They had the Mandate of Heaven until they didn't and someone brought them down. This was a Shadow Mandate, and they lost it on Molino." She looked at something in the distance, or was it in the future? "They just don't realize it yet."

Erik stared at her for a moment, then a grin appeared. "Listen to you. When I met you, you couldn't even shoot a man with a stun pistol. Now you're talking about crushing every new conspiracy that arrives."

"My eyes are open now. Let's just hope Esposito gives us something to work with."

CHAPTER FORTY-NINE

The prison station loomed before them on their final approach. Despite all the emptiness of space, the sensor displays made it clear this slice of the Solar System, L4, was far from empty. The clusters of stations in that orbit weren't close enough for easy transit from one to another, but they formed their own small constellations, masquerading as bright stars in the distance.

"I've imitated Mr. Durn's voice for final approach communications," Emma explained. She'd been invisible for the last few hours. "I did not imitate his annoying manner."

"Because no one can imitate me all the way," Cutter insisted, jerking a thumb toward his chest. "I'm unique and original. That's why I fly ships and don't try to do all that ghost stuff."

Emma raised an eyebrow. "You certainly are unique. No one can escape that horrifying realization."

Cutter chuckled.

Erik found himself transfixed by the prison station

growing closer in front of them. The squat globular central body connected with a dozen arms leading to circular compartments. A few patrol ships, mere specs in the distance, flew past. It wasn't as if someone escaping had much of a chance.

The Fleet maintained a presence in the area and was more than prepared to send destroyers and fighters to intercept anyone who might somehow escape from a prison station, providing them an opportunity for target practice.

"Never been to one of these," he admitted with a chuckle. "We barely had any on the frontier. A lot of colonial governments think it's a waste of resources to house prisoners off-planet, especially if they can use those prisoners for any sort of work."

"I suppose it was inevitable that we ended up on one as cops." Jia nodded toward the station in the distance. "But from everything I've read, on the inside, it's not any different from a jail on Earth."

"Looking the same and being the same are very different." Erik lifted his arm. "Just like with this. A man in jail still knows there is air outside those walls, and he knows he might have a chance at returning to a normal life. A man on a prison station knows there's nothing but death waiting outside."

"I just hope we're not wasting a day being screwed with by Esposito." Jia glanced at Cutter. "You're going to have to stay on the ship. We're the only authorized visitors. They know you're coming, but you can't enter the prison."

He shrugged. "I don't care either way as long as I get

paid. It's not like I was looking forward to hanging out in a prison."

They finished their approach, Emma decelerating until the ship gently floated forward. The large docking bay doors had already opened, the faint shimmer of the temporary oxygen field marking the border of survival.

The docking bay wasn't much more than an expansive open area with several sets of docking clamps. A couple of patrol craft, slender ships not much larger than the MX 60 were parked at the far end of the dock. A cargo ship easily twice as long as the Rabbit was docked in the center.

Emma fired thrusters to maneuver their ship next to the other cargo vessel.

The light from the inside the bay grew brighter, the darkness of space receding from the edges of their view. Proximity alarms beeped, warning of their final approach. The grav emitters smoothed out the impact of the course corrections on the three humans inside, but they all wore harnesses for the final approach.

Emma extended the landing struts, a faint mechanical whir echoing throughout the ship.

The Rabbit glided gently into the docking bay, now subject to the prison station's grav field. Emma brought the Rabbit down to settle near a forward docking clamp. Prison guards in beige uniforms, stun rods on their belts, stood at parade rest, surrounding a tall white-haired man in a dark suit.

"Let's go say hello," Erik suggested. "And hope we didn't waste our time."

"We're not going to be able to bring our PNIUs into the prison," Jia commented. She grimaced. "I hadn't thought of that."

"So?"

"No PNIUs means no access to Emma."

"That does sound questionable," the AI chimed in.

"We'll be fine." Erik unfastened his harness.

"I've gotten used to the backup," Jia admitted.

"I appreciate your confidence and support, Detective Lin," Emma replied.

"Just keep the sensors active, and if anything weird happens, she can hack the prison."

"Hack a prison?" Jia stared at her partner in disbelief. "Are you *insane*? That's not keeping a low profile."

"Only if something happens, and only if the prison staff can't keep it under control. I'm not saying she should do it if there's a riot." Erik inclined his head toward the side of the cockpit. "Emma, open her up. I'm guessing the guy in the suit is the warden."

She sniffed. "It is. I checked his image against the database I downloaded."

With a hiss followed by a loud hum, a side door pulled away from the cockpit. When it was pointed down, a ladder extended until it hit the ground. Erik and Jia disembarked and walked toward the guards and warden.

The man in the suit cleared his throat and extended his hand. "Warden Harris. My pleasure, Detectives."

Erik and Jia shook his hand in turn.

"We're sorry to have to bother you," Jia replied. "But if

Esposito's ready to give people up, this could lead to the case being reopened and a lot of other people going down."

The warden smiled. "No, I'm sorry you had to come all the way out here. We do our best to keep filth away from Earth so people don't have to deal with them. You two have dealt with your fair share of antisocials and others. You know what I'm talking about." He looked over his shoulder. A narrow hallway led from the cargo bay to a reinforced door. "I'm going to be honest with you. You might hate me when I say this since you just flew a half a day to get here, but I think you're wasting your time."

"Why?" Erik asked.

"Because I think this is just Esposito trying to get you to come here so he can cry about his family," the warden admitted, annoyance coloring his voice. "He was already whining to us. I don't know what he expects us to do about it. We're not the ones who committed his crimes."

Erik grunted. "If you think he's just yanking our chain, why did you tell us to come?"

The warden gestured toward the corridor and turned around. "Because if I'm wrong, we get more customers to join the family here in our pleasant hotel. I'm willing to take a few hits to the ego and admit I'm wrong if it means we take down more criminals."

Erik could respect that and said nothing back.

The guards didn't move, so Erik and Jia fell in behind the warden. The other men finally broke their line, forming a semi-circle in the rear. Erik wondered if it was a show of force to impress him.

That he *didn't* respect.

The warden stopped at the reinforced door and placed

his hand on the access panel. Internal bolts thudded, and the door opened to a small room connected to another reinforced door. He stepped inside and waited for Erik and Jia to join him. After they did, the door shut behind them, leaving the guards outside.

The warden gestured to Erik's and Jia's PNIUs. "Sorry, no outside devices. We'll give them to you on the way out. If you have anything else on you, this is a good time to pull it out." He pointed to his eyes. "That includes smart lenses, sorry."

A small door popped open in the side wall and lowered until it was flat. Two thin trays lined it on either side. Erik pulled the small silver card off and set it inside. He carefully popped out his two thin lenses and set them in one of the trays. Jia did the same.

The warden looked satisfied. "Before we go any farther, I have to ask you if you're carrying any weapons."

Erik shook his head, and he wasn't lying. The warden hadn't specifically asked if they were carrying any weapons on the ship.

A blue light illuminated the room. Erik stood in place, letting the weapons scan proceed.

"Clean," announced a voice over a hidden speaker.

"Thank you for your cooperation, Detectives." The warden nodded and the back door slid open, revealing a brightly lit corridor. "That makes it so much easier for everyone involved."

Once they stepped into the corridor, Erik could see guards off to the side, managing a security station with data window feeds from the checkpoint. A half-dozen other feeds showed other locations.

Six-legged security bots crawled past an intersection, their thin legs tapping on the hard, smooth floor. Small drones flew with them, keeping pace.

"Trouble?" Erik asked, waiting for an alarm to sound.

"Just standard patrols. We're not in the cell blocks yet." The warden shook his head. "People can be made into hostages. Machines can't. Consider those a way of amplifying the effectiveness of our staff while reducing risks. Not every prison follows this model, but a few of us have been pushing this strategy. It's cheaper overall. Why spend more taxpayer money on the inmates than we have to?"

Jia narrowed her eyes at the departing bots. "But machines can be hacked."

"Which is why prisoners aren't allowed access to the appropriate tools." The warden's satisfied smile suggested he thought the method flawless. "And you'd be surprised by how secure our systems are. I think you'd need to be a ghost to have a chance."

Erik waited for Emma to make a snarky comment in his ear. A few seconds passed before he remembered he didn't have a direct connection to her anymore. He didn't know how to feel. He'd gotten so used to her omnipresence, he almost felt naked without her—not that he would admit that to her.

The last thing Emma needed was to have her ego fed.

"You've never had any escapes?" Erik asked.

"Sure, but it never ends well for the prisoners." The warden gestured to the security station. "I'm sure you saw them from outside. All those external habitat modules are the cell blocks. The prisoners have no direct docking bay access. Maybe a guy somehow gets his hands on a suit, and then what? Floats until he runs out of air? That's the big advantage of a prison station. All we have to do is keep people from taking the docking bay. Deep space is the most effective prison guard ever conceived, and we don't even have to pay it or spend money to fix it." He chuckled. "No prisoner who has escaped this place since I've been warden has made it far. We either caught them, or we found their body floating near the prison." He clapped his hands. "But enough about us. Let's go to your boy and see if he's ready to sing a new song."

"Come on, Holochick," Cutter whined. "I'm sure you're a great singer."

Emma glared at him. She floated in the air, her eyes turning solid black. She grew transparent.

Cutter looked up at her. "Are you trying to haunt me now?"

"I'm simply adopting an appearance that reflects my current feelings." Emma's nails grew into twisted talons. "I'm not a human, Mr. Durn. And I don't sing *folk songs.* This will be far less annoying for both of us if you simply do not talk to me until the detectives return."

Cutter sighed and slumped in his chair. "This is going to be more boring than I thought." He wagged a finger. "You'll like me eventually."

This time, it was Emma who turned her face away. "Please don't threaten me."

CHAPTER FIFTY

Esposito was already waiting for them in the room. A prison guard stood in the corner, glaring at the inmate, his hand resting near his stun rod.

Jia wasn't sure if the attitude was for their own benefit, but it wouldn't hurt to help convince the prisoner to give up more information.

"You aren't his lawyers, so we're going to be monitoring everything," the warden noted.

"Fine by us," Jia replied with a nod.

Esposito sat at a table, his hands folded neatly atop it and a nervous smile on his face. His wrists were bound, but his legs were free. He took a few deep breaths. His cheeks were flushed.

Erik didn't sit. He moved to the wall and turned toward Esposito. Jia stared at the prisoner. He kept rubbing his wrists and darting his eyes back and forth. Beads of sweat covered his forehead.

"Nervous?" Jia asked.

"Not as much as you might think," Esposito replied.

"But it's hard not to be somewhat nervous when you're about to do something big, don't you think?"

"Why did you call us out here, Mr. Esposito?" Jia asked. "Shouldn't you have called the CID agents who handled your arrest?"

"We both know they weren't the real reason I went down," he responded. He glared at her. "You were the two who shook everything up, so you were the two I needed to talk to. You're the ones who changed everything in Neo SoCal. You're the ones who made it hard to do...*business* there."

"So, is this about Ceres Galactic?" Jia glanced at Erik, who nodded. She was more than content to take the lead on the interrogation.

Esposito licked his lips. "You'd like that, wouldn't you? You'd like to be able to take down more people and show everyone what special cops you are. Destroy more families and not think about the consequences."

"I like taking down criminals." Jia folded her arms. "And you're the one who destroyed your family when *you* decided to commit crimes instead of remaining a law-abiding citizen. Did you call us here to give us information on Ceres or not?"

"Too damned bad for you." Esposito worked his jaw for a moment, grimacing and tilted his head, his attention jumping between the two detectives. His forehead glistened with perspiration. "You flew all that way for nothing. I've got nothing to give you. You wasted your time. How does it feel, Detectives? Knowing you've been set up?"

Jia shook her head.

"That's your big plan?" Erik asked. "You wanted to

waste our time? Not the stuff of epic revenge, Esposito. You should have hired someone to piss on my flitter. It would have hurt more."

The prisoner let out a strangled laugh. "Waste your time? No. Don't you see? I lured you out here. *You're not going to leave.*"

"Threatening two detectives isn't going to get time taken off your sentence." Jia glared at him. "You better start talking, or we're leaving." She narrowed her eyes, her heart rate kicking up.

The guard frowned at Esposito and grabbed his stun rod.

"So, you're going to do what, kill us?" Erik asked. "How are you going to do that on a prison station with your hands bound and without a weapon?"

Esposito slowly stood, sneering. "You think you're better than me, don't you? You're nothing. You're *cops!* I was a senior vice-president of one of the most important corporations on Earth. When you die today, no one will care. You're *insects.*"

"Sit down, Esposito," ordered the guard, raising his stun rod.

"We *are* better than you," Erik replied, still against the wall, his expression bored. "Because we didn't sell our souls to whatever pieces of shit you did. You can't be pissed at us that we caught you. You chose a bunch of garbage as friends, and so you ended up with garbage support in the end."

"So brave." Esposito spat at the feet of the guard. "If you stay out of my way, you don't have to die because you haven't screwed with me." He nodded toward the detectives. "But those two won't leave this room alive."

"I told you to sit down!" The guard walked toward him.

Esposito leapt into the air, easily clearing the table, and snapped his leg up. He connected with the guard's head and the man flew back, slamming into a wall with a grunt.

Esposito landed in a crouch, his eyes closed. He growled, and the veins in his neck bulged.

Jia moved toward the guard's side, but he waved her off.

"I'm fine," the guard shouted. "Time to teach this son of a bitch a lesson." He launched himself at Esposito, swung the stun rod, and caught the man on the head. Esposito twitched for a moment before his eyes snapped open. Odd yellow striations covered his sclera, and his dilated pupils had erased almost any other color from his eyes.

Another swing of the stun rod didn't bring Esposito down. He sank his teeth into the man's wrist.

The guard screamed as the prisoner clamped down with a crunch, blood spewing out of his mouth to drip on the floor.

Esposito opened his jaws and the guard stumbled back, blood pouring from his half-opened wrist. The prisoner spun to deliver another powerful kick. The crack echoed in the mostly empty room, and the guard fell back, his head at an unnatural angle.

Red lights flashed, and alarms screeched.

Jia lifted her hands and shifted her feet into a combat stance. Erik circled around the other side of the table.

"Didn't know you were augmented," Erik murmured. "Why didn't they take that into account?"

"I'm not a Tin Man," growled Esposito. "I'm something

better. They made it so I could have my revenge. I was afraid, but now I'm not."

"They?"

"The people who want you dead." Esposito cackled.

The door slid open, and two other guards rushed in. Esposito leapt onto the table, snarling and slavering, his teeth stained with the blood of the dead guard.

He jumped at the new arrivals, his shoulder slamming into one guard and knocking him into the wall, where he slumped. Unconscious, but not dead.

Jia rushed toward Esposito, dodged a kick, and slammed her foot into his head. He jerked back before jumping up and smashing his head into the chin of the other guard.

The man stumbled back, his eyes rolling up.

Jia's flurry of palm strikes barely pushed Esposito back. He lunged for her, but she spun out of the way and brought up her knee to meet his nose with a crunch. Blood sprayed all over the floor, but he didn't slow.

He just growled louder.

Erik leapt over the table and drop-kicked Esposito. The prisoner crashed into the wall with a resounding thud. The man's face was a mangled mess, covered in blood, both his and others'.

Several of his teeth had been knocked out. He continued to snarl and growl like a rabid animal. Heavy footsteps echoed from the hallway, mixing with the alarm, along with the rhythmic taps of approaching bots and the hum of drones.

Esposito growled louder. One of his arms hung loosely from above his elbow, a huge bulge visible. If he felt any pain from the obvious break, it wasn't slowing him down.

"What the hell is this?" Erik shouted.

When Esposito lunged at him, Erik met him with his left fist. The blow sent the man staggering back, his face half-collapsed, his flesh riven.

The condition of his arm and his uneven gait suggested those weren't his only wounds.

A security bot crawled in from the hallway. It jumped onto the table and then toward Esposito with its long stun rod. The rod made contact, but the prisoner just jerked for a second before snarling and kicking the bot away.

Jia dodged the bot before she delivered a solid roundhouse to Esposito's head, but he barely flinched. "I'm beginning to regret not having a gun."

"Funny how that works," Erik grumbled. "Screw a gun. I wish I had the laser rifle."

The bot tackled Esposito once more, and this time Erik grabbed one of the stun rods on the ground.

"If at first you don't succeed?" Jia asked.

Another bot scampered into the room and rushed toward Esposito. He bit down on the first bot's leg, growling and snarling. Both bots shoved their stun rods against him, trying to incapacitate him, but he kept trying to bite the leg as if oblivious to either their attacks or their being bots.

Several guards arrived outside the door, all holding rods but not entering. Their faces were masks of fear.

Erik stomped toward Esposito and tossed the stun rod into his left hand. "A missile might be nice, too." He brought up his left arm and slammed the rod into Esposito's head with all the momentum the artificial limb could provide.

With a loud crunch, the weapon split the prisoner's skull and entered his brain.

Esposito howled and thrashed. Jia stared, transfixed in horror. The guards outside watched, wide-eyed. One man crossed himself and murmured a prayer under his breath.

Erik brought up his boot and shoved the stun rod all the way through Esposito's head. With that, his head fell back, and he stopped moving.

The alarm fell silent.

No one said a word for a good thirty seconds before the guards crept in, eyeing the prisoner's body.

"He was drugged," one of them muttered. "He had to have been."

Jia shook her head. "I've had a lot of different people try to kill me in the last year, including people on drugs." She pointed to the body as she spoke to the guard. "Have you ever seen anything like that before? That wasn't a drug."

"Yeah." Erik prodded the body with his boot tip. "This wasn't drugs. This was straight-up mutant *yaoguai* shit."

CHAPTER FIFTY-ONE

Warden Harris ran his hands through his hair as the guards were hauled away on hoverstretchers.

One moaned as they guided him down the hall, a medpatch on his head.

Erik figured any man who could still make noise could be saved.

He glanced back into the blood-splattered room. Paranoia had turned into prophecy. This was strange even by his standards. His earlier explanation didn't make sense. Esposito had lived a full and public life. If he was a mutant or changeling that bizarre, someone would have noticed.

Jia's angry gaze bored into the warden. "What just happened?" She flung her arm in the direction of the room. "You were watching the whole thing, right? He was immune to stun rods, and he had to be de-brained to be taken out. That wasn't just an assassination attempt. It was a fight against a monster, and trust me, I've fought my share."

"You don't think I get that?" Warden Harris snapped.

"One of my men is dead, and the other seriously injured. I don't get it. Esposito's been a model prisoner. He's *never* attacked anyone, let alone bitten them."

Erik stomped to the warden and glared at him. Three guards surged toward him but stopped at the warden's upraised hand.

"A lot of people have tried to kill us," Erik growled, his voice low and full of menace. "There are even cops who have purposefully dragged their feet to get us killed."

"What are you saying?"

"You know exactly what I'm saying. Look me in the eyes and tell me you had nothing to do with it."

Warden Harris locked eyes with Erik and squared his shoulders. The men were of similar heights, but Erik's bulk and sheer presence made the other man seem small.

"I pride myself on keeping scum in line," the warden replied, his voice quivering with rage. "And even if I was a corrupt bastard on some syndicate's payroll, you think I'd send my men in there to die?" His finger stabbed in the direction of the bloody room. "What kind of sense does that make? I'm just as pissed as you are."

Erik nodded slowly and stepped away. "Yeah, seems like it."

"None of that changes the fact that a prisoner with no cybernetic augmentations fought off five people and two bots before Erik smashed the stun rod through his skull," Jia stated. "His eyes and veins and earlier behavior suggest something was wrong with him, and it wasn't just adrenaline. Something changed him. I've never seen a drug produce that reaction, but it's the most likely explanation. It's not like he had tons of cybernetic augmentations surreptitiously implanted while he was in a prison in space."

The warden scrubbed a hand over his face. "He had a visitor recently, someone named Hadrian Conners. We did a full check on the guy. He has no record. He's just some businessman. I assumed he was a contact from Esposito's Ceres days. He was scanned, and he didn't bring anything in."

"Obviously, he did," Erik commented.

"You don't know that. It's just a theory," the warden shot back.

"What did they talk about?" Jia frowned. "I'm hoping he didn't say, 'Hey, you want to kill two cops?'"

"I checked the footage." The warden shook his head. "It was just Conners talking about sphere ball and how he was planning to help Esposito's family. It was strange because he's the first visitor other than his wife since he was imprisoned here, but I see that all the time with fallen corp princes like him. Everyone's ashamed to be associated with them, but after a while, they start feeling pity. I figured it was something similar."

"Esposito said someone did something to him, and the point was to kill us. When was the last time his wife visited?"

"Not for several months."

"The footage was probably altered," Erik suggested. "Esposito didn't change himself and call us out of the blue."

The warden scoffed. "Altered footage? You're saying this Conners hacked our systems when he was here for less than two hours? That's impossible."

"I'm not a warden." Erik inclined his head toward the

bloodied meeting room. "I'm a cop, and we go off evidence. Esposito was normal, and then this Conners shows up. Now he's not normal. He didn't pay any attention to us this entire time, and suddenly calls us? That's a lot of coincidences stacking up."

"I'm going to have our doctor examine the body," the warden explained, weariness underlying his voice. "And I can't let you leave until we get this figured out. I don't know if this was drugs or what, but it could be some sort of pathogen you brought aboard."

Jia laughed. "So, it's our fault now?"

"He wasn't biting people and able to ignore pain after his last visitor. I'm not saying you did it on purpose, but your partner's the one who just got done talking about coincidences. If you do have a pathogen, we're going to need to quarantine you until we can get the appropriate personnel here to handle it."

"We need to talk to our people on our ship. Our person, I mean. If you don't want us to leave, just don't release the docking clamp." Erik inclined his head up the corridor in the direction of the docking bay.

The warden took a deep breath. "I'll allow it, but I want our doctor to take a blood sample. After you talk with your pilot, you'll need to come back to the infirmary."

Erik frowned. If the warden was corrupt, he could easily lie about the test results, but he was allowing them to go back to the ship temporarily, so there was no point in fighting him.

"Fine," Erik muttered.

Cutter eyed Erik with suspicion. "So, you don't have space rabies? You sure? Maybe you're a carrier."

Jia rolled her eyes. "You just flew with us for twelve hours."

"The passive pathogen filters aren't detecting anything unusual," Emma reported. "It's not impossible that a pathogen is present on the *Pegasus,* but it's extremely unlikely."

Jia frowned at Cutter. "If we were the cause, you'd already be trying to bite our throats. This was an assassination attempt. I'd suggest you keep the doors closed on the ship, though, and recycle your air just in case. If it is some sort of bioweapon, it could be in the prison air, and it might be contagious."

"Sorry." Erik shook his head with a laugh. "I can't do it."

"Do what?" Jia asked.

"I'm not kissing you if you grow a mustache or try to bite my throat."

"Duly noted," Jia replied with a wry smile. "Shoot me instead."

"Seriously?"

"No, not seriously." Jia threw up her hands. "We need to figure out what's going on. If it's a disease, we need an antidote. I might end up trying to eat your face instead of kissing you."

Erik blinked. "I have no idea how to respond to that."

Jia groaned and placed a hand on her face. "Don't. I wasn't thinking where that would go. It sounded better in my head."

"I'm presuming this is now a sufficient emergency to warrant special procedures?" Emma asked.

"Yeah," Erik admitted. "I don't know if the warden's in on it, but this Conners is the key."

"Unfortunately, that wouldn't be so simple," Emma admitted, sounding embarrassed. "And potentially not even possible."

"What?" Erik shook his head. "What do you mean? Since when is something like that impossible for you?"

"The system is almost completely locked down from the outside," Emma explained. "I probed a little when the alarm went off. Given the nature of this facility, I expected it, but it's still disappointing."

"The alarm went off even out here?" Erik asked.

"No, but I was using the ship's sensors to do my best to monitor unusual noise from the inside," Emma explained. "Since I wasn't directly in communication with you, it only seemed prudent. You *do* tend to attract trouble. I was expecting conventional gun goblins, not hungry inmates, but that doesn't change the trouble you encountered."

Jia sighed. "I was afraid of that. If it was not well protected, there would be too much risk of a criminal ship getting close and hacking things. I'd read about that, but I'd hoped Emma could overcome the system."

"You're telling me she can't?" Erik asked.

Emma snorted. "I'm saying if you want efficient manipulation of the system, I'll need direct internal access, which will require me to accompany you physically. This isn't unprecedented in our encounters. Remote access always requires a certain set of assumptions on behalf of the initial system designers."

Erik's gaze dropped to the core matrix protruding from an IO port below the main control panel. "They're not going to let us walk in there with you. It doesn't even matter if they know what you are. They'll get that you're something that might be trouble, and if anything, they're on higher alert now."

"Then there's little I can do for now, Detective Blackwell. I could potentially access the docking clamp and override locally, but they would know immediately."

Erik shook his head. "We don't need that when we're running under fire or from a horde of weird-eyed hungry freaks."

"Things would get boring if we only dealt with regular criminals, I suppose," Jia muttered.

"Emma, Cutter, stay on standby." Erik cracked his knuckles and looked out the front window at several prison guards waiting near the security door. "I have a feeling by the time this is over, we'll be bringing in more extra goodies than just Emma's matrix."

An hour later, Erik, Jia, the warden, and the prison doctor, Matthews, stood in the infirmary. Esposito's body was quarantined in a storage locker. The middle-aged doctor had brought up various data windows showing different scans and images from the body. He pointed at a gray graph.

"I think this might be the cause," Doctor Matthews explained. "It's not a pathogen, or at least not in the conventional sense."

The warden squinted to read. "Average nanite concentration?"

The doctor nodded. "Esposito's serum nanite levels were very, very high. Much higher than you'd expect, even for someone who'd had several medpatches applied and was being actively treated in a medical facility, and he had *none* of that. Not only do we have that concern, but I isolated some of the nanites, and they're like nothing I've ever encountered, let alone any medical nanite I've ever seen." He shook his head. "I don't have the necessary equipment to begin to figure out what they are or where they came from."

Warden Harris closed his eyes and took several deep breaths. "Was this some sort of attack?" he asked. "Is it contagious?"

"I checked the guards, including the one who was bitten. There are no detectable nanites in the wound or their blood samples." He nodded at Erik and Jia. "Nor were nanites present in their blood samples."

"Then it was just Esposito," Jia concluded. "Conners did something to him during their meeting. He must have injected him with the nanites then. There might have been an incubation period or even something Esposito was doing to keep them under control until he could release them. We need to see the footage of their conversation."

"What's the point?" Warden Harris stared at the nanite concentration graph. "I told you already; they weren't doing anything like that. They didn't even touch each other. We didn't have a guard stationed in the room, and maybe that was a mistake, but this isn't something he could have spread through the air."

"This is all you speculating." Jia pointed at the doctor. "He just mentioned he doesn't have the equipment to identify the nanites. You're operating blind and ignoring the most obvious clue."

Warden Harris scoffed. "And you have the equipment to figure it out?"

"No, but we do have equipment that would tell us if the footage was altered," Jia insisted. "If we can reconstitute the original recording, it might shed light on what happened."

"Even if what you're saying is true, there's no way I'm letting you bring outside devices into this prison, especially after what just happened. I've already got one dead guard because we were lax." Warden Harris looked to the side for a moment before returning his attention to Jia. "I'm not accusing you of anything, Detective, but I need to get this situation under control, and adding more variables to the problem isn't going to do that. Once I have a better idea of what's going on, then we can call for outside assistance."

"I get that you don't want us bringing equipment in here the prisoners might get their hands on." Jia furrowed her brow, frustration obvious on her face. "But you must have spare data rods. Copy the footage to one, along with the relevant access logs, and we'll take it out and examine it with the equipment on our ship. If we fail, we fail, but if we succeed, we'll have a better idea of what is going on here. That helps you, it helps us. We're not just investigators. We were the obvious targets."

"How do I know this isn't about you trying to get away? It'd make sense for you to run if you were the targets."

Jia glared at him. "You control the docking clamp, right? I'm just trying to do what a detective does best: figure things out."

Erik was glad he'd told Emma to wait on trying to hack the clamp. The warden was more with it than he'd anticipated. He nodded at his partner, smiling at her confidence. A woman who would stand up to her captain wasn't going to be cowed by a warden.

"She's right," Erik added. "Your job is to keep criminals inside this place. Our job is to figure out how they do things. Give us the footage. If we find nothing, we find nothing. We can't get out of here without you releasing our ship, and we both want to figure out who juiced that con up on experimental nanites to try to kill us."

Warden Harris turned to Doctor Matthews. "Is there anything more you can figure out?"

"I can send my results out and ask for help," the doctor replied.

"We're not sending anything out to anyone until we know what the hell is going on," the warden insisted. "They could jump to the wrong conclusions." He grimaced and turned to Jia. "All right. You win. It's not like you're just anyone. You're two of the top detectives in the NSCPD. I'll give you the footage, but if you start showing any symptoms, you need to come back here immediately to be restrained."

CHAPTER FIFTY-TWO

"This is one of those situations where I have both good and bad news," Emma declared. She lowered the external forward shutters, blocking the windows.

"Why are you doing that?" Erik asked, eyeing the closing blinds. "Is that part of the news?"

"Partially." Emma appeared. "It cuts down on the possibility of someone reading lips or realizing you're talking to me, even without my holographic form. I assume we want to minimize that information, especially given the events now unfolding and potential links to other bad actors."

Jia folded her arms and tapped her foot. "What about the good and bad news?"

"I always like hearing the bad news first," Cutter interjected. "That makes everything after it seem better in comparison." He nodded, the tip of his tongue poking out of the corner of his mouth.

"The bad news is I can't reconstruct the original footage," Emma explained. "Not based on the recording, at least, either the video or audio data. If I had full access to the system, I might be able to do it off the backups, but not from the data provided."

"There's no way they're going to let us plug anything into their system." Erik grunted and kicked at a seat. "Damn it. So we don't know—"

"No," Jia interrupted. "Did you hear what she said? She couldn't reconstruct the original footage. That sounds like she confirmed it was altered. That is useful to know."

"That would be the aforementioned good news." Emma smirked. "It's definitely been altered. It's an impressive bit of work, and I can see how a human analyst would miss it, even with good algorithmic tools. However, there are many subtle clues that confirm my conclusion, both from the data and the logs they provided. It's always nice when my opponent is worth my effort."

"That gives us the who and the when, and we already know the how," Jia mused. "It's enough proof for a follow-up. Hadrian Conners flew all the way here. He had to have left a trail we can follow."

"There is more bad news." Emma shrugged, something approaching an apologetic smile on her face.

"Of course," Erik muttered. "What is it?"

"Given the nature of the alterations and the time series data associated with it, I'm dubious this was an outside hack," Emma explained.

"Conners smuggled something inside to pull it off?"

Emma shook her head. "The required level of familiarity with the system on top of the technical skill makes it unlikely. Note it's not just a matter of spoofing the feed, but also of changing the supporting logs and backup data."

Erik gritted his teeth. "You're saying Conners had inside help."

Cutter clapped, eyeing the two detectives. "Man, this is better than watching a cop drama. Usually, it's just like, 'Cutter, take us to this remote location so we can kill all these terrorists.'" He pointed to his head. "No inside-the-brain thinking, you know. The cool stuff." He withered under everyone's glares. "Just saying," he muttered. "It's a good thing."

"Setting aside a certain annoying fleshbag's comments," Emma continued, "that's exactly what I'm saying, Detective. Without knowing more about the personnel stationed here, I can't give you a better direction than that, but it's highly likely this mysterious Mr. Conners was aided by someone on prison staff with systems access."

"I don't think it's the warden." Erik rubbed the top of his lip and frowned. "We've both looked into the eyes of a lot of criminals in the last year, and I dealt with terrorists and other killers for decades in the military. Those weren't the eyes of a man who knew he was sending men to their deaths. It also doesn't make sense to send a guy in there. The fewer people in there, the easier it would have been for Esposito to try to kill us."

Jia dropped into a seat. "It could be anyone with systems access, which is basically most of the prison staff. And we're well outside of our jurisdiction. Even if the warden was willing to let us examine the footage, do you think he's going to let us question everyone, just because we say our mysterious equipment tells us the data has been altered?" Her brow furrowed, and her jaw tightened. "The Esposito incident is forcing him to be a bit more open, but that's very different than saying he's got someone working for him who is a criminal."

"It's not our job to investigate corrupt prison officials," Erik pointed out. "You heard the doctor. Whatever this was, it sounds like it was a one-time thing. There are no nanites in anyone else. It was a targeted assassination attempt. But..."

"But if they went through all that trouble, and they have someone on the inside, would they really give up that easily?" Jia raised an eyebrow. "If this is the conspiracy, they've got something else up their sleeve."

"Exactly. Shit." Erik glanced at the control panel. "We could contact the captain and try to get him to send CID agents. The attempted assassination of two detectives on a prison station is worth their attention, even without our evidence. The warden can only stonewall them so long."

"Internal alarms are now sounding inside the prison," Emma announced.

Jia jumped out of her seat. "*What?*"

"A short-range transmission is coming in," Emma reported. "I'll connect it via the cockpit comm."

"Detective Blackwell, Detective Lin, are you there?" It was Warden Harris' panicked voice.

"We're here," Jia replied. "What's going on?"

"That damned idiot doctor was wrong," the warden yelled. "There are more like Esposito. A lot more."

"The guards who were attacked?"

Jia and Erik exchanged annoyed glances. There was nothing worse than an enemy who didn't know when to quit, especially when it was a hungry enemy who wanted to bite your neck or hand off.

"No," the warden answered. "It's all prisoners, but it's not a riot. They're showing the same symptoms and immunity to stuns. We've lost a couple of guards, and I've pulled a lot of them back. I tried to send bots, but the system isn't taking my commands. I can't even lock down the prison. I tried to flood the cells with gas, but I can't do it. The damned system is just not accepting the commands."

"Not sure gas would work on those things," Jia mused.

"Do you have anything better than stun rods?" Erik asked. "A weapon that doesn't require the system? Something with some actual bullets? I'm assuming a station like this can take a few bullets without risk of a breach."

"Yes, we have rifles and shotguns in the emergency armory, but we're cut off from that room right now by the infected prisoners," the warden explained. "I'm with a few of my men in my office. The damned doors won't close, but we're holding them off with furniture while we try to work the manual override."

"And the prisoners? Can they get into the armory?"

"There's no way they're getting into it without me, but I don't think these prisoners care about guns," the warden replied. "I'm trying to transmit a request for external assistance, but I can't—"

The forward shutters started rising.

Emma pointed out the front. "The transmission is being jammed. It's also affecting my ability to transmit. If we could get out of the docking bay, I could align the ship with a repeater beacon and perhaps use a laser signal."

Cutter patted the control panel. "We're not getting out of here with the docking clamp in place."

"We don't have time anyway." Erik headed toward the

back. “We need to arm up. If there are more like Esposito, we can’t hide here and wait for the Fleet to show up. Everyone might get their throats ripped out in the meantime.”

“No offense, but I didn’t sign up to fight crazy nanite-infected prisoners.” Cutter folded his arms, offering his best laid-back version of defiance. “I’m just the pilot.”

“Jia and I will handle it.” Erik reached into the IO port. “And we’re taking Emma with us.”

“What if we can’t get through it?” Jia asked.

“Then we test the missile launcher on a security door.”

CHAPTER FIFTY-THREE

Cho swallowed as he watched the carnage unfold on the data window.

Rabid prisoners rushed to other prisoners and guards, biting and clawing, shrugging off stun rods and blows like they were machines. He'd never seen anything like it, and he'd been in the thick of riots before.

Everything had gone to hell in under twenty minutes.

The maximum-security breach alarm continued to scream, the red lights flashing. Most of their feeds were dead. The current horror show had lasted only long enough to see a prisoner tackle another prisoner and bite his leg before the feed died. Cho didn't know why the feeds were failing. It wasn't like the cameras were exposed.

Cho tried to connect to the warden. They'd lost a feed earlier that showed a corridor where Warden Harris was running from crazed prisoners, along with some guards. It didn't make sense. The prisoners, crazed or not, shouldn't have had freedom of movement, but most of the doors in the prison were open and systems errors were popping up all over.

CONNECTION ERROR. PLEASE RETRY.

He tried different commands. A thin transparent barrier rose inside the security checkpoint. The shrill cry of the alarm died, now sounding like a distant noise. Cho and his partner were safe for the moment, but that didn't fill him with confidence.

"This is crazy," muttered Rich, the man beside him. "What do we do?"

"We wait for the warden," Cho insisted. "That's what protocol states since the damned system isn't working." His fingers flew as he entered commands, but the system spat back more error messages. He slammed his fist on the control panel so hard it throbbed. "I can't access anything in the main system anymore." He pointed to the lone data window with a camera feed. "That's all we've got left, other than what we can see with our two eyes."

The remaining feed showed the area in front of the entrance checkpoint. The Rabbit remained parked there, but ever since they'd closed their cockpit shutters, the guards couldn't tell what was going on. Had the warden told the detectives to escape? Should the guards try to leave with them?

Rich shook his head. "The warden's dead, and we both know it. We need to figure out some way to call for help. We need the Fleet to drop off a bunch of badass soldiers in exoskeletons."

"Without main systems access, we can't do that. And we need an official override order." Cho groaned. "Crap. There are no patrol flights out right now. One was supposed to launch fifteen minutes ago, but the pilots never came. I flagged it, but they were still within the window. We've also got no scheduled deliveries today. No one's going to know what's going on here."

"Nothing's going on," Rich insisted. "It's just a riot with a few crazy prisoners. The other guys will get it under control."

"Just a riot? People are trying to *eat* other people, man! It's some damned Orlox bioweapon making people crazy, that's what it is. I read about this kind of thing on the net. The government doesn't want anyone to worry, so they don't admit how vulnerable we are."

"How is an Orlox going to sneak a bioweapon all the way into the Solar System? To a prison station?" Rich looked at Cho like he'd lost his damned mind.

"But what if it is?"

Rich closed his eyes and took a deep breath. He blew it out his nose. "It doesn't matter what it is. We can't let anyone in or out."

"We shouldn't be letting anyone in or out until the warden gives the order anyway. There are pilots among the prisoners, and we've got two decent-sized ships out there in the docking bay they can take, not to mention all the patrol craft." Cho stared at the Rabbit. "No, we protect this place, and make sure none of those prisoners get out until we get official orders."

In the cargo bay, Erik finished strapping the laser rifle to his carryaid.

He would have preferred a full exoskeleton for fighting whatever the hell they were about to fight, but the mechanized backpack, combined with the tactical suit he found in one of Alina's provided boxes, would have to do.

He slung his TR-7 over his shoulder.

He'd stuffed all the magazines he could into the carryaid, along with extra power cells. He wasn't going to risk explosive grenades on a space station, and he didn't think stun grenades would stop the prisoners.

He couldn't help but glancing Jia's way as she shimmied into the formfitting tactical suit, her shirt and pants lying on the ground. Erik shook his head. It wasn't the right time to be thinking about his partner's tanned body.

They had crazed super-prisoners to take down.

Jia finished putting on her tactical suit. She'd already filled her carryaid and hung her rifle on the side. She knelt, slipped her arms through the straps, and stood.

Erik tapped his PNIU, which he'd grabbed on the way out of the prison. He looked at Cutter, who was watching them arm up with the excitement of a child. "Cutter?"

"Yeah, Blackwell?"

"I'm sure you're a smart enough guy to disable that docking clamp if you really want to."

Cutter chuckled. "I'm sure Emma could do it faster."

"She's not going to because she'll be with us," Erik explained. "But if it hits the fan, I'm not going to ask you to stay and die for no reason. That said, I'd prefer it if you stick around. I'd like the option to evac if this goes bad."

"If you flee, I'll haunt you, fleshbag," Emma insisted.

"Can she do that?" Cutter eyed the speaker her voice came out of.

Erik laughed. "I don't know. She's one of a kind. I wouldn't put it past her."

"I better not chance it," Cutter concluded. "I've been in rough situations before. I'll try to stick around in case you need evac. I should have known it'd end up this way."

"Why is that?" Erik slid a magazine into his TR-7.

"Because this job was too easy," Cutter replied. "And the universe has a way of balancing things."

"Okay, Emma, open the back," Erik ordered. "There's no way we're climbing down the ladder decked out in all this stuff."

The cargo bay door groaned open, then descended until it became a ramp. Erik and Jia bounded down the ramp and jogged toward the security door, both performing a quick check of the docking bay. There were no crazed prisoners, just the patrol craft and the docked cargo ship that had been there since before their arrival.

"Let us in," Erik shouted. "I know you can see us in there. We know what's going on, and we know your people got cut off from the armory. You need serious reinforcements, and that's what we are."

"We can't let you in here with that gear, Detective," came a voice over a speaker. "Those are unauthorized lethals. No lethals allowed except those from the armory. We need an official override order, and you can't give it."

"Who am I speaking to?" Erik asked.

"Uh, I'm Cho," the guard replied.

"Cho, did you hear what I just said? The warden contacted us. He's cut off, and those crazy-ass infected prisoners are going to take him down. Someone's jamming transmissions outside the prison, and I'm betting you've noticed by now that there's something wrong with the system. The warden tried to knock everyone out with gas, and it wouldn't let him. The bots aren't working, either." Erik pulled his rifle down. "Someone has fucked you all over and is going to get you killed unless you let us in. Screw your official override order. Let us in there so we can take those things down."

"Y-you can't bring outside lethals into the prison," Cho replied. "Without the override order."

"Have you seen one of the infected prisoners in action?" Jia shouted. "Stuns don't work. We had to destroy his brain to stop the last one."

"We can wait for reinforcements," Cho insisted, his voice shaking. "Someone will figure it out. There are confirmation signals that go out. If the system's not working, they won't go out. They can send the official override order."

"Someone has hacked your system." Jia pulled her rifle off her carryaid and held it in both hands. "If they're smart enough to do that, they're smart enough to spoof whatever signal they need to send out. If we wait, those *things* are going to overrun the prison. I don't need to see everything, but let me ask you one question. Are the normal locks active and in place?"

Cho groaned. "I don't know. I don't think so."

Erik patted his TR-7. "I'm sure a burst with four bullets to the brain will take one of those things down nice and quick. If you want anyone to live through this, you're going to open that door."

Jia added, "Let me summarize your position for you. You have multiple prisoners infected with some sort of bizarre nanites that enhance their ability to take damage and make them irrationally violent. The guards' only available weapons don't work, and your backup, the stupid bots, aren't helping. We, however, have heavy weapons and are prepared to risk our lives when we could just be getting on our ship, hacking your docking clamp, and fleeing and sending a message to someone else to handle it, while leaving you all to get eaten."

Cho didn't respond.

Jia turned to Erik. "Could we blow the door with the launcher or plasma grenades?"

The security door bolts thudded, and it slid open.

"We're letting you in," Cho announced, "but if you come in here, we can't let you out until the situation is under control, or we get an official override order."

Erik switched off his safety. "Sounds like a good plan. It's time to pacify some prisoners."

CHAPTER FIFTY-FOUR

Jia had wondered if the guards intended to trap them in the inspection room, but the second door opened once the first door had closed. She and Erik jogged forward, glancing toward the security station, where Cho and his partner sat, temporarily safe. She couldn't resent them for hiding from danger.

They wouldn't last thirty seconds against one of the infected.

"Look for an IO port," Emma recommended. "Note that due to the jamming, I won't be able to communicate with you if you're more than a short distance away, or otherwise in a long, uninterrupted line-of-sight where I try something in the optical or infrared ranges."

"Understood," Erik replied.

The detectives jogged forward a few meters until Jia found a panel. She pulled it up to reveal an IO port. "Here we go. That was easier than I anticipated."

Erik pulled the crystalline matrix that was Emma's heart out of his pocket and slid it into the IO port. "The best bet is for you to work on regaining control of the prison systems. If that's going to take you some time, we'll leave you here to do it. We can't wait around while those things are killing people."

"Interesting," Emma replied. "This might be more difficult in some ways and easier than others."

"Why?"

"Because I'm seeing various subsystems failures. I think the overall system isn't under the control of another. It's less that it's been hacked than it has been disabled because of damage to the underlying systems' programming. I'm attempting to reroute around the damage, but it'll take time to make decent progress."

"Can you give us the blueprints?" Jia asked, watching the long corridor for signs of movement.

Emma chuckled. "Yes, because I already had that information. Transmitting now."

"Without Emma in control of the system, we're blind. The warden might be able to help her, or she might be able to help him regain control sooner. We should head toward his office." Jia tapped the PNIU to bring up the blueprints in a data window. They didn't trust the smart lenses with the jamming, so they hadn't put them back on. For all they knew, the nanites might mess with them.

Jia jabbed the aerial map. "It's a hike, but at least it's not on the other side of the station."

Erik patted his weapon. "I wouldn't bother with anything like knee shots. Aim for the brain if you see one."

They hurried down a long hall before turning into a new one that ran past open doors that mostly led to offices or storage rooms. Distant screams echoed throughout the area, their sources impossible to trace.

Jia took a deep breath. Her heart didn't race.

Killing twisted monsters had become part of the job. They needed to focus on regaining control of the prison, and that started with the warden and Emma.

"This is like a *jiangshi* attack out of a bad horror movie." Jia advanced alongside Erik, keeping a firm grip on her weapon. "I get weird *yaoguai* in the Scar, but on a prison station in the middle of space?"

"More like a zombie. Nanozombies." Erik nodded with a satisfied look. "Perfect place for an artificial outbreak."

"Nanozombies. Perfect. But the question is, why are there more? If it's not spreading through a bite or the attack, how *is* it spreading? The nanites are Talos tech if I had to guess, but we still don't know a lot about them." Jia raised her weapon as they approached an intersection. The security door that normally would have blocked access was wide open, almost taunting them.

Erik frowned as they turned a corner. "Emma, can you still hear us?"

There was no response.

"Damn," he muttered. "We don't know that it's spreading, Jia."

"There's more than just Esposito," Jia pointed out. "That implies it is."

"If it didn't infect the guards or us earlier in the small room, I doubt it spreads."

Jia nodded. "True."

"It's not hard to persuade lifers to go nanozombie for some money for their families." Erik crept closer to another open security door with a frown. He flattened against the wall and waited, then spun, sweeping his rifle back and forth. "Got a body."

Jia cleared the doorway. A guard's corpse lay on the ground in a pool of blood. It was obvious more than a few bites had been taken out of him, and he was missing a hand. She spun toward the sound of heavy footfalls.

"They got this far?" she whispered. "That security checkpoint at the front might not hold."

"It's not like these things are going to fly a ship out of here," Erik replied. "There's a docking bay, then nothing but space for thousands of kilometers."

The detectives continued to advance, their next turn taking them closer to both the warden's office and the cell blocks. More remains of mauled and mangled guards littered the ground, but the occasional inmate's body lay on the ground as well, their wounds resembling those of the guards. The corpses who still had eyes didn't show any sign of the nanoinfection.

Panting and footsteps sounded from around the corner. The path led to the warden's office. Jia and Erik backed up, both aiming their weapons high. Heart shots might stop the nanozombies, but they couldn't be sure, and finding out in the middle of a fight would be suboptimal. The footsteps and panting grew louder and closer.

Jia held her breath, her heart beating fast. She selected burst fire mode and waited. The noise grew closer.

A form rushed around the corner, his bright uniform marking him as a prisoner. He skidded to a halt and dropped to his knees, putting his hands behind his head.

"I'm not one of those fucking things. Don't shoot. For the love of all that's holy, don't shoot."

"Show me your eyes," Erik ordered.

The prisoner stared at him—no striations, no bulging veins. He whimpered rather than growled or snarled.

Jia gestured for him to stand with her rifle. "What are you doing out here?"

He let out a hysterical laugh. "Are you fucking kidding me? You just checked my eyes. You know what's happening. Guys have gone nuts. They're eating people. They're crazy strong. I saw one guy all but tear Kevan's arm off, and Kevan's a big guy. And that's before..." He doubled over and vomited.

Jia wrinkled her nose. She waited politely while the prisoner emptied the contents of his stomach. "What are you doing in this part of the prison?"

"I was part of a work detail." The prisoner shook his head. "Suddenly alarms are flashing, the doors are all opening, and people are eating people. I looked for the guards for protection, but their stun rods weren't doing shit." He licked his lips, a hungry smile on his face as he eyed the guns. "But you've got real guns. You can protect me, right? I don't care how strong a guy is or what he's on. You blow his head off, and he'll stop moving."

"We're going to the warden's office," Erik explained. "We lost contact with him. If you want to tag along, that's fine."

The prisoner ran his hands through his hair. "But *they* are that way. The warden's probably already dead, and they're having dinner."

Erik let out a quiet grunt. "Maybe, but he's also one of our best bets for regaining control of this place."

Loud growls and snarls sounded in the distance. Quick, rhythmic steps came right after.

The prisoner shook his head, tears running down his face. "No, no, no. I'm not staying here."

"There are plenty of offices and storage rooms," Jia mused. "You work here. Go find one and hide. We'll handle the nanozombies. Just don't come out until you hear normal people talking."

"Nanozombies?" The prisoner groaned, spun on his heel, and sprinted away.

Jia sighed. "I miss the days when it was just drunks trying to run me down."

CHAPTER FIFTY-FIVE

A massive pack of nanozombies swept around the corner.

Blood covered their faces and shredded clothes. While the new enemies had the same bulging veins and oddly colored eyes as Esposito, the mottled gray skin tone and dark purple of their veins suggested further degeneration.

It made no sense. How had the staff not noticed?

But the hows and whys would have to wait until they were no longer a threat.

The pack growled and bared their teeth at Erik and Jia. The nanozombies hesitated, suggesting some thin strands of intelligence recognized the heavy weapons. Given the speed Erik had seen with Esposito, the monsters would be able to close quickly, but a decent distance separated them.

There was no way, even in the best scenario, the nanozombies could win without heavy casualties.

"They aren't attacking each other and rushing us," Erik whispered, slowly raising his weapon. "They're not mindless."

"But they *are* attacking other prisoners," Jia replied.

"More like animals that recognize their own kind and their threats than humans showing careful tactical planning."

"It'll have to do. I don't care how we win, as long as we do."

The nanozombies rushed forward on all fours, an awkward loping gait that propelled them at a surprising speed. Erik fired a burst. The shots blew out a knee, complete with blood and bone, dropping the zombie to the floor.

A normal man would have been wailing in pain from such an injury.

The wound didn't matter. Snarling louder, the creature continued crawling toward them in an even more bizarre mix of one-legged hopping and pulling. Erik's next four TR-7 bullets almost took the zombie's head off.

At the same time, Jia offered some lead to a target on the opposite side of the pack. Her rifle didn't produce the satisfying hole of the TR-7, but the nanozombie collapsed, tripping a few of his comrades behind him.

Anything that slowed the pack meant more opportunities to attack.

Erik sorely missed the clearance power of grenades as he snapped up his rifle to line up with the next target and fired. His target took the rounds in the shoulder, jerking back and snarling while his comrades continued forward. Erik blew the head off another one before taking aim at his original target and ending his twisted new life.

Jia's rifle fired rapidly, quick, careful shots through the head that left more of the pack on the floor, twitching and dying. Another burst went into a nanozombie's chest, but other than an initial stumble, he continued advancing.

"Head it is," Jia grumbled.

The pack had closed half the distance when Erik ejected his magazine and slapped in a new one. Loud, constant gunfire overlapped and echoed in the narrow hallway.

The challenging din didn't distract him as he continued precision-firing.

Fewer enemies were falling as quickly as in a typical fight, but Jia had just proven he couldn't risk anything but a headshot to finish them off.

Neither partner spoke as they kept firing, each aiming at their own side of the pack. For all the viciousness of the enemy, headshot after headshot diminished their threat, whittling them down to half-strength, then quarter-strength, and finally only a few. Those were now within striking distance. The ever-present stress of battle had stretched a brief encounter into what felt like an unending wave of mindless killing.

Jia nailed one of the survivors and ejected her magazine.

Erik decapitated another with a burst to the neck. The last remaining nanozombie leapt for him, snarling and dripping blood-flecked spittle. He threw up his left arm and caught him by the throat. He bit into the sleeve of the tactical suit, but couldn't penetrate. The nanozombie shook like an angry dog, trying to dig his teeth deeper. The small amount of intelligence left in the infected man didn't seem to extend to understanding the strength of Erik's and Jia's defensive outfits. He'd half-wondered if the tactical suits were pointless.

Now he had his answer.

Erik shoved the barrel against the hungry nanozombie's head. "You wouldn't want to eat me. I'm full of beer, beignets, and spite." He pulled the trigger, and his opponent's body fell limp. He tossed it to the floor. The more zombies he killed, the more a sour stench filled the air. It wasn't the smell of normal death. He'd run into that plenty of times in his career.

"Yeah, always new, messed-up stuff to kill and smell," he commented.

"Better to kill and smell than die and smell nothing." Jia surveyed the corpse-filled hallway with a mix of fascination and horror on her face. "You know, if you had mentioned nanozombies were in my future a couple of days ago, I would have asked what you had been taking. Now it's starting to feel like a normal Tuesday, and I'm wondering what I need to start taking. I don't know what that says about my life."

"It says you're a survivor, and that's the best thing you can be." Erik loaded a fresh magazine into the TR-7 and looked at his sleeve. The teeth marks were surprisingly deep. "The nanites must strengthen everything, not just their muscles and pain tolerance." He held up his sleeve. "The average person trying to bite into a tactical suit would more than likely break a tooth. I'm almost impressed. If they weren't brain-dead, they might be a serious threat."

Jia turned her head back and forth, her eyes narrowed. "I still hear growling, but it sounds farther away than before."

Erik listened for a moment and nodded. "Let's take this chance to get to the warden. He's our best bet until Emma comes through."

He had no doubt the AI would, if only to prove something to her fleshbag partners, but it wouldn't hurt to have a backup plan. Every minute that passed with nanozombies running loose meant more people could die.

Erik and Jia broke into a jog, weaving between the piles of bodies in the hallway. The poor bastards had all once been men. Not good men, given they were in prison, but at least human.

The nanites had reduced them to mindless, ravening beasts.

"This shit smells like Talos," Erik noted. "Using technology to make people into enhanced killers?"

Jia glanced over her shoulder as they left the final body behind. "Moving up from full-conversion cyborgs? I didn't even know this kind of thing was possible. I've read all the horror stories about medical nanites going wrong, but those were just people dying painfully, not getting stronger."

"I think it's less about it being impossible and more about why anyone would want to use this under normal circumstances."

"You're right." Jia grimaced and swallowed. "It's not like no one anticipated this application. They've made it difficult and illegal to pull off, but that's not the same thing as impossible."

"Exactly," Erik replied.

They turned the final corner leading to the warden's office. Dead guards were intermingled with a smaller number of dead nanozombies and non-infected prisoners. A heavy wooden desk lay on its side in front of the door, blocking the entrance to the office, covered in deep gouges and bloodstains. The nanozombies were nothing if not persistent.

"Anyone alive in there?" Jia called out. "It's Detectives Lin and Blackwell! We have weapons that can kill those things."

No one replied.

Tension suffused Erik's shoulders. He wouldn't be surprised if the warden was dead, but he'd hoped he wouldn't be. The situation was barely stable as it was.

"Cover me." He slung his TR-7 over his shoulder. "I'm going to move it, even if I have to get loud."

"You think that'll attract more of them?"

Erik shook his head. "If the constant gunfire didn't, I don't see why this would."

Jia backed away from the door, looking up and down the hall for advancing enemies. Erik wasn't worried. Even if his efforts attracted more of the creatures, they'd hear the nanozombies coming long before they saw them.

He advanced on the desk and used his left arm to push, but it wouldn't budge. He brought back his fist and slammed it into the desk, cracking it. Several more blows launched chunks of wood into the air and produced a nice fist-sized hole. He shook out his hand.

Erik peered through the hole. Chairs and a large wooden table had been jammed in between the desk and the wall to hold it in place. Warden Harris and a couple of guards were slumped against the wall, covered in blood, their clothes ripped and wounds on their chests and arms. Despite their awful state, they still seemed to be breathing. There was hope.

"Okay, time for the real effort," Erik muttered.

He backed away from the desk and charged forward, his left shoulder leading, and slammed into it with a grimace. The arm might feel reduced pain, but that wasn't the same thing as none. He backed up and collided with it again. A loud crack accompanied his fourth hit, and the desk toppled over. Jagged pieces of wood from the chairs, table, and desk showered the floor, victims of the cybernetic arm.

Erik reached into his pocket to pull out all the medpatches he had on him. "So much for the warden helping us." He applied the patches to the man's most grievous wounds. "It's better than nothing."

Jia produced patches from her pockets and applied them to the guards. "I hope these will keep them stable. If we don't regain control of the system soon, it won't matter. Right now, we don't know how many of those things are out there. If most of the prisoners have been infected, we'll run out of ammo before we stop them all."

Emma's holographic form appeared. She looked down at the warden with a frown. "This is, some might claim, fortuitous timing, but I think it's simply a reflection of my vast superiority as an intelligent being."

Erik stood and walked toward her. "You've got control of the prison?"

She shook her head. "I've regained partial access to some systems, including the cameras and doors. I don't know the exact method the hacker used, but much of the underlying systems code has been completely obliterated, and actively sabotaged in others. It was surprisingly thorough and destructive. I'm trying to actively rewrite it all, which will lead to questions later, but I assumed you'd prefer successful system access over plausible deniability."

"You're right. We'll worry about that once we don't have a bunch of nanozombies trying to eat our faces."

Jia wrinkled her forehead. "Wait. You're here, and we're not in line-of-sight. Does that mean the jammer is down?"

Emma nodded. "Yes, I located the device once I restored the camera feeds. It was connected to the main power grid, so I killed power in that area. Don't worry, there's no one there."

"What about the bots?" Erik asked. "They're not great, but we could at least use them to swarm them like you did with my drones."

"I'm prioritizing door and cameras," Emma noted, "due to the previously observed ineffectiveness of the security bots, as just noted. The gas might be useful, but it's suffered even higher levels of system damage, and there seems to be physical damage near the storage tanks."

"Sabotage," Jia hissed in irritation.

"I'd assume."

Erik looked around the office. "I hope we can find the son of a bitch responsible for all this."

"I had Cutter send a distress call." Emma snickered. "That way, there are fewer questions about him later, and he doesn't have to remember the details secondhand. We used wide broadcast mode, but we've made it clear this situation is beyond mere reinforcements from other prisons. We've also requested active military intervention from any Fleet assets nearby."

"Good try, but it's not that simple." Erik shook his head.

"The Fleet's not going to send a ship over here just because of a prison riot."

"I had Cutter be selective with the truth. I had him say terrorists had smuggled *yaoguai* into the prison. I thought they might doubt the truth, despite the unsettling nature of its reality. Uniform boys can be so stiff in their thoughts."

Jia eyed Emma for a moment, her look of confusion turning into one of respect for the AI. "It's close enough to the truth. Good job."

"Even if they believe Cutter, it might be a couple of hours or more, depending on where they are." Erik inclined his head toward the warden. "And he's out, so it's up to us to keep things from getting worse."

A three-dimensional holographic map of the prison appeared, filled with scattered white, blue, and red dots. There was a heavy concentration of blue and white dots in a large room in the central portion of the station, with a thick grouping of red dots surrounding them.

Emma pointed to a white dot. "Non-infected prisoners." She moved to a blue dot. "Prison staff. The red dots represented infected. I'm locking anyone alive in a room where they'll be safe. I've tried to seal infected off, but most of them have already converged on a central location. It's like they're calling to each other."

Jia nodded at the map. "And where is that?"

"The cafeteria. Prison staff and noninfected are working together to fight off infected. It's almost heartwarming."

Erik frowned. "Can't you seal it?"

A flash of irritation crossed Emma's face. "I've been trying. There seems to be physical damage to some of the doors in that area, and there's unusually severe damage to the systems code concerning that part of the station."

"That sounds like more sabotage." Jia stepped closer and circled an area on the map with her finger. "This is where we are?"

Emma nodded, and two golden dots appeared.

"There are no active nanozombies left on this level," Jia noted. She quickly pointed to scattered red dots. "And it looks like you've got them mostly trapped, except for the cafeteria."

"That is an accurate assessment."

Erik frowned. "We still don't know how it's spreading."

Emma summoned a large data window. Prisoners and guards stood side-by-side, bracing tables stacked together as barriers. Others punched, kicked, or slammed stun rods into nanozombies that were trying to clamber over the makeshift barrier. A nanozombie cleared the table and leapt onto a guard. A prisoner rushed over and kicked the monster off before shoving a shiv into his head several times and yelling in triumph.

"I reestablished partial camera feeds before killing the jammer," Emma explained. "Most of them are direct lines. I had time to observe, and I haven't noted any active conversions since then, regardless of the nature of the contact."

"They can't pass it through bites or the air," Jia surmised. "Or if they can, there is a major delay before the transformation takes place. For all we know, they could have all been exposed weeks ago. It could have been when Conners visited."

"We should have just brought our breathers," Erik suggested.

Jia blinked and laughed. "I didn't think of that."

"It doesn't matter now." Erik nodded at the door. "They need our help in the cafeteria. If we thin out that horde, that should buy us all enough time until reinforcements arrive."

"Assuming we survive," Jia replied.

"Yeah, always a big assumption." Erik chuckled and traced a path on the map. "We'll come from this approach. That should give us the most targets, and a better angle to shoot at the zombies without hitting the survivors."

She looked at him, a small smirk gracing her lips. "Ever miss when gangsters were our worst problem?"

He smiled. "Nah. This keeps things interesting."

CHAPTER FIFTY-SIX

What started as distant snarls and growls grew in volume until it sounded like an entire zoo packed with rabid, out-of-control animals was nearby.

The screams of dying men and yells of those refusing to die joined the noise. The din swallowed Erik's and Jia's heavy footsteps as they sprinted toward the cafeteria and granted them an unexpected element of surprise.

Bloodstains and crimson foot- and handprints grew more common as they drew closer, along with bodies. They were mostly non-infected, although not as many as they would have expected.

Occasionally, they spotted a collapsed security bot or a downed drone. Whether it was superior wisdom to have less staff and potential victims or arrogance that led to a lower chance of controlling the bizarre situation remained unclear. For now, it didn't matter.

Jia and Erik were the only ones in the entire prison with effective weapons.

"If we start taking down the nanozombies, they might

leave the others alone," Jia suggested between breaths. "But that means they'll come after us."

"If not, it'll be easy to pick them off, and I kind of expect them to come after us. They're idiots. We can win." Erik nodded ahead to an upcoming intersection. One more right turn would bring them behind the largest concentration of nanozombies in the entire station. He slowed and looked at Jia. "You ready for this? I'll try to trip some and hope we get lucky, but mostly I'm going to stick to headshots."

"It's just a horde of nanozombies," she joked. "They don't have missiles or giant sentry bots. It's like taking on a room full of schoolkids."

"Nanozombies are like schoolkids?" Erik stared at her. "Your fancy elite schools must be far scarier than I thought."

"You have no idea." Jia jogged to the intersection and flattened herself against the wall. "Any of them moving our way, Emma?" She'd not realized just how used she'd gotten to Emma providing active tactical information via her smart lenses.

A woman never appreciates a military-grade AI as much as when she is facing off against a nanite-infested horde of ruthless, bestial killers.

"No, they are continuing to attack the breathing flesh-bags in the cafeteria," Emma replied. "Who, I should admit, are mounting a valiant defense, all things considered."

"Three," Jia began. "Two. One." She pivoted around the corner, rifle at the ready.

Dozens of zombies growled and clawed at survivors and their barricades. Despite the hundreds of noninfected men in the cafeteria, the horde was pressing them in with sheer intensity. Dead, mauled bodies lay strewn about, most lacking the mottled skin of the advanced nanozombies. Prisoners and prison staff continued to punch, strike and stab at the horde with makeshift weapons, but every enemy forced back left two or three men wounded or dead. They wouldn't survive without aid.

Jia and Erik lifted their weapons and moved to the side of the hallway. They needed to aim so their bullets wouldn't pass through the barricades. This was as much about saving lives as it was ending zombies. Without a countdown, they both opened fire simultaneously. One nanozombie's head popped like an overripe fruit. Another who had been climbing over the barricade lost most of his neck and tumbled backward, losing his head when he hit the ground. Cheers erupted from the prisoners and staff.

"Yeah, take those things out!" screamed a wiry prisoner. "If I had a gun, they wouldn't be doing so well. I can tell you that."

The horde spun almost as a unit toward Erik and Jia, their snarls and shrieks reverberating off the walls. The nanozombies rushed forward, loping on all fours again. Jia's stomach knotted at the inhuman sound of their shrieks and growls, but it didn't slow her response. Wherever and however she died, it wouldn't be at the hands of a bunch of mindless monsters on a prison station.

If she did, her mother would follow her to the afterlife to complain.

Jia backed up slowly but took her shots quickly, moving from target to target with practiced ease. Erik's TR-7 spat a river of bullets on full automatic.

He aimed low, the bullets ripping into the legs of the front of the horde. Zombies fell to the floor, stumbling over their fallen allies. His plan was working.

He slapped another cartridge in and continued his torrent of death, concentrating on slowing them while Jia delivered the coup de grace: a shot to the head. They could do this.

They could win.

The horde continued to move forward, and Jia's jaw tightened.

Well, maybe not.

There were far more than they'd fought near the warden's office, but there was nothing to do now but fight and win. There would be no mercy from the enemy.

Her body moved on its own as she shifted from closest target to closet target, barely hearing her gunfire or the enemy. The TR-7's loud bellow continued beside her, the sound almost sweet, given the situation.

Missile explosions would have been nice, but she understood the logic of avoiding hull breaches in deep space, especially when the grav and oxygen fields might not be stable.

Erik and Jia continued to back up, leaving a trail of casings and empty magazines close to them and bodies farther away. They'd already thinned the horde by half. Jia had never been so grateful for the mindlessness of an enemy.

Her partner's gun fell silent after two bursts ended with two kills, giving the enemy a chance to advance. A nanozombie pounced at him, but he batted it off with the TR-7.

Jia twisted and put three bullets through its brain before it hit the ground.

More enemies surged forward, shrieking for blood. A trigger pull followed, then another. The former men fell, spared their hellish existence.

Jia fired again, but her gun had run dry. A zombie closed to within a couple of meters before Erik's freshly reloaded rifle added a new large hole where a brain had once resided.

"This is intense." Jia ejected her magazine and yanked another from her carryaid. She slapped it in and started shooting again, almost without aiming.

The convergence of her fire and Erik's shredded the remaining nanozombie vanguard, leaving them on the floor either dead or twitching before dying.

The horde and survivors were now silent. The hallway and the cafeteria were also quiet, except for the ragged, short breaths of exhausted men and one woman. Then a round of cheers ripped through the cafeteria and corridor.

Erik crept forward. "How we doing, Emma?"

"All infected have been neutralized in your immediate vicinity," she reported. "I've successfully contained the others that are spread out over the station, but combined, the remaining strength represents one-fourth of what you've just defeated. I have now restored normal function to all door systems."

A prison guard poked his head above one of the tables. "Are you with the Fleet?"

"No," Erik called back. "We're *cops*."

"The door systems have been restored," Jia announced. "An...associate of ours stationed in the docking bay can lead you to a safe place. There are some remaining nanozombies, but we've got them contained."

"Nanozombies?" a bloodied prisoner asked. "That's crazy. I kind of wish I hadn't tried to rob that flitter dealer now."

Another prisoner stared at the heap of corpses filling the hallway. "Screw this." He put his hands behind his head. "I demand the guards take me back to my cell where it's safe. I didn't commit all those crimes just so someone could eat my face. That's messed up." He looked at the headless corpse near him, still leaking blood. "*Really* messed up."

Other men raised their voices in agreement. The surviving guards were few in number. In a normal riot, the prisoners could have overwhelmed them with ease. Guards shook hands with prisoners and patted them on the back.

Each group had earned the respect that only facing death from a merciless undiscriminating enemy together could bring.

"Emma, can you lead the guards and prisoners back to their cells, where they'll be safe?" Jia asked. "Erik and I will clean up the rest of the nanozombies, then we'll go back to the Rabbit."

"I didn't want to distract you during the battle, but the Fleet has responded, and the uniform boys and girls are on their way. The UTS *Lightning* was in the area and is responding. They have infantry aboard and seem to be taking the situation seriously. Their ETA is one hour."

Erik rested his rifle on his shoulder and wiped some blood off his face. "If Emma's got the last few zombies contained, let's just let the reinforcements handle them. I say we head back to the docking bay and wait. I've had enough of shooting zombies."

Jia watched as a guard led a group of prisoners away. Weariness laced her voice as she kicked a casing toward the wall. "Yes. For once, let somebody else handle the cleanup."

CHAPTER FIFTY-SEVEN

Erik and Jia were about a minute away from the security checkpoint when a data window popped open in front of them. They skidded to a stop, exchanging glances before looking at the window.

"What's going on?" Erik asked.

"I'm sorry," Emma reported. "I thought this would be the most efficient way to get the information across."

The data window showed a feed of Cho and Rich in the security station. Emma provided full audio as well.

"Can you believe this?" Cho commented with a smile. "We're going to make it through this. We're damned lucky Lin and Blackwell are here. Otherwise, we'd probably be lunch for those things already."

"You idiot." Rich sneered. "It's because Lin and Blackwell are here that this is happening." He reached under the control panel. "They're screwing things up. They should have just died in that meeting with Esposito and saved us trouble."

"Screwing things up?" Cho pointed to a feed showing

the detectives advancing down the hall. "They've got some of the systems restored, and you saw what they did in the cafeteria. If they'd died earlier, we would have all been screwed. Nobody can get near the armory right now."

"All they did was save a bunch of trash," Rich muttered.

"Hey, our guys were in there, too." Cho frowned. "Man, what's wrong with you? I don't know what happened, but they saved our asses. Somebody obviously dropped the ball, and it wasn't Lin and Blackwell."

Rich pulled a gun from under the control panel and pointed it at Cho.

The other guard raised his hands. "Whoa. What the hell are you doing? If you had that all the time, you should have been out there helping."

"Why would I help something *I put in motion*?" Rich scoffed. "Just consider everyone sacrifices to my retirement." He fired three times into Cho's face and sneered as the other man slumped forward, dead.

"That was thirty seconds ago," Emma reported as the feed vanished.

"We found our inside man," Erik grumbled. "Surprised it was one of those guys, but a lot of things make sense. No way I'm letting that bastard get away after everything he did."

The detectives sprinted down the hallway toward the security station, their weapons at the ready. The door to the inspection room and the door to the docking bay both stood open. Blood drops led away from the security station. Gunfire rang out from the docking bay.

"What was that?" Jia asked.

"I showed Mr. Durn what was going on so he had situational awareness." Emma sighed. "I didn't anticipate he would attempt to engage the guard."

Erik and Jia ran into the docking bay. Cutter was on one knee, holding his chest, his jaw clenched. A pistol lay near him. They rushed over to him.

"It's okay." Cutter grimaced. "I've had worse. It's not fun, but I'll live." He inclined his head toward the other transport. "He ran into the back, up the loading ramp. Give him a few lumps for me."

"Damn it." Erik pointed his rifle at the transport. "He probably can release the docking clamp himself."

Jia reached into her pocket. "I'm out of medpatches."

Cutter stood, his teeth gritted. "It's fine. I'll get one from the Rabbit. Like I said, this isn't my first time getting shot. Or stabbed." He looked up in thought. "Or thrown across a room." He shook his head. "Maybe I've made poor life choices."

"I question the wisdom of your engagement, Mr. Durn," Emma commented quietly, "but I respect your bravery for facing that gun goblin. I would almost think it a net loss if you were killed. Almost."

"Thanks, Holochick. That *almost* makes it worthwhile." Cutter managed a pained grin as he headed toward the Rabbit. "Show the bastard what's up." He gave them a thumbs-up.

"He's not getting away." Jia clutched her rifle. "We won't let him."

"The *Lightning* can intercept him," Erik suggested. "If he doesn't surrender, they can blow his transport to pieces."

"That wouldn't be as satisfying," Jia told him. "Esposito was part of it, but none of this would have happened without an inside man. Somebody put him up to this, or he works for the conspiracy. I'd like to ask him a few questions."

Erik grinned. "I hear you. Let's see if he's smarter than the zombies." He pulled the TR-7 around. "There's no point in running," he shouted. "If you surrender to us right now, we can guarantee you don't end up dead. We need to interrogate you. I'm sure you've got a lot of interesting stories to tell us. Even if you can fly that thing out of here, there's a Fleet destroyer on its way, and you can't outrun them. They're almost here."

A bloodcurdling scream erupted from the back of the transport.

"I'm scarier than I thought." Erik frowned, considering the other likely possibility. "I hope. Emma, do you have a visual on the back of that transport?"

"No, the cameras were physically disabled in that part of the docking bay," she reported.

"Part of his plan, probably. Yeah, fun."

Heavy footsteps thudded in the back of the transport, and a loud, inhuman growl filled the air. Something tossed Rich's body out. It was missing its right arm, except for a bloody stump. The body landed, the remaining limbs bent in unnatural directions.

"You didn't say anything about nanozombies being out here," Erik complained, lifting his gun. "And so much for your interrogation, Jia."

"I wasn't looking inside the ship," Emma replied. "There must be a compartment that is shielded, much like you have." She sounded annoyed. "This was a rather thorough effort in many ways."

A dark-gray form ambled down the loading ramp, its elongated body hunched over. The creature had once been human, but black veins covered its exposed, mottled flesh. Its solid black eyes took in the world. It snapped at the air, spraying thick black spittle.

"Is that what happens after long enough with those nanites?" Disgust took over Jia's face.

"Who the hell knows?" Erik lifted his TR-7. "Won't be our problem soon enough. Let's send him to join all his friends."

He fired. The creature's head jerked to the side, but it didn't fall, instead snarling in rage. When he turned back toward Erik, there was no large hole, only a few scratches.

"Oh, that's new," Jia commented. "Not good-new, annoying-new."

"Concentrate fire," Erik shouted. "It's just a guy with a lot of nanites."

Their combined efforts forced him back but again didn't produce any serious wounds. The few seeping scratches on the super-zombie's face began to seal.

"And I thought the hordes *were* their backup plan," Jia griped. "This is truly annoying."

"What's above truly annoying?" Erik asked.

"I add colorful metaphors my mother wouldn't approve of."

"So, you talk dirty?" Erik grinned.

"Something like that," she admitted, firing once more.

The super-zombie threw his head back and shrieked. The grating sound echoed around the docking bay.

There was no way they were going to beat the super-zombie the way they'd taken out the enemies within the prison. At this point, they needed something more powerful than the TR-7, something they might use to take out a vehicle.

Erik whipped his left hand to his carryaid and yanked off the laser rifle. He dropped the huge weapon on the deck with an unceremonious *thud* before running toward the super-zombie in a zigzag pattern and firing intermittent bursts, yelling at the top of his lungs.

"What the hell are you doing?" Jia shouted.

"Distracting it. *You* finish it."

The super-zombie scurried toward Erik with an earsplitting shriek. He halted its advance with another headshot before shifting to a circular running pattern that momentarily confused his opponent.

Jia tossed her rifle to the ground as she sprinted toward the laser rifle. She dropped into a slide and tapped the side of the rifle to extend the tripod. With a grunt of exertion, she pulled the huge weapon until it was upright and rolled behind it, narrowing her eyes on her prey.

The super-zombie jumped, bringing back its arm. Erik raised his TR-7 to block the blow, but it knocked the weapon out of Erik's hands. He only didn't lose it because of the strap. He threw a punch with his left arm and connected, but the hit barely staggered the monster.

"Oh, that's not good," he muttered.

The creature responded by backhanding him so hard he flew backward and landed with a grimace several yards away, pain spiking through his chest and back from the hit and the carryaid slamming into him. Much like Cutter, he filed it under the "he'd had worse."

Any hit that didn't remove an arm or almost kill him was classified that way.

"Stay the hell away from my partner," Jia shouted and pulled the trigger. The deadly invisible beam did its work, boring a hole through the chest of the super-zombie.

The creature responded with a loud roar and stalked toward her, twitching but not falling.

"Oh, come on. Die already." She fired again, this time burning a clean hole through its head, but it kept walking toward her.

"This has moved to the top of the list of annoying." Jia fired again, this time taking out its knee. The super-zombie fell to the deck but continued crawling toward her. She fired three more times into the monster, draining the cell and adding three new holes, including another in what was left of its head, but that somehow didn't kill it, only slowed it. She dropped the laser rifle and backed up.

"There's evidence of nanite-based regeneration," Emma reported. "Both of you hurry to the inspection room. I'll close it once you're inside. I have a plan to dispose of the enemy that won't require heavy weapons."

"Is it a stupid plan?" Erik called to her.

"I prefer the term 'desperate.' Detective Blackwell, but take the laser rifle with you. Mr. Durn, secure the ship unless you want to die."

The ladder retracted on the Rabbit, and the door lifted to seal the cockpit. Erik forced himself to his feet, ignoring his pain.

He limp-jogged toward the rifle and scooped it up with his left arm, continuing toward the inspection room. Jia sprayed the crawling super-zombie from the room with her assault rifle, but the creature continued moving, determined to punish her for her attacks. Once Erik stepped into the inspection room, the security door slid closed.

A feed of the docking bay appeared in front of them. The bay doors rumbled and began to part. Red lights flashed in the bay.

"Warning!" announced a soft female voice. "Oxygen field and backup grav field are inactive. Overrides are in place. Warning! Loss of atmospheric containment is imminent."

Erik grinned. "Damn, Emma, that's *cold.*"

"Yes, and soon, our friend will be too," Emma replied.

The docking bay doors continued opening. Unsecured crates tumbled through them, sucked into space by the rapid decompression of the bay.

The patrol craft shuddered but didn't move thanks to their docking clamps. Rich's arm flew out of the docking bay, followed by his body. The super-zombie shrieked in defiance as it hurtled backward, waving its arms. It snagged a docking clamp with its fingers and continued its snarling and shrieking.

The sound died as the last of the air evacuated the docking bay. It wasn't much longer before the creature slipped into the cold, dead darkness of space, flailing the entire time.

Erik laughed. "Nice, Emma."

CHAPTER FIFTY-EIGHT

Soldiers in exoskeletons clanked through the docking bay, inspecting each ship individually. They were ready to open up with armor-piercing death against any nanozombie popping up from a hidden cargo hold. At least a dozen soldiers had already boarded the larger transport to perform a sweep. There had been no gunfire or screaming.

All evidence suggested the super-zombie had been the last backup plan.

Erik sat in the cockpit in the Rabbit next to Jia and a pale but recovering Cutter. They'd already given their report to the commanding officer of the boarding team, a stern-faced and professional woman.

Emma had disengaged from the system but had repaired enough that the surviving prison guards could help coordinate the military cleanup of the remaining nanozombies. They'd tried to take a few alive, but in the end, the soldiers eliminated the few survivors and confirmed the surviving prisoners had all returned to their cells.

Erik turned toward Cutter. "You got shot. You think a few medpatches will be enough? We should get you to the prison infirmary or the sickbay of the *Lightning.*"

"Come on, Blackwell," the pilot replied, gesturing at the patch on his chest. "It's not like you go to the hospital every time you get shot. Sometimes a man takes some lead and just sleeps it off."

"True enough. You know your body best."

"Are you sure?" Jia asked him. "That isn't a hangnail."

"The bullet passed right through." Cutter smiled down at his wounds. "I just need some rest and the patches. I'll sleep on the way back and let the nanites do their things. After we get back to Earth, there's a place I'll go for follow-up." His smile faded, and he winced. "Damn. After everything that happened, I kind of don't like the idea of the nanites doing their things. If I come back as one of those things, don't dump me into space. Blow my brains out, so I have a respectable death."

Erik gave him a polite nod. "Full burst, four-barrels, right between the eyes. It'll be quick. I promise."

"Thanks. I appreciate that, Blackwell." Cutter stood. He swayed as he made his way toward the crew cabin. "That makes me feel better. If I'm going to die, might as well be at the hands of a legend and not some random monster."

"I wouldn't say I'm a legend," Erik called to the man.

Cutter shook his head. "The Goddess of Death wouldn't want your help if you weren't. It's just, this time, you became a legend before the Directorate came sniffing around." He turned back toward the door.

"Cutter, wait," Jia called.

He stopped. "What's up, Lin? Want to give me a kiss?"

"In your dreams." Jia rolled her eyes.

"Probably not even then," Cutter admitted.

Jia chuckled. "I wanted to thank you for not leaving. I have a feeling that docking clamp wouldn't have stopped you for more than a couple of minutes if you had really wanted to go, and this wasn't a normal situation, even by the standards of what Alina might have you working on."

"Hey, I don't bail on a job just because a few guys start eating people." Cutter scoffed. "I'm a professional, and I have standards. I'd never live it down if I got a rep as a guy who cuts and runs when things get a little hot. For now, though, I need some sleep." He slapped the access panel and stepped into the crew cabin, closing the door after him.

Jia laid her head back on the seat. "Did you imagine when you woke up this morning that something like this would happen?"

"Depends." Erik ran his tongue around the inside of his mouth as he thought. "You mean, exactly like this? Nanozombies, and Esposito being the first one?"

She looked his way. "You're saying you imagined something that was even in the same neighborhood?"

"Kind of." Erik waggled his hand left, then right. "I figured it might be a trap. After Molino, I got the message I'd let myself forget during my career, that even the easiest milk run can end in something unexpected. But no, I was thinking more like Esposito might have implanted explosives, or something like that, not—"

"Nanozombies," Jia finished for him.

"Yeah, nanozombies. I don't know if they're better or worse than *yaoguai*, but I'm not sure it makes a difference."

Erik watched a few troops walk past, rifles in hand and bored looks on their faces as they headed into the prison. "Sometimes I'm impressed by how together the UTC has managed to keep things. There's a lot of stuff people can do with tech that they don't officially allow. That doesn't stop all of it, but it's stopped a *lot* of it. I don't imagine this is the first time someone thought of something like this."

"I suppose," Jia murmured. "I wish that tech would stop trying to kill us, though." She rolled her head his way and grinned. "I know we poke our noses into things voluntarily, but I'm starting to take some of the Lady's taunts personally."

"Yeah, she's a bitch sometimes." Erik laughed. "And it'd be nice to only have to worry about normal enemies. But hey, at least it wasn't fake bikini-babe space raptors."

"No, it wasn't those, for certain," Jia replied. "I'm not sure I wouldn't have preferred fake bikini-babe raptors."

"Nanozombie or Zitark?" Erik tossed out for fun. "They both want to eat you."

"I hadn't thought of that," she admitted. "Being eaten isn't at the top of my list of ways to die."

They sat in companionable silence for a few minutes before Erik turned to look at her. "Would you prefer to be eaten by an alien or a zombie?"

Jia stuck her hands behind her head and looked at the ceiling of the ship. "Do I have to be eaten?"

"For purposes of the question, yeah." Erik snickered. "It's not fun otherwise. You could choose to have your neck broken or be stabbed by a Zitark."

Jia smirked. "How about I kill all the aliens or zombies before they eat me, break my neck, or stab me?"

"That's one way out of it. Probably the best way." Erik sat up. "We need to be more careful going forward. This one was a little closer than I would have liked, but hey, we're still breathing, and everything they sent to kill us isn't."

"I know." Jia sighed. "They really are out of control. I can't even believe they thought up this kind of plan."

"When the obvious doesn't work, try the not-so-obvious. Nothing worse than smart criminals."

"This goes well beyond criminals," Jia suggested.

"Detectives," Emma interjected. "Warden Harris is attempting to call."

"Put him through," Erik ordered. "I'm surprised he's up so soon."

"Detective Blackwell? Detective Lin?" The warden's voice sounded strained, not surprising, considering the injuries he had suffered.

"Sorry you missed all the fun at the end, Warden," Erik answered. "But glad you're up so soon."

"That's only because of you two. You also saved those two guards with me. We would have bled out for sure without your help."

"We were just doing our jobs," Jia commented. "Protect and serve, even in space against nanozombies."

"That's easy for you to say," Warden Harris offered. "But I've got dead guards and prisoners to justify. We let contraband in here, not to mention a corrupt guard. If it hadn't been for your quick actions, things would have even been worse, and the oversight failure was on my part. So, thank you for covering my ass."

Erik frowned. "I hate to do this to you, Warden, but I

doubt you only had one bad guard. There's no way one man pulled all that off by himself."

"I know. I have no idea how you managed to partially repair the system so quickly, but I'm not complaining. Based on what my people are telling me, it's going to take weeks to fully restore everything, and we'll be transferring most of the prisoners to other facilities because we'll still need to check everything to make sure there are not hidden backdoors left inside the systems." The warden audibly swallowed. "You're right. I doubt one mid-ranking prison guard would have the capability of pulling all that off by himself. I'll be doing my best to cooperate with the CID investigators when they arrive. We need to find Hadrian Conners. I don't know what syndicate he works for, but based on what I heard, they had another of those things hidden in that transport, which means the guy went all-out to mess this place up. Thank God you sucked it out into space."

"Yeah," Erik replied. "Somebody from the Fleet's going to pick it up. They're tracking the body now. You can check with them if you're dying for more info."

"That's...okay," the warden replied. "I'm not all that interested in the fine details of the monsters."

"I haven't heard any alerts," Erik commented. "I take it there were no more nanozombies? The soldiers look pretty calm, but I wasn't sure if you were just trying not to get everyone too worked up if new ones popped up."

"Nothing. None of the survivors who were bitten or scratched have any evidence of infection. The air quality is steady. There must have been something else. I recommended that they let you go immediately, but I'm no longer making that call, given the emergency, and the fact you called the Fleet in."

"Yeah, we were told we needed to stick around for a little bit." Erik chuckled. "It's not a big problem. We're not in a hurry. We're just glad they're not sticking us all in quarantine."

"It's surprising, is what it is." Jia eyed the people moving past their ship. "It's almost like they've dealt with this kind of thing before and knew what to look for."

Erik frowned. He hadn't thought of that, but once she said it, it made perfect sense. There was no longer any such thing as "too paranoid" in their lives. Jia noticed him looking at her and shrugged in response to his unasked question.

"I fully expect to be fired for what happened," the warden admitted. "But I want to be clear. I don't blame either of you for anything, and I'm grateful you two were here and risked your lives to save not only my staff but also the prisoners. Did you want to help investigate the other prison guards? I'm sure if I push, I can convince the CID."

Jia half-closed her eyes. "This is well outside our jurisdiction. I think we'll leave that to them. I'm comfortable being the victim being assisted by other law enforcement."

"You're hardly victims. You're heroes."

Erik stared at her for a moment, the corners of his mouth twisting into a playful smile. "I agree with my partner. Sometimes you want to handle everything yourself, and sometimes you just want to take a long rest."

"I understand, Detectives," the warden offered. "I need to handle a few things. If you need anything else while you're here, just let me know, and I'll do what I can."

He signed off.

Erik and Jia sat in silence for a couple of minutes, reflecting on the events of the trip. Exhaustion weighed heavily on their faces, despite their satisfaction at handling the problem. It might have helped if they hadn't made a half-day flight beforehand.

"Make me a promise," Jia whispered. "For the future?"

Erik looked her way. "Promise you what? I can't promise you no more surprises."

"No, I expect surprises. I just want no zombie simulations."

Erik laughed. "Even bikini zombies?"

"Especially bikini zombies. They're even worse than bikini space raptors."

CHAPTER FIFTY-NINE

September 14, 2229, Neo Southern California Metroplex, Police Enforcement Zone 122 Station, Office of Captain Alexander Ragnar

The captain didn't look preoccupied or angry.

That was a good start to the day.

He'd been nothing but concerned during their immediate calls after the incident the week before, and when he'd called them in right after their return to work, neither was sure what it might mean. He'd had days of contact with only the briefest of comments. At this point, there wasn't much to say.

"I don't get you." The captain nodded to both detectives. "You two could have taken a few days off, you know. You didn't have to come back immediately and start working a new case. You've had a busy couple of months."

"It's good to be able to concentrate on normal work," Erik offered, "after nearly getting eaten by nanozombies."

Captain Ragnar chuckled. "If that sentence came out of anyone else's mouth, it'd sound ridiculous, but somehow it's reasonable that you two keep ending up in situations like that."

"It's not like we're trying," Jia half-argued. "It's just how things work out. And the last thing I wanted to do was sit around in my apartment and obsess over nanozombie prison riots."

"Good. If you're not having trouble, then it's as good a time as any to talk about this." The captain offered them a warm smile. "I have to debrief you. The CID seems obsessed with handling this incident through channels, which is why they haven't contacted you directly. I've fielded their requests to keep you from being bothered."

Erik rubbed the back of his neck. "Is this about the reports and the hacking? Look, Captain, I didn't want to explain to the CID in detail about Emma. I'm sure somebody high up knows about her, but I can't say that about every random agent between the field and the very top."

Captain Ragnar shook his head. "Don't worry about it. I made it clear you were testing various experimental devices on behalf of other government agencies, and that seemed to satisfy them. Plus, I called some friends, and from what I understand, a couple of people already pulled strings on your behalf. The thing is, the CID doesn't want to press you too hard. I'm sure they want you two to stay as far away from this as they can manage."

"Why?" Jia frowned. "You think there is a cover-up?"

The captain barked a laugh, his beard shaking. "It's nothing like that, for once. This is too high-profile to cover up, even if they're massaging the details." He shook his head. "No, it's because it makes the CID look bad for the Esposito collar to begin with. They want to write it off as terrorism, but it's obvious you two were direct assassination targets of someone using specialized and advanced resources. They've also found two other guards who were involved in sabotaging the prison and helping smuggle items inside."

Erik nodded. "That makes sense."

"Those were in addition to the guard who died during the incident, and a medic who was working with them. They've all testified about being approached and offered large sums of money to help with smuggling a few things. They don't seem to be aware of what the overall plan was. Most of them were under the impression they were helping bring in drugs."

"I'd hope they didn't understand what they were doing." Jia's nostrils flared. "After all, agreeing to let someone turn people into monsters and murder their fellow guards is far beyond smuggling in items to help someone escape. I'm still confused about how they turned the prisoners into those things."

"Based on their testimony and what the CID investigators uncovered, those nanites were injected into the prisoners," Captain Ragnar explained.

"The medic," Erik concluded. "That's why they needed him."

Captain Ragnar nodded. "Yes. He also falsified medical reports, but no one's sure yet if any of the prisoners other than Esposito volunteered for the procedure. Most of the infected were men who had recently gotten physicals."

"But why did they change so suddenly?" Jia asked. "This all happened shortly after our arrival."

"They're still investigating that. Apparently, one of the

guards was told to activate a device at a certain time. The working theory is the nanites responded to some sort of signal. Esposito had only gotten the injection that day."

"That explains why he wasn't as messed up as the others," Erik commented.

"None of them claim to know where the super-zombie came from, but two did admit they knew they were smuggling in something large the day before." Captain Ragnar tapped his PNIU, and a still image of the super-zombie in space appeared. "This one wasn't a prisoner. DNA match points to a low-level enforcer for a Martian syndicate. He was reported missing by his wife several weeks ago. No sign his family received any money. I don't think he was a volunteer. The CID says he doesn't fit the profile."

Jia tapped her lips, deep in thought. "I assume it's too much to ask that the CID has been able to follow up on whatever payments were made to the prison staff?"

"Sorry, Detective Lin. There was a lot of special care put into hiding the money trail," Captain Ragnar replied. "All we know is, someone had a lot of money and a lot of skill in financial crime."

Erik folded his arms. "Not surprised. This was advanced biotech. If it's not Talos, then it's someone very much like them, and people like that know how to cover their trail. I wouldn't be surprised if we can never follow the trail to the end, especially if they made sure to keep a lot of it flowing through off-Earth banks."

Captain Ragnar looked down at his desk, his brow tightening. "They also have no line on Hadrian Conners. The man with that name and with accounts linked to activity in recent weeks has been dead for several years."

"That's...fitting." Erik smirked.

Jia gave him a confused look. "Why do you say that?"

He looked at her. "Zombies and dead people kind of go together."

Captain Ragnar grunted. "If he were a real zombie, it'd make more sense. Amazingly, we've got no video footage of the man at the prison. It's like he's a—"

"A ghost?" Jia raised an eyebrow.

"Something like that. The only thing I can tell you two is that you need to be careful. Damned careful." Captain Ragnar stared at the super-zombie image. "Sounds like someone really wants you two dead, and they're willing to do pretty twisted stuff to get that done. Now we've got everybody from the military to the CID involved, and I'm sure the Intelligence Directorate is sniffing around, too. That gives you some cover, but only a little. If someone released those nanozombies in the middle of a city where they couldn't be as easily contained, who knows how many people might be killed? If it was Talos, they might not pull this stunt again, but that doesn't mean they won't try something else just as nasty."

"Careful?" Erik chuckled. "We're always careful, Captain. It's the other guys who keep trying to make our lives difficult."

The holographic avatars of the members of the Core surrounded their meeting table.

Some looked on with boredom, others irritation and fascination, as they reviewed a feed of the events on the prison station, ending with the advanced nano-modified prototype experiencing the painful joys of explosive decompression.

Shoji threw his head back and laughed. "Now *that's* creativity. You have to admire the Last Soldier and his allies. Most would have given in to despair when faced with such an opponent.

Sophia glared at him. "You find this amusing?"

"Yes. That was why I laughed." Shoji gave a bemused look. "You don't find it entertaining at all?"

"I think this is a setback, and I don't find setbacks entertaining...ever."

Shoji sighed. "Your loss."

Farad folded his arms. "She's right. This was a failure, and an expensive one. The test subjects were supposed to kill the Last Soldier and his partner, but instead, they defeated even the advanced prototype, and now the ID is undoubtedly scouring *every* piece of evidence on that station. We've exposed ourselves with this."

Shoji flicked a wrist, a dismissive look on his face. "And they'll find nothing. There's no trail that leads directly back to our researchers. They'll have what they always have—supposition and suspicion that combine into nothing concrete. You consider it an expensive failure, but I contest that. It wasn't a failure. It was a wonderful success." He looked around. "You people need to change your perspective."

"What strange world do you live in where that was a success?" Farad blinked and shook his head, his face twisted in anger and disbelief over the utter foolishness coming out of the other man's mouth.

"I live in the same world as the rest of you." Shoji gestured at the image of the super-zombie. "As I said, modify your perspective, Farad. As an assassination attempt, it failed, but it was a useful field test of a potential tool. You'll live longer if you don't stress out over unnecessary jokes." He snickered. "Sorry, I couldn't pass up the opportunity."

Ivan scoffed. "This was how you wanted to test it? If it was a test, we should have used it against the government factions that stand against us, not a pointless prison station filled with rabble."

"Why not?" Shoji waved a hand. "It's the perfect test for what you're describing. We were able to infiltrate a highly secure, controlled facility and infect a number of subjects. If we'd tried a different target, we might have failed." Shoji licked his lips, his smile growing. "We were also able to deploy the tools through third parties with minimal training, proving the viability of the tool for a variety of targets and applications. The project requires additional research, but now we have useful and practical field data on the abilities of the test subjects, up to and including heavy weapons use. What is that but a rousing success?"

Sophia swept her hand through the air, and the super-zombie image vanished. A large holographic depiction of Molino appeared.

"We must be more cautious in the coming months," she stated. "Although we've tied up several loose ends, some of our recent efforts have failed, and we must expect blowback from our enemies. The Last Soldier and his partner are irritants, but they can make us vulnerable to others with substantially more bite."

A beautiful woman with blue-black hair named Julia leaned forward at the other end of the table. She was dressed well even by the standards of a Core meeting, with an elaborately embroidered silk dress showing off her pale, delicate shoulders.

Sophia frowned and looked her way. No one in the Core could be completely trusted, but Julia was more unpredictable than most. She also hadn't cared to speak during their last two meetings.

"What?" Sophia asked, the word coming out with the intensity of a curse.

"Have you considered another option?" Julia's words came out with warmth and sweetness. The feigned sincerity sickened Sophia.

"Another option? Such as?"

"The Last Soldier and this partner could be useful tools. I think you're all focusing so much on his elimination that you keep forgetting." Julia motioned toward the hologram of Molino. "If he believes he's found the people responsible, and we provide him the evidence, he would be in our debt, and we could steer him toward our targets with greater ease."

There was a sudden silence.

"Delicious," Shoji declared, his face lit with joy at the idea.

"That's nonsense," Sophia countered. "He won't be so easily manipulated. If we were to deal with him that directly, even through proxies, all we would do is lead our true enemies straight to us. No. For now, he's too dangerous. We should let things lie. Let him believe he's wounded us, and let him drown in the banal realities of normal police work. We can use our agents to continue field operations."

"You're missing an opportunity," Julia insisted. "One that might not arise again."

"No, we're being wise. No one should take action against either the Last Soldier or his partner without all of us agreeing." Sophia swept the table with her gaze. "Understood?"

"Clarity has never been one of your problems, Sophia." Julia offered her a soft smile. "Understood."

CHAPTER SIXTY

Jia's heart pounded as she grabbed a beer from her refrigerator. She headed back into her living room and offered it to Erik. "I know it's not your favorite brand, but…"

She wasn't sure why she had beer other than Erik's favorite brand in her refrigerator. It wasn't like she drank it unless he was around. Was it to fool her family when they came over and worried about her taste?

Erik smirked. "But old princess habits die hard and you drink expensive beer when you're alone?"

"Something like that." Jia considered grabbing one for herself but decided against it. She needed a clear head for the conversation she wanted to have.

Erik took the beer with a smile. "Booze is booze." He looked around with a frown. "But I'm not seeing any duck. That's the real problem."

"Duck?" Jia took a seat next to him. "I didn't say anything about duck when I invited you over. Did I?" She shook her head. "No, there's no way. I would have remembered. I don't take duck lightly.

"I assumed that was why you wanted me to stop by. Whenever you've asked me to stop by without explaining things in the past, that's *always* been the reason." Erik took a sip of the beer. "But free beer is always welcome, even expensive, fancy, rich-person beer. And it's not bad. It lacks a certain…something, but I'm not going to complain."

"I've been thinking about everything that happened the last couple of weeks," Jia explained. "That was what I wanted to talk about."

"That's always dangerous, especially for Lady Overthink." Erik swallowed significantly more beer this time. "And what does your thinking tell you?"

"That Esposito wasn't just trying to kill *you*." Jia frowned. "He was also trying to kill *me*."

Erik searched the coffee table for a coaster. Jia had already set out one with an elaborate floral pattern. He put the beer down.

"Plenty of people have tried to kill you before." He shrugged. "What's the big deal? Someone tried to kill you on the day we met. He just wasn't very good at it."

"That's true." Jia looked away. "But before, it was either incidental or related to my work as a detective. This time, it felt like the conspiracy was targeting both of us. We're not talking about hiring a lone hitman, but people willing to use something as elaborate and dangerous as nanozombies. It's not something I can just blow off."

"True." Erik nodded slowly. "So, where are you going with all this?"

Jia reached over and placed her hand on top of his, and he struggled for a moment to focus. He overcame the synapse problem she had caused just before she started talking. "We're not famous cops anymore, Erik. We're targets. And because we're targets of a ruthless conspiracy which is willing to do anything and use anyone, we might end up being more of a liability than a help to the NSCPD. Not just you, but also me. Nanozombies aren't the kind of thing we can handle as detectives." She sighed. "If we didn't possess those barely legal weapons, we wouldn't have been able to handle Delta 97. If we hadn't ignored procedure to let an experimental AI hack a prison station, a lot more people would have died, probably including us. I've tried to ignore that, but I can't anymore."

Erik looked down at her hand. "That's all true."

"If this is what we're up against, we need to face them a different way," Jia insisted. "We can't do that as cops. I've accepted that now, *fully*. Because of that, I think we need to take Alina up on her offer."

Erik smiled and pulled his hand away. "Are you sure? It's not like you'll be able to walk back into the station six months from now. I'm not saying this is impossible to come back from, but we're talking about the ID, not changing to a new corp."

Jia locked eyes with him, her heart pounding. Her entire life was about to change even more than when he'd first fallen into it. If she were honest with herself, she found that more exciting than frightening.

"I'm sure," she declared. "I think I have been for a while."

"Then I'll contact Alina," Erik replied softly. "We should also see if Malcolm's interested. The ID's already vetted him, and it'd be nice to have the beginnings of a support team. We'll need to work out the details about how to best do this, but it's not like we need to have it figured out tomorrow."

"You're right." Jia looked away. "I'm not claiming I'll never regret this, but I have a feeling I'd always regret it if I *didn't* take the chance."

"I'm glad," Erik murmured. "I don't want to do this without you."

Malcolm stared at Erik, his mouth open as he leaned forward in his chair. He looked around his office as if they were behind one-way glass. "Should we be talking about this kind of thing at work?" he hissed. "I mean, this is, like, serious ghost stuff."

"I've handled the privacy, Technician Constantine," Emma explained, merely a voice in the air. "Unless someone along the lines of the ID is attempting to spy on you, I doubt you have anything to worry about."

Erik grinned and clapped Malcolm on the shoulder. "You knew it was coming to this, didn't you? I figured you knew that from the minute you found out the truth about Camila."

"I wasn't sure about quitting my job." Malcolm groaned. "I'm not the kind of guy who wants to fight zombies in space or crazy monsters in a sewer."

"You don't have to fight zombies in space or monsters in a sewer. That's what Jia and I do." Erik stepped away. "We need you for what you do now: help with investigations, data, and records." He motioned toward the data windows floating above Malcolm's desk. "Nothing new, and no firefights. With you and Emma working together, we'll be able to go through evidence like it was nothing. And we don't care about what shirts you wear." He grinned. "Come on, Malcolm. You've been interested in doing this since before you even knew what I was involved in."

"I don't know, Detective Blackwell. I mean, this is crazy." Malcolm chewed his lip. "Super-crazy."

It was time for one final push.

Erik leaned close to Malcolm's ear to whisper, "Let me ask you one thing. You banging Camila yet?"

Malcolm blinked several times, his eyes flicking to Erik's face. "W-what did you just say?"

"I asked if you were banging Camila. Because if you aren't, leaving behind your old job to help the Intelligence Directorate is a definite turn-on for a woman like her." Erik leaned back, a huge grin on his face. "Just saying. It's time you put your skills to the test, and it'll help you look cool for your girlfriend."

Malcolm shook his head once, then twice. Then he shrugged, smirked, and threw his hands in the air.

"Well, when you put it that way, sign me up!"

Erik stared up at the huge waterfall cascading down the tower and flowing into an artificial lake. Everything about a waterfall park atop a metroplex tower was absurd. It was simply an expression of the arrogance of humanity in building something without practicality just to show they could. On most days, Erik might even admit that was why he liked it. The story of humanity was the story of struggle and survival.

And that was what he was: a survivor.

Jia smiled at the waterfall. Her smile vanished, and her hand moved into her coat as someone emerged from behind a nearby tree. Erik went for his gun. Both relaxed when they spotted a familiar cyan ponytail.

Hair swaying, Alina sauntered up to the detectives with a slight smile. "Good morning. I'm glad to see you two are always ready to take down assassins."

"It keeps us alive when people send cyborgs and zombies to kill us." Erik frowned as he looked around. Something was off.

Something had changed, but what?

Jia glanced his way with a knowing look. "We can't hear the waterfall anymore."

"More ghost shit. Got you." Erik chuckled. "I'm surprised you're not here in disguise, Alina."

"I've made sure this area is controlled for the moment, which is why you haven't seen anyone else since coming here." Alina inclined her head toward the waterfall. "And loud noises offer their own excuses for why people can't hear things. Sometimes the best place to hide is in plain sight. Sheer audacity can make for spectacular intelligence successes."

Erik nodded. "Fine. We might as well get this over with. We're ready to take your offer. We'll be your contractors or whatever you want to call it, but that doesn't mean we're pawns. We're doing this in exchange for a focus on the conspiracy, whether it ends with Talos or goes deeper than that. Malcolm's onboard as well. We can figure out the details going forward."

Alina nodded. "So Camila told me. I'm surprised they ended up together. He doesn't seem her type. It goes to show you that even an intelligence agent can get people wrong."

Jia walked over to a nearby bench and took a seat, then crossed her legs. "You never thought Erik would say no."

He looked at the women but didn't speak.

Alina shrugged. "I think I made an offer that provides something for everyone involved. There was little long-term reason not to take it. Both of you have stared directly into some very nasty truths, and I knew it wasn't long before you'd want a bigger sandbox to play in to confront those truths. And here we are."

"The nanozombies pushed me over the top," Jia admitted. "Somehow..." She shook her head. "At least the mutants were born that way, but what the conspiracy did this time was a new low."

Alina stared at the waterfall, a distant look in her eyes. "Give it another year or two, Jia, and you'll find there's no such thing as 'a new low' for some people. But I understand where you're coming from. I also have information that's relevant to the incident on the station."

"Was it Talos?" Erik asked.

"We're not sure, but there are technological innovations involved that we've previously seen from them." Alina tore her attention away from the waterfall, a haunted look on her face. "I'll be blunt. Things are worse than they appear."

"Of course they are," Jia muttered. "That's why you're grabbing police officers to turn into rent-a-ghosts."

"It's beyond that." Alina pointed at Erik's left arm. "Most people buy into some form of Purism, and there are laws against various types of technology. I want to be totally honest with you. There are elements of the government who keep an eye on certain technologies in particular applications."

"Advanced genetic engineering and cybernetics?" Jia guessed.

Alina nodded. "It's not enough to make things illegal. A record of a technology is as good as immortality for the technology, and certain things are…well, you've seen them. *Yaoguai*. Nanozombies. What's the point of improving on things like that? You don't have to be a Purist to be disgusted. A law is a fiction enforced by the strength of the government, but if the knowledge never existed as far as society is concerned, it's easier to contain."

Erik shook his head, letting out a hearty laugh. "Conspiracies within conspiracies. I'm surprised I'm not dizzy."

"Yes." Alina gave him a defiant look. "The Intelligence Directorate got our hands on samples from those nanozombies. We wanted to confirm who might be involved, but we also wanted to confirm something else: the baseline technology used."

Jia narrowed her eyes. "You've seen it before."

Alina nodded. "There was a government super-soldier project a few decades back, code-named 'Dragon Fire.'" She gritted her teeth, her body trembling with barely concealed rage. "They wanted the perfect soldier, stronger, faster, able to heal. The researchers involved decided the existing limits on nanotechnology were too confining. They wanted to employ different types of nanites."

"But there were side effects," Erik suggested. "Bad side effects."

She nodded. "Yes. The human body can accommodate a lot, but the more you change things, the more you have to compensate for the changes." Alina took a deep breath. "We don't know how Talos has beaten cybernetic psychosis syndrome, or if they truly have, but we know they didn't solve the problems with the Dragon Fire nanites. I also refuse to believe it's a coincidence that they had nanites from a program halted decades ago."

"Someone in the government leaked them to Talos."

Alina nodded. "This is what we're fighting. The enemy isn't an army wearing uniforms. The enemy looks and sounds like a loyal member of the UTC government, all the while conspiring with a terrorist organization to make disgusting weapons that pervert the very nature of humanity."

Erik snorted. "Who gives a shit?"

Alina blinked. "Huh?"

"I don't care what they look like. We'll find them, and we'll end them." Erik eyed her. "It's as simple as that."

Alina let out a light chuckle. "Really? It's as simple as that?"

Erik bobbed his head. "It's not right that the government is screwing with research, but I know the other side is worse, and they were involved in killing my people on Molino. For all I know, we stumbled onto a nanozombie lab on that moon, and that was why they ambushed us."

Alina turned to Jia. "What about you? Things aren't always going to be black and white, Jia. You'll have to make some hard calls, and you won't be able to hide behind the law when you're working for me."

"Those using nanozombies and *yaoguai* aren't the kind of people I'm going to lose sleep about taking down." Jia gave a resolute nod. "I'm with Erik. Things might change after we track down whoever is responsible for Molino, but until then, I know we'll be doing more to help the UTC than harm it."

"We've already thought about this a lot, Alina," Erik explained. "We know what we're getting into."

The ID agent smiled. "Good. Who am I to say no to qualified help? I suggest we ease you out over the next couple of months. Sudden moves will get the wrong kind of attention, and like you said, we need to work out the details. Sound good?"

Erik looked at the moon in the distance. It wasn't Molino, but it was a reminder of his promise and duty to his soldiers. "Yeah. Sounds good."

CHAPTER SIXTY-ONE

Jia carried in the silver tray from her kitchen. A perfectly roasted duck, the skin crispy, sat on the tray. A perfect comingling of spices filled the air, and her stomach rumbled at the scent. She moved over to the dining room table where Erik sat and put the tray in the center.

"Since you complained last time you were here about not having duck," she commented.

Erik laughed. "I'm just saying, if you invite a man to your place, you should give him duck. Especially since you cook it so well." He stood and picked up a knife to carve the bird. "The last time you invited me, it was because you'd made a big decision." He cut down the side. "Have you made another big decision?"

"I have been thinking," Jia admitted. "Even if we tell the captain we're not leaving for a few months, it's going to seem sudden, and a lot of people are going to notice that we're leaving together."

Erik finished carving the duck and set some meat on

his plate. There was an open beer in front of him already. "So?"

"Don't you think they'll link it to the prison attack?"

"Maybe they will, but it doesn't matter. The official media report is playing it up like a *yaoguai* thing, with the nanites a minor factor. No official nanozombies exist," Erik answered. He speared a bite of duck with his fork.

"I suppose that's part of them suppressing technology." Jia shook her head.

Erik swallowed his duck. "This is damned good duck."

Jia smiled warmly. "Thank you."

"In this case, though, it's a good thing we're leaving so soon after that crazy crap." Erik pointed with his fork toward himself, then her. "They're not going to think about strange conspiracies. They're going to think we got fed up with always being in the middle of weird and dangerous incidents, and we decided to do something else with our lives. It makes sense if you think about it."

"We'll no longer be symbols." Jia picked up her glass of wine. "We'll be keeping a lower profile for our work with Alina. People will forget about us."

Erik shook his head. "No, they won't forget about us. We'll become something better."

"Better?" Jia set the glass down after taking a sip. "How?"

"Because we'll be the best kind of symbols—the kind people can project their own meaning onto." Erik smiled. "And we probably won't be around for reporters to hassle to get the truth."

Jia let out a quiet laugh. "I hadn't thought of it that way." She smiled at him, her expression softening. A contented sigh escaped her lips. "Is it strange that I feel relaxed about quitting my job to gallivant across the UTC, working for a ghost?"

"Focus does wonders for personal satisfaction." Erik took another bite of duck. "I wish we had a sexier ship, but maybe we can raid some Talos accounts and buy ourselves something better." He looked up from his plate, his gaze fixing on Jia's soft lips. The words of the old woman from the park popped into his head.

Jia's breath caught as if she could sense the change in his mood. "What is it?"

"I was just thinking about something someone told me before all that nanozombie crap happened." Erik furrowed his brow and stared at Jia. "About complicating things."

"Complicating things? Like having bacteria as friends?"

Erik chuckled. "Not quite. About feelings and the future."

"Feelings?" Jia swallowed. "And the future?"

"I don't know why we're faking anything anymore. I can't guarantee you anything, Jia. I can't even guarantee we'll be alive in a few months, but I'm changing my mind about dating for real."

"I see." Jia took several deep breaths. "I can't say I'm disappointed. I've told you what I want. Why the change?"

"Because I've been trying to tell myself I'm protecting you." Erik chuckled. "But what am I protecting you from? If we can go through everything we've gone through together, we can at least try things out and see where they go."

"You and me against the universe?" Jia joked.

Emma winked into existence, her holographic form

sitting in an empty chair at the table. "I'll be the logical one, while you two are full of fleshbag hormones that make you say and do idiotic, foolish things."

Erik groaned and scrubbed a hand down his face. "Talk about killing the mood."

"What? You wanted to bang tonight?" Emma scoffed.

Jia blinked. "'Bang?'" A few seconds later, she burst out laughing.

Erik pointed his knife at the smirking Emma. "I swear I'm going to find a black hole and dump you in it."

AUTHOR NOTES - MICHAEL ANDERLE

MARCH 7, 2020

Thank you for reading not only this book but through the end to these *Author Notes* in the back!

Where do we go from here?

Right now, this book will come out in April 2020. I'm busy editing book 06 as we fly from the US to the UK (London) for what is left of the London Book Fair week.

It's going to be a bit sparse because the London Book Fair canceled the event. However, I'm a speaker at a live event on Monday, and while the concern is running full tilt in the United States, my wife and I have looked at the statistics, and here we are.

Note: We live in Las Vegas, and 80,000 people or more fly into the city every day. The fact that we aren't already showing more cases in our city is shocking to me. Or, they aren't being listed as Covid-19. I'm probably going to be safer in London.

This whole episode had me thinking when I saw a book called *Zombie: Indiana* (great title, Scott Kenemore.) You see, I come from Texas, and I think this is how a Zombie outbreak would happen down where I came from.

<This has NOTHING to do with anything other than where my mind takes me at times.>

Large group of Texans at a BBQ, when one of the guys comes from a hunt complaining about some bad food he ate the day before. He comes up to three of his friends, sweating horribly.

One of his friends notices that George is quiet, and his health is subpar.

"George, you're looking a little flushed, man."

George looks up, his eyes all white. *"Brainszzzz."*

"Awww hell, George." Three pistols get yanked from their holsters.

BLAM! BLAM! BLAM!

The man shakes his head. "Dammit George, you still owed me $10 for beer last week."

Game Over:

Zombies: 0

Texans: 1

Zombie patient 0 just eliminated. Zombie Infestation stopped. Please resume your normal activity.

Having a zombie story set in Texas would make for a very short Zombie Apocalypse story indeed.

Editing tonight

So, back to flying over. It is dark outside, and I can only assume we are flying over the U.S., but we *could* be taking a trip over the Pole, I suppose.

OH!

(I rarely use the tv in business class, but I remembered that I

could look at a map and pulled it up. Looks like we are going to go over Canada and then past Greenland.)

This explains why I need a blanket over my shoulders to stay warm so early into the flight. It is minus 53 degrees Celsius outside the plane at the moment, and it will get worse as we fly north.

I'm not looking forward to when we fly over Canada and I feel like an author-popsicle.

Where do we go from here?

If you are looking at the covers (aren't they fantastic?), we just finished covers for stories 7 & 8 (preorders up now, Go buy, go buy!).

Well, to be fair, Gene Mollica and his team finished covers 7 and 8. There was very little "me" in that 'we' designing and creating *ANY* art whatsoever. *I get credit for names and concepts only.*

My Job

Titles and Strategy are what I'll claim I am responsible for. "Yes, we need Erik and Jia on the cover. Emma will be a <redacted> in book 09, so we need to start a new model for her body."

That's my involvement. High-level everyone…where the big bucks are, *#AmIRight*?

Or I could express my job as *High-level, where-those-who-don't-have-a-lick-of-art-talent-for-designing-great-covers-work.*

Hey, I am man enough to admit I can't hold a candle to what Gene and Sasha accomplish. All I can say is thank goodness for Gene Mollica Studios and

Judith for working on our side to accomplish the amazing art.

I look forward to seeing you at the end of Opus *Z* (hahahaha). Ok, ok fine. No *Opus Zombie* stories.

See you at the end of Opus X Book 06!

Ad Aeternitatem,

Michael Anderle

BOOKS BY MICHAEL ANDERLE

For a complete list of books by Michael Anderle, please visit:

www.lmbpn.com/ma-books/

CONNECT WITH MICHAEL ANDERLE

Michael Anderle Social

Website:
http://www.lmbpn.com

Email List:
http://lmbpn.com/email/

Facebook Here:
https://www.facebook.com/groups/lmbpn.opusx/

www.ingramcontent.com/pod-product-compliance
Lightning Source LLC
Chambersburg PA
CBHW020225110726
47898CB00004B/1155
9781642024067